"Suffused with the dark, moody rhythms of the jazz that Resnick loves, *Off Minor* is a treat."—Alix Madrigal, *San Francisco Chronicle*

"In order to show the devastating impact of murder on everyone it touches, however peripherally, Mr. Harvey packs his narrative with subplots and uses abrupt scene shifts to bring them in and out of focus. Through such cinematic techniques, he isolates his characters and then strips them to the psychic bone. Suspects, cops, grieving relatives, alarmed teachers, creepy kids from the neighborhood—no one escapes the glare of the author's insights or the warmth of his compassion for the pathetic frailties of human nature."—Marilyn Stasio, *The New York Times Book Review*

"Harvey's approach is to present a dozen different characters in a shifting, scattergun style. This is a difficult trick to pull off, and Harvey does it masterfully. . . . A certified winner."—John Dunning, *Rocky Mountain News*

"Harvey imbues a satisfying police procedural with a level of characterization not usually found in the genre, resulting in a moving story far removed from the formulaic."—Steve Paul, *Kansas City Star*

"*Off Minor* is a major work, a police procedural plotted on acts of gross inhumanity yet infused with uncommon humanity. These characters are breathing entities, so convincing and compelling that crime detection and absorbing personal dramas become one and the same in this book."—Sherryl Connelly, *New York Daily News*

OFF MINOR

JOHN HARVEY

A Marian Wood / Owl Book

HENRY HOLT AND COMPANY / NEW YORK

Henry Holt and Company, Inc.
Publishers since 1866
115 West 18th Street
New York, New York 10011

Henry Holt® is a registered trademark
of Henry Holt and Company, Inc.

Although this novel is set in a real city, it is a work of fiction
and its events and characters exist only in its pages
and in the author's imagination.

The lines on pages 197–98 are from "Infinite Beasts"
by Rhona McAdam, collected in *The Hour of the Pearl*
(Saskatchewan, Canada: Thistledown
Press, 1987), and reprinted here with permission.

Library of Congress Cataloging-in-Publication Data
Harvey, John.
Off minor / John Harvey.
p.   cm.
ISBN 0-8050-5498-7
I. Title.
PR6058.A6989035   1992   91-33697
823'.914—dc20   CIP

First published in hardcover in 1992 by
Henry Holt and Company, Inc.

First Owl Books Edition 1998

A Marian Wood / Owl Book

Designed by Katy Riegel

Printed in the United States of America
All first editions are printed on acid-free paper.∞

1   3   5   7   9   10   8   6   4   2

TO COLIN:
FOR HAVING THE FAITH
AND KEEPING IT

OFF MINOR

1

He sat across the bar from Raymond, staring, daring him to walk over and say something: the youth who had stabbed him, the one with the knife.

Six weeks back it had been, Saturday night like this one, but colder, Raymond's breath on the air as he turned down past the Royal, heading for the square. No reason to notice them then, no more than any others, four young men in shirt sleeves, nineteen or twenty, out on the town; white shirts and new ties bought that morning at River Island or Top Man, hands punched down into pockets of trousers that were dark and loose at the hip. Loud. Voices raised at girls who scuttled past and laughed, short skirts or shorts, rattle of high heels.

"Hey, you!"

"What?"

"You!"

"Yeh?"

Raymond had bumped into one of them, hardly that, shoulder no more than brushing his shirt as he swivelled past, close to the glass of Debenham's window.

"Watch where you're fucking going!"

"Okay, I didn't . . ."

The four of them closing round him, no room for explanations.

"Look . . ." A gesture of pacification, Raymond raising both hands, palms outwards: a mistake.

The nearest one struck him, more a push than a punch, enough to drive him back against the cold flat of the glass; the jolt of fear across his eyes enough to draw them on.

"Bastard!"

All of them then; punches he hardly felt, except that he was down on his knees and one of them, swaying back, kicked out his polished shoe, causing Raymond to cry out, and that, of course, they loved. The four of them wanting some piece of him, a good kicking while the rest of the city veered round them, a few more pints, a few more laughs, the night not half over and everyone wanting some fun.

Raymond clung to a leg and hung on. A heel stomped down on his calf and he closed his teeth around the trousered thigh and bit hard.

"Jesus! You bastard!"

"Cunt!"

A hand grabbed at his shirt, hauling him on to the punch. A face wide with anger. Pain. Stumbling back towards the window, Raymond saw the blade, the knife. Then it was out of sight inside the pocket and they were gone, a cocky strut across the street which broke into a run.

Raymond was looking at the same face now, brown eyes, dark beginnings of a moustache; his attacker sitting at a table with three others, heads close together as a girl with purple bites and permed black hair struggled to finish her joke without cracking up. But the youth that Raymond had recognised was not really listening, knowing who Raymond was now, remembering; with a swagger he got to his feet and walked towards the counter, empty glass in hand. Ordering another pint of lager, Heineken draught, paying for it, waiting to receive his change, scarcely shifting his eyes the whole time from Raymond's face. Smiling with those eyes now as he straightened, mouth set tight. Come on, you ponce, you shirtlifting piece of shit, what are you going to do about it?

What Raymond had done, that evening weeks before, was ease himself into a sitting position, leaning back against the window while people stepped over the spread of his legs, over or around. He was frightened at first to feel where the blow had landed, the soft flesh above his hip where the knife had cut. Unsteady on his feet, pausing every dozen paces, he had passed the circle of shrubs festooned with someone's discarded knickers, mushy peas and pizza crust, containers from Kentucky Fried Chicken and Burger King, on past the toilets to the taxi rank at the bottom of the square.

"Queens," he said, wincing as he eased himself into the seat.

"Which entrance?"

"Casualty."

A conga line in fancy dress danced over the pedestrian crossing in front of them—Minnie Mouse, Maid Marian, Madonna—somebody's hen night in raucous celebration.

When they arrived at the hospital the driver cursed Raymond for leaking blood onto his seat and tried to charge him double fare. The receptionist had to ask him to spell his name three times and each time Raymond spelled it differently because he wasn't about to give her his real name, was he? They cleaned him up enough to apply a temporary dressing, gave him some paracetamol and sat him in a corridor to wait. After almost an hour, he got fed up hanging around, picked up another taxi on the upper level and went home.

The first few days, each time he went to the bathroom, he would prise back the plaster he'd used to keep the dressing down and check for any sign of infection, without really knowing what that might be. All he saw was a darkening scab, no more than an inch, inch and a half across, round it a bruise that was changing colour even as it began to fade.

Raymond went back to work and, except when he stretched or lifted something heavy like a side of beef, came close to forgetting what had happened. Except for that face, fast against his when the blade sank home. Raymond wasn't about to forget that—especially when it was no more than twenty feet away from him, like now, the youth sitting back with his friends, but still the eyes flicking back to Raymond every once in a while. *What? You still here?* All right. The last thing Raymond wanted him to think, that he was in any sense afraid. He made himself count to ten under his breath, set down his glass, one to ten again and stand, wait until the youth is looking right across at him and hold his gaze—there—then walk directly out of the bar as if he didn't care about a thing.

Only once Raymond was out in the corridor, instead of turning left towards the street, he went the other way and ducked down the stairs towards the Gents; one man in there in a short-sleeved check shirt, arm extended against the wall, leaning forward to take a blissful piss.

Raymond tried the first cubicle, no lock, let himself into the second and quickly slid the bolt across. He unzipped the front of his leather jacket—forty pounds at the stall close alongside the fish market and unlikely to be repeated—and reached into the inside pocket. The cross-hatch pattern of the Stanley knife handle was comforting against his fingers, the palm of his hand. The thumbnail with which he flicked up the blade had been bitten low, almost to the quick. Outside in the urinals someone was singing "Scotland the Brave"; next door somebody was trying to be sick. Raymond slid the blade deftly up and back, up and back. With the point he carved his initials into the wall below the cistern, finally altering the R into a B, the C into a D.

As the knife scored the paint, he thought of coming face-to-face with his attacker, somewhere crowded, or quiet, that didn't matter. All that did was that when Raymond cut him, he knew who it was. "Raymond Cooke." The way he would say it. No need to shout, the lightest of whispers. "Raymond Cooke. Remember?"

Back in the front bar, busier now, it was several moments before Raymond realised the youth had gone.

2

The girl had been missing since September. Two months. A total of sixty-three days. Resnick's first home game of the season. He had taken his place in the stands at Meadow Lane, suffused with the annual early enthusiasm. A new player at the centre of the defence, signed during the summer lay-off; their twin strike force smiling from the back page of the local paper, each vowing to outdo the other in their chase for thirty goals; good youngsters bubbling up from the youth team, the reserves—didn't two of the team have Under-21 caps already? Walking away from the ground after the final whistle, numbed by a nil-nil draw with a bunch of cloggers and artisans from higher up the A1, Resnick had considered calling in at the station, but thought better of it. Rumour was that Forest had won 4–1 away and he could do without the sarcastic reminders of his colleagues that he was supporting the wrong team. As if he needed them to tell him; as if that wasn't most of the point.

Which meant that it was not the detective inspector, but his sergeant, who was the senior officer in the CID room when the call came through.

Graham Millington shouldn't have been there, either. By rights, he should have been at home in his garden, stealing a march on autumn before it did the same to him. His garden or Somerset. Taunton, to be precise. He and the wife should have been in Taunton, drinking some ghastly mix of Earl Grey tea and eating egg-and-salad sandwiches while his wife's sister and her excuse for a husband went on at great length about the rising crime rate, the ozone layer and the diminishing Tory vote. Oh, and Jesus. Millington's in-laws, the original right wing, Christian conservationists, sitting up there at the Green right hand of God, like as not offering him another wholemeal lettuce-and-cucumber and some advice about keeping acid rain well clear of the hem of his garment.

Millington's long face and protracted warnings about traffic hold-ups on the M5 had finally had their effect. "Right," his wife had declared, metaphorically folding her arms across her chest, "we won't go anywhere." Promptly, she had shut herself in the front room with an illustrated companion to the Tate Gallery, a new biography of Stanley Spencer and a set of ear plugs: this term's course on art history was beginning with a new look at British visionaries. Millington had staked a few dahlias, dead-headed what remained of the roses and got as far as seriously considering putting top dressing on the back lawn. The weight of his wife's umbrage bore heavy on him, sullen-faced on the newly recovered settee with those awful paintings she'd shown him. What was it? The cows at bloody Cookham. Jesus Christ!

He hadn't been in the office ten minutes, less time than it took to boil a kettle, set the tea to mash, when the phone rang. Gloria Summers. Last seen on the swings at Lenton Recreation Ground a little after one o'clock. Relatives, neighbours, friends, none had set eyes on her; not since her grandmother left her to walk to the shops, no more than two streets away. Stay there now, there's a good girl. Gloria Summers: six years old.

Millington wrote down the details, took a taste or two of tea before raising Resnick on the phone. At least once the boss was involved he'd likely talk to the kiddie's parents himself; one thing above all else that turned his stomach, Millington, looking into those collapsing faces, telling lies.

The summons saved Resnick from a difficult decision: Saturday night propping up the bar at the Polish Club, wishing all the while that he'd stayed home, or Saturday night at home, wishing now he'd gone to the club. He spoke to Maurice Wainright, making sure all uniforms had been alerted, car patrols diverted, nothing new in the way of information yet obtained. Six o'clock: he guessed the superintendent would be listening to the radio news and he was right.

"See your team started well, Charlie," Jack Skelton said.

"Couldn't seem to get going, sir."

"Leave it too late as usual, like as not."

"I daresay, sir," Resnick said, and then told him about the missing girl.

Skelton was quiet: in the background Resnick could hear the disembodied newsreader and, laid over it, a woman's questioning voice, Skelton's wife or daughter, he didn't know which.

"Five hours, Charlie. One way or another, not such a long time."

She could have jumped down from the swing and realised her gran was no longer there, panicked and gone looking for her, got lost. Somebody's mum, someone who should have known better, might have bundled her back with friends for cake and cola, a rented video of cartoons, anthropomorphic animals perpetrating unspeakable violence upon one another while the little girls laughed until they were crying. She could even be sitting up the road in the Savoy, hands sticky from too much popcorn, roped in on another's birthday treat. All that was possible, they had known it all before.

Then there was the other set of possibilities . . .

Neither Resnick nor Skelton needed to voice what was nagging at their minds.

"You'll go to the home," Skelton said, not a question.

"Directly."

"Keep me informed."

Resnick set down the small cat that had climbed into his lap, the back of whose ears he had been absentmindedly stroking, and headed for the door.

Outside it was darkening. Lights here and there at the windows of the high-rise gave it the appearance of an unfinished puzzle. Resnick turned off the main road between the twenty-four-hour garage and the cinema and parked beyond the slip road's curve. A desultory group of youngsters, the eldest no more than fourteen, evaporated at his approach. He was surprised to find the lift working, less so by the sharp stink of urine, the promises of love and hatred graffitied on the walls.

Someone had painted the door of number thirty-seven a dull, dark green which petered unevenly out a brush stroke from the bottom, as if either the paint or the energy had suddenly run out.

Resnick rang the bell and, uncertain whether it was working, rattled the letter box as well.

The muffled sound of television laughter became more muffled still.

"Who is it?"

Resnick stood back so that he could be seen more easily through the spy hole in the door and held up his warrant card. In the fish-eye distortion of the circular lens, Edith Summers saw a bulky man, broad-faced, tall inside the uneven folds of his open raincoat; the slack knot of his striped tie several inches below the missing button at the neck of his shirt.

"Detective Inspector Resnick. I'd like to talk to you about Gloria."

Two bolts were fumbled back, a chain released, the latch slipped on the lock.

"Mrs. Summers?"

"You've found her?"

A slow shake of the head. "Afraid not. Not yet."

Edith Summers's shoulders slumped; anxiety had already forced out most of her hope. The corners of her eyes were red from rubbing, sore from tears. She stood in the doorway to her flat and looked at Resnick, half-broken by guilt.

"Mrs. Summers?"

"Edith Summers, yes."

"Perhaps we could go inside?"

She stepped back and showed him along the short hall into the living room: a television set, a goldfish tank, some knitting, photographs lopsided in their frames. On the TV, barely audibly, a man in a white dress suit and a wig was persuading a middle-aged couple to humiliate themselves further for the sake of a new fridge-freezer. In one corner, beneath a square table with screw-in legs and a gold-painted rim, the arms and heads of several dolls poked from a green plastic bag.

"You're Gloria's grandmother?"

"Her nan, yes."

"And her mother?"

"She lives here with me."

"The mother?"

"Gloria."

Resnick tried to blank out the thud of a poorly amplified bass from the upstairs flat, hip-hop or rap, he wasn't sure he knew the difference.

"You've seen no sign of her yourself?" Resnick asked. "Nobody's been in touch?"

She looked at him without answering, plucked at something in the ends of her hair. Resnick sat down and she did the same, the two of them in matching easy chairs, curved wooden arms and skinny cushions, upholstered backs. He wished he'd brought along Lynn Kellogg, wondered if he should find the kitchen, make a pot of tea.

"She's always lived here along of me. It was me as brought her up."

Edith Summers shook a cigarette from a packet in her cardigan pocket; lit it with a match from the household box on top of the gas fire. Turned low, the centre of the fire burned blue.

"Like she was my own."

She sat back down, absentmindedly straightening the loose skirt of her belted dress over her knees. The cardigan draped across her shoulders had been cable stitched in black. On her feet were faded purple slippers with no backs and an off-white puff of wool attached to one of them still. Her hair was less than shoulder length and mostly dark. She could have been anything between forty and fifty-five; probably, Resnick thought, she was around the same age as himself.

"Someone's taken her, haven't they?"

"We don't know that."

"Some bastard's taken her."

"We don't know that."

"We don't know bloody anything!"

Sudden anger flared her cheeks. With a swift wrench of the controls she turned the television volume almost to full, then sharply off. Without explanation she left the room, to reappear moments later with a long-handled mop, the end of which she banged against the ceiling hard.

"Turn down that sodding row!" she screamed.

"Mrs. Summers . . ." Resnick started.

Someone above turned up the sound still further, so that the bass reverberated through the room.

"I'll go up and have a word," offered Resnick.

Edith sat back down. "Don't bother. Soon as they see you go, it'd be twice as bad."

"Gloria's mother," Resnick said. "There's no chance she might be with her?"

Her laughter was short and harsh. "No chance."

"But she does see her daughter?"

9

"Once in a while. Whenever it takes her fancy."

"She lives here, then? I mean, in the city?"

"Oh, yes. She's here all right."

Resnick reached for his notebook. "If you could let me have an address . . ."

"Address? I can give you the names of a few pubs."

"We have to check, Mrs. Summers. We have to . . ."

"Find Gloria, that's what you've got to do. Find her, for God's sake. Here. Look, here." She was on her feet again, picking up first one photograph, then that, cutting her finger on the edge of the glass before she could free one from its frame.

Resnick held in his hands a round-faced little girl with a pale dress and spiralling curls. It was the picture that would appear on the front pages of newspapers, that would be beamed into millions of homes, often accompanied by Resnick himself, or his superintendent, Jack Skelton, looking suitably severe and patrician, pleading for information. The information came, for almost two weeks they were flooded with sightings and rumours, accusations and prophecies, but then, when little seemed to happen, attention waned, instead of the photograph of Gloria now there was a single paragraph at the foot of page 5, and, after the police had followed every lead, sifted through everything they had been told, there was nothing.

No clue.

Nowhere to go.

No Gloria.

The photograph could still be found on posters round the city, smeared, stained and torn, ignored.

Some bastard's taken her.

Sixty-three days.

3

Whenever Raymond lifted his fingers to his face, he could smell it. Living there. His arms, too, inside, where the meat slapped against him as he struggled to free it from the hooks that swung from the conveyor running along the covered yard. No matter how hard he scrubbed, scouring his skin with pumice stone, harsh bristles of the brush, he could never drive it out. Fingers and arms, shoulders and back. Smell of it in his hair. Never mind the shampoo, the soap, deodorant and after-shave, splash-on, spray or douse, Raymond carried it with him, a grey film, a second skin, like gristle.

"Here, Ray. Ray, c'm here. Listen. You want, I can fix you up."

"Leave him, Terry, leave him. Don't waste your breath."

"No, no. Serious. I'm serious. He wants a job, I know this bloke, I can put in a word."

"Wanted a job, he'd haul himself out of bed of a morning."

"He hasn't got the need . . ."

"My boot up his arse, that'd give him need enough."

"Jackie, he's not a kid anymore, he's a grown man."

"Grown! Look at him."

"What's wrong with him?"

"What's bollocking right, more like."

"All he wants is a job."

"And the rest."

"Jackie!"

"Any road, he's not interested. Jobs, he's had them till they were running out of his ears. And how long did he ever spend in any of them? Three weeks, no more. Maybe a month. Once, I think maybe once, he stuck it for a month. I tell you, Terry, son of mine or not, put yourself out for him and you're the one'll end up with his hands in the shit. He's not worth it."

"Your flesh and blood."

"Sometimes I wonder."

"Jackie!"

"What?"

"Give the boy a chance."

"You're so keen, you give him a chance."

"That's what I'm saying. I can help him. Ray, Raymond, here, listen. This bloke I know from snooker, I could pull a favour, only one thing, you got to promise not to let me down."

"Some chance."

"Jackie!"

"What?"

"What about it, Ray? You interested or what?"

Raymond's father and his uncle Terry talking about him in the public bar of their local, almost a year before. A pint of Shippos, pint of mixed, for Raymond a half of lager he'd been sitting over the best part of an hour. Not wanting his old man going on at him for never paying his wack, standing a round.

"Butcher's. Wholesale. Over by the county ground."

"That's the abattoir," Raymond's father said.

"It's *near* the abattoir."

"I don't fancy working in the abattoir," Raymond said.

"You don't fancy working anywhere," his father said.

"It isn't *in* the abattoir," said his uncle. "Near it. Close. Suppose you could say, alongside."

"Handy," his father said.

Raymond had walked past there at night, turning right by Incinerator Road: steady hum of electricity through the wall, a warm smell that seeped into the air, sometimes so strong that you choked and held your breath and hurried past before your stomach heaved, your eyes began to water.

"Ray-o," his uncle said, draining his glass as he stood to get in another. "What d'you reckon?"

"Tell you what," said his father, passing up his own glass, "he thinks when he can carry on sponging off me a bit longer, why bother?"

"Talk to him," Raymond said to his uncle. "Tell him I'll do it."

"Good on you!" His uncle grinned and scooped up Raymond's glass too.

"What the fizzing heck you want to do that for?" his father hissed, face close into his. "Why the hell d'you want to tell him you'll work in the sodding abattoir?"

"Least it'll get me out from under your feet," said Raymond, not looking into his father's eyes. "Stop you getting on at me all the time."

"You great pillock! Half the time you'd never think to wipe your arse without someone there to tell you."

"We'll see."

"Aye, we'll see right enough. See you come wingeing home with your tail between your legs, that's the only thing we'll like to see."

"Here we are then." Raymond's uncle splashed the drinks down onto the table. "Sup up. Let's drink a toast to the new working man. Good as." And he reached down and gave Raymond's ear a tweak and broadly winked.

The house was in a cul-de-sac east of Lenton Boulevard, nursery school to the right, pub to the left. High-rise blocks of greying concrete poked from the grass and tarmac ground behind. Like most of the terrace, it had been bought cheap, barely renovated, rented out to working men or students—"professionals" or "graduates" graced the Park, the suburbs, lived in flats instead of rooms.

Raymond's was the first floor back. Space for a narrow bed, a melamine wardrobe and three-drawer chest, a chair. The landlord's promise of a table had never materialised, but supper was something eaten on his knees, eyes fastened on the faintly flickering images of a black-and-white set, breakfast instant coffee and curled toast he swallowed down while getting dressed. What else might he want a table for?

In the shared living room a sagging three-piece suite, burn marks on its arms, was arranged around the communally rented TV, the VCR, rented copies of *Casual Sex, Desire and Hell at Sunset Motel, American Ninja 4: The Annihilation*. Unwashed mugs and encrusted bowls spilled from the sink and draining board onto the kitchen floor; the bacon fat layered round the grill pan could have greased any one of them through a cross-Channel swim. Every so often one of the shifting group of five tenants would draw up a rota and stick it to the door of the fridge; within a few days it would be pulled down to write a note for the milkman, light a cigarette.

Raymond kept himself to himself, mumbled "Hi" and "Bye"; only got on the others' nerves the way he would lock himself into the bathroom after work for hours, run the hot water till the tank was empty, all the taps were running cold.

On this particular Saturday, Raymond had restricted himself to forty minutes, though he would have stayed longer had the door not been subjected to a series of sharp kicks and the air blue with suggestions as to exactly which perversions he was practising under the cover of excessive cleanliness.

He hurried out and down the threadbare stairs to his own room, probing the passages of his ears with a Q-Tip as he went. The small, frameless mirror propped on the windowsill revealed a curving line of pimples—whiteheads rather than blackheads—at the corner of his left eye. He popped these with his fingernails, wiping them clean under the arms of his deep blue sweatshirt, where it was unlikely to be seen. He was wearing brown cords, ten quid in the sale at H&M, black shoes with toe caps that might have been Doc Martens but weren't, red-and-brown paisley pattern socks; he lifted his leather jacket down from its wire hanger in the wardrobe, feeling good about the way the jacket tilted just a fraction to one side—the weight of the knife.

4

As yet the Polish Club was quiet; recorded music filtered through from another room. The line of vodka drinkers at the bar was only one deep. Resnick allowed himself to be guided to a corner table, well clear of the crowd to come, the dancing that would inevitably start. He had been no more than mildly surprised at Marian Witzak's call, glad enough that the responsibility for a decision had been removed. A bone of contention from years before, when he had been a young DC and married to Elaine, that his nights off were so few and far between. Now they seemed so many.

"You did not mind that I telephoned?"

Resnick poured the rest of the Pilsner Urquel into his glass and shook his head.

"Such short notice."

"It was all right."

"I wondered, perhaps, if you might think it rude."

"Marian, it's fine."

"You know, Charles . . ." She paused and her fingers, narrow and long, moved along the stem of her glass. Resnick thought of the piano near the french windows of her living room, sheet music for a polonaise, the slowly yellowing keys. ". . . sometimes I think, if it were left for you to contact me, we would not very often meet."

Although she had been in England all of her adult life, Marian still talked as if her English had been learned from watching untold episodes of *The Forsyte Saga* in scratchy black-and-white, from lessons spent mimicking the teacher's words.

This is a pencil. What is this?

This is a pencil.

She was wearing a plain black dress with a high neck and a wide white belt, tied at one side into a loose bow. As usual her hair had been tightly drawn back and pinned precisely in place.

"You know, Charles, I was to go to the theatre tonight. Shakespeare. A touring company from London, very good, I think. Highly spoken of. All week I have been looking forward to this. It is not so often there is something cultural coming now to the city." Marian Witzak sipped her drink and shook her head. "It is a shame."

"So what happened?" Resnick asked. "It was cancelled?"

"Oh, no."

"Sold out?"

Marian sighed a small, ladylike sigh, the kind that would once have made drawing room pulses race. "My friends, Charles, the ones who were taking me, late this afternoon they telephoned. I was choosing already my dress. The husband is ill; Frieda, she has never learned to drive . . ." She looked sideways at Resnick and smiled. "I thought, never mind, I shall go on my own, I can still enjoy the play. I run my bath, continue to get ready, but all the time, here in the back of my mind, I know, Charles, that I can never go there alone."

"Marian."

"Yes?"

"I'm not clear what you're saying."

"Charles, which night is this? It is Saturday night; Friday, Saturday night, it is no longer safe to go into the city, a woman, a woman like myself, alone."

Resnick glanced at the glass and the Pilsner bottle alongside it; both were empty. "You could have ordered a taxi."

"And coming home? I telephoned the theatre, the performance finishes at ten thirty-five; you know the only places I can get a taxi at that time of the evening, Charles. All the way down to the square, or by the Victoria Hotel. And every pavement, everywhere you go, there are these gangs of young men . . ." Two bright spots of colour showed high on her cheekbones, accentuating the paleness of her face, her concave cheeks. "It is not safe, Charles, not anymore. It is as if, little by little, they have taken over. Bold, loud, and we look the other way; or stay at home and bolt our doors."

Resnick wanted to contradict her, say that she exaggerated, it simply wasn't so. Instead he sat quiet and toyed with his glass, remembering the senior officer at the Police Federation conference warning that the police were in danger of losing control of the streets; knowing that there were cities, and he did not just mean London, where bulletproof vests and body armour were routinely carried in police vehicles on weekend patrol.

Marian touched his hand. "We do not have to think back so many years, Charles, to remember gangs of young men marauding the streets. It was right to be afraid then."

"Marian, that wasn't us. It was our parents. Grandparents, even."

"And so we should forget?"

"That wasn't what I said."

"Then what?"

"It isn't the same."

Marian's eyes had the darkness of marbled stone, of fresh-turned earth. "Because of those young men, our families fled. Those who were not imprisoned, not in the ghetto, not already dead. If we do not remember, how can it not happen again?"

Raymond had been sitting in the Malt House for the best part of an hour, two pints and a short, watching the women flocking in and out again, brightly coloured and shrill voiced. Off to one side of the room, a DJ played songs Raymond half-remembered, without ever knowing either the singer or the words. Only now and again something would strike a chord, Van Halen, ZZ Top, one of those white bands that came straight at you with plenty of noise.

Raymond was getting fidgety, trying not to notice the youths near the bar, putting the eye on him every so often, wanting him to stare them back, cock an eyebrow, respond. Oh, he knew they'd not start anything right there; they'd wait till he got up and go and follow him out onto the street. A few shouted remarks as he turned down towards the Council House, jostling him then as they fanned out around him, pushing past.

He'd seen another lad bundled into a dress shop window just the week before, right there, that street. By the time they'd finished with him, both eyes were closing fast, his face like something Raymond might heft onto his shoulder at work, blood smearing his overalls.

Not that they would deal with Raymond that easily; not like before. Not now that he had something with which to strike back.

He walked around to the far side of the bar; one more half, then time to make a move. A girl, laughing, swung her arm back into him as he passed and laughed some more, dance of permed blonde hair as she swivelled her face towards him, eyes, quick and greedy, summing him up, dismissing him out of hand. Raymond waited to be served, half-watching the girl, blue dress with straps, finer than his own little finger, running tight along the pale skin of her back. Watched as for a moment her eyes closed, singing along with the music, some soul shit from last year's charts. Always the same crappy lyrics, always "touch me, baby," always "all night long." Raymond stepped clear of the bar with his glass. The girl was perched on a stool now, his age, younger. Raymond remembered watching the singer, his video on TV, one of those bloated coons in ruffled shirts and bow ties, dress suits. He thought it was the same one, what was the difference? Women wriggling out of white knickers, throwing them up onto the stage so he could wipe the sweat from his face. Raymond staring at the girl now, feeling sick.

"Here! What d'you reckon you're looking at?"

He put down his unfinished drink and left.

"Charles, you should not leave now. It is still early." A smile, small but imploring. "We could dance."

The last time Resnick and Marian had danced at the club, his ex-wife had interrupted them on their way back off the floor. Elaine's voice recognisable instantly, but not her face: not her hair, always so carefully tended, set and brushed and teased out with a comb, now stiff and dry and chopped with neither rhyme nor reason; not the blotched skin nor the stained clothes; not her face. Her accusing voice.

All the letters I sent you, the ones you never answered. All the times I rang up in pain and you hung up without a word.

If he had not left then, he would have struck her, the only wrong thing he had never done.

Resnick didn't think that he would dance. He said good-bye to

Marian and touched his mouth to her powdered cheek. Back home the cats would be eager to greet him, jumping onto the stone wall for the warmth of his hand, running between his legs as he neared the front door. Of course, he'd fed them before he left, but now he had come back, hadn't he, and surely there would be a shaking of Meow Mix, shavings of cheese if, as often, as usual, he made himself a sandwich, milk for them warmed gently in the pan, if he were feeling soft at heart.

Dark beans of Nicaraguan coffee shone rich and smooth inside his hand. It was still minutes short of ten o'clock. Elaine had stepped out of the darkness and back into his life, back into his house, and he had not wanted her, only as a vehicle for his anger, his storehouse of pain, yet after she had told him about the abortion of her remarriage and all that had come after, he had wanted nothing more than to wrap his arms about her and seek absolution for them both. He had not done even that. She had gone away again, not telling him where she was going, refusing, and Resnick had seen, had heard, nothing of her since.

Resnick carried his coffee into the living room, poured himself a healthy scotch, set mug and glass on the floor on either side of the high-backed armchair. He had not switched on the overhead light and the red dot of the stereo burned bright. Without really knowing why, he began to play Thelonious Monk. Piano, sometimes vibes, with bass and drums. Hands that attacked tunes from the corners, oblique and disarranged. "Well, You Needn't," "Off Minor," "Evidence," "Ask Me Now." "Sounds as if he's playing with his elbows," Elaine had once disparagingly remarked. Well, fair enough, sometimes he did.

Raymond had tried for a last drink at the Nelson, but one of the bouncers had taken against him and refused to let him in. So it was he ended up in the same pub where he'd encountered his attacker, just the week before. Brave enough this far into the night to half-hope him there again. But no. Raymond stood squashed up against the furthest end of the bar, the ledge behind him overcrowded with empty glasses and hard against his back. Only when he was able to manoeuvre himself a little to the left did he notice the girl. Not dolled up, tarty, like the one in the Malt House, her hair brown and straight and cut to frame her face, the face itself just this side of plain.

She was sitting at a crowded table, chair angled away as if to make it clear she was on her own. Legs crossed, her black skirt rode above her knees; white top hanging outside the waist of her skirt, silky and loose, the kind that would be good to touch. In the half-pint glass beside her elbow, the drink was oddly red; lager, Raymond guessed, and black currant. When she realised that Raymond was staring at her she did not look away.

5

"Sara, then?"

"Yes, Sara."

"With an *H*?"

"Without."

"My cousin, she's Sarah. Only she's got an *H*."

"Oh."

Raymond couldn't believe his luck. Waiting for her to finish her lager and black, he'd edged his way across the bar, caught up with her before she reached the door.

"Hello."

"Hi."

They had stood several moments before the phone boxes, across from Yates Wine Lodge, from Next. Others jostled round them, heading out for the clubs, Zhivago's, Madison. Engine running, a police dog van idled at the kerb. Raymond knew she was waiting for him to say something, not knowing what.

"If you like, we could . . ."

"Yes?"

"Get a pizza?"

"No."

"Something else then. Chips."

"No, you're all right. Not hungry."

"Oh."

Her face brightened. "Why don't we just walk? You know, for a bit."

They went up Market Street, midway down Queen Street before doubling back up King; on Clumber Street they joined the crowd in McDonald's, stood in a line twelve or fourteen deep, six lanes working, Raymond couldn't believe the money they must be taking; finally he came away with a quarter-pounder and fries, Coke and apple pie. Sara's was a chocolate milk shake. Benches all taken, they leaned up against the wall that led down to Littlewoods's side entrance, Raymond chewing on his burger, watching Sara prise the lid from the container, tip the shake right into her mouth, too thick to suck up with the straw.

When he told her he worked at a butcher's, wholesale, she did no more than shrug. But walking on towards Long Row later, she said: "At work, what d'you, d'you, you know, the meat and that, d'you have to chop it up?"

"Into joints, you mean?"

"I s'pose."

"Carcasses?"

"Yes."

Raymond shook his head. "That's skilled work. I mean, I might. Like to. It's a lot more money. But, no. Mostly I'm just humping stuff around, loading, packing, jobs like that."

Sara worked in a sweet shop down near the Broad Marsh. One of those bright, open-plan places painted out in pink and green, the kind where you're encouraged to go round and make your own selection, have the assistant weigh it at the end. That was when quite a few people got funny, Sara told him, seeing their paper bag resting on the scale, about to cost them seventy-five p, a pound. Then they would ask her to tip some out, get it down to something more reasonable, and she would have to explain, being patient, keeping the smile on her face and her voice level the way the manageress had told her to, how difficult it was when they'd chosen from as many as ten different kinds to take them back, put them into their respective containers. Are they sure they wouldn't like to go ahead and pay for them, just this once? She was sure they wouldn't regret it, all the sweets were really lovely, she sneaked one or two herself all the time.

Raymond's attention wavered more than a little in the course of this, steering Sara from one side of the pavement to the other, so as to avoid whichever bunch was hollering at the tops of their voices, blocking their way so they would have to step out into the road. That and glancing sideways at her skirt, even now she was walking, still above her knees; the silk flash of her blouse beneath the dark, unbuttoned jacket that she wore, swell of her small breasts. Waiting for the lights to change at the bottom end of Hockley, that was when he touched her for the first time, his hand moving against the inside of her upper arm, circling it there.

Sara smiling: " 'S good of you to walk me home."

"No problem."

She squeezed her arm to her side, Raymond's fingers trapped warm between.

The wasteland off to one side of the road, Raymond's uncle had told him once it all belonged to the railway, like as not still did. A murky scattering of buildings, large and small, all manner of stuff that people had junked dumped in between. After dark, flatbed lorries would back in, vans with names repainted over and over on their sides; next morning others would come with prams and handcarts, picking through the debris, hauling away whatever they could use or sell.

Sara shivered, her breath blurred on the air, and Raymond took and squeezed her hand; the bones of her fingers tiny, brittle like a child's.

"C'mon," he said, pulling her past a pile of broken masonry towards the hulk of a disused warehouse, bolstered up towards the sky.

"What d'we have to go in there for?"

" 'S all right."

Raymond scooped up a stone and hurled it high; there was the splintering of glass, small and distant, as the last fragments of window fell away; the fast flutter of pigeons taking off, sudden and abrupt.

Off to the left, distant, Raymond saw a cigarette glowing through the dark. He moved his hand and touched Sara's blouse at the back, beneath her coat: under the slide of silk, knots of her spine. Inside the building he bent his head to kiss her hair and she turned her face and instead he kissed her mouth, the edge of it first, not quite right, moving till his mouth was over hers, taste of chocolate from the faint hairs on her upper lip.

"Ray, is that what they call you? Ray?"

Raymond smiling, feeling for her breast. "Ray-o."

"Ray-o?"

"Sometimes."

"Like a nickname?"

"Yes."

He took off his coat and then hers, laying them on the ground, concrete and packed earth from which the boards had long been ripped.

"What's this?"

"Where?"

"Sticking in my back."

He eased her up, unzipped his inside pocket and removed the knife.

"Ray, what is it?"

"Never mind."

In little more than outline, she could see his face; see the metal object in his hand.

"It's not a knife, is it? Raymond? Is it?"

Looking down at her, the sharp, almost pretty features of her face as his eyes grew accustomed to the scarcity of light.

"Is it? A knife?"

"Maybe."

"Whatever d'you want a knife for?"

He dropped it from sight into his trouser pocket and reached towards her. "Never mind."

Less than five minutes later, the front of his cords unzipped, he had come against her hand. As they lay there, not speaking, he could feel her rib cage rise and fall as she breathed.

"Ray-o."

He rolled over and sat up and she fumbled a tissue from her bag.

"What's that?"

"What now?"

"That smell."

He felt himself blushing and got hurriedly to his feet, embarrassment in his voice. "I can't smell nothing."

"Yes. I'm certain. Back in there."

She was staring where the back wall disappeared into the darkness, past piles of rotted cardboard, sodden sacking and old boxes. And though Raymond didn't want to admit it, he could smell it too, not unlike the tubs where he worked, brimful of all the tubes and offal ends, the guts, the tripes and lights.

"Where are you going?" Alarm in Raymond's voice.

"I want to see."

"What for?"

"I do. That's why."

One hand clamped across his nose, he followed her, thinking all the time that what he should do was turn round, walk away, leave her.

"Fuck's sake, Sara, it could be anything."

"No need to swear."

"Dog, cat, anything."

Sara took the lighter from her bag and held it high above her head, snapping it to life. The stench had already raised tears in her eyes. In the furthest corner a wooden door had been wedged at an angle between floor and wall; behind it, broken planks and cardboard had been stuffed and piled.

"Sara, let's get out of here."

Her lighter went out and when she clicked it on again, a young rat wriggled from beneath the pile and raced away along the line of the wall, its belly hanging low.

"I'm going."

And as Raymond shuffled back, Sara, unbelievably, took two, then three, then four more paces forward. When at last she stopped it was because she was certain of what she saw: the heel of a child's blue shoe, what might once have been the fingers of a hand.

6

"What's the matter, Charlie? You look distracted."

Resnick was sitting in one of three chairs across from the superintendent's desk, one leg crossed above the other, mug of lukewarm coffee in
his hand.

"No, sir. I'm fine."

"Fashion statement then, is it?"

Resnick realised that Skelton was looking towards his feet, one black
sock, thin nylon, the other a washed-out grey. Resnick uncrossed his
legs, sat forward in the chair. When the phone had rung, wrenching him
from sleep, he had been in a hospital ward with Elaine, his ex-wife
strapped down in the bed, a mixture of terror and pleading in her eyes,
while Resnick, in a white doctor's coat, had looked down at her and
shaken his head, instructed the nurse to expose the arm, prepare the
vein, he would administer the injection himself.

Even the shower, switched from blistering hot to cold and back
again, had failed to lift the sweat from his body. The guilt.

"Run it by us, Charlie. What've we got?"

The others in the room aside from Resnick and Jack Skelton were
Tom Parker, the DCI from Central Station, and Lennie Lawrence, chief
inspector and Skelton's deputy. Tom Parker was nine months short of
retirement, mind set on a smallholding in Lincolnshire, him and the

wife and a few dozen chickens, pigs, possibly a couple of goats. His wife was partial to goats. If this hadn't cropped up, Sunday morning, he'd have been out at his allotment, not a great deal to do but pull some potatoes, get his fork down into the compost, keep his back in shape for all the digging that was to come. Len Lawrence would be going out on just about the same day, off to help his son-in-law run a pub on the outskirts of Auckland, even this far ahead the tickets booked, deposit paid. The last thing either man wanted, their last winter on the force, was this.

"Couple came into the station, sir, little after two. Reported finding what they thought was a body in an empty building, that waste ground in Sneinton."

"Why report it here?" Lawrence interrupted. "Central's more obvious, closer."

"Seems there was some question about reporting it at all. They must have come across it a couple of hours before, nearer twelve. One of them, the lad, he's got a room in Lenton, our patch. When finally they decided to come in, that was where they were."

"The body, Charlie," said Parker. "Identification?"

Resnick shook his head. "Difficult. Apparently been there quite a while. A lot of natural decomposition, though this cold snap's helped us some. Body seems to have lain largely undisturbed. Whoever put it there had wrapped it inside two large plastic bags . . ."

"Bin bags?" asked Lawrence.

Resnick nodded. ". . . covered those over with a piece of old tarpaulin and then built a kind of shelter round it, planks of wood, whatever was around." For a moment the mug of coffee was less than steady in his hand. "Without all of that, the body wouldn't have stayed as intact as apparently it has; that whole area's alive with rats."

"They never got to it at all?"

"That's not what I said." Resnick got up and walked across to the coffee machine, helped himself to another half a mug. So far, he'd only spoken to Parkinson, the Home Office pathologist, on the phone, but what he had heard had been enough to twist his guts into a knot.

"I'm not clear what you're saying," said Tom Parker. "Are we going to be able to make an identification or not?"

"We're not going to be able to look at a photograph and say yes, that's her, that's the kiddie, that's one thing we're not going to do." Resnick realised, too late, how high his voice was raised.

Tom Parker looked at him, only mildly surprised.

"You think it's the little girl who went missing," Skelton said, lining up the paperweight against the picture of his wife and child.

"Yes." Resnick nodded and sat down.

"Gloria."

"Summers. Yes."

"September, wasn't it?" Len Lawrence shifted his weight in the chair. Sitting too long in one position gave him cramps; privately, he was dreading the flight to New Zealand.

"Yes," said Resnick. "Nine weeks now. A little over."

"No leads," said Lawrence.

"Till now."

"You can't be certain, Charlie," Skelton said. "Not yet."

"No, sir."

But he was.

Resnick was conscious of the comparative silence outside the room, the virtual absence of traffic on the normally busy road outside; a lull between the usually omnipresent ringing of telephones. Most people were turning over in bed for an extra half hour, going downstairs in dressing gowns and bare feet to put on the kettle, fetch the paper from the front door mat, let in or out the dog or cat. They sat there in that first-floor room, four middle-aged men, talking about murder. The next time it was officially discussed there would be maps and photographs, computers, newly opened files and many more personnel. Too many people, Resnick thought, not wanting the silence to break; knowing that when it did he would have to get out on the street, the next step in the investigation.

"At least," Kevin Naylor said, pointing his fork in the direction of Mark Divine's plate, "it hasn't cost you your appetite."

Divine grunted and cut diagonally across his second sausage, forking up one end and using it to break the yolk of his second egg. He carefully wiped this around the juice of his tinned tomatoes and baked beans before lifting it to his mouth.

"Something like this," Divine said, "what it does to you," wiping his chin with a convenient slice of fried bread, "makes you think about being alive. You know, savouring it."

Naylor, who had restricted himself to two rounds of toast and a large tea, nodded understandingly. He remembered his father telling him, an unusually unguarded moment, how after his wife's, Kevin's mother's, funeral, all he could think of was hustling his aunt Mary into the spare bedroom and giving her one. Nine months later, the two of them were married and, from what Naylor could make out on his rare visits to Marsden, his dad was still trying.

"Tell you what," Divine said through a mouthful of breakfast, "that feller wrote that book about serial murder, you know, the bloke who skins 'em alive and wears them like a shell suit, according to him, what you do, keep the stink from turning your gut, like, it's carry round this little pot of Vicks and rub it round inside your nose. Bollocks! Half a ton of it wouldn't have kept this from wellying the old nerve ends. Stroll on! Worse than a bevy of bottled farts well past their sell-by date."

He speared three miscellaneous pieces of egg white and the last of the sausage. Divine had been one of two CID officers on duty when the report had come in. He had talked briefly to Raymond Cooke and Sara Prine, sending them off with a promise to come back and make a full statement around mid-morning. By the time he got out to Sneinton, the whole area had been roped off, lights were being set up, the scene-of-crime boys eager to move in and shoot a video that would fetch a small fortune if copies ever found their way onto the snuff market. Parkinson had driven down from a dinner party in Lincoln, still wearing his evening dress, rat droppings and worse making a right old mess of the bottoms of his trousers, patent leather shoes. Not that there was much the pathologist could establish there and then. Most of his work would have to take place in more clinical conditions.

"You know what I think," Divine said, voice lowered and leaning close. "Next time something like this crops up," glancing across the canteen now to where Diptak Patel was standing alongside Lynn Kellogg in the queue, "we ought to send Sunshine out there, all that oil and incense, stuff he has to eat, like as not he wouldn't even notice."

Finding Gloria Summers's mother the first time had not been as difficult as the grandmother had suggested. Susan had been living with a girl friend in a second-storey housing association flat in one of those conversions that lined the upper edge of the Forest. This time, mid-morning on a Sunday, the friend was there, but Susan had not returned.

"Since last night?" Resnick asked.

"Since a lot of nights."

"Any idea where she might be?"

"Oh, yes." Resnick had the impression she might have grinned at him, including him in the joke, if she had not been so obviously bored. "A lot of ideas."

"Boy friends?"

"If you want to call them that."

Resnick's notebook was in his hand. "Where shall I start?"

"What might be a good idea, get a bigger book."

He struck lucky with his third call. A bleary-eyed West Indian opened the door, scratching himself beneath the voluminous arm of a kaftan top. Resnick identified himself and told the man he was looking for Susan Summers.

The West Indian smiled and ushered him in.

Susan was propped up against several pillows, not too fussed about the way the sheet was covering her body. The bed was a mattress stretched across the floor, take-out cartons and Red Stripe cans strategically around it. An ashtray the diameter of a dinner plate was close to overflowing.

"Cup of tea?" the man asked, smiling now at the way Resnick was looking at Susan, trying not to look.

"Thanks, no."

"Suit yourself."

"Remember me?" Resnick said to the young woman in the bed.

The last time he had spoken to her, asking if she had any idea where her daughter might have gone to, asking if she had seen the girl herself, Susan Summers had replied: "Ask that cow of a mother of mine, why don't you? She's the only one good enough even to wipe the shit from her precious little arse."

Now, when Resnick told her he didn't want to upset her, but there was a chance that a body they'd found that night might be that of her daughter, what she said was, "About fucking time!"

7

Raymond had called work early, spoken to the under-manager; told him he had a cold, heavy, he was planning to go back to bed, dose himself up with aspirin, hot milk and whisky, the way his father had told him, sweat it out. Sure, he'd be back tomorrow. No problem. Last thing he was about to do, let on that he was going to the police station, make a statement. You did what? You found *what*? There'd be enough of that later on, once the news got out.

Raymond spent almost as long in his room that morning as he usually did in the bathroom, standing in front of the tacky little wardrobe, drawers of the chest half out. It was the kind of occasion he wasn't sure what you wore. In the end he plumped for a grey shirt with a pinkish tinge, courtesy of the launderette; the brown jacket, too long in the sleeves, his uncle had given him for his interview at the butcher's.

"Why don't I go down the shops," Raymond had said, straight-faced, "buy a couple of pounds of pig's liver, squeeze it out all over your old decorating overalls, go along in those."

"Ray-o," his uncle Terry had said, "this is serious."

Wrong.

This was serious.

He hadn't arranged it, seeing Sara climbing into a police car in the early hours to be driven home, but Raymond figured he would get back to the station before their eleven o'clock appointment, hang around, talk to her before they went in. Other considerations aside, he wanted to make sure she wasn't pissed off with him about last night, dragging her off to some place where there were dead bodies, for fuck's sake; he'd liked the way her eager little hand had found its way inside his flies, the way she hadn't complained afterwards when he'd shot his load.

That was the other thing, he didn't want her rabbiting on to the detectives about too many details. At least, let them use their imaginations. Let them think he'd got her in there and given her one, proper, not some weasely little hand job.

Two officers came out in uniform, pausing for a moment at the top of the short flight of steps, and Raymond turned away, wandering down towards the bus stop, the spiritualist church in the basement alongside it. When he looked again, there she was, hurrying over the pedestrian crossing as the little green man flashed its warning, head down and legs moving fast, almost as if she were running. Though he knew her the minute he saw her, she wasn't the same. Trotting along in this little pink suit, low black heels, black leather handbag dangling from one crooked arm.

"Sara."

"Oh. Ray."

"Hi."

"Am I late?"

"No, you're early."

"I thought I was late."

He showed her his watch, still only ten to. "So," Raymond said, "what're you going to say?"

The way she looked at him made Raymond think she might be short-sighted. Though not as bad as his auntie Jean: one Christmas his uncle Terry had come into the room in the middle of *The Sound of Music* with his thing hanging out, a piece of coloured ribbon tied round the end of it in a bow. "Terry," Raymond's aunt had said, reaching for another Quality Street, "whatever's the matter with you? Your shirt's still hanging out."

"What d'you mean?" Sara asked.

"About last night."

"I'll tell them what happened, of course. What we saw."

"That's all?"

"You can wait here if you want," she said. "I'm going to get it over."

From the foot of the steps Raymond asked: "You're not going to go shooting your mouth off about, you know, what we . . . ?"

The look she gave him was enough to stop him in his tracks, keep him there after Sara had pushed open the main door, let it swing closed behind her.

"This is it," Mark Divine had announced, making sure that everyone else in the CID office heard him, "your big chance; half an hour from now, follow me to one of those secluded rooms along the corridor and do me the ultimate favour."

A roar went up from the half-dozen in the room, all eyes now, eager to see how Lynn Kellogg would react. On one legendary occasion she had stopped Divine's mouth with a punch and ever since the whole of CID had been waiting for her to throw another. "Next time," Divine had sworn, "I'm going to thump the stupid cow back."

"Lynn," winking into the body of the room, "what d'you say?"

Lynn was typing up a report of visits she made before the weekend. An old man in his eighties had been collected by ambulance for his three-monthly checkup and one of the nurses had noticed bruising around the lower back, high on the inner arm; the former was consistent with a fall, but the rest . . . ? At first the man's daughter, close to her sixties herself, had refused Lynn permission to talk to him, and when she had he had been so confused it had been difficult to get much sense out of him. The social worker had made a face, pointed at the case files overflowing her desk; she had last visited the home some five months ago, an application by the daughter for hand rails to be fitted to the bath. Yes, as far as she'd been able to tell, the old man had been fine.

"Lynn?"

Divine was a pain in the arse, incorrigible, ineducable—though he had used the word *ultimate*, jeans adverts obviously having more going for them than recycling old Motown numbers.

"The couple who found the girl's body, you want me to take one of their statements?"

"Yes."

Lynn whipped the sheet of paper from the machine, pushing back her chair as she stood up. "Why the fuck didn't you say so?" She left the room without bothering to give Divine another look, this time the office roar solidly with her, for all that Mark Divine was giving her the finger behind her disappearing back.

Lynn Kellogg was late-twenties, the kind of build that would have had Betjeman in paroxysms of desire. Thighs like flour sacks was Divine's description, but then he was no poet. Her last, and only, live-in lover had spent more time trying to get her onto the front of a tandem than anything else. In the end, she hadn't been able to cope with a man who shaved his legs more than she did herself.

Getting into CID had not been easy, staying there twice as hard. The perennial question: all the sexist jokes, the constant innuendo, was it best to laugh along, show that she wasn't a prude, prepared to be one of the lads, or did she make a stand? That's offensive. It offends me. Cut it out. Like others, like, in a similar way, Patel, she supposed she wobbled uneasily between the two, reining in what she was truly feeling until, as sometimes happened, it went too far. One thing seemed true, the better she did her job, the less conspicuous the remarks; which didn't exactly prevent Lynn from regretting that to gain what respect she had, it had been necessary to try twice as hard.

"Sara Prine?"

"Mm."

"I'm Detective Constable Lynn Kellogg. Why don't you have a seat?"

"Oh. No, you're all right, I . . ."

Lynn smiled, put the witness at ease, wasn't that what it said in the handbooks, those who've come in voluntarily to make a statement. "We're going to be here for quite a while."

"Oh, I thought, you know, I'd be through by lunchtime."

"Then we'd best get started, shall we?"

When the girl did sit, Lynn noticed, it was almost primly, knees under the hem of her suit skirt drawn tight together. Her handbag she rested in her lap, hands, at first, clasped across it.

"What I want you to do, Sara, is tell me what happened last night leading up to you finding the body . . ."

"I already . . ."

"Do it in your own way, take your own time; when you've finished I might ask you a few questions, in case any part of it seems unclear. Then I'm going to write down what you've told me on one of these forms.

Before you go, I'll ask you to read it through and sign it; once you're happy that it's all correct. Now is that okay?"

The girl looked a little stunned. Ten years back, Lynn was thinking, what would I have been like in her position? Little more than Saturday shopping trips into Norwich to broaden my horizons, holidays at Great Yarmouth.

"Okay, then, Sara, in your own time . . ."

For God's sake, Divine thought, what's the matter with the youth? Squirming round on that seat like he's got Saint Vitus's dance. As if I'm about to give a toss what he did to his little tart and why. Bloody miracle was that she went with him at all. Face like a lavatory floor at close of business and whenever he leaned close Divine got this whiff of him, like opening a tin of cat food with your nose too sharp to the tin.

As for the jacket . . . Oxfam job if ever he saw one.

Divine stifled a yawn and tried not to make it too obvious he was looking at his watch. Come on, come on, get to the point. Only another six hours and he'd be over in the pub with the lads, sinking a few pints, curry later, that's what he fancied, put a bit of spice into the evening. Somebody reckoned The Black Orchid the place to go early in the week, good pickings, but look, these days, it paid to be careful where you were sticking it, didn't do to take too many chances.

"Hold up!" Divine spread his hands on the table, interrupting his own line of thought. "Let's have that bit again."

"What?"

"What you just said."

Raymond looked perplexed. What *had* he said?

"You said," Divine prompted him, "as soon as you saw the shoe . . ."

"Oh, yes, I guessed what it was. You know, under there."

Divine was shaking his head. "Not exactly. What you said was, you *knew*."

Raymond shrugged, fidgeted some more. "Knew, guessed, I don't know, what's the difference?"

"One means you were certain. If you knew, you . . ."

"That's right, I did. Least, I thought I did. Wasn't just the shoe, there was this . . . hand, I s'pose it was, a hand, part of her hand. And the smell." Raymond looked away from the table, where he'd been staring at his own chewed fingers, the bitten-down nails, and flush into Divine's face. "Had to be her. Didn't it?"

"*Her?*"

"The little girl, the one who went missing, ages back, you know."

Divine held his breath. "What you're saying, Raymond, right off, it wasn't simply you knew what was hidden in that corner was a body, you knew whose body it was."

Raymond stared back at him, not squirming anymore, quite calm. "Yes," he said. "Gloria. I knew her. Used to live near me. See her mornings, on her way, like, in to school. Weekends, off down the shops with her nan. Yes. Gloria. I used to watch her."

8

"Here," the pathologist said, "take one of these."

Resnick slipped one of Parkinson's extra-strong mints inside his mouth, pushing it high against his palate with his tongue. It was quiet enough in the small office for Resnick to hear the tick of the old-fashioned fob watch Parkinson always wore, attached by a chain at the front of his waistcoat. Only when he had to don an apron did the pathologist remove the jacket of his three-piece suit; the only occasion he removed his cuff links, rolled his shirt sleeves carefully back up, was when his assistant was holding out a pair of flesh-coloured surgical gloves.

"Quite a mess, eh, Charlie?"

Resnick nodded.

"As well we found her when we did."

Resnick nodded again, trying not to visualise the bite marks on the body; the front of the face, one way or another, laid bare almost to the bone.

"What helped most, of course, either it's my damned age or this is set to be one of the chillest winters we've had for years. Building like that, no heating, much of the time it would have stayed the right side of forty degrees."

They had identified Gloria Summers from her dental charts and by comparison of bones from an X ray that had been taken a year earlier, when she had fallen and broken a bone in her right ankle. Resnick had asked her mother if she wanted to come to the mortuary and see the body and Susan Summers had looked at him with raised eyebrows and said, "Are you kidding?"

"How definite can you be," Resnick asked now, "as to cause of death?"

Parkinson removed his bifocals and proceeded to give them an unnecessary polish. "One thing's positive: strangulation. Without doubt the windpipe has been fractured; the other signs you'd anticipate are clearly there. Haemorrhaging in the neck, close by the hyoid bone. Some evidence of swelling in the veins at the back of the head, caused by the increase in pressure when the blood is unable to escape."

"Then that was what killed her?"

"Not necessarily." Satisfied, Parkinson set the glasses back upon his nose. "There is also a severe fracture at the rear of the skull, acute extradural and subdural haematoma . . ."

"Fall or a blow?"

"Almost certainly a blow. The way the haemorrhaging's below the fracture. While she could have sustained a similar fracture as the result of a fall—she was only a wee girl remember—the force of that kind of accident jolts the brain hard against the skull and I'd be looking to find bleeding further forward, scarcely any underneath the fracture at all."

Resnick crunched the last fragments of mint between his back teeth. "So, your report, which one will you be opting for, principal cause?"

Parkinson shook his head. "Either, or." He put his hand into his waistcoat pocket, offered Resnick another mint. "Come the end of the day, I'll be surprised if it greatly matters."

Resnick got back to the station to find Graham Millington closeted in his office with Kellogg and Divine. Millington hadn't quite dared to take Resnick's chair, but hovered near it instead, as if he might be invited to sit at any moment. Divine, of course, sportsman that he was, had been working his way through Benson and Hedges Silk Cut, giving a pretty fair impression of Sellafield on a cloudy day.

"Sorry," Millington said, straightening not quite to attention, "like open house out there."

Resnick shook his head. "I assume you're not in here to discuss the dinner and dance?"

"No, sir."

Resnick wafted the door back and forth a few times, settled for leaving it partly open. "Better fill me in," he said.

Millington looked pointedly at Mark Divine and waited for him to start. Resnick listened, observing carefully: the way Divine leaned forward, shoulders hunched as if locking into a scrum, the eagerness in his voice; Lynn, more centered on her chair, soft scepticism on her face; and Millington—outside of the moral righteousness that went with a well-tended garden and a clean shirt, whatever he might be thinking was a mystery. Aside from the fact that he'd been sergeant for too long now, couldn't understand why the promotion he surely deserved still seemed so far away.

There was a moment after Divine had finished that they looked, all three of them, directly at Resnick, leaning back behind his desk. Outside, officers answered telephones, identifying themselves, rank and name; a single laugh, harsh and loud, broke into a raking cough; someone whistled the chorus of "Stand By Your Man" and Resnick smiled as he saw Lynn Kellogg bridle.

"He actually said that?" Resnick asked. " 'I used to watch her'?"

"Very words. Look." He held his notebook towards Resnick's face. "No two ways about it."

"No chance you had a tape running?" Millington said.

Divine scowled and shook his head.

"Clearly, you think it means something," said Resnick.

"Sir, you should have seen him. When he said it, about watching her. He didn't mean, yes, well, I used to bump into her in the street, knew who she was. He didn't mean I used to *see* her, casual like. What he was on about was something more."

"You didn't question him about that? Try to confirm your suspicions?"

"No, sir. I thought if I did, then, I mean, he might, you know, clam up."

"Where is he now?"

"One of the plods is treating him to a cup of tea."

"Thinking he knew who it was, lying there underneath all that debris," Resnick said, "that doesn't have to be so surprising. He'd have had to be a blind man not to have read about it, seen her face. And if he knew her anyway, by sight at least, there might have been more reason for her to stick in his mind than most."

"But this other, sir . . ."

"Yes, I know. We'll talk to him again, clearly." Resnick was suddenly conscious of the churning of his stomach; just because the morning with the pathologist had turned his mind away from food, that didn't mean his body had to agree.

"Lynn?"

"Sounds a bit odd, right enough. Then again, if there was anything iffy, would he come right out and say it?"

"Stupid or clever," suggested Millington.

"The girl," Resnick said to Lynn, "Sara. Did she say anything about the youth's reactions when they realised what they'd found?"

"Only that he was frightened. They both were. It took them over an hour, you know, before they made up their minds to come in and report it."

"Did she say which one of them was hanging back?"

"Says it was the lad, sir."

"Mark?"

"He never said exactly, just that they spent ages wandering around; he did say as the girl was upset, that's why they went back to his place, calm her down before walking round here."

"All right." Resnick got to his feet and Divine and Kellogg did the same; Graham Millington moved his arm from the filing cabinet where he had been leaning. "Mark, have another word with him, low-key. Lynn, why don't you sit in with them? See if you can establish just what his relationship with the girl was, supposing it was any more than he's said. And that warehouse, maybe it was a place he's used before, somewhere handy for a bit of fun after closing. Let me know how you get on."

Resnick's phone rang as they were going out of the door. He lifted the receiver from the cradle, but cupped a hand over the mouthpiece.

"The girl, Lynn, she's not still here?"

"Afraid not."

"No matter, we can talk to her later."

Lynn took her time about turning away again, something she had to get off her mind. "I'm not sure if this is the way we're thinking, but if this Raymond did know Gloria Summers was in that building, wouldn't it have been the last place he'd have taken his girl friend for a snog?"

"Depends," Divine said quickly, "on just how much of a pervert he is."

"So, Raymond, how was the tea? Okay? Good. This here's my colleague, Detective Constable Kellogg. Like I say, we won't keep you long now, just a couple of little things we need to get sorted."

Raymond finally left the station at seven minutes after three. His shirt was stuck to his back with sweat and he could smell his armpits and his crotch with every movement, every step. Underneath the tangle of hair, his scalp itched. Pain reverberated, sharp and insistent, beneath his right temple, causing his eye to blink.

On and on they had gone at him, mostly the man, but the woman chipping in too, all the same questions, again and again. Gloria, Gloria. How well had he known her? When he said that he watched her, what did he mean? Perhaps he used to baby-sit? Help her grandmother with her shopping? Do odd jobs? Collect Gloria sometimes from school? How well would he say he knew her? The mother? Gloria. Would he, for instance, describe her as a friend? Daft! How could some kid of six be his friend? All right, then, Raymond, what was she? You tell us.

He wanted to go home and wash. Take a long bath, slow. He wanted something cold to drink. He bought a can of Ribena from the cob shop over the road and walked back across Derby Road to drink it, sitting with his back against the wall of the insurance offices.

She was a kid he'd noticed first through the shock of fair hair that seemed, more often than not, to spring from her head in all directions. Blue, blue eyes. Like a doll's. Raymond wondered why he'd thought that? Never had a sister, never had a doll in his life. Handled one: held it. Once he'd spotted her—running along the street towards him, lolly waving in her hand, her nan, her mum he'd thought it was then, calling, "Be careful, be careful! Oh, for goodness' sake do be careful. Oh, look what you've done. Just look at you now." He seemed to see her everywhere he looked. In the Chinese chippy, on the rec, waiting at the bus stop with a hand in her nan's, swinging from it and kicking out this leg and then that, never still. One day he realised that if he angled his head from the window at a certain angle he could see one corner of the school playground. Gloria with all her little friends, laughing and shouting, playing games, skipping, two-ball, kiss chase.

9

Resnick had opted for the southerly route, leaving the A153 before the potential bottlenecks of Sleaford and Tattershall Bridge. B roads would take him past the furthest outreach of the fens, safely through Ashby de la Launde, Timberland and Martin Dales; after Horncastle the choice lay between Salmonby and Somersby, then it was Swaby, Beesby, Maltby le Marsh and he was there. Returning home, he'd promised himself the high road through the rolling Wolds; Louth and then the cathedral tower at Lincoln, its lights burning for miles through the steadily gathering swathes of mist.

That would come later.

A necessary balm for what he was about to do.

Right now, there was a flask of coffee on the seat beside him, sandwiches in greaseproof paper he'd picked up from the deli. Emmenthal and slivers of prosciutto ham, so fine that they would fold back and wrap around a finger like gold leaf; a thick-ridged pickled cucumber, sliced and lain across corned beef, further spiced with a liberal splash of four-grain mustard. Four small cherry tomatoes, ready to burst into his mouth, sweet pulp and tiny seeds. Resnick slowed to allow a Land Rover to swing past on the broad stroke of a bend; another impoverished farmer late for the bank.

Fumbling the cassette one-handed from its box, he slotted it into place and swivelled up the volume. The Basie band at its first prime, 1940, America still to enter the war. A swirl of riffs teased along by the leader's piano, the soloists stabbing and soaring, the last, Lester, leaning back against the beat.

Lester Young.

On the road with the band, he had avoided military call-up until 1944, when a presumed fan turned out to be a draft officer in disguise. Despite an examination which revealed syphilis and an addiction to alcohol, barbiturates and marijuana, Lester was inducted as Private 39729502. Within six months, he would be dishonourably discharged by a military court and imprisoned for almost a year. Prior to sentence, he was diagnosed as being in a constitutionally psychopathic state: the condition for which ten months in the U.S. Army Detention Barracks, Fort Gordon, Georgia, was a guaranteed cure.

Resnick steadied the flask between his legs, unscrewed the cap, took a long swallow and rewound the tape so as to listen again to "I Never Knew." One of those tunes Gus Kahn likely tossed off at his piano between cigars. The trombone takes the first solo, sliding between slur and rasp: then it's Lester, tenor angled steeply to the mike, paving his way with a stepping-stone of single notes before striking for home with thirty-two bars of pride and beauty, making the melody, the moment, his own. Resnick can see him, in his mind's eye, sitting back in the section with the slightest of nods, a too-thin man with reddish hair and green eyes, wearing a band jacket that is perhaps too large, while behind him the brass rises to its feet for the flag-waving finale.

What is it that causes us to take a man who, despite disease and self-doubt, can create such glory and throw him into the stockade, denying him everything, a thirty-four-year-old, light-skinned black man in deepest Georgia? Take a girl with china-blue eyes and blonde hair and break her body, bury her in bin bags in the wasted dark?

I Never Knew.

Resnick lowered his foot on the accelerator, turned up the volume of the tape until the sound trembled on the edge of distortion, closing out all other noise, all thought.

Mablethorpe, less than twenty miles up the coast from Skeggy, and forever its poor relation, welcomed Resnick like a Dickensian pallbearer wintering away from the poorhouse. Along the length of the single main street, boarded-up shop fronts vainly promised lettered rock and candy floss, jumbo hot dogs and fresh-made doughnuts, five for a pound. A white-haired man in an old RAF greatcoat nodded at him, his wire-haired fox terrier showing a passing interest in Resnick's ankles. Up ahead, the broad concrete promenade had all the friendliness of the Maginot Line. And beyond that, all but lost in mist, the North Sea rolled coldly in, inexorable, more like sludge than sea.

Edith Summers had swopped her high-rise flat for a 1930s bungalow with a pebble-dash facia, three doors down from a corner café advertising fresh-caught local cod and chips (tea included, bread and butter extra). She didn't say anything when she recognised Resnick standing at her front door, shoulders hunched against the drizzle and the wind.

She had brought her fish tank and gold-rimmed table with her; hired a new TV, bolted onto a black metal trolley, and, in poorly mixed colour, Petula Clark was gazing wistfully at Fred Astaire, singing "How Are Things in Glocca Morra?" in a failing Irish accent. Edith left Resnick in the low-ceilinged room and returned with a flowered cup and saucer.

"I've not long mashed."

When he was sitting, sipping at the lukewarm tea, she said: "I know why you're here."

Resnick nodded.

"I was right, wasn't I?"

"Yes, but . . ."

"What I said."

"Yes."

At first, he thought she was going to control it, brave it through until he'd gone, but, sitting in front of him, a distance that could be spanned too easily by an outstretched arm, he watched her face crumple inwards, a balloon from which the air was being slowly released.

While the first sobs were still raking her, he set down his cup and saucer, knelt beside her, reaching up, until she buried her face in the crook of his neck, cheek fast against the rough collar of his coat.

"Had he, you know, molested her? Interfered with her, like?" It was later, dark pressed up against the windows; Resnick had made the tea this time and the pot sat before the bars of the electric fire, knitted tea cosy not quite in place.

"We don't know. Not for certain. The length of time she'd been left. But, yes, you have to think it's possible." A shiver coursed through him, nothing to do with the cold. "I'm sorry."

Edith shook her head. "I can't understand it, can you? How anyone in his right mind . . ."

"No," Resnick said.

"Then, of course, that's it. They're not in their right mind, are they?"

He said nothing.

"Sick, sick. They need whipping, locking up."

He began to reach a hand towards her.

"No, no. It's all right. I shall be all right."

Inside the room it seemed airless. The fire was burning Resnick's right leg, making no impression on the left. Despite himself, he was thinking of the long drive home, the murder incident room the next morning.

"The funeral," Edith said suddenly. "Whatever's going to happen about the funeral?"

"Perhaps Gloria's mother . . ." Resnick began and then stopped.

"It's my fault, you know."

"No."

"It is. It is my fault."

"No one can be expected to watch over a child all the time. Where you left her . . ."

But that wasn't what Edith Summers meant. She meant her daughter, Susan, born late, virtually ignored by her father for the first nine months of her life, nagged and harried for the eighteen after that until he left, setting up house in Ilkeston with a woman he'd met on the checkout in Safeway, old enough to indulge him and count the consequences. He scarcely ever came round after that, not all the while Susan was growing towards her teens. Not that Edith encouraged him, better at gritting her teeth and bearing it than she ever was at reconciliation.

When Susan reached ten, rising eleven, all that seemed to change. Her dad's relationship had broken up and he was back in the city, sharing a house with a couple of taxi drivers who lived at Top Valley and driving a cab himself. "Edith," he would say, smiling his way round the door on his increasingly frequent visits, "Edie, lighten up. She's my daughter, too. Aren't you, princess?" Offering Susan the comics, the chocolate, the Top Twenty singles to play on the Taiwanese music centre he'd bought her as a Christmas present. "Eh, her dad's girl."

Three years it lasted, lightning visits whenever one of his fares left him over in the right direction, time to call in and sweep his daughter off her feet all over again. Then the Saturday he kissed Susan on the top of the head and said to her mother, "Right, c'mon. Get your coat, we're off round the pub. Nothing for you to worry about, princess. Back in a couple of shakes."

Over a pint of mixed and Edith's gin and Dubonnet, he told her about America, the woman he had met when she was over here on holiday—"Just picked her up in the cab, short fare from the Lace Hall to Tales of Robin Hood, who'd have thought it?" She was the one who'd invited him over, reckoned she could put in a word, get him fixed up with a job, someone who would vouch for him, see that he settled.

"And Susan?" Edith had managed.

"She'll be able to come over, won't she? Holidays. You see; I'll send the fare."

What he sent were postcards, once a Mickey Mouse that lost a leg in flight. Susan sulked and cried and claimed she didn't care: right up to the time she first stayed out all night and when she arrived back home next morning, dropped off by a twenty-five-year-old in a purple-and-gold Cortina, said to her mother's face, "It's my life and I'll do what I want with it and there's nothing you can do to stop me." Not so many days short of her fifteenth birthday.

Edith looked at the teapot by the fire through blurred eyes. "I don't suppose there's anything in there worth drinking?"

Resnick tried for a smile. "I'll make some more."

"No," getting to her feet, "let me. It's my house. Bungalow, anyhow. You're the visitor, remember?"

He followed her into the tiny kitchen; whenever she needed to reach for the packet of PG Tips, the carton of UHT milk, Resnick had to suck in his stomach, hold his breath.

"Sixteen she was when she fell for Gloria," Edith said, waiting for the tea to draw. "I was only surprised it hadn't happened sooner. If ever I asked her, you know, said anything about taking precautions, all that happened was she told me to watch my mouth, mind my own business. I suppose I should have stood my ground, made a scene, dragged her off screaming and kicking to the doctor, family planning, if that's what it needed." She sighed and gave the pot a final stir before beginning to pour. "But I didn't, I let it alone. Look," handing him the cup and saucer, "you're sure that's not too strong?"

Resnick nodded, fine, and they moved back into the other room.

"Turned out," Edith said, sitting down, "she'd got in with this particular gang of lads, old enough to have known better; they'd been passing her round like some blanket you use to take the chill out of the grass when you lie down. Any one of them it could have been and, of course, none of them stood up for it. Susan was too concerned with being sick, being angry to think about pointing fingers, blood tests, any of that."

Edith leaned forward from her chair, shaking an inch of ash from her cigarette onto the beige tiles surrounding the fire.

"She could've had an abortion, but I think she was too frightened. All she could talk about was adopt, adopt, adopt. I suppose somewhere inside I hoped that once she'd had the baby, held it, she'd think different. No. The only feelings Susan ever seemed to have were for Susan. Anything that was going to cost her more than opening her mouth, opening her legs, she didn't want to know."

Edith rattled down her cup and looked Resnick in the face. "Whatever made me think, after the mess I made of bringing up one daughter on my own, I could do better with another?"

Resnick took away the cup and saucer, stubbed out the cigarette and held her hands. "Listen," he said, "what happened, it wasn't your fault."

She was a long time replying. She said: "No? Then who was it ran off and left her there? Off round the corner for a packet of fags? Who?"

Only when his arms were numb, the heat from the fire on his leg so strong that he could smell the material of his trousers beginning to singe, did Resnick seek to loosen her grip, let her go.

Outside the rain had stopped and the wind that cut across the street was keen as a knife. Hesitating for a moment before getting into his car, Resnick could just hear the swish and fall of the sea, dull roll of the undertow. And because there was nothing else to do, he turned his key in the lock, the ignition, released the hand brake, adjusted the choke, indicated that he was pulling away.

10

"D'you see this?"

"What d'you say?"

"I said, did you see . . ."

"Lorraine, it's no use, I can't hear a word you're saying."

Lorraine remembered not to sigh or shake her head, pushed the local paper a little to one side and sipped at her red mug of Nescafé, Gold Blend decaffeinated. On the ceramic hob, potatoes and carrots were simmering nicely; five minutes' time, she'd empty some frozen peas from the large family pack into a small pan of boiling water, add a teaspoon of sugar and a shake of salt, the way her mother always did. She would check the oven at the same time; if the fish was ready inside its foil packet, move it down onto the lower shelf and adjust the temperature ready for the Sara Lee Danish Apple Bar, Michael's favourite, served with double cream and custard both.

"You're always doing that, you know," Michael said, still towelling his hair as he walked into the room.

"What?"

"Talking to me while I'm in the shower, as if you expect me to understand what you're going on about."

"Michael, I wasn't going on."

"All right," aiming a kiss towards her face and missing, "whatever you were doing, I didn't hear it."

They had bought the house a year ago, five thousand short of the asking price in a declining market and glad to get it, carpets and curtains thrown in. Though, as Lorraine had informed Michael at the time, as soon as they could afford it she was going to throw them out again; not her taste at all. Another thing Lorraine had insisted upon, new units in the kitchen, proper surfaces, wipe off and keep clean, electricity instead of gas. There was a small room off the kitchen, surely it wouldn't cost a fortune to have it fitted out with a shower? That way they needn't be getting under one another's feet in the mornings.

And Michael, just married for the second time, a younger woman this time and with ideas of her own, bound to have, did what he could to ensure they managed. All the mistakes he'd made before, himself and Diana, he wasn't about to let them happen again.

Besides, the extra shower was a good idea. Although he left the house quite a bit earlier to catch his train, Lorraine liked to be up too; partly to make sure he had a proper breakfast, but also as she enjoyed sitting over her coffee after Michael had gone, washing already in the machine, dishes stacked away, reading the *Mail* in her own time. There was always some little tidbit she could slip into her conversation with the other tellers at the bank, the customers even. "Did you read about . . . ?" while she was weighing the bags of change. It made it more personal, as if she were making contact, not one of those machines set into the wall.

"What's for dinner?" Michael asked, wandering through into the other room and coming back with the scotch bottle in his hand. Lorraine wished he wouldn't do that, knew he would have had one or two already on the train; once she might have said something but now she knew better. What you did, bit your tongue and kept mum.

"Fish," she said.

"I know fish, but what kind?"

"Salmon."

He paused and looked at her, then poured a couple of fingers of scotch into the solid-bottomed glass.

"It's fresh," Lorraine said. "Sainsbury's."

"Steaks?"

She shook her head. "A whole fish."

"Must've cost a quid or two."

"It was on special offer."

"Needing to get shot of it, then. You're sure it's okay? Fresh?"

What did he think she was going to do, pay out over six pounds for fish that wasn't fresh? "This morning's catch, his word on it."

Michael added a little water to his scotch, not too much; where was the sense in buying good whisky only to water it down? "You can never believe them," he said. "Salesmen. Say whatever it takes. Stands to reason, it's their job, selling. If you have to bend the truth a little, well . . ." tasting his drink, ". . . you bend the truth."

Michael was a salesman, sort of, himself. Machine tools, he had tried to explain in detail once, but gone off in a huff when she'd been slow to understand, accusing her of being thick. She stopped herself from thinking about Michael, the occasions when he might be tempted to bend the truth.

"Anyway," she said, "he's not a salesman, he's a fishmonger."

Michael laughed and slipped a little more whisky into his glass. "Wears a striped apron and straw hat, does he?"

"Yes, as a matter of fact, he does."

Michael leaned over and gave her a kiss; not on the mouth, but a kiss all the same. She wished he wouldn't patronise her so much.

"How much was it then, this whole salmon?"

"Only four pounds. I told you, it was a bargain."

Michael sniffed. "Four pounds. Better be good."

After dinner, Michael liked to stretch out in the lounge, swing one of his legs over the side of the armchair. When Lorraine had been growing up, it was something her mother had been forever telling her about, the way it stretched the covers out of shape. Together they would watch TV for a while, once Lorraine had finished in the kitchen. Usually she would have to nudge him awake and then they'd probably watch the headlines on the news and if there was nothing special, like a plane crash or another pile-up on the M1, start to get ready for bed.

Sometimes, especially at weekends, they lingered downstairs and Michael would put some Chris DeBurgh on the CD player, Chris Rea, Dire Straits.

The first time he had made love to her, in the studio flat he'd moved to after separating from his wife, he had programmed "The Lady in Red" and then pressed the repeat button. This will be our song, Lorraine had thought, but never said.

Now, there were still times when, as she was getting undressed, moving between the dressing table and the bathroom, Michael would lean on one elbow, reach out a hand towards her and touch the inside of her leg as she passed, fingers stroking the inside of her thigh.

Fridays. Occasionally Saturdays, especially if they'd been round for dinner with friends, Michael passing round the third bottle of wine and staring down the front of someone else's wife's dress.

Lorraine remembered once, a month or so back, she had been feeling especially loving, had put a CD on the machine herself and sat, cross-legged, on the carpet near Michael's chair, resting her head against his knee. When "The Lady in Red" had come on, she had asked, something of a wistful quality in her voice, "Do you remember, Michael, when we first heard this?"

"No," Michael said. "Should I?"

Lorraine sat in front of the mirror, dabbing a ball of mauve cotton wool around her eyes. She could hear Michael urinating in the bathroom, one thing her mother would never have stood for. She would go on and on at Lorraine's dad, telling him if he couldn't direct his flow quietly against the sides of the bowl, then please be thoughtful enough to run the cold tap until he was through performing. Michael didn't even close the bathroom door.

And as for farting . . . well, she didn't think her mother acknowledged that the word existed, never mind the deed. Not in the nice part of Rugeley, where they lived.

"Tired?" she asked, as Michael rolled into bed alongside her.

"Knackered!"

"Poor sweetheart!"

She reached under the duvet and began, lightly, to stroke his stomach, just gently, but he grunted and rolled over, shrugging her away.

That was that.

If she'd been Julia Roberts in *Pretty Woman*, Lorraine thought, she wouldn't allow herself to be so easily dissuaded. She would run her fingers down his back, but firmly, carry on till she was past his buttocks, wait until his legs widened apart.

As they surely would: if she were Julia Roberts.

Now Michael curled away onto his side and was beginning to snore.

"Michael," she said, nudging him with her toe.

"I was just getting off to sleep."

"What I was going to say before, you know, when you were in the shower . . ."

"That was hours ago."

"I know. Only . . ."

"Only what, for heaven's sake?"

"That little girl, the one that went missing. You know, it was all over the papers . . ."

"What about her?"

"They found her body. She'd been murdered."

Michael turned over sharply, facing her. "Of course she had. What else did you think had happened?"

When Lorraine woke, the clock at her side of the bed read 3:28. At first she thought Michael had stirred, disturbing her, either that or she needed to go to the bathroom and relieve her bladder. When she realised it was neither, she slid her legs out from beneath the duvet and found her slippers on the floor. Her dressing gown was hanging behind the bedroom door.

Emily lay upside down with one leg hanging over the side of the bed, the other beneath the pillow. Her head was pushed against the wooden base, strands of auburn hair trailing down. Her nightie had become rucked up in the tangle of sheet around her waist, and Lorraine, careful not to wake her, eased it back over her legs.

Since Michael had been forced to take a job almost two hours away, his daughter was frequently in bed before he returned home; the only time he got to see her was forty-five minutes in the mornings and at weekends. It was Lorraine who fetched her from school, who made her tea and listened to her chatter; said, "Ooh! Yes, lovely!" at her paintings—great sploshes of red and purple on grey paper, which later were stuck to the fridge-freezer door.

It was Lorraine, more often now than not, who dropped Emily off at Diana's house; Diana, Emily's mother, Michael's first wife. Lorraine who collected her, seven hours later, trying not to notice the older woman's face, the dark and swollen eyes, the tears.

Lorraine wasn't sure how long she stood there in the half-dark, looking down at her stepdaughter, while the images conjured up by the news report nibbled away at the edges of her mind.

11

Patel had been out on the street for less than an hour on a dull, run-of-the-mill end-of-year day, the kind that promises nothing, other than sooner or later it will end, when someone spat in his face.

He was on his way to interview the assistant manager of a building society near the corner of Lister Gate and Low Pavement about a recent robbery, wondering if, while he was there, he might ask about applying for a loan, moving upscale to something a little quieter, less prone to woodworm and suspect drains.

On the descent past M&S, shaking his head politely, sorry, no, at the part-time market researchers who hovered hopefully with their clipboards and part-time smiles, Patel paused to look down at the painting a young man was reproducing in chalk on the flagstones, a Renaissance madonna and child. A little further on, close by the crossroads, a muscular black mime artist, in singlet and sweatpants despite the temperature, was making slow-motion moves to the taped accompaniment of what Patel understood to be electrofunk. Quite a crowd had gathered in a rough, mostly admiring, circle. Patel walked around the outer edge, taking his time. The clock above the Council House had not long sounded the quarter hour and his appointment was for half past. He was reaching into his trouser pocket for a coin to throw down into the performer's hat when a blue van, descending Low Pavement towards the pedestrianised cross street, braked sharply to avoid colliding with a pram.

The woman, thirties, black Lycra pants and a fake-fur coat, cigarette trailing from one hand, swerved the pram sharply round, its rear wheel finishing only a foot or so away from the off-side wing of the van.

"Great daft bastard!" she shouted. "What the 'ell d'you think you're doing? No right to be driving down here any rate. Not like that, you're sodding not."

"Lady . . ." tried the driver through his partly wound-down window.

"Nearly ran smack into me, you know that. Right into the effing pram."

"Sweetheart . . ."

"If I'd not had me eyes about me, you'd have gone right sodding over it, baby an' all. Then what would you be doing?"

"Darling . . ."

"Up in bloody court on bleeding manslaughter."

"Look . . ."

"You effing look!"

Shaking his head, as if to suggest to the crowd deserting the mime show for this new drama that he wasn't wasting any more of his breath, the driver wound up his window and engaged gear. The woman promptly stepped away from her pram and planted a kick low on the door, hard enough to dent the panel.

The driver rapidly wound his window back down. "Watch it!"

"You effing watch it! Who you telling to watch it? You're the one, came down here, sixty miles an hour. Selfish bastard!" And she kicked the door a second time.

"Right!" The driver wrenched open the van door and climbed out. The crowd fell quiet.

"Excuse me," Patel said, stepping forward. "Excuse me," setting himself between them, "madam, sir."

"Fuck off, you!" shouted the woman. "Who asked you to butt your nose in?"

"Yeh," said the driver, giving Patel a push in the back, "one thing we don't need, advice from the likes of you."

"All I am trying to do . . ." Patel tried.

"Look," the driver said, moving round him. "Piss off!"

"I . . ." said Patel, reaching into his pocket for his identification.

"Piss off!" said the woman, and, with a quick backward arch of her head, she spat into Patel's face.

"I am a police officer," Patel finished, blinking away phlegm and saliva.

"Yeh," said the woman. "And I'm the Queen of Sheba."

Patel let his fingers slide from his warrant card and reached for a tissue instead. The driver got back into his van and the woman reversed her pram around him. Within moments, they were on their respective ways and most of the crowd had gone back to watching the mime or were wandering off to continue window-shopping. Only Lynn Kellogg stayed where she was, in the doorway of Wallis's, doubtful if Patel had spotted her and wondering whether the tactful thing would be to slip away unnoticed.

It didn't take her long to decide; he was still in the same position when she touched him lightly on the arm and smiled. "Wonderful, isn't it?" Patel nodded, tried to smile back. "Try to help and that's what happens."

He screwed up the tissue and pushed it down into his pocket. "It doesn't matter."

"Got time for a coffee or something?"

Patel looked at his watch. "Not really, but . . ."

They walked through the ground floor of a small shop dedicated to the sale of potpourri, expensive wrapping paper and cardboard cutouts of benign-looking cats, upstairs into a small café largely patronised by women from Southwell or Burton Joyce wearing floral print dresses and good camel coats.

"Why didn't you carry through with it?" Lynn asked, stirring sugar into her cup.

"Warrant card, you mean?"

Lynn nodded.

"Didn't seem a great deal of point. 'Excuse me interrupting your little confrontation but I am a police officer.' Not given their first reaction." Patel tried the coffee and decided it tasted of very little. "Whatever I had showed them, if I had said I was in CID, a detective, I don't think they would easily have believed me."

Lynn allowed herself a wry smile. "Any consolation, Diptak, I doubt they'd have believed me either."

The walk-through sweet store was full of small children tugging at their parents' hands: "I want! I want! I want!" Lynn chose a small scoop of old-fashioned striped bull's-eyes, some black liquorice with soft white centres, barley sugars, chocolate limes and a few strawberry fizzes filled with pink sherbet. She could always hand them round to the rest of the office; no law said she had to eat them all herself.

"How much for these?"

Sara Prine looked young in her uniform, more a fuchsia than a regular pink; a false apron, striped, at the front, meant to summon up some addled vision of bygone days, where everyone knew their place and kids' treats weren't squeezed from single-parent income support and excessive sugar didn't rot your teeth.

"One pound, forty-eight."

Lynn raised an eyebrow, handed over a five-pound note. "Remember me?" she said.

Of course, she had; those tight little cheeks sucked in tighter still, slight tremor of the hand as she gave Lynn her change.

"I'd like to talk to you."

"Not here."

"You'd prefer to come back to the station?"

Sara's shoulders tensed as she gave a quick, terse shake of the head.

"When do you get a break?"

"I'm on early lunch."

"How early?"

"Eleven-thirty."

Early enough to be late breakfast. "I'll meet you outside. We can find somewhere to sit."

Sara nodded again and took the bag from her next customer, setting it on the scale. Lynn popped a bull's-eye into her mouth and left.

"And the weapon?" Patel was saying.

"The gun."

"Yes. You say he took it from his pocket?"

"His inside pocket, yes. A blue . . . donkey jacket, I suppose that's what you'd call it."

"Like a work jacket, similar to that?"

"Smarter. I mean, he didn't look as if he'd nipped in from a building site. Besides, there was none of that reinforcement they have, real working ones, across the shoulders."

Patel nodded, wrote something in his book.

The assistant manager had turned out to be an assistant manageress.

He had waited at the corner of the inquiry desk until the buzzer sounded and he was waved through, escorted into a narrow, windowless room, barely large enough to hold a desk and two chairs, the chairs on which they now sat, Patel and Alison Morley. When he had asked her name, she had simply pointed to the badge pinned at an angle over her breast.

"You don't know, I mean, what kind of a gun?"

"No. Except that it was . . ."

"Yes?"

"Black. It was black."

"Long?"

She shook her head. "Not very." A pause. "I mean, I suppose it depends what you're comparing it to."

Patel set down his pen and held out both hands, sideways on, approximately eight inches apart.

"Is that long?" she said.

"It depends."

"I mean, I've seen that film, on television, more than once. Clint Eastwood. He can't get to finish his hamburger on account of this robbery taking place on the other side of the street. Anyway, there's all this shooting and cars crashing, and then he's standing there with this gun . . ."

"A Magnum," Patel said.

"Is that what it is? Anyway, he's pointing it down at this gangster, bank robber, whatever he is, pretending he doesn't know if there are any bullets left or not. Which I think, well, it's funny, but also it's stupid, because if he's a policeman, I mean a professional, he must know how many bullets he's got left in his gun. Don't you think so?"

Patel nodded. "I suppose . . ."

"I mean, if you were on duty and armed, you'd know how many bullets you had left, wouldn't you?"

Patel, who had never been armed on duty and earnestly hoped that he never would be, told her that, yes, he hoped that he would.

"Anyway," Alison Morley said, "that gun was big."

"A forty-five Magnum, the most powerful handgun in the world," Patel said, quoting from the film as accurately as he could remember. "And the weapon the man pointed at you through the glass, it wasn't that size."

"Nothing like. But frightening enough all the same."

"You were scared?"

She looked back at Patel, smiling at the corners of her mouth. "I thought I was going to wet myself," she said.

Lynn Kellogg and Sara Prine were sitting on a bench not far from where Sara worked; they were dipping into Lynn's diminishing bag of sweets as they talked. Lynn chatting to her about her job at first, trying to get her to relax a little, some chance.

"There isn't anything else I can tell you," Sara said, selecting a strawberry fizz. "About finding that poor girl's body. I've been over it again and again in my mind."

"I wanted to ask you about your boy friend," Lynn said.

"Boy friend?"

"Yes, Raymond."

"Raymond isn't my boy friend."

"I'm sorry, I thought . . ."

"That was the first time I'd ever seen him. That evening."

"Oh," said Lynn, looking at her half-profile, Sara less than keen on eye contact, "I thought . . ."

"I'd known him longer?"

"Yes, I suppose . . ."

"Because I went with him?"

"I suppose so."

Sara looked at Lynn then, a dart of the head, round and away. "We didn't do anything, you know."

"Look, Sara . . ."

"I mean, nothing happened."

"Sara . . ."

"Nothing serious."

Just for a moment, lightly, Lynn touched the girl's arm. "Sara, it's none of my business."

Sara Prine got to her feet, brushing puffs of pink sherbet away from the front of her uniform. Higher up the street, outside C&A, a busker wearing a comic hat and a red nose was singing "There's a Blue Ridge Round My Heart, Virginia," accompanying himself on banjo. It wasn't the version Lynn had heard in the station canteen.

"Sara," she said, trying for the intonation of a friend, an older sister. Sara sat back down.

"Where you and Raymond went, the sidings, did you get the impression he'd been there before?"

She thought it over, nibbling at a hangnail on her little finger. "I hadn't really thought about it, but, yes, I suppose . . . He knew where he was taking me, yes. I mean he wasn't stumbling around in the dark."

"And the building itself?"

"Oh, I don't know. He could've. Yes. Though we didn't really go far in, you know, not at first."

"When you were . . ." Lynn paused. "Kissing?"

"Yes."

"So up until the time you suspected there might be something very nasty in there as well, what would you say was Raymond's mood?"

Sara chewed at the flesh inside her lower lip. "I don't know what you mean."

"Well, was he . . . for instance, was he excited, was he nervous?"

"He wasn't nervous, no. Only after."

"After you found Gloria's body?"

Sara nodded.

"Up to that point, then, he wasn't apprehensive at all?"

Sara frowned, not certain she understood.

"Raymond, he wasn't frightened?"

"No. He had no need to be, did he? Specially not when he had the knife."

Lynn was aware of the skin at the back of her neck beginning to prickle. "Knife, Sara? What knife was this?"

"So," Alison Morley said, hands on the table, fingers spread, "shall I be talking to you again?"

"I don't know," Patel said. "If we find somebody, make an arrest, then yes, it is possible."

"An identification parade?"

"Possibly."

Alison Morley nodded once; getting to her feet, she gave the sides of her skirt a discreet downward pull.

"Thank you for your time," Patel said, suddenly self-conscious that she was watching him stow away his notebook and pen, push back his chair.

"You're not from here, are you?" she said.

Patel shook his head. "Bradford. My family, they come from Bradford."

Alison nodded. "I thought it was more a Yorkshire accent."

"Well, yes."

"I've a cousin, comes from somewhere outside Leeds."

"Yes." He glanced round at the door, began to back away. "Well, thanks for being so helpful."

"Wait a minute."

She took a small handkerchief from her pocket and nodded at the lapel of his jacket. "You've got something down you."

Patel watched as, carefully, she dabbed it away. The badge engraved with her name was so close to touching his other lapel. She had, he noticed, a tiny mole immediately below one corner of her mouth and level with the cleft of her chin.

"There," she said, satisfied, stepping back.

"Look," Patel said, blurting out the words too quickly, "you wouldn't like to come out with me some time?"

"Why not?" said Alison Morley, stepping back. "We could always talk about your mortgage. See if it isn't time for you to think about an extension."

12

Resnick had emerged from Jack Skelton's office inspired. Back from a brisk two-mile run, the superintendent had unfolded from their neat foil wrapping two pieces of dry plasterboard, which turned out to be Swedish crisp bread, three sticks of green celery and an apple.

"Hear that report on the radio this morning, Charlie?" Skelton had asked, slicing the apple scrupulously into four and then four again. "Two thirds of the country setting their health at serious risk through sloppy eating habits. Cancer of the colon, cancer of the bowel."

Resnick had entered the deli committed to good intentions. Nothing wrong, after all, with a salad sandwich on wholemeal bread, no dressing, no mayonnaise, hold the butter. Cottage cheese, not many carbohydrates in that, specially if you went for the low-fat version. Course, it didn't taste of a whole lot, but where a healthy body was concerned, the sacrifice of a little flavour was a small price to pay.

"That'll be two pounds, thirty-five."

It was the second sandwich, the one with tuna and chicken livers, radicchio in a garlic sauce, dark rye bread with caraway, that was what put up the price. That and the wedge of Cambazola that had been standing there so temptingly at the edge of the board.

" 'Lo, Kevin."

"Sir."

Naylor walking away from the area of the cells as Resnick came back into the station, heading for the stairs.

"Going all right?"

"Sir."

"Wife okay?"

"Sir."

"Baby?"

"Sir."

Naylor held open the CID door for Resnick to walk through, then hurried towards the safety of the far end of the office and began shuffling forms and papers over the surface of his desk.

Resnick used the sole of his shoe to push his own door closed and set his lunch down alongside the duty roster, licking at his fingers, where grease had seeped through the paper bag. Kevin Naylor had come to see him several months before, unofficial inquiry about a transfer. To the best of Resnick's knowledge the young DC had never pursued it further, but rumours that all was not well at home had persisted, ructions between Debbie and himself, even some difficulties with Debbie and the baby. Resnick had asked Lynn Kellogg about that once and Lynn had said, yes, as far as she knew, Debbie had been suffering a bit of postnatal depression but she understood things to be sorting themselves out. Naylor did his share of drinking off-shift, nothing that wasn't par for that particular course. If he'd taken to going over the side, at least he hadn't been shooting his mouth off about it in the canteen.

Even so . . .

Resnick chewed thoughtfully, half a mind to call Naylor in, see if there wasn't more to get out of him than the same single-syllable word. He was still thinking when his phone rang and he had to swallow hastily before picking up.

"I don't know," he replied, after listening to what Lynn Kellogg had to say, "youth like that, out in the city on a Friday, Saturday night without a knife of some kind about him, that might be more of a surprise. Even so, a few more questions likely wouldn't hurt. . . . No, no, let Mark have another go at him. Besides, I've got other plans for you. How'd you feel about a bit of a bucket-and-spade job? Quick trip to the seaside?"

Lorraine wished she knew if the right thing to do was tell Michael about it or not. She knew, at least she was pretty certain she knew, what his reaction would be. It wasn't that he was an irrational man, Michael, and not violent, no, not that, absolutely not, not normally; but where his ex, where Diana, was concerned, it was different. There had been the period when she had kept sending Emily letters; not letters, really, more little notes, usually no more than a few words written on one of those notelets, the kind with flowers around the border. And it didn't matter, wasn't as if Emily could read them properly, Diana's handwriting not being of the best. She had been able to understand the bottom part, though: Mum; *love and kisses*, Mum; and then lots of Xs, just to underline the point.

Michael had torn them up when he'd found them, which hadn't been for the first couple of weeks, Lorraine having decided that what Michael didn't know wouldn't harm him, the post arriving after he'd left to catch his train.

"However long's this been going on?" he'd demanded, glowering at Lorraine as if it all had been her fault. And when she'd told him, "Suffering Christ!" and he'd wrenched the drawer right out, showering them down onto the bed and the floor. Of course, Emily had cried when he'd torn them up, sobbed her heart out. "See," Michael had said, pointing. "See?" Vindicated. "How upset it gets her."

And then there had been the phone calls, Diana's voice at first, calmly inquiring if she might speak to Emily.

"Diana, I'm not positive that's such a good idea," Lorraine had faltered.

"Keep this up and I'll get the law on to you," Michael had said. "Keep this up and see if I don't."

After that, she never spoke, simply waited ten, fifteen seconds before ringing off. Michael had said it was some pervert, a heavy breather going through the phone book, getting his sordid little kicks. Lorraine had nodded, maybe, knowing it wasn't that, whatever desire and longing might be at the other end of the line was of a different kind altogether.

Now it was this: three afternoons out of the last four, after Lorraine had collected Emily from the school and driven home, there she was, waiting across the street—Diana. The first time it had given Lorraine quite a shock, seeing her standing there in that bottle-green coat she always seemed to wear, the one with the hood. Lorraine had hesitated, expectant, waiting for Diana to walk towards them, imagining perhaps that something had happened, something important. But no. No movement. No sign of recognition. Aside from the fact of her being there: there and watching.

Lorraine had busied Emily into the house; she could go back later and put the car in the garage, plenty of time before Michael would be home. She made Emily her usual home-from-school treat, four or five assorted biscuits with the profiles of different animals embossed on them, each arranged round a piece of Marks and Spencer Swiss roll at the centre of her Peter Rabbit plate; then she'd shooed her off into the living room with this and a glass of banana-flavoured milk, switched on the TV. Outside, Diana hadn't moved. She was standing on the opposite pavement, close by an overgrown cotoneaster, three doors down. Her hands were in her pockets and her face looked cold, expressionless and cold. Lorraine had to fight a sudden impulse to go over and talk to her, say hello, invite her into the house. Perhaps it would be possible for them to sit down in the kitchen, sit over a pot of tea and talk.

She had never really talked to Diana.

"You don't talk to Diana," Michael had said. He had made it absolutely clear. "You take Emily, you drop her off. The only conversation you need to have, make sure she knows what time you'll be there to pick her up. That's it. Understood?"

Perhaps if she were able to talk to Diana, she might be able to understand Michael a little better. Try and make sure that whatever it was went wrong with the two of them, Michael and Diana, didn't happen again. But she knew she couldn't do that. It wasn't real. What it was, the kind of thing that happened on television, *Neighbours, Brook-side*. Besides, it would probably mean they would have to talk about the time Diana went into hospital and Lorraine didn't think she wanted to know about that.

"Only surprising thing," Michael had said when he'd heard, "is that she didn't end up there years ago. Best place for her."

Lorraine turned away from the kitchen window, swilled boiling water around the pot and emptied it into one side of the twin sink, dropped in a tea bag and three-quarters filled the smaller pot. When she looked out again, Diana had gone.

Three days later, she was there again; and two school days after that. Lorraine began to find excuses for not bringing Emily straight home, something she'd forgotten from Sainsbury's, why didn't they go into town and have tea out, a treat? The days shortened and Diana was little more than a shadow, something glimpsed over Lorraine's shoulder as she hurried Emily into the house, a blotch of pale face above a formless patch of darkness, darker than the rest.

Something choked in Lorraine's throat: what was she doing? Scurrying a six-year-old girl away from her mother's reach, out of her sight.

"Mummy!" Emily had called out once, as Lorraine was urging her through the front door.

"What about her?" Chubb lock against her back, holding tight to Emily's hand.

"I saw her."

"Yes, the other Sunday."

"No. Now." Emily pointing towards the door, Lorraine scooping her up into her arms. "Nonsense, sweetheart, you just imagined it." Sweeping her through to the rear of the house.

The noise would have been enough to shatter the plaster from the walls, if it hadn't been for over a decade's cigarette smoke and nicotine holding it glued together. Residents had long since given up complaining; turned up their TV sets, their stereos instead; arranged their nights out around the pub's live music. Tonight was blues night: take your basic three chords and a few flourishes and process them through the amps at a volume that defied criticism.

Naylor made it back through the packed bar without spilling more than a few inches from each pint glass.

"What's this?" Divine shouted over the din. "You order halves?"

If he heard, Naylor chose to offer no comment. He squeezed back alongside Divine, sharing his section of the bench seat with a broad-faced Rastafarian and a scrawny student type sporting a string of political badges, a wisp of beard and a navy-blue peaked cap that sat sideways on his head.

"What the hell we doing here?" Naylor asked.

"Keeping our eyes open, remember?"

A month before the drugs squad had intercepted a couple of padded envelopes on their way to a known dealer who lived above a video shop off the Alfreton Road. One appeared to have been posted in Canada, the other in Japan; the original source of both turned out to be Pakistan. Bribe a few officials, infiltrate items into the postal system as if they had started out in countries that aroused little customs and excise suspicion—bingo! Your friendly, international mail-order drug company. While Interpol and the National Drugs Unit were hauling in the bigger fish, Naylor and Divine were supping dubious bitter and watching out for a few minnows.

It didn't look as if it were going to be one of their nights.

"If that fat bastard," Divine yelled in Naylor's ear, indicating the middle-aged white man at the piano, "sings another word about going to Chicago, I'm going to take him down the station personally, stick him on the fucking train."

They left thirty minutes short of closing, sound ringing in their ears.

"Fancy anything?" Divine asked, eyes on the kebab place across the street.

Naylor shook his head. "Got to get home."

"Debbie waiting up for you?"

Naylor shrugged.

"Better still," Divine winked, "waiting in bed."

Naylor had left his car at the station; he knew he probably shouldn't be driving, leave it there till morning, take a cab. What the hell! Lights shone from the first-floor windows and for half a moment, Naylor considered going back in, passing the time, make himself a coffee, black. Instead he backed the car out onto the road and headed for home.

Only the small light burned above the front door.

There was a pint of milk open in the fridge and Naylor drank it right down, scarcely moving the carton away from his lips for air. He thought about opening another, making himself some cereal. Inside a bowl, covered over with a small plate, there was some tuna and he took that through into the front room and switched on the TV, volume low. Faces snarled at one another from banked rows of seats, a serious political presenter egging them on. Asian men and women in black-and-white costumes and subtitles, talking, talking, talking. *Soccer Special*. *Newsnight*. He switched the set to an empty channel and finished his flakes of tuna staring at the moving speckles of the screen, listening to the hum.

Wife okay? Baby?

As far as he knew, they were fine.

13

Raymond lay there, that narrow bed in his twelve-by-fourteen room, seeped in semen and his own stale sweat, trying not to think about the girl. Smiling face and the bright hair and the slightly chubby hands that seemed eager always to reach out and touch.

"Ray-o!"

Sitting on the wall outside the pub, he had told her his name, his nickname, and she had shrieked it aloud, gleeful, her whole body shaking as she danced up and around.

"Ray-o! Ray-o! Ray-o!"

Without thinking he had whisked her off her feet and whirled her round, like a carousel at Goose Fair, round and round until he lowered her gradually down, laughing and shaking, excitement tinged with fear. The next time he saw her, days later, she had tugged at her nan's hand and pointed across the street—"Ray-o!"—and he had quickly waved and walked on.

Now he threw back the blanket and the skimpy sheet and pulled on a T-shirt and yesterday's pair of pants before climbing to the bathroom, not yet light.

When he left the house fifty minutes later, leaving through the back door, careful to avoid the dog shit on the square of weed and grass, the rawness of the air took him by surprise. He had no sense of the black Sierra, parked amongst others at an angle to the road; no awareness of the camera focusing over inches of wound-down window, his steps along the pavement masking its whir and click.

"I wonder if you recognise him, Mrs. Summers?"

Lynn Kellogg spread the prints across the table, a group of hastily processed ten-by-eights, the central one, the close-up, sharp enough, though, to pick out the ghost of the subject's breath as it left his mouth.

"Oh, yes," Edith Summers said. "It's that boy."

"Boy?"

"The one Gloria took such a shine to."

"Oh."

"Yes. Ray-o."

"That's his name?"

"It's what she called him, Gloria. Raymond, I suppose his real name was. Ray. He was a nice enough lad, not like some."

As Lynn had been driving into Mablethorpe, a burst of sun, shocking in its brightness, had split the clouds that had hung over her the length of the journey. Edith Summers had been outside at the front of the bungalow, sweeping the short path that led from the gate with a long-handled brush. She had insisted on opening a new packet of digestives, brewing tea.

"What did you mean, Mrs. Summers," Lynn asked, "when you said Gloria took a shine to Raymond?"

"Oh, you know, she would chatter on about him sometimes, she seemed to get a kick out of seeing him, I suppose that's what it was. I mean, Raymond, he would make a point of calling out to her if ever he saw her, waving and that. Playing the fool."

"Where was this, Mrs. Summers?"

"I'm sorry?"

"When Gloria and Raymond saw one another, where would this be?"

"Out round the boulevard, down by the school. Sometimes, the rec."

"The recreation ground?"

"Yes, he was there sometimes."

"With friends?"

"No. Least, I don't think so. On his own, more like. As I recall, he always was. I never remember seeing him with anyone else."

"And he would be where, the times you saw him in the rec?"

"Oh, I don't know. Why? Why does this all matter anyhow?"

"Near the swings?"

"Yes, I daresay he might have been near the swings. But . . ."

"And did you notice him being friendly with any other little girls by the swings, or . . ."

"Now, look . . ."

"Or was it just Gloria?"

"Look, I'm not daft, I can see what you're thinking. What you're saying."

"Mrs. Summers, I'm not saying . . ."

"Yes."

"All I'm interested in doing . . ."

"Yes, I know."

"If he took a special interest in Gloria, if she trusted him . . ."

"Look, I've told you. He was a nice boy, a nice young man. Polite. What you're suggesting . . ."

"The day you left Gloria playing on the swings, Mrs. Summers, the day she went missing, you can't remember seeing Raymond there then?"

"No."

"You can't remember for sure, or . . ."

"No, he wasn't there."

"You're certain of that?"

Edith Summers nodded.

"Quite certain, because . . . if he'd been there, I would have seen him. Gloria would have seen him." She took a breath. "If Raymond'd been there none of this would have happened."

"Why's that, Mrs. Summers?"

"Because I should've left her with him, of course. Asked him to keep an eye on her, like I'd done before."

Divine had spoken to Raymond's boss on the phone, not a major inquiry, hardly anything at all, certainly nothing to bother mentioning to the youth himself, but if it was possible to establish . . .

"You better come down," the manager said.

Divine parked his car on the opposite side of the road, fifty yards down. No telling what you might get splashed across your paintwork, driving in amongst the delivery vans, offal on electric blue not one of his favourite colour combinations.

"Mr. Hathersage won't be long," the middle-aged secretary told him, walking him across the yard to the manager's office, little more than a cubicle with orders spiked in three piles on a high desk, a couple of meat packers' calendars on the wall, the one waving a fork through her legs worth a second look.

Divine eased the door back open a crack and listened to the refrigerators hum.

Hathersage was a stocky man in a smeared white coat, fiftyish, one eye swollen, its pupil floating in yellow rheum. The hand that shook Divine's was firm and strong.

"I'd never have took him on if I hadn't owed Terry a few favours. That's his uncle, like. I hope I'll not have cause to regret it."

"You haven't so far?"

Hathersage gave a slow shake of the head. "Youth's willing enough, I suppose. Not the sort to go prancing out the door the minute the second hand slips into place. Not bright either, but who is nowadays, types we get in here, job like his."

"Reliable, though?"

"Oh, aye. What's he done?"

Divine didn't answer. He asked the manager to tell him about Raymond's hours of work instead.

It transpired that some of the more skilled employees worked shifts, including nights. Raymond, though, for him it was a straightforward day, eight till four or four-thirty.

"Five days a week?" Divine had asked. "Six?"

"Five and a half as a rule, sometimes Sunday on top."

"Regular half day?"

"Clockwork."

"And in our boy's case?"

"Tuesday."

Divine wished he could remember the day Gloria had disappeared, couldn't even get the date straight in his head. Still, easy enough to check later on. For now, Divine glanced at his watch, checked it against the clock on the wall at right angles to the manager's desk.

"Serious, is it? This trouble youth's in."

Divine shook his head. "Shouldn't think so."

"Nothing for me to worry about, like?"

Another shake of the head.

"Petty thieving?"

"Your cash box is safe."

The manager grunted disparagingly. "What I got in there, take it, you might say, and welcome to it." He tapped the fingers of a stubby hand on Divine's knee. "I've had sides of beef disappearing out of here like they've risen from the dead. Three hundred, four hundred pounds' worth a week. In the end we took on this security firm. Night patrols. That's when it were going missing, like. It were one of your chaps solved it. Come by here in his Panda car, shortcut over the bridge; funny, he thought, loading that time of a night. Flashed his torch on a dozen and a half carcasses bedded down in the back of a Mitsubishi estate. Chuffing security bloke holding open the boot, splitting it fifty-fifty. Feller as was behind it, been here six year, courting my lass for last three of 'em. Got real shirty, she did, when I allowed as how I wasn't coming to no wedding."

Divine wondered idly what she'd had in her bottom drawer: couple of sets of silk underwear and half a dozen chump chops.

"You can wait for him here," the manager said. "I'll whistle him over."

"It's okay. Take the time to stretch my legs."

"Gets to you, doesn't it?" The manager smiled, opening the office door.

"What's that?"

"The smell. Wife swears if she's born again she's going to latch on to a vegetarian. Wouldn't do no good, I tell her, fart twice as bad as anything I bring home with me. Not their fault, mind; beans and the like."

Divine waited by the canal, leaning on the parapet watching an old man and a boy gazing at their rods, lines descending into the still flatness of water. In twenty minutes, none had moved: man, boy or lines. If that was all life had to offer, Divine thought, I'd as soon jack it in now. He turned just as Raymond was rounding the corner, floodlights at the visitors' end of the County ground rising up behind him. Divine made no other move, waiting for the youth to recognise him, hesitate, flustered, before making his way over.

"Is it me you're waiting for?"

Raymond stood, shoulders stooped beneath the bargain leather jacket, stitching starting to give at several of the seams. Here and there, particles of pork fat, freckles of dried blood, clung to his face and hair.

"Off home," Divine said. "Car's over there, I'll give you a lift."

Raymond blinked at him, uncertain. "No, you're all right. Sooner walk."

Divine reached out a hand towards Raymond's arm. "After a day's work? You'll not want that."

"Yes. I do." Divine's fingers round his elbow. "The walk, I like it. Helps me clear my head."

Divine let his hand fall away. "Suit yourself."

Raymond nodded quickly, blinked and went to step round Divine, but the detective shifted his balance, blocking Raymond's way. "We'll sit in the car instead," Divine said.

"So, Raymond, Ray," Divine relaxing now, opening the nearby side door so that Raymond could slide in, "how's the job going? Pretty well?"

Raymond sniffed and leaned forward, staring through the windscreen.

"Get on all right with the boss?"

"Hathersage? 'Side from he shouts all the time, he's okay."

"And the rest?"

Raymond glanced around. What was he after, asking all this stuff? Wasn't exactly like being on Youth Training Scheme. "All right, I suppose. Don't have a lot to do with them, really. One or two of them, though, been there for years, think they know everything, you know how I mean?"

Divine nodded helpfully.

"Least there's no blacks, one good thing." Raymond's fingers were seldom still, now pulling at the material of his trousers, now flexing, now tightening into a fist. "Wouldn't be right, would it? Working, you know, with meat and that. Wholesale. Go down the butcher's for a piece of steak, topside, whatever, you don't want to think some nignog's had his hands all over it, do you?"

Divine had to admit the youth had a point there.

"Where d'you keep it, Raymond? Somewhere at home, or d'you carry it with you all the time?"

Gob-smacked. "What?"

"The knife."

"I don't have no knife."

"Raymond."

"I haven't got a knife."

Divine staring at him, enjoying it now.

"What'd I want a knife for? What kind of knife, anyway? I don't know anything about no knife."

"Under the bed? Jacket pocket? For all I know you've got it with you this minute."

"No."

"No?"

"It's in the drawer."

"Which drawer's that?"

"In my room."

"Along with the socks?"

Raymond wanted to get out of the car. He didn't understand why the police were so interested in any knife, what that had to do with anything.

"What d'you want a knife for, Raymond? Not taking your work home, trimming away surplus fat?"

"Protection."

"Who from?"

"Anyone."

"Girls?"

"Course not girls. What would . . ."

"Had it with you that night, though, didn't you?"

Sweat breaking out along Raymond's forehead, starting to run down onto the bridge of his nose. "What night?"

"You know." Divine smiling.

"No."

"The night you were with Sara; the night you found Gloria."

"There's no law against it."

"Oh, Raymond, that's where you're wrong. Carrying an offensive weapon, intent to cause malicious damage; get the wrong magistrate, you're looking at time inside."

It was hot inside the car now, hot and getting hotter; Raymond could smell the warm smell of flesh, his own and others', his own sweat. "I'm going," hand reaching round for the door catch. "I want to go."

"You haven't ever used it to threaten anyone, Raymond? Force them into doing something against their will?"

Raymond pulled clumsily and the door swung outwards, releasing him onto the street. At first he thought the policeman was going to come after him, haul him back. But all he did was sit there, arms folded across the top of the steering wheel, grinning at Raymond as he backed, half-running, across the street.

All the way along London Road, cutting through past the station, scuttling along the tow path by the canal, Raymond kept looking round, all the while expecting to see Divine suddenly there, behind him and closing. By the time he had fumbled his key into the lock, dropped down onto his bed, Raymond was shaking so badly he had to squeeze his hands hard against his sides, not moving until the shirt beneath his jacket was stiff and cold.

14

Of course, it wasn't going to be that easy. The day that mattered, the day in question, proved to be Saturday and never Tuesday, no matter how many times Mark Divine took the dates of the month, the days of the week, and shook them around, spilling them out across his desk hoping for bingo. It always came out the same: Saturday. Between one and one-fifteen. Divine had checked back and there was nothing that put Raymond as missing that day, not as much as a couple of hours. By the time he had checked out, the earliest, Gloria Summers had been missing for at least four hours.

That aside, what else was there?

A spotty kid, a nervous disposition and BO.

Big deal.

A youth who sweated a lot and carried a blade.

What rankled Divine most was the certainty that if it were Lynn Kellogg, Patel even, urging them to ride a hunch, never mind there's no evidence for now, I feel it in my water, they'd likely do it. But Divine . . .

As far as Resnick was concerned, Millington even, he was a set of muscles with an attitude problem and not a great deal more. Get yourself sorted or you're out: it had been implied more than once; stated outright the time his prisoner had been found in the cells, blood all over his face.

He went berserk, sir. Those injuries; they were self-inflicted.

Asking Resnick to believe that had been a bit like persuading the Archbishop of Canterbury that Mother Teresa did a little hooking on the side.

"Ease up, Mark," Millington had said, doubtless passing down the word from on high. "We know where your Raymond is. Minute anything else points in his direction we'll have him so fast he'll think he's grown wings."

So Divine went back to helping the rest do something about improving their crime clear-up rate, now wavering around the thirty percent mark, despite the whining willies at the Home Office who kept announcing to the world that it was in single figures. Which is to say that he went back to wasting more than sixty percent of his time with unnecessary paperwork; whoever dreamed up PACE, Divine thought, was a stationery freak whose fantasy was a fifty-foot-long form to be filled in in triplicate. And as for the bright idea of recording interviews on tape, instead of having some poor bugger with an aching wrist and a splodgy Bic trying to get down every word—great! Terrific! Saved no end of time during the interview, preserved the flow, course it did. Made it less likely some lying bastard was going to get his brief to accuse you of fitting him up, sure it did. What nobody seemed to have bothered thinking about was the amount of time it took to transcribe the things, every spluttering cough, every sodding word. Playing it through a second time, checking for mistakes. Rumour was, more civilian staff were being taken on to help cope, but rumour, Divine knew, didn't do shit.

In the office that morning, Patel was beavering away under a pair of headphones, Lynn Kellogg was writing up a summary for court, which was where Naylor was kicking his heels, waiting to give evidence against a bloke who'd been poncing auto parts and not even sure if he'd get called. Likely as not, the sergeant was pressed up against the mirror in the Gents, clipping his moustache, and Resnick was behind his desk wrestling with an oversize ham sandwich. So who was out there, getting it done?

If he had his time over again, Divine thought, he'd use his head: take up rugby professionally, either that or be a brain surgeon.

Resnick had finished his sandwich and was looking again at the final report from Forensic. What had been recovered from the railway sidings had been in such a state it had taken days, not hours, to pick it through, isolating anything that had come into contact with Gloria's body. Most of the fabric that had been painstakingly recovered from inside the plastic bin liners had been contaminated with mould and was unlikely to provide anything useful. From beneath Gloria's fingernails, however, the path lab extracted several minute fibres of woven material, red and green. A carpet? A rug? Though nobody was placing bets, the wise odds were on the latter.

What? Had the killer wrapped her body in the rug before moving her elsewhere? Prior to the plastic bag? If so, how had she been transported? By car, along the rear seat, or stowed, like excess baggage, in the boot? Someone with access to a van?

It was possible, Resnick realised, that the assault had taken place on the rug itself; the assault which had resulted in Gloria's death, in addition to whichever others might have taken place beforehand.

Before what?

Resnick, on his feet, walked round his desk once, twice, caged by visions of what he didn't want to see. Before what? Before the girl had panicked, refused, screamed, struggled and struck out; before she had to be restrained, quietened, silenced, finally stopped. Although the rug from which those fibres had come had almost certainly been destroyed, that was not necessarily the case. It was not impossible that it lay still in the centre of some perfectly ordinary room; the room where Gloria Summers had ended her short life.

Resnick sat back down. One thing he felt sure of: somewhere in the city, Gloria's killer was walking around, leading an apparently normal life. One thing he was frightened of: before they caught him, that person might be driven to strike again.

Raymond's first instinct had been to go right down there, have it out with her. Tell her what for, smack in the centre of the hazelnut whirls and mint cream imperials. But he knew that was wrong. Temper. He'd had to learn to control his temper. More than once, his uncle Terry had had to take him off to one side, explain the facts of life. *Ray-o, you can't go on like that, flying off the handle. It's not like you're a kid, not anymore. You carry on that way, people are going to think there's something wrong.* Well, there wasn't. I mean, that's nonsense. A load of bollocks. He was all right.

The water had started to run cold, so Raymond stepped out of the shower and began to towel himself down. Hair first, good hard rub, then his back, shoulders, legs and arms. One thing he couldn't stand, putting any of his clothes back on before every square inch was properly dry. Kind of thing you had to be careful with, didn't want to catch a cold; worse, that flaky skin between the toes, athlete's foot; start walking around in wet clothes, sitting down, next thing you had piles.

Raymond sprayed deodorant in the direction of his underarms, down towards his pubic hair. He shook a little scented talc onto one hand and patted it between his legs, around his balls.

A kick on the base of the door. "Leave it alone, Raymond, and give someone else a whack. You've been in there over half an hour."

He had meant to iron his blue shirt, but he pulled a crew neck jumper on over the top so that only the collar and an inch or two of cuff were visible. The jumper had worn through on one elbow, but his jacket would take care of that. He wondered what Sara would be wearing, hoped it would be something casual, not that suit she'd worn to the police station. Like it was church or something.

He took a position close by one of the lions, keeping that at his back, that way he had a clear view past the fountains up to where the bus came in, the one he thought Sara would likely take. Punks sat on the steps, calling out at the occasional passerby. Sticking safety pins up your nose and sniffing glue, all that was ridiculous, aside from unhygienic, no one carried on like that anymore. Pathetic!

He stepped away as Sara paused at the edge of the pavement, trying to pick him out. Really nice, she looked, loose black trousers, black jacket over a red blouse. The last thing he was going to do, risk spoiling the evening, say anything about the knife.

"What did we have to come and see this for?"

"Shh. Watch this bit. It's terrific. Look."

"Where?"

"There, coming through the door. Look!"

"Oh, God!"

Sara twisted sideways in her seat, covering her face with her hand almost as quickly as the seminaked hero magicked a sword from the ether in perfect time to slash the throat of one attacker right across while connecting a flying kick to the jaw of a second, finally disembowelling the third with all the skill of a pathological Vietnam vet and master butcher, the dying man's entrails slithering off screen, silver-grey and red.

"Amazing!" breathed Raymond, lost in admiration.

"I just didn't like it," Sara said. "All that violence."

"It wasn't that bad," Raymond said. "I've seen a lot worse." He meant *better*, but he wasn't about to say so. Get too far up Sara's nose and he wouldn't even get a feel from her on the way home.

They were in Pizza Hut, the smaller one, up near Bridlesmith Gate. The other one, above Debenham's, was better, but Raymond didn't have good memories of walking down there this time of a night.

"I don't want to be snobby, Raymond, but it's just not my kind of film, that's all."

"Oh, so what is?"

"I don't know . . ."

"Something all romantic, I suppose?"

"Not necessarily." Sara chewed her garlic bread with mozzarella topping and thought about it. "Something with more to it, I suppose."

"You mean, serious?"

"Okay, if you like, serious."

"Well, what about what we just saw, then? All that stuff about how they kept him buried underground for weeks at a time, absolute blackness, nothing to eat except for rats he had to catch and kill himself."

"What about it?"

Raymond couldn't believe it. Was she stupid or what? "It shows you, doesn't it? Explains why it happened."

"What?"

"Why he turned out like he did. Dedicated to vengeance. No feelings. It's like," pointing his fork at her, "his motivation. Psychology and that. Can't tell me that's not serious."

"One deep-pan medium with extra beef topping," announced their waitress, Tracey, wafting the platter between them. "One thin and crispy vegetarian."

Raymond was sure she'd ordered that on purpose, get him all riled up.

"Table for two?"

"Please," Patel said.

"Smoking or non?"

Patel glanced sideways at Alison, who said, "Non."

"Do you mind sharing?"

"No," said Patel.

"How long would we have to wait," Alison asked, "to get somewhere by ourselves?"

Raymond had finished his pizza, every slice, garlic bread, more than his share of the salad; now he sat nibbling on a piece of Sara's vegetarian, didn't taste of a thing. Since they'd argued about the film, she had scarcely said two words, beyond complaining about the dressing he'd spooned over their bowl of salad, how she preferred the blue cheese to the Thousand Island any day of the week. Next time, get it yourself, Raymond had thought, saying nothing. What sort of an idiotic name was Thousand Island for a salad dressing anyway?

"Listen," he said, leaning towards her.

"Yes?"

"That knife of mine; what d'you have to go bloody talking to the police about it for?"

Alison paused in the midst of explaining the relative merits of a fixed-rate mortgage.

"You're not listening, are you?"

Patel felt himself beginning to blush. "Yes, I am."

Alison shook her head. "You're staring."

"I'm sorry."

She smiled. "It's all right." And reached out her hands. "Now all you have to do is stop fidgeting with that knife and fork."

"I'm . . ."

"I know, you're sorry. Are you always so apologetic, or is it something to do with me?"

"I'm sorry, I'll try to be more positive."

"Good," Alison said, still smiling at him with her eyes. "Do that."

"Are you ready to order?" the waiter asked.

"Er, I don't think so," said Patel. "Not quite."

"Yes," said Alison. "We'll order now."

Patel smiled, and then he laughed.

"I hate that," Raymond said.

"What?"

"Over there?"

Sara turned her head, following his stare. "What about it? I don't see . . ."

"The girl sitting with that Paki." Raymond grimaced. "Kind of thing I hate to see."

15

"What's the matter with you this morning?"

"Nothing. Why?" Lorraine, turning away from the kitchen window, busying her hands with her apron.

"Three times I've come in here now, three times you're just standing there, staring."

"I'm sorry." Heading for the dishwasher now, to finish loading it up with the things from last night's dinner party, every fork and glass and plate, she didn't know how her mother had managed for so long without one.

"You're sorry?"

"I was thinking."

"What about?"

"Oh, I don't know. Nothing special."

Michael lifted the kettle, making sure there was sufficient water before switching it on to boil. "That's what she used to say."

Lorraine trapped the word, *who*, before it left her tongue. Of course, she knew.

"Came in once, don't know where I'd been, somewhere, I don't know, local, not far, maybe taking a load of stuff down the tip, Diana was in the front, the lounge. She was wearing her outdoor clothes, raincoat, red scarf she'd had for years; standing there in front of the windows, she'd got this shovel, little garden shovel, blue-handled, in one hand. 'Diana,' I said, 'what d'you think you're doing?' And she just turns to me and smiles, like I was the last person she expected to see. 'What are you doing?' She's got nothing on under her coat, not a stitch. 'Nothing,' that was what she said. 'I don't think I was doing anything.' And then, 'It's turning quite cold. I shouldn't be surprised if we weren't in for some rain.' "

Lorraine, listening, couldn't look at her husband's face; instead, she concentrated on his hands, the way, slowly, he spooned coffee into the two mugs and, after the kettle's click, added the water, one spoon each of sugar, the milk.

"What she was going to do," Michael said, "was start digging. Digging for James."

Lorraine wanted to throw her arm round him, give him a hug, tell him that it was okay, she knew that it still got to him and that was all right, she could understand. But she knew that if she did, he would shrug her off and frown and give her his look that said, Don't, don't, just leave me alone.

Taking her coffee from the work top, she brushed the outside of his hand with her own.

"I'm sorry," he said, looking across the room.

"There's no reason."

"Just, when I walked in and saw you . . ."

"I'm not Diana," Lorraine said, wiping at the surface where the mugs had left a faint ring. "I'm nothing like her."

"I know."

"So."

Michael sipped his coffee; it was still too hot. "He was only eight days old, James. That's all he ever was."

The muffled whine of a power saw aside, it was silent for some little time; then, through the door, the shriek of sudden laughter, Emily watching Sunday morning television. Lorraine set down her mug and crossed the room to switch on the dishwasher. "If I'm going to get that stuff out back sorted," Michael said, "it'd better be now."

If God had meant me to be a plumber, Millington thought, He would have set me on this earth with a full set of washers and a neck that stretched easily around U-bends.

"Graham!" his wife called from the foot of the stairs. "Is it coming along all right?"

Millington confided his reply to the spider with whom he was sharing the space beneath the bath and fumbled for the correct adjustment to the wrench.

"Whatever happened to that nice young man you met at that garage? You know, the time you had that trouble with your exhaust. Somewhere your side of Grantham."

"Nothing, Mum."

"I thought he was going to take you out for dinner or something? He did fix the exhaust for free."

What he had done was squeeze on some rapid-dry sealant, pack some black gunge around it and try for a quick feel while her Nova was still jacked up to head height. Dinner had been a Berni's three-course special offer, prawn mayonnaise, rump steak with jacket potato and watercress garnish, black forest gateau. He'd hardly been able to wait to get Lynn out into the car park and show her that he hadn't earned his Kwik-Fit mechanic-of-the-month certificate for nothing.

"So there's nobody else on the horizon, then?"

"No, Mum. Not just at the moment."

"Oh, Lynnie," her mother sighed. "I do hope you haven't left it all too late."

"And not before time," Patel's father said, unable to keep a smile of second-degree pleasure from his voice. Patel could imagine his father's face, his mother and his sisters standing near.

"You must bring her up to visit us."

"Look, I don't know . . ."

"Soon."

Sara's mother spent her Sunday mornings at the Church of Jesus Christ of Latter-day Saints, a former community hall with a corrugated roof and a view of the racecourse. Her dad spent his Sundays in bed with the *News of the World* and the *People*—*Only chance I get to have a good read*—least till the pubs opened.

"What's he like, then, this Raymond?" Sara's mother asked, sliding a three-inch-long steel hat pin from the folds of her permed hair, the soft grey felt of her church hat. "Educated, is he? Nicely spoken?" She pursed her lips into a smile. "As long as he isn't common."

Divine gripped the white porcelain, willing himself not to throw up a third time. His throat felt as if it had been scraped out with a blunt instrument and his head was a ball that had been punted eighty yards upfield. If ever he got back up from his knees, he had to stagger down to the corner shop for a couple of pints of milk and the twenty Bensons whoever it was in his bed had been asking for ever since raising her head from his pillow, mascara and eye shadow smeared right across it. Half-light of day she looked seventeen, office junior somewhere, the two of them last night, stuck out on the dance floor, one minute jiggling around to some electrocrap, the next rubbing up against her to Phil Collins. "You're not really a copper, are you?" *No, darling, I'm Leonardo da-fucking Vinci!*

Kevin Naylor had been up since short of seven, ironing his work shirts in the kitchen while he listened to the *Bruno and Liz Breakfast Show*, pair of them flirting like mad over the microphone, likely didn't say a word to one another once it was over, separate taxis home to Surrey or wherever. He had hoovered all of the upstairs and about half of the down, stupid bag had jammed up and he'd torn it taking it out, no spares under the sink and his attempt at a running repair with Sellotape had ended in disaster and dust at the foot of the stairs he'd had to sweep up with a dustpan and brush.

When finally he phoned, of course it was her mother who answered; he'd thought she wasn't going to let Debbie come to the phone at all.

"Three-thirty, then?"

At the other end of the phone, it was ominously quiet.

"Debbie?"

He could feel her mother standing there, exaggeratedly mouthing words for Debbie to say.

"You're still bringing the baby for tea?"

He had gone into Marks and Spencer and bought one of those battenburg cakes that she liked, chocolate éclairs, a pair of them in a cellophane-topped box. He'd queued forever at Birds, in a line of old women and older men, to buy sponge mice with eyes and little tails, each in different coloured icing, a malt loaf, gingerbread men. In case Debbie didn't bring any with her, he had got tins of baby food desserts, rhubarb and apple, rice pudding, apple and plum.

Now he grabbed them from the cupboard shelves, the fridge, tore at their wrappings, hurling them into the sink and squashing them against the sides, pummelling them with his fists.

"Bloody hell, Ray-o! What d'you call that?"

Raymond struck the end of his club against the ground and watched as the ball bounced yards past the twisted metal flag and ran down the slope underneath the hedge at the edge of the municipal putting green.

"Thought you'd be better getting it in the hole than that." His uncle Terry winked.

"Thinks he's Tony bloody Jacklin, that's his trouble," Raymond's father said, dropping his own ball on the spot.

"Stop bloody moaning," Raymond said. "Took you five shots at the last one and then you had to knock it in with your foot."

"That's what the real pros do, you ignorant twat," his father said.

"How do you know?" said Raymond scornfully.

"Because I've watched them."

"In your dreams."

"On the tele."

"My shot," said Terry, moving forward.

"Only pros you've ever watched," Raymond said, "are the ones up by the Forest. Fiver for a quick gob job in the back of the car."

"Hey!" Raymond's father went for him with his club, but hit his uncle Terry instead.

Raymond threw down his own club and went storming off across the green, hands in pockets, head down, ignoring the shouts of other players lining up their putts.

"Ray-o!" Terry shouted. "Come on back here."

"Good riddance!" his father said. "Don't waste your breath."

Really surprised, Lorraine had been, when Michael had touched her neck and said, what did she think, maybe they could slip up to bed, have a little rest. Surprised, but pleased. She could scarcely remember the last time they'd made love in the afternoon; when first she'd started seeing him, seriously at least, seemed to be all they'd ever done.

"Where you off to now?" Michael had asked, undressed beneath the duvet, eager to get on with it but thinking maybe Lorraine thought she'd need the K-Y jelly, Vaseline.

"Just checking," Lorraine said, peeking through the drawn curtains, Emily with her dolls spread out all over the rear lawn, the little pushchair and the pram. She could just hear her voice, pretend adult, telling them they should be more careful with their clothes, asking them if they thought money grew on trees.

She walked back from the window slowly, knowing that Michael was touching himself under the covers, watching the movement of her breasts.

Twenty minutes later, sitting on the toilet in the bathroom, hearing Michael whistling as he put back on his clothes, Lorraine said: "Give Emily a shout, there's a love. Wash her hands before tea."

16

Michael, lighting a cigarette, pushing his shirt down into his trousers, thinking, another six or seven hours, the damned weekend's good as over. Alarm'll be going and there I'll be, fighting for car-park space before seeing the same old faces on the train. The ones who nod and climb behind their *Telegraph*; those who want nothing more than to talk about their round of golf, their kids, their car; the four who had the cards shuffled and dealt before leaving the station, bridge at a penny a point.

"Michael!"

Thinking: Sheffield, that'd be better. Chesterfield, even. Easier. Worth dicing with the traffic on the M1 for a chance to get home at a decent hour, get back to living a proper life.

"Michael!"

He rested his foot on the board at the foot of the bed, so as to tie the lace. If Lorraine and I weren't forever rushing off in different directions, if we had a bit more time to relax, going to bed wouldn't be such a rare event. Thank God, at least when they did it was still pretty good. He tied his other lace. Lorraine, she'd never needed a lot to get her going; certainly not back when they'd started.

"Michael!"

"Hello!"

"You're not still there, are you?"

"No, I'm on my way."

Emily's dolls were scattered here and there on the back lawn. Her pushchair was skewed sideways in the gravel passage that ran between the side of the house and their neighbour's high creosoted fence. Michael couldn't see the doll's pram at first, but then there it was, pitched onto its side near the garage door.

"Emily!"

He hurried fifty yards in either direction, finally back to the house, front and rear gardens—"Emily!"—all the while calling her name.

"Michael, whatever's the matter?" Lorraine in the doorway, sweater and jeans, pink towel in her hand as she rubbed her damp hair.

"Emily, she's not here."

"She's what?"

"Not bloody here."

Lorraine stepping out, towel to her side. "She's got to be."

"Yes? Then show me where she bloody is."

They searched the house, top to bottom, every room, bumping into themselves in and out of doorways, on the stairs, faces increasingly pale, drained.

"Look."

"Where?" Michael swivelling anxiously round.

"No, I mean . . ."

"I thought you'd seen something."

Lorraine shook her head, came forward and took his hand and he shook her away. "Just for a minute," she said, "we ought to sit down."

"I can't bloody sit down."

"We need to think."

"Out there looking for her, that's what we need to be doing."

"You said you'd done that already."

"And I didn't bloody find her, did I?"

His eyes were wild and his hands were beginning to shake. He surprised Lorraine by letting her lead him into the kitchen, though when she pulled out a stool and sat down, Michael remained, agitated, on his feet.

"We should make a list," Lorraine said. "Places where she might be."

"What places, for Christ's sake?"

"Friends. Megan Patterson, for instance."

"That's half a mile away."

"Not if you take the cut-through before the end of the crescent. She could easily have walked there in the time we were upstairs."

"Screwing," Michael said.

"That's got nothing to do with it."

"Of course, it's got something to fucking do with it! If we hadn't been up there, leaving Emily alone, this wouldn't have happened." He was leaning forward, glaring at her. "Would it?"

Lorraine got to her feet.

"Where d'you think you're going now?"

"To phone Megan's mother."

Val Patterson hadn't seen anything of Emily, not since a few days ago, and besides, Megan was off at her riding lesson, her father had dropped her off there over an hour ago. Why didn't Lorraine try Julie Neason, didn't Emily and her Kim go to school together sometimes? Lorraine rang the Neasons', but there was no answer. The front door slammed and she knew that Michael had gone back out to look for Emily again. While Lorraine was looking in the phone book, fingers sliding awkwardly over the pages, she heard the car being backed out of the garage, driving away.

In the ten minutes that followed, Lorraine spoke to every one of the parents in the area that she knew and with whom Emily had any kind of contact. Clara Fisher's dad had been driving past half an hour ago and seen Emily pushing her pram across the front lawn. No, he couldn't be positive about the time, not to the minute, but he was sure it had been Emily.

"Did you notice anybody else?" Lorraine asked. "Anyone close by? Another car?"

"Sorry," Ben Fisher said. "I didn't notice a thing. But then, you wouldn't expect to really. You know as well as I do what it's like round here Sunday afternoons, quiet as the grave."

Outside, a car drew up, the door slammed and there was Michael, shoulders slumped forward, distraught. "Well?"

Lorraine looked away.

"I've been four times, up and down the crescent," Michael said. "Checked everywhere between Derby Road and the hospital. Stopped anyone who was around and asked."

"We should look again," Lorraine said. "Inside the house. I mean, really search. Cupboards, everywhere. She might have been hiding, a game, got too frightened to come out."

Michael shook his head. "I don't think she just went wandering off."

"That's what I say, she's somewhere here . . ."

"She's gone off with someone," Michael said.

Even though he was standing close to her now, close in the carpeted square of hall, the telephone table they had bought from Hopewell's to match the little chest Lorraine's parents had given them as a wedding present, she could scarcely hear what it was he'd said. Not wanting to hear the words.

"She's gone off with someone," Michael said again, taking hold of her arm below the elbow.

Lorraine shook her head emphatically. "She wouldn't do that."

"There's nothing else, is there?"

"But she wouldn't."

Michael released her arm. "How can you be so sure?"

"Because we've told her, time and time again, both of us. It's been drummed into her ever since she could walk. Don't talk to people you don't know, anyone who comes up to you in the park, in the street. Don't take anything, no matter how nice it looks. Ice cream. Sweets. Michael, she just wouldn't do that."

He reached out his hand towards her face, brushing back a few strands of hair. "Someone's taken her," he said.

Lorraine's stomach hollowed out and a fist tightened inside her throat.

Michael reached past her.

"What are you going to do?"

He looked at her, surprised. "Phone the police."

"But if she's not been missing for an hour?"

"Lorraine, how long does it take?"

He was dialling the number when she started, a little breathlessly, gabbling her words together, to tell him about Diana.

All the years that Michael and Diana had been married, they had lived on Mapperley Top, a three-bedroomed end-terrace, all they had chosen to afford at the time, not wanting to sink everything into the deposit and the mortgage. Two holidays a year that had meant, not having to stint on going out; clubs, that's where they went in those days, Diana liking to let her hair down, have a bit of a dance. Afterwards a curry at the Maharani, the Chand; sometimes, if they were feeling especially flush, the Laguna.

After the trouble, the divorce, Michael had found his studio flat and Diana had stayed on in the house, a FOR SALE board outside, though not too many people bothered to come looking. Then, when Michael had wanted to buy somewhere with Lorraine, of course he'd had to insist that Diana leave; if the only way they could get shot of the place was dropping a few thousand, so be it.

Diana had moved outside the city to Kimberley, a small town where once the men had mostly worked in the pits and the women in the hosiery factories and now they were fortunate to be working anywhere.

Diana's house was little more than a two-up, two-down, open the front door and you were standing in the middle of the front room, another couple of paces and you were in the back. Michael turned right past the mini-roundabout, left again onto a narrow street running parallel to the main road. Three lads, ten or eleven years old, were chasing their second-rate mountain bikes up and down the kerb, practising wheelies. Michael stood for some moments outside the house, looking up at the lace curtains at all but one of the windows. Back across the street, someone was sharing this week's Top Twenty with all but the clinically deaf.

Michael walked past the overgrown privet hedge, through the gap where the gate was supposed to be. The bell didn't appear to be working and there wasn't a knocker, so he rattled the letter flap instead, hammered the side of a fist against the door. Please God, let her be here!

"She's gone away," called a neighbour two houses down, setting her milk bottles on the front step.

"She can't have."

"Suit yourself."

Several doors along there was an arched passageway, leading to the backs of the houses. Michael stepped around the dustbin and peered through the square of kitchen window, what looked like breakfast things stacked alongside the sink, that didn't prove anything one way or another. He knocked on the back door, leaned his weight against it: bolted and locked.

By clambering onto the narrow, sloping sill outside the back-room window, he could see through a gap in the curtains. Scrubbed pine table and assorted chairs, a towel draped over the back of one; dried flowers stood in a wide-bellied vase in front of the tiled fireplace. On shelves in one of the alcoves, paperbacks jostled for space with cassettes and magazines, scrapbooks, photograph albums. On a table in the further alcove stood photographs of Emily, souvenirs, most of them, of her fortnightly visits to her mother. Emily reaching up to stroke a donkey, face uncertain; Emily in her costume beside an indoor pool; Emily and Diana on the steps of Wollaton Hall.

There were no pictures of the three of them together, Michael, Diana and Emily, as they had been then, a family.

"Hey-up! What the heck you doing up there?"

Michael turned and jumped back down; the flush-faced man was standing by the fence of the house that backed onto the alley.

"Seeing if there's anyone in," Michael said.

"Aye, well, there's not."

"D'you know where she is, Diana?"

"Who wants to know?"

"I'm . . . I was her husband."

"Oh, aye."

"I need to see her, it's urgent."

"Not been here all weekend, far as I know. Most likely off away."

"You don't know where?"

The man shook his head and turned back towards his own house. Michael hurried along to the archway, on through to the front of the house. The woman from two doors down was standing to admire her handiwork, step now spotless, rubber kneeling pad in one hand, brush in the other.

"Diana," Michael said, trying to control the anxiety in his voice.

"Away for the weekend."

"Know where?"

"Can't help, duck."

"You sure she's not been here at all?"

"Far as I know."

"And a little girl? You haven't see Diana with a little girl, six, reddish hair?"

"That's Emily. Her daughter. Well, seen her, course I have, many a time, but, like I say, not these past couple of days."

Michael shook his head, turned away.

"It's what she does, you know. When the kiddie's not with her. Take off for Sat'day, Sunday. Sad, if you ask me."

"How's that?"

"Bloke she were married to, it's him as stops her seeing the kid more often. Breaks her heart."

Michael phoned Lorraine from a call box, fumbling the coin into the slot. "She's not here. Nobody's here. You've not heard from her?"

"Nothing. Oh, Michael . . ."

"I'll call on the police on the way home."

"Should I come too, meet you there?"

"Someone's got to be home in case."

"Michael?"

"Yes?"

"Be as quick as you can."

He broke the connection and ran to the car. Emily had been missing an hour and a half, maybe a little more. Pulling onto the main road, he had to brake sharply to avoid a builder's lorry, heading down the hill towards Eastwood, its driver calling him all kinds of bastard through the glass. Slow down, he told himself, get a grip; you're not going to help anything if you can't hold yourself together now.

Lorraine sat in the kitchen, gazing out through the front window, hands tight around tea which had long since gone cold. All the while she had been sitting there, the streetlights had shone more and more strongly. Each time a car entered the crescent, the adrenaline coursed through her: someone had found Emily and was bringing her home. And each time the headlights of the car swept past. Whenever there were footsteps on the pavement, she craned forward, waiting for figures to turn in to the path, the anxious running of feet, fevered knocking at the door.

That little girl, the one who went missing, you remember?

It was something you read about in the paper, saw on the television news, shocking, the faces of those parents, pictures of their child. The pleas for a safe return.

They found her body.

And Michael suddenly staring at her, so sure.

Of course . . .

As though there were no other possibility, no other end.

What else did you think had happened?

The cup slipped from her fingers onto her lap and shattered on the floor. Lorraine did nothing to pick it up, left the pieces where they lay.

When Michael finally arrived, it was in convoy, a police car in front, white with a blue stripe, an unmarked saloon bringing up the rear. The two uniformed men were out of their vehicle quickly, moving briskly after Michael as he came, half-running, towards the house. A young woman wearing an anorak stepped from the third car and opened the rear door for a bulky man who stood for a moment on the pavement, pulling his raincoat around him.

Lorraine, face close to the window, was aware of this man, whoever he was, looking back at her, hands thrust down into his pockets, bareheaded, there in the broken dark. Then it was Michael with his arms tight round her and long, raking sobs, his mouth pressed against her hair, repeating her name, softly, over and over, Lorraine, Lorraine.

17

The great thing about Sunday lunchtimes in the city, back when Resnick had still been walking the beat, was the number of bands you could hear for the price of a pint. Often not too much variety, it was true: New Orleans and Chicago by way of Arnold and Bobbers Mill, but when you weren't paying admission, it didn't pay to be fussy either. Besides, after a tough Saturday night, the familiar strains of "Who's Sorry Now?" or "Royal Garden Blues" had a lot to commend them. Two choruses of ensemble, solos all round, a couple more with everyone going for broke, finally four bar breaks in the last of which the drummer would likely throw his sticks into the air, shout "Ooo-ya! Ooo-ya!" and miss them coming down.

Resnick had persuaded his father to go along once, knowing that if he'd said anything about the music beforehand, the older man would have refused. So they had ordered at the bar, Resnick expressing surprise when half a dozen men came wandering in with instrument cases in various shapes and sizes. His father, a Semprini man if anything, and whose idea of acceptable jazz had never extended beyond Winifred Atwell and Charlie Kunz, had lasted until the third number, a partic-ularly clumping version of "Dippermouth Blues." At the unison shout of "Oh, play that thing!" Resnick Senior had pushed his unfinished pint of mild aside, withered his son with a look of true scorn and left.

Thereafter, it was referred to disparagingly as "that melodious ragtime!" Resnick refraining from the satisfaction of informing his father he had both words wrong.

Still, leaving the Bell this particular Sunday afternoon, some of the musicians he had been listening to the same as on that earlier occasion, it was his father Resnick found himself thinking of, rather than this solo or that. Never a man to encourage displays of affection, nor any excesses of emotion, there had been little physical contact, other than the occasional shaken hand, between the two of them for years. Crossing the broad edge of the square, Resnick remembered now leaving his father in hospital for the first time, an exploratory operation, braided wool dressing gown loose over new-bought paisley pyjamas that buckled against his slippered feet. "Bye, son," his father had said, and on whatever impulse, Resnick had clasped him in his arms and kissed his unshaven cheek. He could still hear, through the muted traffic, the gasped cry of surprise, see the tears welling in his father's eyes.

Walking home now, Resnick turned left through the ever-spreading Polytechnic and entered the Arboretum, a few parents wheeling their kids past the aviary, holding them, pointing excitedly, close against the bars. He sat for a while on one of the wooden benches facing the cannon, weathered black and impressive, which the local regiment had captured in the Crimea. The daftness of it, a man not so far short of middle age, sitting alone on that early winter afternoon, rehearsing all of the things he wanted to say to his father and now never could.

When he walked in through his front door, thirty minutes later, cats swirling round his feet, the telephone was already ringing.

You couldn't see them so well that time of an evening, but Resnick knew the houses well enough, two-storey, detached, each with its own garage, gardens front and back; most of the front lawns with a cherry tree or something close, soft petals that drifted out onto the curve of pavement, purple or pink. Family homes that went up—what?—twenty years ago, twenty-five? Resnick would drive round there sometimes, using the crescent as a cut-through, and think it was like a movie set. The fifties' Hollywood ideal. Crusty old pop, forever chewing on his pipe; mom with flour on her apron, a great line in advice and pies whose pastry rose just right; the daughter with a soft spot for dogs and crippled kids and the leading man, who was pretty much of a ne'er-do-well, but who saw the light in time to find his way to the altar. If Resnick could ever remember their names, he'd know her—round-faced, fair-haired, sort of catch in her voice she most likely developed when she was just another band singer, sitting stage left near the piano, patiently waiting till she was called to the microphone. Dinah? Dolores? What was her name?

Michael Morrison guided the young woman in from the kitchen towards them. "This is my wife, Lorraine."

Resnick guessed her to be early twenties, but the result of all the crying had been to render her younger, late teens.

Resnick introduced Lynn Kellogg and himself, suggested they go somewhere and sit down; there were questions they had to ask.

With Michael's permission, the uniformed officers were already making a thorough search of the property, top to bottom. Police in another part of the country had recently gone to a hostel, looking for a kidnapped four-year-old boy, had checked the room in which he was being kept and driven away empty-handed, leaving the cupboard in which he was hidden undisturbed.

"I don't understand," Lorraine said, "what you're doing. She isn't here."

"We have to check, Mrs. Morrison," Resnick said.

"They have to check, Lorraine," Michael said.

"Perhaps we can start," said Resnick, "with the last time you saw her."

"Emily," Lorraine said, twisting the ends of her hair around her fingers.

Resnick nodded.

"She's got a name."

Yes, thought Resnick, they always have. Gloria. Emily.

"My wife's upset," Michael said. He touched her arm and she stared at his hand as if it belonged to a stranger.

Resnick's eyes and Lynn's met. "The last time you saw Emily," Resnick said.

"Lorraine saw her," Michael said. "Didn't you, love?"

Lorraine nodded. "From the bedroom window."

"And where was she? Emily?"

"In the garden. Playing."

"That would be at the front?"

Michael shook his head. "The back. The main bedroom, it's at the back."

"And what time would this have been?"

Michael looked at Lorraine, who was still twisting her hair, staring at the floor. Heavy footsteps walked across above their heads. "Three, three-thirty."

"You can't be more accurate than that?"

"No, I . . ."

"Five past three," Lorraine said with sudden sharpness.

"You're sure?"

"Look." Lorraine suddenly on her feet. "It was three o'clock when Michael said why didn't we go to bed. I know because I looked at the clock. I went straight up to the bathroom, then into the bedroom and that's when I saw Emily. Five minutes, okay? Six. Seven. What does it matter?"

Michael tried to grab her, prevent her running out of the room. "I'm sorry," he said.

"It's all right," said Resnick. "I understand."

Lynn Kellogg looked over at Resnick and when he nodded she went to look for Lorraine.

"We'll need a detailed description," Resnick said, "a photograph, recent, head and shoulders. The sooner we get it circulated the better. A list of Emily's friends, those she'd be most likely to play with, visit. Relatives—we know of course about her mother, there's an officer at the house now, waiting for her return. Anything else you think is relevant."

Resnick smiled reassuringly. "She'll be all right, Mr. Morrison. We'll find her." But Michael was not reassured.

Lynn Kellogg tried the kitchen, the bedrooms; standing to one side on the narrow landing as the constable went by, she asked him a question with her eyes and was answered by a setting of the mouth, a quick shake of the head. Finally, Lynn found Lorraine in the rear garden, cardigan around her shoulders, one of Emily's dolls tight within her arms. Lights showed, orange and yellow, in most of the adjoining houses; silhouettes of people proceeding, undisturbed, with their lives. *The Antiques Road Show. Songs of Praise. Mastermind.* What remained of the chicken, the roast, covered with foil and placed in the fridge. Tomorrow saw the start of another week.

"She's not mine, you know. Emily."

"I know."

No tears now: all cried out.

"We were . . . we went . . . we were making love."

"Yes."

"Oh, God!"

Fingers pressing deep into her palms, she turned towards Lynn and Lynn held her in her arms. At either side of them, officers with torches were making their slow search among the shrubs, along the borders.

Back inside the house, Michael, with some hesitation, was telling Resnick about Diana, his first wife.

18

"Should have called me sooner, Charlie."

"Chances were, found her first couple of hours."

"Yes. But we didn't, did we?"

Skelton set his overcoat on the hanger behind the door, running his hands outwards along the shoulders to ensure it hung smoothly. He had been settling into a book when Resnick had got through: Alexander Kent, naval yarns that knocked Forester and Hornblower into a cocked hat.

"Dad, for you." His daughter, Kate, leaning round the door, black T-shirt and lipstick to match. Six months now she'd been going around with what Skelton had been informed was a Goth: a first-year physics student at the university with a taste in loud music and necromancy. Weekends it was down to London and Kensington Market, clubs like the Slimelight. More than likely drop out next year and take Kate on a tour of Transylvania.

Skelton had finished his sentence, put his bookmark in place and gone to the hall telephone, receiver dangling from its cord as Kate had left it.

The first tones of Resnick's voice and he had known it was serious. "All right, Charlie, I'm coming in."

Now Skelton stood behind his desk. "Mother's not turned up yet?" Resnick shook his head.

"Who's out there?" Skelton angled the chair away from the desk and sat down, indicating that Resnick should do likewise. The overhead light burned brightly, the clear hundred-watt bulb reflecting off the white inside of the coned shade. The raw facts, such as were known, lay typed inside the folder on Skelton's blotter, together with the photocopied face, Emily's age and description, last seen . . .

Almost three months ago they had sat in the same room, the same situation. Twenty-four hours. Forty-eight. The autopsy report on Gloria Summers still lay in the top drawer of the superintendent's desk.

"Patel, sir."

"Last in contact?"

"Twenty minutes back."

Skelton opened the folder and slid the papers out, fanning them across the desk like a deck of cards. Resnick leaned forward, for a moment resting his head against a hand, elbow on his knee.

"The mother, anything to go on outside the father's hunch?"

Resnick straightened. "Some psychiatric history, hospitalization."

"Recent?"

"Few years back now."

"Do we know anything more specific?"

"Depression, Morrison says."

"Jesus, Charlie! We're all depressed."

Five percent of the population at any one time, Resnick thought, and that was just those clinically diagnosed. Sit most people down in front of a standard HAD test and get them to check off the answers, how many thousand more would be standing in line for their lithium, their Tryptizol?

"The wife . . ."

"Which one?"

"The second. Lorraine. She says the girl's mother's been acting peculiar for quite a while, phone calls and the like. Recently, she's taken to hanging round the house."

"What doing?"

Resnick shrugged. "Not a lot, apparently. Watching."

"That's all?"

Nod of the head.

"No approach made to the girl?"

"None."

"Could be she was building up for it."

Resnick glanced at his watch. "Neighbour Patel spoke to, reckoned she was always home this side of eight o'clock."

"And if she's not?"

Resnick didn't answer.

"If she's not," Skelton said, "we have to assume she's snatched the kid."

Of all the variables tripping over themselves inside Resnick's mind, it was the one to be infinitely preferred. Even though it was less than a minute since he had looked, he checked his wrist again. Twenty minutes short of nine o'clock.

Patel kept the engine running for fifteen minutes at a time, heater turned up high. In between, he would climb out of the car and pace up and down, clapping his hands together, warming them with his breath. Normally, going out on obs, he would take a large thermos, in this weather a pair of long johns under his grey trousers; this had been so sudden, there had not been time to find even his gloves.

A woman came out from one of the terraced houses with a Snoopy mug. "Coffee, all right?"

Patel smiled thanks and sipped, giving her an immediate questioning look.

"Brandy. We'd got it in for Christmas. Only a drop, duck, don't you fret. That or a cuddle to keep out the cold, eh?"

Patel had phoned Alison from the call box on the main road. "Look, I'm sorry, but I'm not going to be able to make it."

"Oh, well," Alison had replied, "another evening trying to master macramé. You don't know anyone who wants half a dozen slightly skewwhiff plant holders, do you?"

Back in the car, Patel contacted the station: nothing to report either way. He switched on the radio and failed to find anything worth listening to. A car turned into the street, headlights wavering and widening in Patel's wing mirror; hand on the car door, he held his breath, relaxing only when it had turned again, this time out of sight. These weekends that the little girl's mother went on so regularly, wasn't the most likely thing that she was off to see someone she knew? He patted his pocket, checking his notebook was in place; time to knock on a few more doors.

House-to-house near the Morrisons' home had come up with three vehicles parked close by during the afternoon and so far unaccounted for: a transit van, dark green; a black Sierra with a rear stabiliser and fancy trim; and a red hatchback, possibly a Nova.

There were also two reports of strangers. Four different people remarked on a man wearing sports clothes—blue running gear, track suit trousers and a hooded anorak top—jogging up and down both sides of the crescent. Two said the hood had been up, one said, no, definitely down, the fourth was uncertain; one claimed to have seen a wispy beard. It was not impossible that they had seen more than one person running; increasingly, it was what people did on Sunday afternoons, those who weren't sleeping in front of the television, taking a nap with their respective husbands or wives.

The other sighting was of a woman, early middle age, nothing remarkable about the way she was dressed, but she had seemed to have been wandering along talking to herself. Yes, out loud. No, not loud enough to hear what she had been saying. Wait a minute, though, now the officer mentioned it, she did seem to have been paying some attention to the Morrison house, looking into the windows as she went past.

The police knocked on more doors, asked the same questions, wrote down the replies. Overtime was all well and good, especially something like this, a kiddie gone missing, but nothing to be gained from hanging about, not with the chance of getting in a pint or two before closing.

Patel's voice was indistinct, the connection poor, but the jist of what he told Resnick was clear. As far as any of the neighbours knew, Diana spent her weekends away in Yorkshire, though exactly where was more debatable. There were two votes for Hebden Bridge, one for Huddersfield, one Heptonstall and a rather halfhearted suggestion of Halifax. At least the H was consistent. Diana had said something to the woman two doors down, possibly the closest in the street to a friend, that she had been seeing someone in the course of these weekends.

"Staying with him?"

"Oh, I don't know, duck. She didn't offer and I say it's none of my business to ask, but you know what they do say, nature will have her way."

"You never saw this man? He didn't come and see her down here?"

"Not as far as I know."

"And his name? She didn't mention his name?"

"No, lovie, sorry."

"Get yourself home," Resnick said. "Catch a few hours' sleep. Be back out there first thing. If she doesn't show, we'll call Yorkshire, see if we can't track her down."

Patel disappeared beneath a crackle of static and Resnick went off in search of a road map, an atlas. When he had been a DS and Skelton a DI, he'd allowed himself to be talked into a couple of days walking on the Pennine Way. Aside from blisters, he seemed to remember that Hebden Bridge and Heptonstall were close together. Wasn't one down in the valley, the other up on a hill? If he had to go up there again, he'd make sure it was by car, not an anorak, not a rucksack in sight.

The crime reporter from the city paper knocked on the Morrisons' door a little shy of ten o'clock. A decent man wearing a sombre expression and a brown suit, it didn't take him long to persuade Michael that the kind of coverage his paper would give to Emily's disappearance would do nothing but good.

He sat and drank tea, made bluff sympathetic noises, made notes. Lorraine—"red-eyed and stricken with grief"—said very little, but Michael—"clearly distressed, but determined to be hopeful"—talked willingly about his lovely daughter as he showed the reporter photos from the family album—"a happy child with beautiful red hair."

Making sure he got permission to come back the next morning with a photographer, the reporter hurried off to get his story ready for the first edition. On his way he used the car phone to contact a colleague from the local radio newsroom, a favour returned like money in the bank.

So it was that the first broadcast of Emily Morrison's disappearance went out as second lead on the eleven o'clock news, sandwiched between rumours of a half percent cut in the bank lending rate and a near fatality on a local golf course during a thunderstorm.

Resnick heard the item driving home and wondered if the Morrisons were in any way prepared for the media attention their daughter's disappearance would inevitably bring. More especially, since the body of another girl of similar age had so recently been found. Another girl who had lived in the same part of the city, their homes less than a mile apart.

19

Resnick woke to the sounds of birds outside. Except that these weren't birds. Clusters of notes, grey, like sparrows at first light: soft insistence of sound. Faint splash of wings in shallow water, dusty cymbal strokes. Fragmentary. Minor chords at angles to the night.

He sat on the side of the bed, listening, wondering at the irregular rhythms of the heart. Someone attacking Gloria Summers with force enough to splinter bone.

There had been a bird: a skeleton he had found inside the house; white and smooth, perfectly proportioned and perfectly matching, translucent, bones that had become dust inside his hands.

I don't understand how anyone in his right mind . . .

Resnick knew a man who, in a single uncharacteristic moment, had brought a hammer down smack between his mother's eyes. Now, after nine years locked away, he reported to his probation officer, changed the flowers on his mother's grave, lived a productive, blameless life. He knew another who had killed a man with the broken end of a bottle in a pub brawl, an argument over nothing that had ended in a starburst of arterial blood. On the third day of his parole he had quarrelled with a taxi driver over a two-pound fare and bludgeoned him to death.

How anyone . . .

Resnick stood at the window looking out and all the other windows he could see were curtained across and dark. There was a place in most people's lives where they were capable of every evil thing.

I wished you dead, Charlie, does that shock you?

Wherever Elaine was now he hoped that she was sleeping and not awake like him, hung on the edge of something he could neither ignore nor fully understand; something that, even when he closed his eyes and ears, still echoed discordantly inside his mind.

"Off Minor."

Lorraine had been awake since grey dawn, watching the troubled movement of Michael's sleeping face, the winking eye of the digital clock. When she reached out to smooth the tightening frown around her husband's eyes, he jerked instinctively away, unwaking, numbed by the enormity of what had happened.

Lorraine continued to lie there, remembering the first occasion she had seen Emily's face: pressed up against the rear window of her father's car, dark eyes surrounded by startling red hair. Michael had taken her with him to the shops and, on his way home, detoured by the bed-sitter where Lorraine lived. She and Michael had been seeing one another for about a month. Stubborn, the little girl had refused to leave the car, say hello to Daddy's friend. Lorraine thinking, as they drove away, I can't handle this—a man with his marriage on the point of disintegration, a small child—this is not what I want.

"For pity's sake!" her father had exclaimed. "Is this what we brought you up for? Educated you for? Somebody else's leftovers?"

"What he's doing to his wife," her mother had said, "who's to say he won't do the same to you?"

At the wedding they kept themselves to themselves, stood stiff-backed at the reception, left early because of the long drive home.

Emily had been so excited, so pleased with her new dress, which, as the afternoon wore on, became smudged with trifle, ice cream and wedding cake. When the music had begun, Michael had danced the first dance with Lorraine, the second with Emily, swinging her safe and wide and laughing in his arms.

Michael grunted something loudly and rolled over, covering his face with his arm. Softly, Lorraine slid out from beneath the duvet and crept downstairs. When she eased the curtain back a crack, the first camera crew was hurrying across the front lawn.

———

Raymond lay late in bed that morning, tired and horny, trying to summon up clear images of Sara but others insisting on getting in the way.

"All right," Skelton began, "wide awake, let's have your attention."

The appropriate section of the city map had been enlarged and attached to the wall behind him. Photographs of Gloria Summers and Emily Morrison on either side. Coloured pins flagged their homes, the last places they had been seen alive. Ribbon marked the journeys they would have taken to their respective schools, the roads along which they might have been taken to the rec.

"Two girls," Skelton was saying, "similar ages. Slip a shoehorn between their birthdays if you're careful. Missing within three months of one another. Homes, schools, no more than three-quarters of a mile apart. Coincidence?"

The superintendent looked at the faces of the officers, grim beneath an early morning haze of cigarette smoke.

"We're running the Summers case back through the computer, looking for connections. Up to now, the second incident, the mother's our best bet. We've got a lead to West Yorkshire, DC Patel's on his way there now, liaising with Chief Inspector Duncan, Halifax CID. The rest of you, you know the priorities: three vehicles—a red hatchback, Ford Sierra, green transit—and two individuals, the jogger and a woman who might or might not prove to be the girl's mother.

"Questions?"

There were none.

Chief Inspector Lawrence spelled out the rest. Uniformed officers would back up CID on house-to-house, double-checking, broadening it beyond the immediate vicinity of the Morrison house. Others, along with civilian volunteers, would begin to search the wasteland along the canal and beside the railway tracks; divers were standing by. A watch was being kept at the house in Kimberley in case Diana Wills returned under her own devices.

Skelton was on his feet again. "I don't need to tell you the urgency here: we want the girl found and as soon as possible."

He didn't add: *While she's still alive.*

He didn't need to.

———

"Michael."

He pushed away Lorraine's hand and rolled towards the far side of the bed.

"Michael."

"What?"

"There's people outside, filming the house. I asked them to go away and they refused." He was sitting upright now, staring at her; all the while he had been sunk in sleep it had been possible to think that it had not really happened. "They say they want us to talk to them, make a statement."

A stone clinked against the window.

"Mr. Morrison! Wakey-wakey! Rise and shine!"

20

There's a statue of J. B. Priestley in the heart of Bradford, an imposing figure in a loose raincoat, not unlike Resnick, Patel had thought on more than one occasion. He had never read a word of Priestley, knew little enough about him, but he had, fifteen, been taken by the school to an afternoon performance of one of his plays. At the Alhambra: *When We Are Married*. A kind of sit-com, Patel remembered it, bluff-talking folk who smoked cigars and talked of brass, a maid in uniform, adultery—except it wasn't really that—endless high teas. He had tried to tell his parents about it later, but his mother, unable to follow Patel's tenuous grasp of the plot, had kept asking him to go back to the beginning; his father had queried what it had to do with education, suspected it of preaching values that were decadent, immoral.

One thing you could do if you were standing alongside the statue: lift up your head and see, above the furthest ridge of housing, the green of hills. Patel had grown up with this, woollen towns built in a valley, the power of water, streaming down. Even though that industry had largely gone, changed, the towns lived on. Bradford. Wakefield. Halifax.

Patel had been swept past the police station in the swell of traffic that sped around the broad ring road. His apology had been on his lips before Chief Inspector Duncan looked ostentatiously at his watch.

A thin-lipped constable drove them out along the valley road towards

Hebden Bridge, past stone walls and blackened stone chapels, tiny chippies that seemed to have been built into the front rooms of people's houses, factories that sold sheepskin coats and clogs, fishermen in green plastic, glimpsed here and there along the canal.

Duncan sat alongside Patel in the back of the car, gazing through the window and saying next to nothing. Sheep stared back at him, bedraggled, from steeply sloping fields.

"That photo you faxed up," Duncan offered, passing through Mytholmroyd, "next to bloody useless."

It had been a colour snap, eight or nine years old, just about the only picture of his former wife Michael Morrison had kept.

"I were your boss, I'd have 'em beating a path through the woods with sticks, dredging the local reservoir, the canals."

Patel nodded politely, said nothing.

"Another kiddie, weren't there? Not so long back?"

"Sir."

"Where was it they found her?"

"Old railway sidings."

"That's it then. That's the place to be looking. Not having us chasing us tails with a needle-and-haystack job up here."

HEBDEN BRIDGE, the sign read, THE PENNINES CENTRE.

Elsewhere, the day began well. One of the Morrisons' neighbours, eight doors down, called the station and told the duty sergeant about the transit van that had been parked outside their house. A couple of men had been doing some decorating; on Saturday they had stripped the wallpaper from the living room and prepared it for a fresh coat of paint. They left the van through Sunday, prior to returning on Monday evening.

Divine found the pair through a contact number, the two of them moonlighting from their regular jobs with a large building firm, currently engaged in transforming one of the Victorian factories in the old Lace Market area into exclusive flats and offices. Where the original owner had installed a chapel in the basement and paid his workers to attend between seven and seven-thirty each morning, the new entrepreneur was thinking along the lines of a squash court and sauna.

"Yes," conceded one man, "old green van. That's ours. Not a problem, is there? Not the tax? In the post."

"Doing a little job out there," the second man said. "More a favour than anything else. Friend of a friend, you know? Look, you don't have to say anything about this to Inland Revenue, do you? VAT?"

Graham Millington had been halfway to his car, heading off towards the house-to-house, crack the whip a little, when the constable called him back. A Mrs. McLoughlin, sounded quite distressed, wanted to talk to somebody working on the investigation. Not just anybody.

Moira McLoughlin was waiting behind the door as Millington drew up, a house not unlike the Morrisons', just two short streets away. She opened the front door and drew Millington swiftly inside. She was a small woman with swollen ankles, with soft permed hair and a beige dress that fastened all the way up to the neck.

"This is about the missing girl?" Millington asked.

"Please," she said, anxiety wobbling her voice between registers, "come through to the other room."

They sat in a dralon dream lounge with the standard lamp burning, curtains drawn, not yet eleven in the morning.

"It's the car," Moira McLoughlin said.

"Car?"

"The car that was parked in the crescent. You were asking about it on the news."

"The hatchback? Nova?"

She nodded, a forward dart, like a bird at a feeder.

"What about it?"

The woman's fingers steepled momentarily, then crumpled into one another, a movement of swelling knuckles and rings. "You see," she said, not looking at Millington, looking anywhere but at him, "we parked it instead of outside here . . ."

"We?"

"He. My . . . friend."

Sweet Jesus, Millington thought, that's what this is all about. She's having an affair.

"It wasn't often that he came to the house and when he did, he always parked the car in different places, so as not to attract suspicion." Her mouth was dry and the pale pink of her tongue kept sliding across it. It didn't make any difference, Millington was thinking, not age, nor appearance, not a damned thing. There they were, half the population, shedding their marriage vows as easily as they could shuck off their knickers. Even women like this, wouldn't guess she'd had a sexy thought in her life, wouldn't think another man would look at her twice. For a moment, as Moira McLoughlin continued talking, Millington realised he was thinking about his own wife, all those evenings in stuffy class-rooms learning about Russian verbs or Barbara Hepworth's bronzes, the chatter afterwards over coffee, articulate young men with degrees and aspirations who weren't compelled to work strange hours, then come home smelling of beer and other people's cigarettes.

"I wasn't going to say anything at all, you see, but I knew that Alan never never would, and you did say, the police report on the news, it did say it was important." She touched her fingers to the loose skin bunching at her throat. "That poor child."

Millington uncapped his pen. "The gentleman in question, er, Alan, how long would you say he was here?"

"I don't know. I suppose until five. It must have been until five. My husband, his mother is in a nursing home, you see, all the way down in Hereford, and he travels down to see her. Sundays. Some Sundays. After lunch."

Soon that's where we'll all be, Millington thought, tucked up in wheelchairs up and down the country, slobbering over our Sunday mashed potato and trying to remember who it was we committed adultery with and why.

"You won't have to contact him, Sergeant? You see, I thought if I told you myself, that would be all right."

"I'll just take a note of his name and address. It shouldn't be necessary to speak to the gentleman himself, but if it is I assure you we'll use the utmost discretion."

A job for Divine, Millington thought: Oi, which of you's been humping the dwarf with the swollen legs? He wrote the details carefully into his book and rose to his feet. "We're very grateful that you came forward. Now we can forget about the car, at least."

"Do you think you'll find her?" Moira McLoughlin asked at the door. "I mean before . . ."

"I don't know," Millington replied, a slow shake of the head. "I honestly don't know."

21

"Are you married?"

Lynn Kellogg shook her head. "No."

"Must be difficult, a job like yours. If you were, I mean. Shift work, things like that."

"Yes," Lynn said, "I suppose so."

"Still," Lorraine Morrison tried for a smile and missed, "plenty of time yet."

Tell that to my mother, Lynn thought.

They were sitting at the back of the house, the living room, french windows out onto the garden towards which Lorraine's eyes kept returning: as if Emily would be miraculously there, the same old game continuing, dolls and babies and mummies and prams, happy, happy families.

"I was nineteen," Lorraine said, "when I met Michael. We were in this restaurant. Mama Mia. I'd gone there with a bunch of girls from where I worked. The bank. Somebody's leaving-do, you know?"

Lynn nodded. The traffic noise from the main road nearby was ever-present, dull, cushioned by double glazing. They had been sitting there long enough for their too-weak coffee to grow cold, for Lynn to marvel at the correctness of everything in its place, the vases, the cushions with their bright floral blues and greens, the print of pink ballet dancers on the wall. Earlier that day, when Lynn had first arrived, she had found Lorraine lifting ornaments and picture frames and dusting underneath. She imagined Lorraine as a child, following her mother from room to room with the hoover, watching, cleaning, falling into step. Here she was, younger than Lynn by a good six years, already married, a husband, a house, a missing child . . .

"I suppose we must have been making a lot of noise," Lorraine was saying, "the way people do, evenings like that. Michael was there with this other man, business. After a while he came over, tapped me, you know, on the shoulder. He and his friend had been having a bet on what it was we all did. I told him and he laughed and called out that he'd won. Next day, I looked up from the counter and there he was, halfway down the queue. 'You didn't tell me which branch,' he said, when he got to the window. 'I've been walking my feet off all over the city centre.' The cashiers either side of me were listening, one of them laughed and I could feel myself going red. He pushed a cheque through to me and it wasn't even the right bank. I asked him what he was doing. 'I thought you could endorse it,' he said. 'Address and telephone number on the back.' As much to get rid of him as anything else, I did."

" 'You're asking for trouble,' one of the other girls said. 'Married man. He is good-looking though, nice clothes.'

" 'How d'you know he's married?' I said. He hadn't been wearing a ring, I had noticed that.

"First time I went out with him I asked him and he laughed and said, 'No, what kind of a bloke do you think I am?' After we'd been seeing one another for maybe a month, he told me that he was. I went mad, really screaming at him, calling him a liar, all sorts. 'Steady, steady,' he said, catching hold of my hands. 'I didn't tell you before 'cause there wasn't any point.' 'What do you mean?' I said. 'I wasn't in love with you then,' he said."

Michael had phoned in and asked for time off, compassionate leave. When Lynn had arrived at the house, he had been on the point of going outside, running the gauntlet of the news photographers, the video cameramen. She had persuaded him it was not, perhaps, the best idea, since when he had stayed in the kitchen, blinds closed, chain-smoking and working his way through a bottle of Bulgarian wine.

"Fifteen years older than me, Michael. It's all my mum could think about, that and the fact that he'd been divorced. Fifteen years." She glanced at Lynn. "I don't think that's a lot, do you?"

Lynn shook her head. "Not necessarily."

" 'By the time you're thirty,' my mum used to say, 'he'll be forty-five. Middle-aged. Have you thought of that?' " Lorraine was on her feet by the french window: a robin was squatting near the edge of the lawn, so still that it could have been a plastic toy. "It's not as if," Lorraine said, "he acts his age. Not, you know, old. Only since he lost his job, had to take another miles away, all the travelling, well, he gets tired. I mean, he's bound to. Anybody would. His age, that's got nothing to do with it."

Lynn stood up, smoothing down her skirt. She didn't know about Michael, but being around Lorraine somehow made her feel young and old at the same time. Lorraine was the kind of girl Lynn hated sharing a communal changing room with whenever she was buying something to wear; there she'd be, struggling into a size twelve, glance up and there's this kid with a model-girl figure sliding down into a ten with inches to spare. Remember Michelle Pfeiffer in *The Fabulous Baker Boys*? The scene where they take her out for new clothes and one of the Baker Boys, one of the Bridges brothers, says to her, "What are you? An eight?" and she just looks at him and says, "A six."

Lynn loved the film, had seen it three times, but that really got to her. A six!

Lorraine had time and money to spend on herself as well; hair done each week and more than the occasional hour on the sun bed. Where else was she going to get that tan, that shine on her skin?

"If I could use your phone," Lynn said, "I'll check in with the station."

Raymond had been fifteen minutes late for work and Hathersage had given him a proper bollocking in front of half a dozen others, enough to bring tears to the corners of Raymond's eyes as he stood there, head down, smarting. An inch away from chucking it all in, asking for his cards, walk right out of there and go into town, maybe Sara was on early lunch. But he stuck it out, as much afraid of what his father would say when he found out, his dad and his uncle Terry, organising his life for him between rounds at the pub.

Raymond kept his head down and kept on working: the day hadn't been invented that lasted forever.

All around radios crackled about him as he moved, none quite tuned to 96.3, their sounds all but drowned beneath the loud, mechanical swearing of the men, the high whine of electric saws, the thump of cleavers hammering down. Off-loading a fork-lift truck, Raymond missed Emily Morrison's name on the news report, but registered what had happened, a young girl missing from home.

"Look at you now! Clumsy young bugger!" bawled Hathersage, passing through. "Want to keep your mind on what you're sodding doing!"

Raymond's mumbled apology went unheard, scrabbling as he was, down on his hands and knees amongst ox livers, deep dark red.

22

Hebden Bridge seemed to be tearooms closed for refurbishment and antique shops presided over by damp little men with grubby hands and sunken faces. Perhaps things brightened up in the summer when the walkers came in from Manchester and Leeds, greedy for barm cakes and fresh air. What Patel did find, close by the canal, was a record shop that stocked the devotional Sufi songs of Nusrat Fateh Ali Khan and he left there happily with two CDs in a recycled Pricerite plastic bag. Chief Inspector Duncan had long since departed for Halifax, leaving Patel the services of two uniformed constables and an ominous "Good luck, Sunshine. Catch anything here aside of a stinking cold and sore feet, you're going to need it."

Passersby barely stopped to glance at the blurred picture of Diana Wills before shaking their heads and moving on. In the pubs, provision shops, the chemists staffed by pleasant-faced women in sensible shoes and spotless pink uniforms, it was the same. Even the caretaker of the Calder Valley Spiritualist Church could offer no hope of a sighting. It was only when Patel, weary of the omnipresent drizzle that came down from the hills in waves, ducked into a café for shelter that he struck lucky. At the counter he ordered a pot of tea and two slices of toast, then took a seat to wait. The only other customer was a woman in a duffle coat, mechanically rocking the handle of her pram as she forked her way through a large piece of passion cake.

A second woman, the one behind the counter, carried over Patel's order on a tray. She was setting the teapot on the circular table when her hand stilled in midair.

"What's this, then?"

She was looking at the slim sheaf of pictures near Patel's arm.

While Patel explained, she continued to unload her tray. "Oh, yes," she said, finished. "Regular, comes in all the time."

"You're sure?"

"Weekends."

"Every weekend?"

"No," picking at a loose cotton on her apron. "Not every. Every other, maybe."

"She was here this weekend, just gone?"

"Let me see, I . . . No. No, I'm certain I'd remember. Pot of tea, like yours, but weak, extra water. Always takes out the tea bag as soon as pot's on table. Paying over good money for something tastes of nothing's not my way of doing things, but there's some you get in here, worse habits than her, so I never say a thing. Good morning, hello, maybe a few words about the weather. Yes, pot of tea and a slice of carrot cake."

"Diana Wills," Patel said.

"Is that her name? It's not often I know people's names."

"But you are sure this is the woman you know?"

She picked up one of the sheets and looked at it carefully. "Terrible likeness, but it's her right enough."

"And when she's here," Patel said, "weekends, I don't suppose you would have any idea where she stays?"

"What's she done, then, this—what did you say?—Diana Willis?"

"Wills."

"Wills."

"Nothing."

"Seems an awful lot of fuss to go to about nothing."

"We want to get in touch with her, the police, something we have to tell her. It is important."

"I used to like hearing those messages on the radio," the woman said, taking a chair opposite Patel. "After the news. We have an urgent message for so-and-so, so-and-so, at present on a caravaning holiday in so-and-so, so-and-so, will she please get in touch with so-and-so hospital, where her mother, Mrs. So-and-so, so-and-so is seriously ill. You don't get them so much anymore. Wonder why that is?"

Patel took a deep breath. "You have no idea, then, where she stays?"

"Don't say I said so," the woman said, rising, "but why don't you ask at that book shop back down on the main road? That's where her friend is, the one she comes to see."

"Which shop exactly?" Patel asked. As far as he remembered there were three, possibly four.

"Up the hill by the Heptonstall turning, past the whole-food place. That's the one."

Patel started to move and she rested a hand on his shoulder. "They'll likely not pack up and go within the next five minutes. Meantime that tea'll be stewed and your toast's curling up and going cold."

Against his wife's and Lynn's advice, Michael Morrison had left the house, waving off the reporters and threatening to punch a cameraman who positioned himself outside the garage and refused to move. Within twenty minutes he was back: crossing the bridge by the marina he had seen men with sticks, clearing a path slowly through the reeds.

"Investigation!" he yelled at Lynn Kellogg as he slammed back into the house. "You've already made up your sodding mind!"

"That's not true."

"No? Then what's all that going on out there?"

"What d'you mean?"

"Search parties, that's what I mean. You don't carry on like that, looking for anyone you reckon's still alive."

"Michael," Lorraine said. "Please don't."

"Emily!" Michael shouted full into Lynn's face. "Everything else is a cover-up. You think she's bloody dead."

"Mr. Morrison, Michael, that isn't true."

"Don't lie to me. I'm her father, so don't." For an instant Lynn thought he was going to lash out at her, but he banged his way out of the room instead.

Lorraine followed him into the kitchen, where he was opening a fresh bottle of wine. "Do you think you should . . . ?" she began, but the look in his eyes when he rounded on her was enough to choke her words.

"It's routine," Lynn explained when Lorraine came back into the lounge. "Cases like this."

Lorraine slowly nodded, never quite believing. "It's all this stress," she said, "why Michael's drinking. Before he lost his job, had to move, he scarcely drank at all."

In the kitchen Michael lit a fresh cigarette and poured another glass of wine. Sitting at the breakfast bar, elbows on the speckled surface, in his mind he was hurrying into the hospital and seeing the truth on Diana's face before either nurse or doctor could intercept him, take him quietly to one side, explain. "We're desperately sorry, Mr. Morrison. We did everything we possibly could. I'm afraid James slipped away from us."

Slipped away.

For an instant Michael could feel again the earth at his hand's centre, wet and cloying, hear the spatter as it struck the tiny coffin and rolled away.

"It's all right, Diana. Diana. Diana, it'll be all right. Give it time, you see. We have to give it time. We can have another baby, when we're ready. When you're ready. You see."

But it had never been all right, not really. Not after that. And then Emily had been born and each time she cried to be fed she reminded Diana that James was dead: each and every waking hour a living rebuke.

Michael splashed wine over his hands slamming the glass down and barked a shin against a stool on his way to the kitchen door. He was in the car and backing out of the drive when Lorraine came running, cameras clicking; Lynn in the doorway watching. Both women knowing where he was going.

"It's Morrison, sir," Lynn said to Resnick on the phone. "Gone off like the start of the Grand Prix. And he's been drinking pretty heavily. I'd say he's on his way to his ex-wife's place."

She put back the receiver to find Lorraine looking at her, dark-rimmed eyes primed for more tears. Lynn reached for her hands and when the younger woman tried to shake free she didn't let her go. "I don't know about you," Lynn said, "but I'm famished. I wonder what you've got that would be good on toast?"

And she stood there, holding on to Lorraine's hands, until Lorraine said, "Baked beans, there's always loads of baked beans. Marmite. Cheese. Sardines."

23

The name over the door read "Jacqueline Verdon, Bookseller." There were books under a canopy outside, paperbacks in crates, dog-eared and damp, ten pence each. In the window, more expensive, volumes on astrology, astronomy, motherhood and diet, the lives of the great composers, forgotten women artists. If Patel had ever known the name of a woman artist, he had forgotten it. A bell jingled above the door as he went inside.

The interior smelled of slow-burning incense. From the back of the shop there was music playing, chimelike and repetitive. On a central table several vases of dried flowers were surrounded by a display of maps. Almost the entire wall to Patel's left was crammed with green-backed books published by Virago.

"How may I help you?" The woman lifted her glasses from her face before she spoke, treating Patel to a welcoming smile. She was in her forties, he thought, neat brown hair, one of those essentially English women whose good manners impelled them towards liberal attitudes on race relations and capital punishment. When Patel had first moved to his present station, he had lodged with one, bran flakes for breakfast and the toilet bowl had shone; the day she had caught Patel with a Cape apple in his room, she had reacted as if he had been enjoying sexual congress with her miniature schnauzer.

"There's a lot more stock upstairs. You're welcome to just browse. But if you're in any kind of a hurry, it might be best to let me know what it is you're interested in."

Without her glasses she seemed to be staring at him, accentuating the frankness of her gaze. She smiled again and moved her head slightly, so that the circular earrings that she wore brushed against the sides of her face, reflecting such light as there was.

"You are Jacqueline Verdon?" Patel asked.

"Yes." Less certain now, questioning.

"I thought perhaps you could tell me something about Diana Wills?"

Her hand jerked sharply sideways, sending her fountain pen skittering across the desk where she had been working and leaving a line of tiny blots across her papers, each smaller than the last.

Patel rounded the display table, drawing his identification from his pocket.

"What's happened?" Jacqueline Verdon asked. "Diana. What's happened to her?" Alarm clear in the hazel of her eyes, the rising voice.

Resnick got stuck behind a ready-mix concrete lorry going over Bobbers Mill Bridge and was kept fuming in a single line of traffic that stretched from the ring road as far as Basford College. On his radio, the infirm and over-sixties were gamely phoning in to Radio Nottingham, reminiscing about real Christmas trees and real holly, mince pies half a dozen for half an old crown, goodness knows how many shopping days to Christmas and they were bitching about it already. "I remember the time," croaked one, "when there was a Santa Claus in every store in the city": the last Santa Resnick had been in contact with had been up on a charge of molesting small boys in his grotto.

He changed to Gem-AM, sixteen bars of Neil Sedaka and switching off wasn't very hard to do. A gap appeared in the traffic ahead and he accelerated into it, earning the upthrust middle finger of a peroxide blonde delivering auto parts. He arrived in Kimberley in time to find the nineteen-year-old constable sitting on the kerb, helmet between his knees, while the woman who had slipped Patel his brandy-laced drink dabbed at this young man's cut forehead with cotton wool and Germolene.

"What the hell happened here?"

"Oh, the poor love . . ."

The PC blushed.

"He's old enough to answer for himself," Resnick said. "Just."

"Excuse me!"

"He must've broke in round the back, sir . . ."

"Who?"

"Morrison, sir. Least, that's who I think it is."

"How did he break in?"

"Window in the door, sir. Key must've been inside."

"You didn't see him? Hear him?"

"Only after it happened, sir. See . . ." glancing warily at the woman, who was now fitting a piece of Elastoplast over the treated cotton wool, ". . . I was taking a break, like."

"You what?"

"No more than a cup of tea and a cheese cob," the woman said.

"I wasn't gone above five minutes, sir."

"And the rest."

"Don't be so hard on the lad."

"However long it was," Resnick said, "time enough for the mother to've been in and gone."

"Sir, I don't think so, sir. I . . ."

"Don't think is just about right. How do we know she's not in there now, with him? Well?"

The constable looked unhappily at the crown of his helmet. "We don't, sir."

"Exactly."

"There's been no shouting, sir. Nothing like that."

"What has there been?"

"Bit of breaking, I think, sir. Things being thrown around."

"One or two in your direction, by the look of it."

"Poor lamb . . ." the woman began, till Resnick's expression made her think better of it.

"I stuck my head through the door, sir. Calling for him to come out."

Resnick shook his head slowly, more in sorrow than in anger. "You did phone it in?"

"Yes, sir. They said someone was already on the way."

Resnick nodded. "That was me." He turned towards the house. "Come on. If you're through being cosseted, let's see what's going on."

"He's still inside," said the cloth-capped man, leaning against his back fence.

Resnick nodded thanks and carried on into the rear yard. There was no sign of life in the back room or kitchen, but the floor of the former was littered with pages torn from scrapbooks and hurled about. Photographs were jumbled together on the table. A shattered vase, presumably the one that had struck the PC, lay on the quarry tiles in the kitchen.

"Michael Morrison?"

Aside from a dog barking higher up the street and the thrum of traffic, it was disturbingly quiet.

"Michael Morrison? It's Detective Inspector Resnick. We talked yesterday." A pause. "Why don't you come and let us in?"

No response.

To the young constable, Resnick said quietly, "Round and watch the front."

Resnick reached through the broken pane of pebbled glass and tried the handle of the door. The top bolt had been slid into place but he could just reach it with finger and thumb, ease it back. The soles of his feet crunched lightly on china shards. The room smelled slightly musty. Quarry tiles, Resnick reckoned, laid directly onto the packed earth, encouraging the damp.

"Michael?"

Bending towards the rough grey scrapbook sheets, he glimpsed pantomime tickets, a sticker from the Wild West Adventure Park, a souvenir programme from *Babes in the Wood*. On the torn pages of an album there were small square photographs of a man and a woman with a small child, a baby: Michael and Diana, Emily.

"Michael Morrison?"

The front room was snug and dark. It would have been possible to lean in all directions from one of the easy chairs and touch all four walls. The PC's anxious face, strips of plaster incongruous beneath the peak of his helmet, looked back at Resnick through patterned lace.

On the stairs, the edges of carpet had all but worn through.

"Michael, it's Inspector Resnick. I'm coming up."

He was in the bedroom at the front of the house; two beds side by side with enough room for Michael to be sitting between them, back against the wall. The bed closest to the window, Resnick guessed to be Diana's: an alarm clock on the plywood cabinet beside it, two mugs containing an inch or so of long-cold tea, orange now around the edges, a paperback on stress, another, shiny reflective cover, on the subject of assertiveness. On the second bed soft animals crowded round the head. A cushion embroidered with a multicoloured cat lay near the foot. On the adjacent straight-backed chair there were slim books with vivid covers: *Teddybears 1 to 10*, *Morris's Disappearing Bag*. Scattered over both beds were more pages ripped from the albums and scrapbooks Michael Morrison had found below, his family in pieces all around him. His first family. He sat there, not looking up at Resnick, an almost empty half-bottle of whisky tight between his knees.

"Michael."

The eyes flickered towards him, then away. The fingers of Michael's left hand were curled around a doll, round, flat face and hair like straw. A striped dress, yellow and red.

"Michael."

In his other hand was a knife. Serrated edge, the kind more commonly used for slicing bread.

Resnick leaned towards him, careful not to startle, not to draw attention to his own hands.

"It's my fault," Michael Morrison said.

"No," Resnick said and shook his head.

"My fault!"

"No!"

Resnick saw the tensing in Michael Morrison's eyes, and grabbed for the knife too late. The point of the blade plunged fast at the doll and missed, driving hard into Morrison's own thigh.

There was a vast intake of breath, pitched like a sigh: a shout building to a scream.

"Christ!" The word no sooner from Resnick's mouth than Morrison had pulled the knife back out and, fingers buckled open, dropped it to the ground.

Resnick plucked the knife clear and slid it back over the thin carpet, out of reach. Blood was beginning to well, surprisingly bright, through the tear in Michael Morrison's trousers, the puncture in his leg.

Resnick wrenched back the clasp, threw open the window. "Ambulance!" he yelled. "Fast." And then he was hurling off the blankets, looking for a sheet to make a tourniquet.

24

"Thank you," Lorraine said, her voice scarcely more than a whisper.

There in the hospital corridor, porters and nurses hurrying round her, she looked more like someone's daughter than anyone's wife. Whatever makeup she had been wearing had long been cried from her face. Hands like moths around her body, never still.

"I didn't do anything," Resnick said.

"The doctor, he said that without you Michael would have lost a lot more blood."

Resnick nodded. The wound had been less than two inches deep and surprisingly clean. There seemed little reason for them keeping him in overnight.

"Come on," Resnick said. "I'm taking you home."

"I can't." A blur of hands. "Not without Michael."

"Michael's sleeping. When he wakes they'll check him over, phone you."

"Even so."

"You can't do anything here. And if you don't rest yourself you're not going to be much good to him when he gets home."

He could tell she wanted to argue, but she no longer had the strength. Within two days she had suffered a stepdaughter abducted, now a husband hospitalized at his own hand. If she stood there much longer, she would keel over and Resnick was going to have to move smartly to catch her. He put his arm across her shoulders instead. "I'll drive you back."

Between car and house she faltered, only one cameraman hanging on, ready to get a picture of Lorraine fainting on her own front lawn. But she rallied herself, depriving the nation of a front-page splash. Resnick waited, patient, while she found the door keys. My fault, Michael Morrison had said; he wondered what he had meant by that.

"You look as if you could sleep for a week," Resnick said, inside the hall.

"I only wish I could." She smiled wanly. "As it is, I doubt if I'd sleep a wink."

Resnick followed her through the house. "How long is it since you had anything to eat?"

"I don't remember."

"Okay. Sit down somewhere. I'll see what I can find."

Again, she was about to argue and, again, the necessary energy deserted her. Resnick left her in the living room, legs tucked up beneath her. The kitchen looked like something from an advertisement for modern living. The kind, Resnick thought ruefully, that Elaine would have aspired to for the pair of them: except she had fostered other ambitions, altogether more affluent. Why else fall for a high-flying estate agent with a holiday home in Wales and a Volvo big enough to allow easy adultery on the rear seat? Jesus, Charlie! Resnick thought, cracking eggs into a bowl, you can be a self-righteous son of a bitch at times!

When he went back into the living room, omelettes and coffee on a tray, Lorraine was fast asleep. Smiling, he put his own plate and mug down on the floor and turned quietly towards the door. He was turning the handle when Lorraine spoke.

"Where are you going?"

"Put this in the oven to keep warm."

"Were you looking at me? Just now, I mean."

"Only for a second."

"That's funny. I thought someone was standing over me. Staring. It woke me up."

"Come on," Resnick said, "you might as well eat this while it's hot."

Lorraine regarded the omelette with suspicion, pushed at it with her fork listlessly. After a few mouthfuls her appetite revived.

"What's in this?" she said, surprised.

"Oh, nothing much. Tomato, onion, a small turnip I found to grate. Garlic. I sliced up your last rasher of bacon, I'm afraid. Oh, and I finished the cream."

"But what's this on top?"

"Parmesan. I sprinkled a little on after adding the cream. If you cook it the last couple of minutes under the grill, it gets that sort of crust."

Lorraine was looking at him as if she couldn't believe him, quite. "Where did you learn all that?"

"Nowhere special." Resnick shrugged. "Picked it up, I suppose."

"I learned from my mother."

"If I'd learned from mine, it would have been dill and barley with everything, so many dumplings I would've been twice the size I am now. If that's possible."

"You're not fat," said Lorraine politely.

"No." Resnick smiled. "Just overweight."

"Anyway," Lorraine returned his smile, "this omelette, I've never tasted anything like it. It's wonderful." And speaking through another helping, a habit of which her mother would most certainly have disapproved, added, "Thank you very much."

For a few seconds, Resnick caught himself thinking maybe his life would be better if there were somebody else to provide for, look after, someone other than his cats.

Jacqueline Verdon had shut up shop. It had not taken her long to convince Patel that she and Diana Wills were close friends or that, at that particular time, she did not know where Diana was.

"She was to have been here this weekend. The arrangements were the same as usual. Except that when I went down to the station to meet the train, no Diana. I met every train until eleven o'clock. I tried to contact her, waited for her to ring. By midday Saturday, I'd managed to convince myself she wasn't coming." The eyes held Patel fast and he knew she was telling the truth. "I haven't heard from Diana since she was here a little over a fortnight ago. I have no idea where she is. I wish I had."

The truth or something very close.

The hospital rang to say they were sending Michael Morrison home in an ambulance within the next half hour. Lorraine had fallen asleep almost as soon as the last mouthful had passed her lips. Resnick lifted the plate away before it slid from her fingers. At six, Michael still not returned, he switched on the TV news, volume set to a whisper. There was a photograph of Emily, some footage of the house and neighbourhood, mention of a woman the police were anxious to interview. Outside in the hall he called the station, letting them know he would be there within the hour. He took a coat from the hall cupboard and spread it across Lorraine's knees. If he and Elaine had had a child straight off, she wouldn't have been a lot younger than her. As he clicked the living room door gently closed, he heard the ambulance draw up outside.

25

Naylor had been in and out of schools the entire day. Cups of tea with harassed secretaries while he waited to sit across the desk from even more hard-worked and harassed head teachers; more tea in the furthest corners of staff rooms, where he was regarded with deep suspicion and the bourbon biscuits were shielded from his sight. Although everyone was genuinely shocked by what had happened, they could offer very little that was helpful; some even seeming to begrudge the hasty conversations in cloakrooms that smelled faintly of urine and were constantly inter-rupted by a litany of "Miss! Miss! Miss! Sir! Sir! Sir!"

Emily had two class teachers, not a perfect state of affairs, as the head teacher explained, but the authority was quite committed to maternity leave, whatever its drawbacks. So that morning Naylor talked to a proba-tioner with skin problems and a voice that was designed for singing hymns and telling stories in the book corner. She could shed no light on Emily's disappearance—a friendly girl, quite bright, not the sort, she thought, to go willingly to strangers. And no, she hadn't seen anyone loitering around the school, nor Emily with anyone aside from her mother—by that she meant Lorraine. If Diana had been skulking by the gates, she had not been noticed. Naylor thanked her and arranged to return the following afternoon and speak to the supply teacher who took over after lunch.

In the hope that the more recent incident might have jogged something loose in their memories, he travelled the short distance to Gloria Summers's school, there in the shadow of the high-rises where her brief life had been lived. But it had not.

By three-thirty Naylor was exhausted and thought he now knew why so many teachers had the appearance of marathon runners. Losers, at that. More than anything else, it had to be the kids, the sheer numbers, the noise of which they were capable. Racing across the playground or tumbling over the apparatus, sitting cross-legged close to the piano, heads thrown back and mouths wide open. Another thing Naylor had noticed: if there was one white face amongst every twenty Asian or black—every thirty in Gloria's school—it was a surprise.

Naylor trying not to feel that it was wrong, remembering a film set in the States, the South, *Mississippi Burning*. The racist deputy looking at a black child in his wife's arms, their maid's child. Isn't it amazing, he says, how they can look so cute when they're little and grow into such animals. Naylor knew that wasn't what he thought. Animals. Though there were those he worked with that did. Even so—leaving the single-storey building with its copperplate signs in English and Urdu, crossing towards the gate where the mothers in richly coloured saris waited for their children—was this the sort of school he would want his child to come to? His and Debbie's? The only white girl in her class. He didn't see how that could be right.

Not that, if things carried on the way they were, he was going to have a lot of say. Getting into the car, he made up his mind to phone Debbie once he'd finished his report. If it meant he had to speak to her cow of a mother, well and good.

"You mean she's a lessie," Alison said with a laugh.

Patel gestured awkwardly. "Possibly."

"Well, from what she said. And if this Diana's been going up there every weekend, there's obviously something going on."

"Perhaps . . ." Patel began.

"Yes?" Alison smirking at him across the top of her glass. They were sitting in the Penthouse Bar of the Royal Hotel; as Patel had put it, an extra ten p a pint for every floor.

"Perhaps they are simply good friends."

"Like us?"

"Oh, no. I don't think we're such good friends yet."

"Maybe we never will be."

"Oh?"

"Maybe I'm gay, too."

"I don't think so."

"How do you know?"

Patel smiled and sipped his lager; he was thinking of the way she had kissed him the moment they had stepped into the lift, not even waiting for the doors to slide shut at their backs.

"What's the matter with you tonight?"

Raymond scuffed his trainers along the edge of the kerb. "Nothing."

"Well, something's got into you. You've hardly said two words the whole evening."

"It's not the whole evening, stupid!"

"Don't call me stupid."

"Don't act like it then. It's only half eight, if that."

"Yeh, well," Sara scowled, "it feels a lot longer, that's all I know. Hour with you when you're in this mood and it's like forever."

"Yeh?"

"Yes."

"Well, there's one way of sorting that then, isn't there?" And Raymond turned on his heels and stalked off across the square, hands in his jeans pockets, ignoring Sara's belated cry of "Ray-o!" as he kicked out with his foot and sent a score of grubby pigeons into flight over the fountain.

Changing gear as he neared the brow of the hill, Naylor was close to changing his mind as well. Accelerate past the house, drive on round the roundabout, back the way he had come. Back to the place he and Debbie had fixed on together, a starter home on a snug estate, walls so thin there was never the need to feel lonely. Which was what Kevin Naylor had used to think.

He glanced at the mirror, indicated, pulled over. A movement of the curtain as he set the hand brake, released the seat belt, switched off the lights.

Debbie's mother kept him waiting and then greeted him with a face like vinegar. Was it his imagination or did the interior always smell of disinfectant?

"She's in there."

There was the middle room, a dining room, although Naylor couldn't imagine Debbie's mother ever inviting anyone to dinner. Unless it was the local undertaker.

Debbie was sitting in the far corner, close to the drawn curtains of the window, upright in a Parker Knoll chair with polished wooden arms, which had been in the family since before Debbie was born. The table, both leaves extended, stretched almost the length of the room between them, walnut veneer. A pot plant with oval green leaves leaned to the left in a vain search for light.

Debbie was wearing a black cardigan over a black jumper, a shapeless black skirt that covered her knees. No discernible makeup. Naylor wondered if she had taken vows and if so which ones.

"Hi," he said, his voice oddly loud in the room, loud enough to have been heard by her mother if she were standing outside the door—which almost certainly she was. "Debbie. How you feeling?"

She glanced up at his face and then allowed her head to fall.

"How's the baby?"

Now she was looking past Naylor's left shoulder, unblinking.

"Debbie, the baby . . ."

"She's fine."

"So can I see her?"

"No."

"Debbie, for Christ's sake . . . !"

"I said, no."

"Why on earth not?"

"Because."

"What kind of an answer is that?"

"The only kind you're going to get."

He was round the table then, seeing her fingers grip the arms of the chair tight, squeezing her body back, making herself small as possible. Looking at him now, fear in her eyes.

"I'm not going to hit you," he said quietly.

"You better not. You . . ."

"You knew I was coming. You must've known I'd want to see her."

"You've got a funny way of showing it."

"Meaning?"

"Meaning when was the last time you came round here? When was the last time you as much as tried to see your daughter?"

"That's because if ever I do, that bloody mother of yours . . ."

"Leave my mother out of this!"

"Gladly."

"If it hadn't been for my mother . . ."

"We'd've still been back home together, the three of us."

"No."

"Yes."

"No, we wouldn't, Kevin."

"Yes."

"We wouldn't, 'cause another couple of months of that and I'd have been in Mapperley and the baby'd've been taken into care."

Naylor stepped back across the room, banging his hip against the table hard. "Now you're talking bloody daft!"

"Am I?"

"You know full well you are."

"Well, ask the doctor, Kevin. Ask her. It's not an unknown thing for mothers to be depressed after a baby, you know."

"Depressed? You were . . ."

"See what I mean? I was ill and all you could do was stay out late drinking, come home and slam around the house before falling asleep downstairs, going off to work in the same clothes you'd come home in. You never did a thing to help me, you never tried to understand . . ."

"Understand? You'd need to be sodding Einstein to understand you when you're in one of your moods."

"Oh, God, Kevin! You don't even understand now, do you? You really don't. Moods. That's all it ever was to you, moods. What's the matter, Kevin? If there isn't something I can hold up and show, something like a wound, to show that I'm bleeding, why can't you understand that I've been ill?" She wound her arms tightly about her waist and for the first time Naylor could see how thin she had become. "I still am ill."

He pulled one of the dining table chairs awkwardly out and sat down. Inside the wooden clock on the sideboard, time clicked noisily by. What was the point? Kevin Naylor was thinking. I should never have bloody come.

"The baby . . ."

"She's sleeping, Kevin. She only just went off before you came."

"Convenient."

"Don't say that."

"Well, isn't it?"

"She had me up four times in the night, fretted all day. I daren't wake her now."

135

"So I'll come back later."

"Kevin, Mum says . . ."

"Yes?"

"She says I ought to see a solicitor."

Naylor snorted. What had he come to say? Come back home, Debbie. A few days at a time first, if you want. We can make it work, you see. Debbie sitting there, looking at him helplessly. Well, now it was never going to work and that was the end of it. So what were those tears doing, pricking at his eyes?

"Kevin?"

He wrenched open the door and there she was, her precious bloody mother, gloating from the other end of the hall. Naylor knew the only thing to stop him from punching her sanctimonious face was to get out of there fast. He left the front door open wide, had the key turned in the ignition before he was properly in the seat; he was a couple of hundred yards along the road before he realised he hadn't even switched on his lights.

26

When Michael Morrison's brother, Geoffrey, was not so many days short of his third birthday, he came across a large animal living in the back of his parents' wardrobe. It was made from soft, white cuddly material and had yellow beads for eyes and pieces of black thread to mark its mouth and nose and paws. Geoffrey tugged it from the plastic bag in which it had been nestling, through the jumble of his mother's shoes and out into the light. It reminded him of the big white dog their friends, the Palmers, used to take for walks and which they had encouraged him to sit on when he was even younger. At first, little Geoffrey had been terrified, insisting on clinging to his father's hand; the animal twisting and barking beneath him, struggling out from under his weight. But as Geoffrey grew bigger, the dog got smaller and Geoffrey started to enjoy it more, balancing on the dog's back with his toes scraping the ground, striking the dog with his little fists, shouting and screaming with excitement.

It had been then that the Palmers had lifted him off and refused to allow him back on. "Sorry, old sport, too big for that now." Just when it had been fun.

So now Geoffrey hurried down the stairs, travelling backwards, bouncing the new toy after him.

"Oh, Geoffrey," his mother said, looking up from the book she was reading, "wherever did you get that? Darling, look what he's been into now."

"Hmm, Geoff," said his father, coming through from the adjoining room, glass in hand, "up to a bit of exploring, eh?"

"Dog," Geoffrey said, giving it a shake.

"Bear, actually. It's a bear."

"Dog."

"No, bear."

"Dog!"

"Darling, I do wish you wouldn't argue with him."

"Look, Geoff," his father reaching down, "it's a polar bear. You must have seen them, on the box. Those programmes you watch. No? Mummy, we ought to take him to the zoo."

Mummy winced and eased herself round in the chair. No matter what position she got herself into, she was uncomfortable within minutes. "Anyway," she said, "better get it back from him before it gets filthy. Your mother will never forgive us if it isn't squeaky clean for the cot."

Cot? Geoffrey thought. Whatever would it be doing in a cot? He didn't use his cot anymore; he slept in a real bed with his favourite toys all around his head. That was where this new one was going to sleep too.

"You're quite right," his father said, and took hold of the bear's arm. Geoffrey ground his teeth and clung to its legs. "Come on, Geoff. Don't want to hurt him, do we? Not before the new baby's even set eyes on him."

Geoffrey still refused to let go of the bear. What new baby? There wasn't any new baby. There wasn't.

"You see, darling," his father said, "we should have told him before."

His mother groaned and swivelled slowly round to look at her son. "What does he think I'm doing, bless him, all puffed up like an ocean liner?"

Geoffrey's father tutted and laughed and knelt down alongside his wife, stroking the swelling beneath her loose, grey dress. "Look, Geoffrey, come over here. Come and feel Mummy's tummy. Come and feel where the baby lives."

Biting down into the inside of his lower lip, Geoffrey walked to where his mother was sitting. He didn't believe it. He didn't believe there was any baby living in there. How could it? Like a toy bear in a plastic bag at the back of a wardrobe. That was different. The bear wasn't real.

Babies were. Geoffrey swung the bear up and back and hit the mound of his mother's stomach as hard as he could.

So it was that Geoffrey Morrison's nose was first put firmly out of joint; dark-haired Geoffrey, well and truly three and relegated to the sidelines of adult activity and adoration.

"Who loves his baby brother, then?"

Not, Geoffrey would have been moved to answer, bloody me!

But time is a great healer and smoother, and Geoffrey came to realise that younger brothers, like the large white dogs of family friends, do have their uses. And pleasures.

"Geoff's so good with the baby," his father would say. "He really is."

And, the incident in their neighbour's plastic paddling pool aside, Geoffrey did treat his younger brother with a great deal of care and consideration. One result of which was that baby Michael grew up worshipping his brother and would mope and cry forlornly whenever Geoffrey was taken from his sight.

"Michael Morrison," Geoffrey would say, years later, in the course of an interview on Manx radio, "I love him like a brother!" And, once the laughter at his own joke had subsided, added, in all seriousness, "It was my brother, Michael, who was responsible for making me what I am today."

Which was, at the then age of twenty-nine, a near-millionaire businessman with one-fifth of the tear-off perforated plastic bag market in his pocket. "As it were," he laughed to the mid-morning presenter, "I always was the kind of a man who had need of big pockets."

The presenter pressed one corner of his mouth into a smile and cued up something by the Carpenters. Why was it always the biggest pillocks in the world who made the most money? And why did they always end up on his show?

"What I meant to say before," Geoffrey said into the fuzzy end of the microphone, the last sighs of Karen Carpenter disappearing into the ether, "was that up until the day my brother was born, I thought the world owed me a living. I was an only child, idolised, waited on hand and foot. Suddenly—wham!—there's this new model and I'm stuck on the back of the shelf, remaindered. Which was when, and I swear this, all of—what?—three and a bit years old, was when I realised if the world didn't owe me a living, I was going to have to get up off my behind and make one for myself. And I'll tell you," winking at the man behind the console, who said the rest of it along with him, "I've never looked back since."

And it was true.

Not even when he badly overextended his borrowing in 'eighty-seven and was obliged to call in a receiver. Before the ink was dry on that particular bankruptcy declaration, Geoffrey was registering another company under his wife's name. Within a month, he had signed an exclusive contract to supply a northern supermarket company with plastic bags for its new range of serve-yourself fruit and veg. Geoffrey had grinned and bought a new Rover, sent his wife for a fortnight's rest and restoration at Ragdale Hall and achieved similar effects for himself with a course of vitamin injections and a discreet Asian masseuse moonlighting from the Star Sun Lounge, Stockport.

For the next year he played one bank off against another, changed his accountant about as often as most men change their boxer shorts and faked a time-and-motion study at his main factory to persuade his largely immigrant work force to take a cut in pay. Back on top and in danger of becoming too conspicuously solvent, Geoffrey moved house and home some forty miles off the mainland to the Isle of Man. Here, from a six-bedroomed extravaganza on Bradda Head, he could enjoy fresh air, an uninterrupted view across the sea to Ireland and significantly lower tax levels. A private plane, shared with a select group of like-minded businessmen, meant that he could be back amongst the action inside the hour.

At forty, Geoffrey Morrison had a half-share in a couple of race-horses, a steadily improving golf handicap, an open line of credit at a casino in Douglas and several photographs of himself shaking hands with the stars—Frankie Vaughan, Clinton Ford, Bernie Winters. He wore tailored suits, beneath which he flaunted brightly coloured braces, wide silk ties and a relatively flat stomach. Half an hour in the pool three times a week, doing lengths, that and the exercise bike he rode while he was dictating memos.

When he arrived at his brother's house, the morning after Michael had returned from the hospital, Geoffrey was wearing a light grey suit with a dark red stripe, midnight blue braces and a tie in which the predominant colours were yellow and orange. The milkman was still delivering further around the crescent and the lights of the hire car that had met Geoffrey at the airport were still shining. Even the media had yet to arrive.

"Lorraine, sweetheart! You poor darling, what a thing to have happened. It's too much to hope there's any news? And Michael. Where's Michael? My God! What've you done to yourself? You're limping."

Oblivious to his brother's embarrassment, Geoffrey took him in his arms and hugged him tightly; Lorraine, red-eyed, looking on.

"I don't understand . . ." Michael began.

"Of course you don't. How could you? A thing like this, your own child, how could you be expected to understand? How could anyone? Lorraine, sweetheart, you don't mind me saying so, but you look awful."

"That wasn't what I meant," Michael said. "I meant you. What are you doing here?"

Geoffrey's eyes widened with surprise. "The fact neither of you thought to ring me, I can live with. Put it down to the surprise, shock. But that doesn't mean I don't care. I came as soon as I could."

"Geoffrey, I'm sorry I didn't call you," Michael said. "I just didn't think. I haven't been able to think about anything. But, really, there's nothing you can do."

"Do? A time like this." He caught hold of Lorraine's hands and squeezed. "I knew I had to be with you, for now at least, express my sympathy, show how I felt. How we both feel, Claire and myself."

Lorraine had seen Michael's brother no more than twice before the wedding, four or five times after. For the wedding, Geoffrey had sent a small truckload of presents from Harrods, worn a white three-piece suit and had the time of his life splashing champagne into the guests' glasses, dancing with anyone who was fool enough to let him, trying in vain to persuade Michael to join him on the small stage in "All You Have to Do Is Dream," the Morrison brothers in close harmony, Geoffrey singing lead. "Come on, Michael. We used to sing this all the time at home, remember?" Michael swore to Lorraine later he didn't recall singing it once.

They had made one visit over to the island, a week during most of which Geoffrey had been called back to one business meeting or another, leaving Lorraine and Michael in the company of Geoffrey's wife, Claire, and the seals that splashed off the rocks into the coldness of the sea. Since Claire's routine seemed to consist of rising in time for lunch and then immersing her nose in *Home and Garden* or the new Jilly Cooper, the seals proved rather the better company.

That aside, Geoffrey had descended on them occasionally, usually unannounced, staying long enough to drink a cup of tea, make a few phone calls and rebuke Michael for his lack of ambition.

"Lorraine," Geoffrey was saying, "what're the chances of you rustling us all up some breakfast? Times like this, we need to hit the carbohydrates as hard as we can."

Touching a hand to Lorraine's back, he shepherded them towards the kitchen. "And you," he said, looking sideways at Michael, "what the hell have you managed to do to your leg?"

27

Jack Skelton had a freshly jaded look, suffering as he had from his daughter's latest breakfast sport. The game was easy and there didn't seem to be too many rules. The way it was played was to come into the kitchen smiling, brush a kiss across your father's cheek on the way to the Rice Pops, then open the daily paper at the home news, pages 2 and 3. "Oh, look, Dad, I see you've snatched all the headlines again. Black man awarded forty thousand after police beat him up in a racist frenzy and then made up a case against him. Another ESDA test shows officers changed their interview notes to secure a conviction. Accusations of perjury after the police's own video of a demonstration showed evidence of arrest bore little or no relationship to what had actually happened." All of this delivered in the cheery, upbeat manner of Radio One. "Envy you your job satisfaction, Dad. Knowing how much you're respected, admired, working for the good of the community."

Skelton knew what would happen if he argued, tried to explain. The smiles would disappear and in their place would be the face he recognised from their battles of a year before. Only this time, Kate older, the result would be different. How much it would take to drive her from the comparative comfort of her home to join her boy friend in some squalid shared house or squat he didn't know, but he realised it wasn't much. He knew he was being tested and the importance of not being found wanting. A small-scale domestic equivalent of the taunting his officers suffered at the hands of the pickets in the mining strike of 'eighty-four. As Kate delighted in pointing out, the repercussions of that were still being heard, violent retaliation, loss of control.

Skelton was not about to lose control.

He cracked his knuckles as he sat behind his desk, rain whipping against the glass outside. Opposite him, Resnick slumped cross-legged, tired, a piece of toilet tissue hanging from the side of his face where he had cut himself shaving.

Skelton straightened the papers on his desk with the eye of a precision engineer. "This woman up in Yorkshire, the bookseller . . ."

"Jacqueline Verdon."

"No chance she's pulling the wool over Patel's eyes? Mother and daughter stashed away."

"Behind the false book shelf?"

"Something like that."

"Bit Sherlock Holmes, isn't it?"

"But possible."

Resnick uncrossed his legs and according to some strange symbiosis, his stomach rumbled loudly. "Patel reckons she was genuinely distressed, concerned. She could be faking it, but, on the whole, I'd back the lad's judgment. All the same, we have had a word with the local station, asked them to keep an eye."

"And she'd no idea, this Verdon, where Diana Wills might have shot off to?"

Resnick shook his head. "What she did bear out, Lorraine Morrison's tales of her getting more disturbed. Couple of months now, harping on about her daughter, another child she had before as died. Apparently, she'd been talking, Diana, about moving up there permanently. Hebden. Jacqueline Verdon'd been trying to convince her to give a go."

"Maybe she leaned too hard."

"Could be, sir."

Skelton went over to the window, stared down into the street and the two lines of vehicles, almost unbroken, in and out of the city. Diana Wills could be anywhere by now and her daughter the same: together or apart. What did it do to a woman, the court taking away one child after the first had already been lost? Knowing she was there but unable to see her other than at the times laid down. All that he put up with from Kate to keep her another year at most.

"Gut feeling, Charlie?"

For a moment Resnick closed his eyes. "Mother's gone off somewhere, feels she can't cope. I don't believe she's got the daughter with her."

His eyes open again now, both men looking at one another, aware of what that meant.

Geoffrey Morrison had arranged a surprise call on a couple of factories where he had work subcontracted. Catch them with their trousers down; keep them up to the mark. While Lorraine was still clearing away the breakfast things, he got Michael to one side and, not for the first time, offered him a place in the business. A year, eighteen months, you could be running the U.K. distribution, double your present salary, you'd be responsible only to me. As usual, Michael promised he would think about it. All he was thinking about was Emily: where she might be, what had happened to her. All the while he was trying to suppress the pictures of that other unfortunate girl that kept imprinting themselves, like sun spots, behind his eyes.

Resnick walked into the Gents to find Millington adjusting his fly and whistling the theme from the Elgar Cello Concerto. Well, it made a change from *Oklahoma*.

"Wife doing classical music this term, Graham?"

"English art, sir. Plays all that stuff to get herself in the mood. Real catchy, some of it."

"In the Mood," Resnick was thinking, Joe Loss's signature tune. One of the first times he and Elaine went dancing, stumbling over one another's feet to a pumped-up version of "The March of the Mods" at the old Palais.

"You all right, sir?"

Resnick nodded.

"Looked as if you were in a bit of pain. Not prostate problems, I hope?" Millington left, smiling maliciously, Resnick scarcely noticing, certain now that he knew where they would find Diana Wills.

"Who was it you wished to see?" asked the duty officer at the desk.

"For the second and I hope the last time," sneered Geoffrey Morrison, "the senior officer in charge of investigating the disappearance of my niece."

"That would be Emily Morrison, would it, sir?"

"Wonderful, Officer. One of the new graduate entrants, I'm delighted to see."

"There's Inspector Resnick or Superintendent Skelton, sir. Which would you be wanting?"

Geoffrey Morrison counted to fifty in tens. "Which do you think?"

With what bravery Elaine had finally come to see him, to the house where they had lived as man and wife, Resnick could no more than guess at. Her face gaunt in the stairs' light, she had handed him her years of pain. *Once a week we'd sit in this room, all of us and talk, but mostly there wasn't anyone to talk to.* Least of all you, Charlie; least of all, you.

"Lynn! Kevin! In here."

Why hadn't he thought of it before?

"Lynn, go and see Michael Morrison. See if he knows the name of his ex-wife's doctor; if not the present one, the last. Trace it forward from there. One of the reasons he got custody at the divorce was Diana had been having psychiatric treatment. I doubt that he visited her, but he might remember the hospital. Find out when they last treated her; if they're treating her now.

"Kevin, contact all the other hospitals in the area, special-care units, whatever. Right? Let's not waste any more time."

The two detectives had only just left his office when the phone rang and it was Skelton, asking him to step along the corridor.

"Charlie," Skelton said, "this is Geoffrey Morrison, Michael Morrison's brother. Detective Inspector Resnick."

The two men shook hands and stepped back. Fitter-looking than his brother, but older, Resnick was thinking; that aside, you'd know they were family and close. And that Geoffrey spent more on what he was wearing than Michael likely earned in a month.

"Mr. Morrison, quite reasonably, wanted to be sure that we were doing everything to find his niece and I think I've put him at ease on most points." Skelton paused, eyes on Resnick's face. "There is one thing, however . . . Mr. Morrison thinks we would get quicker results if we were to offer a reward."

"Ten thousand for information resulting in Emily's recovery. Safely, of course."

Resnick was shaking his head.

"I assure you it's no idle offer."

"I'm sure it's not."

"I can afford it and if it helps to bring my niece back . . ."

"On the first front," Resnick said, "I don't doubt it. On the second . . ."

"I've explained some of the difficulties as I see them," Skelton said.

"Without doubt," said Resnick, "there would be a huge response. We'd be inundated with calls from all over the country, sightings from the Hebrides to Plymouth Hoe, and the net result would be to tie up personnel and computer time to little actual effect. We'd get hoaxers trying to talk their way into some easy money, psychics with a reputation to prove, worst of all, within hours your brother and his wife would receive their first ransom call. If it can be avoided, I don't think they should be put through that."

Skelton moved around his desk. "Trust us, Mr. Morrison. We're doing everything that can be done."

Geoffrey Morrison looked from one officer to the other. The superintendent had a sense of how an executive should dress, even seemed to keep himself in good trim, but this other one . . . he wouldn't let him within a hundred metres of the board room looking like that.

"You know that if I choose," Morrison said, "I can go straight from here to the office of a national newspaper and it'll be all over their front page by the next edition?"

Both Skelton and Resnick realised that was probably true; neither of them said a word, watching their visitor all his way to the door.

"All right, for the time being, I'm prepared to wait. But you have to know, in case Emily isn't found soon, I'm retaining the reward as an option."

"Thanks, Charlie," Skelton said once Morrison had gone. "Thought I needed a little moral support."

Resnick nodded okay and his stomach lurched loudly.

"Sounds," said Skelton, "as if you could do with something more substantial."

28

Resnick was on his way back into the building with a chicken breast and Brie on rye, a sardine and radicchio with crumbled blue cheese, when he almost collided with a woman standing at the inquiry desk. She was backing away from the square of window, set so low down that you risked slipping a disc bending towards it.

"Oh, sorry!"

"Sorry!"

Resnick lost one of the sandwiches from his grasp, made a lunge towards it and missed, one of his feet sliding out from underneath him so that, off balance, he slipped almost to the floor. Clutching the other sandwich to his chest, he steadied himself against the woman's body, one hand gripping her not insubstantial thigh. If both noticed this, neither saw fit to mention it.

Apologising again, Resnick pushed himself to his feet. Meanwhile, the woman retrieved his straying sandwich, all save for some curls of lettuce which had sprung clear.

"You wouldn't be Inspector Resnick?" she asked.

Do you mean, Resnick wondered, that I have a choice?

"The man at the desk said you'd be back at any minute."

"Here I am," said Resnick. "Not before time. What was it about?"

"The little girl. Emily—is it?—Morrison."

Resnick dumped the brown paper bags on his desk and turned to look at his visitor. She was a little over medium height; dark, almost black hair pierced with grey and cut against the nape of her neck. She was wearing a loose skirt, dark blue, a paler blue sweater under a maroon jacket with deep pockets and padded shoulders. Resnick couldn't be certain, but he thought she might be wearing contact lenses. He put her in her late thirties, early forties, and he was underestimating by a good five years.

"I'm Vivien Nathanson," she said.

All these years and Resnick was still uncertain about shaking hands: did it matter that ten minutes later the person had become a suspect in some heinous crime or was confessing to acts which made the imagination reel? He offered coffee instead.

"I don't suppose I could have tea?"

"Of course."

"Black?"

"Given the usual state of the milk, safest choice." Resnick called into the CID room and Divine stirred himself from the shadow of Miss December to oblige.

"I heard an appeal on the radio as I was driving to work. At the university. I teach."

She didn't look as if she cleaned the floors.

"Canadian Studies."

Resnick was mystified. He hadn't realised there was such a thing as Canadian Studies. What was there to study, after all? Great Canadian inventors? The life cycle of the beaver? Trees? He knew an ambitious detective sergeant from Chesterfield who had arranged a sabbatical for himself, working with the Canadian Mounted Police in Alberta. Reckoned to have spent most of his time watching snow melt.

"You're interested in the identity of a woman seen near where the girl disappeared. I think it might have been me."

Divine knocked on the door and brought in the tea.

"Where's mine?" Resnick asked.

"Sorry, sir. Never said."

"I was in the crescent on Sunday afternoon, some time between three and four. I'm afraid I can't be more specific."

"Visiting?"

"Walking."

"Just walking?"

Vivien smiled. "I don't suppose you know a writer named Ray Bradbury, Inspector?"

Resnick shook his head. "Is he Canadian?"

"American. From Illinois, I believe. And do . . ." as she moved to sip her tea, ". . . start on your lunch."

Resnick opened the bag containing the chicken breast and Brie. He wondered how long she was going to take to get to the point but had already decided, within reason, he didn't much care.

"Anyway," she was saying, "in one of his stories a man is arrested by a prowling police car for walking alone through his neighbourhood. Meandering. Suspicious enough in itself to be considered a crime. When he attempts to argue back, make his case, he finds it's impossible. The police car is fully automated, no human being inside."

"Is that what's called a parable?" Resnick asked.

Vivien Nathanson smiled. "More an extended metaphor. Probably."

"And I'm the inhuman policeman?"

"I hope not. How's your sandwich?"

"Terrific." He gestured for her to take a piece, but she declined.

"Too far into my pre-Christmas diet to stop now."

"What were you doing? While you were walking."

"Oh, thinking."

"Lectures and the like?"

"Uh-huh. Amongst other things."

Resnick found himself wanting to ask which other things. "While you were passing through the crescent, did you see anyone of Emily Morrison's description?"

He passed a picture across his desk and she looked at it carefully before answering no.

"And you didn't see anything unusual going on around the Morrison house?"

"I don't know which one that is."

"The woman who was seen, some of the reports suggest she was showing a special interest in the house."

"But I don't know . . ."

"You said."

"I think," Vivien Nathanson said, "unless I am very much mistaken, the tone of this conversation has changed."

"A girl gone missing: it's a serious matter."

"And I'm under suspicion?"

"Not exactly."

"But if I had a specific reason for being in that area at that time, if, for instance, I were calling on a friend at number, oh, twenty-eight or thirty-two . . ." She stopped, seeing the reaction on Resnick's face. "That's the house, isn't it? Thirty-two. Where they live? The Morrisons."

Resnick nodded.

"I didn't know."

He didn't say a thing, but watched her; a hint of alarm undermining her manner, not a seminar any longer.

"But you didn't see the girl?"

"No."

"Any girl?"

"Not that I remember."

"And you would remember?"

"Possibly. Probably."

"How about a Ford Sierra?"

Vivien shook her head. "I'm afraid the only time I'd notice a car is if it ran over me."

"Let's hope not."

"But I did see a man."

Jesus, thought Resnick, has she been playing with me all this time?

"He might even be the one you're looking for. On the radio, it mentioned someone who was running."

"Yes."

"Well, I was crossing over, you know, towards the footpath that leads through to the canal. He bumped right into me, almost knocked me down."

Like downstairs, Resnick thought, though he had been the one falling. "Your mind on other things?" he asked.

"To a degree. But he was most at fault. Just wasn't looking where he was going."

"Where had he been looking?"

"Back over his shoulder."

Resnick could see the curve of the street clearly in his mind, the direction Vivien had been heading, the path the runner had been following. A man running with his head angled back the way he had come, back in the direction of number thirty-two.

Resnick could feel tiny goose pimples forming all along his arms, hear the shift of register in his voice when he spoke. "You could give us a description?"

"I think so."

"Detailed?"

"It was only for a moment."

"But close."

"Yes, close."

Resnick was already reaching for the phone. "What I'd like to do, as well as taking your statement, arrange for an artist to come to the station, make a drawing under your advice. See how close we can get? Okay?"

"In that case," smiling as she leaned forward, "if I'm going to be here all that time, I will have half of this sandwich."

29

"I didn't know you had that."

Michael shook his head. "Neither did I. Diana must have dropped it in with her things. I doubt she did it on purpose."

"Perhaps Emily took it."

"Could be."

The tag was clear plastic, snapped through at the end where it would have been fastened about the newborn leg or arm: the name written in black felt-tip, *Emily*, the name and the date.

They had been in her room for almost an hour now, sorting through drawers of clothes, some of which, handed on from friends, bought dutifully by Lorraine's parents, Emily had never worn. In a folder there were Instamatic pictures of the first holiday they had taken, the three of them, after their marriage, the divorce.

"D'you remember that?"

Emily on the back of a bored donkey, clutching Michael's hand. Although neither of them would put it into words, each was thinking of Emily as though they would never see her again alive.

"Who was that on the phone earlier?" Michael asked.

"Just my mother."

Michael nodded, wondering by what twists of logic she would have laid the blame for what had happened squarely at his feet.

"She sent you her love," Lorraine said, both of them knowing it was a lie.

"I thought it might have been the police."

"Michael, I would have told you."

Last night it had been Lorraine who had slept heavily, Michael who had turned and turned, his injured leg throbbing; sat finally in the electric light of the kitchen, drinking tea, glancing now and then towards the unopened whisky bottle on the shelf, the empty one on the floor beside the bin. This morning he'd woken Lorraine with grapefruit juice and toast, kissed her on the lids of both eyes, the first time he had done either of those things for longer than she liked to remember.

"Will it always be like this?" she had asked in the heady days of their courtship—or, as her mother preferred to call it, their sordid little affair.

"Absolutely," Michael had said, touching the back of his hand to her breast. Kissing her: "Absolutely."

"Love fades," says the passerby in *Annie Hall*.

"Love hurts," sing the Everly Brothers on their TV-advertised CD *Greatest Hits*. "Love dies."

Their love, Lorraine's and Michael's, had slipped into limbo, fallen somewhere between the late nights and the early mornings, Lorraine forever rushing from her job at the bank to the supermarket to collect Emily from school; Michael turning the car into the drive, exhausted by the stubbornness of clients, the miniature of scotch with which he chased the cans of beer bought on the swaying train.

"I love Emily, Michael, you know I do, but even so, we will, you know, have a baby of our own?"

"Of course we will, of course. We just have to wait until the time is right."

They had not had that conversation for months, more; as far as Michael was concerned, Lorraine doubted that the time ever would be right. She had even begun to live with it. And after what had happened with Diana, what had happened to his son, to James, Lorraine thought that perhaps she could accept, understand. After all, there was Emily.

"What is it? Lorraine, what?"

Michael reached for her as the tears suddenly sprang, but she twisted away from his hand and off the bed where they had been sitting, out through the partly open door and along the landing to the bathroom, leaving him alone. The clock on the chest read 13:22. Tomorrow, if nothing had happened, he would go back in to work: anything was better than being here, breath catching each time a car slowed near the house, waiting for the inevitable walk towards the door, the ringing of the bell.

As Resnick walked along the corridor, yet another conference in the super's office, the door to one of the interview rooms opened and Vivien Nathanson stepped out followed by Millington, a rare smile, broad as Divine's shoulders, lighting up the sergeant's face. Resnick wondered what had passed between them, those moments before leaving the room, and was surprised by jealousy, sudden and sharp, between the ribs, below the heart.

The paintings around the walls were boldly coloured, figures all head and little body, trees whose foliage was a mass of leaves, purple and green, suns blazing so fiercely they threatened to send whole landscapes up in flames. In one corner of the room books were collected in plastic bins or stacked, face out, on shelves that were in the middle of reconstruction. Opposite, a Wendy house offered sanctuary, a place to rest, to act out the already half-mastered rituals of family. Small tables and matching chairs stood in clusters, faced inwards. Flowers. Shells. Fossils. Toy cars. Dolls. Hamsters with pouched cheeks asleep in a cocoon of straw.

Naylor had arranged to meet Joan Shepperd before the start of afternoon school and she looked up from where she was pasting colour supplement pictures onto cards, two or three words of vocabulary clearly written below each one.

She smiled readily as Naylor introduced himself, showed identification, then hesitated, uneasy, uncertain what to do next, remnants of the smile stranded across her broad face.

She was a large woman, motherly, Naylor supposed, brown hair tied back, though wisps folded towards her eyes at intervals and she brushed them automatically away. She was wearing a long cardigan over a print dress; surprisingly, to Naylor, new-looking trainers instead of shoes.

"I still haven't taken it in, not properly. None of us have."

Naylor mumbled something suggesting understanding, leafing through his notebook for the next blank page. The sounds of small children rose shrill through the building as someone opened a door to the outside.

"How well did you know Emily Morrison?" Naylor asked.

"Oh, just the term. She was here before that, of course, nursery, but, no, I'd not taught her before this term."

"But you would have seen her around? In the building?"

Joan Shepperd shook her head. "No, you see, I only started myself at this school in September. Supply. I'm what's called on supply." Hammering started up somewhere beyond the classroom door. Joan Shepperd smiled. "Sit at home waiting for the phone to ring. Well, exaggeration I suppose. If you're lucky it's a term's work at a time. Filling in, you know." She glanced around. "Regular teacher taken sick, that's the usual. Or took time off to have a baby. That's what I'm doing here, somebody having a baby."

"They could ask you to work anywhere then?" Naylor said.

"They could. Inside the authority. Yes, they could. But I like, you know, I don't like to go too far from home." Another smile, more dimpled than the last. "I don't drive. And, well, there are buses, but with a job like this there always seems to be so much to carry."

The hammering stopped and started again. A ball cannoned off one of the classroom windows; a child's face pressed up against another pane until he was shouted away. Naylor went through his questions, never believing it to be any more than routine. At the point where she was asked about strangers waiting outside the school, anyone she might have seen talking to Emily, Joan Shepperd hesitated long enough to give Naylor some expectation, but it was nothing. "Once or twice, I seem to remember she was one of the last to be collected. I think, yes, her mother had been held up, perhaps the traffic or she hadn't been able to leave work dead on. But Emily was good about waiting, inside the cloakroom, I think. Or she would come back in here and help me tidy up. She would never go out onto the street."

The door opened and a man came in wearing brown overalls, a canvas tool bag over one shoulder. "Oh, sorry, Joan . . ."

"That's all right," Joan Shepperd getting to her feet. "This is the policeman, come to talk to me about poor Emily."

"Ah, yes."

"Constable, this is my husband, Stephen."

Stephen Shepperd and Naylor nodded in each other's direction.

"Come around sometimes and lend a hand, odd jobs, you know. These shelves, got into a right state. Wait for council to come along and fix them be like waiting yourself into an early grave. Eh?"

"I do believe the school had been waiting a long while," Joan agreed.

Stephen dropped his tool bag onto a group of tables. "Couple of afternoons and it's all shipshape. Course, got to know what you're doing in the first place."

"Stephen was a joiner," Joan said.

"Not so much of the was. Still am."

"He's not working full-time," Joan said to Naylor.

"Redundant," Stephen explained. "Me and a few thousand others." He pointed towards Naylor. "Nothing as'll likely happen to you. Growth industry, to believe what you hear, crime."

"Don't get onto one of your hobby horses, Stephen."

"If I did, this young man'd tell you I'm right, don't mind betting he would. But I'll not. I'll just leave this lot here and come back when you're through."

"I think we're that already," Naylor said. "Unless there's anything else you've thought of, Mrs. Shepperd?"

Joan Shepperd shook her head. "I only wish there were."

"All right, then. Thanks for your help. Mr. Shepperd, you can get on with your shelves."

In the playground a whistle blew and the clamour of voices stilled.

"Look," Stephen said as Naylor was almost at the door, "I don't want to be pushy, but if there's ever any work you need doing at home, you could do worse than give me a call."

"Thanks," Naylor said. "I'll keep it in mind."

Walking between the lines of children coming back into the school, thinking it would take a lot more than a few nails and a strip of four-by-two to put his home back together again.

Lynn Kellogg called round at the Morrisons' late in the afternoon and told them of the day's developments. The wasteland adjacent to the canal had been searched a second time, as had the railway sidings where Gloria Summers had eventually been found, neither with any success. One sighting of a youngster said to resemble Emily in Skegness had proved incorrect, as had another on the South Coast. There had been three reports as to the probable owner of the black Sierra that had been left for several hours in the crescent on Sunday, but none had checked out. The good news was that a woman had come forward with a description of the jogger observed by the Morrisons' neighbours and this would be released to the media at any time.

Lynn thought that Lorraine looked the more fragile of the two today, as if maybe she had been letting Michael shelter behind her strength and now it was going to have to be reversed. They were to appear on national TV news that evening to make an appeal for Emily's return and Lorraine had tried and discarded five outfits already and was about to do the same to a sixth.

"For heaven's sake!" snapped Michael. "It's perfectly fine."

A cream trouser suit with a pale pink blouse and white, low-heel shoes; it contrasted with Michael's navy jacket and dark grey trousers, highly polished black brogues. To Lynn they looked more like the kind of clothes you would wear to a christening, but she wasn't about to make them any more nervous than they already were. Besides, what exactly was the dress etiquette for occasions like this? She remembered her father turning up at a family funeral tieless and in grubby brown boots, dark speckles of chicken shit unmistakable on his trouser legs. Had it meant that he cared any the less?

Lynn volunteered to accompany them to the television studio and they seemed truly grateful.

Makeup did what they could with the shadows around their eyes, teased some life back into Lorraine's hair. After a few minutes with the producer, they were shown the settee where they would be filmed, side by side. The news report opened with the artist's impression of the runner who had collided with Vivien Nathanson close to the Morrisons' home. Then it was Michael and Lorraine, a photograph of Emily inset over Lorraine's shoulder. "Whoever has taken my daughter and is holding her against her will," Michael said, blinking at the camera, "I'm begging you not to harm her. Whoever you are, please, please, let her go, let her come back home."

Sweat ran visibly down Michael's face, the producer worried that a blob was going to fall from his nose in close shot, not the effect he wanted at all. The moment Michael finished talking, Lorraine put one of her hands over his and squeezed. Pulling back fast, adjusting focus, the camera operator just got it in frame.

"Right!" said the editor, smiling. "There's our out."

30

All day they had been getting after Raymond, chasing him from loading bay to loading bay with their shouts, from cutting room to cutting room, pillar to post.

"Raymond! Here, catch a hold of this, will you?"

"Raymond, why don't you learn to move your bloody self!"

"Raymond, en't you got that order ready yet?"

"Raymond!"

"Ray!"

"Ray-o, damn you!"

"Ray!"

Hathersage caught him by the neck of his overalls and spun him round, Raymond's boots slithering on the blood-strewn floor, legs going under him, only Hathersage's hand, like a ham, holding him aloft. "The Good Lord alone knows what you're thinking about half the time, you godforsaken excuse for a human being, but on my old mum's life I know one thing that it ain't and that's what I'm sodding paying you to sodding do. Here. See here!"

Half-dragging Raymond, half-pushing, he urged him out into the yard, barging him through the hollowed-out carcasses of meat that hung in line and throwing him, finally, hard against the open end of a delivery van.

"Lookit!" Hathersage bellowed. "Look in there and just you tell me what you see? Loin chops, you see that? Freezer packs, wrapped and ready? Chuck steak, best chuck steak? Pork belly? Well?"

Raymond leaned heavily against the van, wanting to rub his hip where it had struck metal, wanting to raise his voice back at Hathersage, tell him take your job and stuff it, tell him he didn't fucking care.

"Look at you, you pathetic specimen!" Hathersage shook his bull-like head. "Christ, if you could see what you looked like, you'd crawl away under a stone and die."

Raymond, still leaning, breathing unevenly, snot dribbling down his face, the faint few hairs that grew along his upper lip.

"Here! Take a good look at sodding this!" Hathersage pushed the copy of the order towards Raymond, who caught at it clumsily, tearing it almost in two.

The manager stepped away, disbelieving; two butchers in white headgear and rubber boots, overalls that had been white at the beginning of the day. "Ray-o," they chanted, softly in unison. "Ray-o, Ray-o, Ray-o."

"Get this unloaded. Check that order, make it right. If you're lucky, I won't be standing at the gate as you clock off, ready with your cards. But don't sodding bank on it."

Raymond spent the time until the close of his shift praying that Hathersage would be there, giving notice, true to his word. That would be an end to it: this much, at least. But all he had seen of the manager was a reddened face, mouth wide with laughter, glimpsed through the office window as Raymond slunk past.

Tonight was the night, more often than not, he went back home, round to his father's, where they would eat sausages and onions, mashed potato, baked beans and tomato sauce. Tea strong enough to stand a spoon in. "One thing your mum could never seem to get the knack of," his dad was like to say, "mashing a good cup of tea."

Never mind, there had been other things she had mastered; getting the measure of his father, for one. Five years married and Raymond rising four, she had realised his dad had already amounted to what little he was going to be. She had latched herself onto a salesman who went from village shop to village shop, small-town store to small-town store; his special lines were household wares, brushes, clotheslines, pegs, three-in-one dustpan sets in hard red plastic. When he wasn't on the road, he lived in a caravan at Ingoldmells. Raymond's mum always had liked the smell of the sea.

The first few years she had sent him cards at Christmas and his birthday. Raymond had kept them for ages, took them out from time to time and ran his hands across the lightly embossed lettering, the fading biro messages: Love from your Mum; Love, Mum; Love, Mum. When he was fourteen he carried them into the back yard and tore them into tiny pieces and left them for the wind to carry away. Even now there were times when he would look inside the drawer, lift out the clothes, expecting them to still be there, safe and flat at the bottom.

Raymond made up his mind: he wasn't going home. No more of his father's and his uncle's jostling, himself caught in the middle. Sara, he knew, was staying in to help her mother wash her hair. He didn't care. After his bath, he could sit in his room, watch TV, play with his knife.

Michael Morrison pushed his dinner around the plate until Lorraine lifted it away and scooped the contents into the rubbish. She gave him two scoops of his favourite ice cream, raspberry ripple, straight from the freezer, and he sat there, watching it slowly melt. Since the television appearance, any remaining energy seemed to have been drained from him, little more than twelve hours and they had changed places again, Lorraine finding the resources somewhere to carry him through what remained of the day. Another since Emily had disappeared, a scattering of dolls in her wake.

Of course, she could still be safe.

Of course.

The telephone broke into life and before Lorraine could reach it, had fallen silent again. She stood staring at it, willing it to ring again.

"Perhaps," she said, back in the kitchen, "we should get in touch with your brother?"

"Geoffrey? For God's sake, why?"

"What he said, the reward . . ."

"No."

"Michael, I don't see why not."

"You know what the police said about that."

"Yes, but there's nothing else. They haven't come up with anything else."

"Even so." He got up and broke the seal on the scotch, daring Lorraine to say anything. What she did was fill the kettle to make herself a cup of tea.

"Look," Michael said, "if I thought it would be any good . . ."

"All I'm saying, I don't see what we've got to lose."

Michael hardly tasted the whisky as it went down; he drank some more. "Ever since I can remember," he said, "my brother has tried to run my life. 'Michael, wake up, you should be doing this, doing that.' 'Michael, Michael, if only you were bright enough, quick enough, had the balls enough, you'd be more like me.' "

"He's only trying to do the best . . ."

"What he wants is for me to get close enough to him that I can see the distance there is between us."

She slipped inside his arms, inside his guard, and kissed the corner of his mouth. "I don't want you to be like Geoffrey."

"I know." Michael closing his eyes, lowering his face against her hair. "I know."

She pressed her fingers lightly against his back, the knot of bone near the base of his spine; when he didn't move away, push her clear, she slid his shirt free from his belt and began to stroke his skin.

"Lorraine," he breathed. "Lorraine."

"All I was thinking," Lorraine said, "even if nothing comes of it, what harm would it really do?"

Two things Stephen Shepperd did at half-past nine every night: lock and bolt both front and back doors, check the latches on the downstairs windows; when that was done he would prepare the tray. Horlicks for Joan, nothing to drink for himself or he'd be up and down like a yo-yo. Four biscuits, buttered, two with a nice piece of mature cheddar, the others with a dabble of jam, black currant or apricot; the cheese were for himself. Rumour was that cheese at night made you dream, but he set no more store by that than he did by any other old wives' tale. It wasn't four years back that Joan had talked him into seeing that fortune-teller at Goose Fair. A long and happy life, she'd said. Expect good news at work, promotion. What he'd got was the sack. Nothing regular since. Pushing fifty—what was he thinking of? He was fifty, gone—most firms didn't even bother to reply. Ah, well, they hadn't settled into such a bad life, after all.

He opened the door first, went back for the tray. He could hear the theme music for *News at Ten* just beginning, just in time.

Lynn Kellogg had been in the car, seat belt buckled, when she realised she didn't want to go straight back. The thought of the bundle of clothes she had left close by the ironing board enough to put her off. Divine and

Naylor were where she expected to find them, Divine over at the corner of the bar, deep in conversation with a tall West Indian, which probably meant that he was after information. Social drinking for Divine rarely extended beyond the colour bar.

She bought a half of bitter for herself, a pint for Kevin Naylor and joined him near the window. From the edges of the room came the electronic clamour of games machines, through the ropey pub stereo Phil Collins was making promises he couldn't keep. Lynn liked Phil Collins: that spring she'd gone across to Birmingham by coach to see him, the NEC, seats had been naff, but he'd been good, really good.

"How's it going?" Lynn asked.

"Don't ask."

She drank some beer and let it be; he'd talk in his own good time or not at all, that was Kevin.

"It's all gone to crap," he said suddenly, moments later. She thought he was talking about the investigation and quickly realised it was some-thing else. "Debbie's back home with her mum, properly moved back in, and she's taken the kid with her. Absolute bloody crap!"

"Oh, Kevin." Lynn took his free hand and gave it a squeeze. "I'm sorry."

"Yes, well, I'm up to here with being sorry and it don't make a scrap of sodding difference."

"Can't you talk to her, reason—"

"Shut it!" Naylor said suddenly, and Lynn jerked back as though she'd been slapped. It was only when she looked at Kevin's face she realised his response had been to the television set above the bar and not to what she had said.

The artist's impression of the man seen outside the Morrison home was still on the screen, a lined face with a strong nose, close shaven, beginning to lose his hair.

"Kevin, what is it?"

"That bloke. I only know him, don't I? I was only talking to him this afternoon."

31

When Resnick had been a boy, eleven, his grandmother had slipped and fallen in the small back room, the parlour. Her arm or leg, some part of her, had dislodged coals from the fire, the coal had smouldered on the carpet as she lay unconscious, stunned by the blow her temple had taken from the polished tiles of the hearth. After not so many minutes a spark attached to the fabric of her dress and flared to life. Resnick's mother, mixing the flour and suet for dumplings in the kitchen, adding water from the measuring jug, a teaspoon of dry mustard, a sprinkling, thumb and forefinger, of dill, had smelled burning. Not the stew. By the time she had found the source, the older woman's clothes were ablaze around her and she had woken to the centre of a dream that was no dream, a nightmare no nightmare, the screams that broke searing from her, her own screams. An old woman with her hair ablaze around her face.

Resnick's mother had responded with the cool control and speed that sometimes visit us in dire emergencies. By the time the fire brigade arrived, the ambulance, the police—and they were quick—all but a few smouldering remnants of the fire had been extinguished. Her mother lay close against the heavy sideboard which stood along the side wall, blankets covering most of her body, shrouding her burnt, blistering head. She was taken to the hospital, sedated, treated for shock, transferred to the burns unit as soon as her condition had stabilised. "You have to understand," the registrar said, "your mother has been through a traumatic experience. It will take time for her to recover." Almost a month Resnick's parents kept to the visiting hours, relations also, a shifting vigil by a largely silent bedside, disturbed only by whimpers of pain whenever she moved. Resnick himself was kept at home, told little of the worst, shielded from upset. When his grandmother did at last open her mouth it was to scream and call her daughter a whore.

There were weeks of silence and sudden, wild accusations, almost inevitably in Polish. In the worst of these, her children were betraying her to the Nazis, she was being dragged headlong from the ghetto, she was bundled into a cattle car on its way to the concentration camp, she could see the ashes floating on the air, smell the burning of the ovens, the sweet pungent smell of smouldering flesh, of skin, of hair.

When, finally, she was allowed home, all that she would do was sit in the kitchen and rock herself slowly back and forth in a high-backed wooden chair, a shawl around her head where her hair had grown back patchily between her scars. Resnick stood once until the blood in his legs sang, hand in hers, uncertain if she knew, not who he was but whether he were even there. After little more than weeks, another ambulance came and she was taken off, this time to the hospital for the mentally disturbed where she would end her days.

On Sundays they would drive and park in the hospital grounds, his father in suit and tie, his mother in her good dress, a bag containing fruit, homemade biscuits, a thermos of soup held at her side. Resnick would be told to lock the doors and stay in the car, while they disappeared into this tall, dark building with turrets at the corners, iron railings ranged along the roof. An hour later they would reemerge, his father shaking his head, mother sniffing, dabbing at the tears. When he would ask them how his grandmother was, his father would fail to reply, his mother would press her lips together and force a smile. "A little better this week, don't you think so, Father? Yes, Charles, a little better." When, after almost a year, she caught pneumonia and died they agreed it was a blessing. For her funeral, the community came out in force, the procession from the cathedral to the cemetery blocking the traffic for almost half an hour.

Now Resnick sat in the car park again.

An early winter evening that promised little more than rain.

The doctor's call had come through to Resnick late that afternoon, hesitant, careful. "An officer was in contact earlier, making inquiries; she referred me to you."

There were lights in one wing of the building only. The remainder stood dark and disused. Despite protest, it seemed likely that within a twelvemonth, the rest would be closed down, most of the patients released into the community. Some would stay in hostels or live together in houses which the authority had bought and renovated specially for them. But many would shuffle, bewildered, between an already overextended network of social workers and volunteers, outpatient clinics and GPs. Soon Resnick would take to recognising their faces on the benches above Bobby Brown's Café, by the fountains in Slab Square; leaning outside the night shelter near the London Road roundabout, asleep amongst the cigarette ends and vomit on the bus station floor.

The nurse who met Resnick was in his late twenties, slight and not far short of Resnick's height; his sandy hair was worn long, eyes clear pale blue. He was wearing loose beige cotton trousers, a faded green shirt over an equally faded T-shirt that swore solidarity to a cause Resnick could not discern. He told Resnick Diana had been admitted the previous Friday, claiming she no longer felt able to cope.

"What with?" Resnick asked.

The nurse looked back at him, somewhat incredulous.

"She's been here ever since? No way she could have gone back outside?"

"She could. But, no, I don't think she has. She hasn't wanted anything to do with anyone or anything. That's the only way we've been able to keep the news away from her." He looked at Resnick earnestly. "I presume you're not proposing to tell her, about her daughter?"

A shake of the head.

"It can't be kept from her forever. It shouldn't, but coming right now . . ."

"You have my word."

"What you have to understand, Diana is under a great deal of stress; she has been for some while. Having said that, a lot of progress has been made. But even so, something like this, it could put her back a long way." The eyes held Resnick fast. "In agreeing for you to see her, we're assuming that you will be sensitive to her condition."

Resnick nodded. "I understand."

"I hope so. She's waiting in one of the quiet rooms, just along here." Resnick followed the nurse down the high-ceilinged institutional corridor. From another floor he could hear the music from *Neighbours*, starting or finishing, he wasn't sure which.

"She is on quite strong medication," the nurse said, lowering his voice outside the door. "She should understand you correctly, but it might mean that some of her responses are rather slow. Also, you might notice some shaking, especially her hands. A side effect of the drugs." He opened the door and stepped inside. "Diana, your visitor's here."

Resnick hadn't been sure what to expect, his mental pictures overlaid in advance by the gaunt shock of his ex-wife's face when finally she had confronted him after years of psychiatric treatment and hospitalization. But Diana Wills looked up at him pleasantly, her smile a little hesitant yet real enough, her face, if anything, fuller than the photos he had seen had suggested.

"I'll leave you for a while," the nurse said.

There were three chairs in the room, a low circular table, pictures on the walls, flowers. Resnick pulled one of the chairs closer to Diana and sat down. "I'm a police officer," he said. "Resnick. Detective Inspector. Charlie."

Diana looked back at him and gave the same quick, nervous smile.

"We were worried about you."

She opened a hand and pulled at the tissue that had been squashed there, used it to dab at the corners of her mouth. She was wearing a button-through dress, soft green, a brown ribbed cardigan. "Worried? I don't understand."

"When you didn't come home."

"Home?"

"At the weekend. The neighbours, they were just a bit concerned. Had a word with the local bobby. We thought you might have had an accident or something."

"Jackie."

"Sorry?"

"Jacqueline."

"Your friend."

Diana pressed the tissue to her mouth again. "You know Jacqueline?"

"I said, we were worried. We got in touch, in case she knew where you were."

"I should have gone to see her."

"Yes."

"This past weekend."

"Yes."

Now both of Diana's hands were beginning to tremble and she slid them from sight. "Was she angry with me?"

"No, not at all. Just concerned."

"You'll tell her where I am?"

Resnick nodded.

"I shouldn't want her to worry."

"Of course not."

"Not Jackie."

"No."

"She'll be so ashamed as it is."

"Why's that, Mrs. Wills?"

"Diana, please."

"Diana."

"What did you ask me?"

"You said that your friend would be ashamed."

"Well, of course she would. Anyone would."

Resnick willed himself to look at her face, not be distracted by the increased agitation of her hands. "Can you tell me why, Diana?"

She sat suddenly upright, eyes widening with surprise. "Because of what I did, of course."

"What you did to whom?"

The sound was faint in the small room, its syllables barely passing her lips. "Emily."

Resnick could feel the dampness gathering in his palms; he was beginning to smell his own sweat. *No way she could have gone back outside?* "What about her, Diana?"

She pushed the folded tissue to her lips. "I didn't want to do it. I didn't."

Resnick's voice, low, not wishing to startle, almost as quiet as hers. "I know that you didn't."

"I knew it was wrong."

"Yes."

"That's why I came here."

"Yes."

"I couldn't think what else to do, where else . . . and I thought, I knew . . . you see, I'd been going there, more and more, I knew it was wrong, but I couldn't . . . couldn't stay away, I had to be close to her, Emily, all the time. He should never have said it was wrong for me, he never . . . I'm her mother."

The hands which had been shaking faster and faster stilled themselves now by grasping Resnick's arms at the wrist, biting tight.

"I had it all planned, I knew what I was going to do. I didn't know yet when, but I knew. Emily and I, on the train. To Jacqueline. She wanted me to go and live with her after all. She kept saying. She couldn't have wanted me to go without my little girl, she would never have expected that. She couldn't, could she? But she kept asking, over and over. It would be better, she said. Nicer. And it would have been, don't you think, Charlie? Much nicer. The three of us together."

"Yes," Resnick nodding as Diana released her grip. "Yes, maybe it would."

"But inside," Diana said, "I knew that it was wrong. But it was as though I couldn't stop myself. Which is why I came back here, to the hospital. So that I wouldn't take Emily away." She wiped her mouth and smiled. "I've been here before, you know. It's nice here. It's quiet. They understand you. They make you better."

For a moment, Resnick hid his face in his hands.

"What is it?" Diana asked. "Whatever's the matter?"

Not so many minutes later, the nurse returned. In the corridor Resnick offered Diana Wills his hand and as soon as, tentative, she touched it with her fingers, he stepped forward and took her in his arms, held her tight.

The rain was falling, further blackening the building, blackening the sky. Resnick engaged gear and sat where he was, engine idling. Ahead of him was a long night that would stretch into the small hours of morning. He would drink coffee black and listen again to Billie with Lester Young, to Hodges and to Monk. Why, when he had refused every one of Elaine's pleas for help, when he had made no attempt to find out where or how she was, even now, did he find it so easy to sympathise with this stranger, to take and hold her in his arms and feel her tears upon his chest, this woman he had never before met?

32

When Naylor's call had cut across the introduction to "No Regrets," a spare few bars of Dick McDonough's guitar before Billie's voice, Resnick had half-rolled, half-slid from the settee and crossed the room, cursing the unwanted interruption. The first chorus of the song barely over, Resnick began to ask questions, steadying the receiver between chin and shoulder as he sought to button his shirt, straighten his tie. Naylor's voice again, excited, and, across the room, Artie Shaw's stop-time clarinet phrases were flowing out of the ensemble in the instrumental break. "You've got the address? . . . Good. Who's there with you? . . . Tell her to pick me up." Resnick put down the phone, went back across the room and onto one knee, searching for his other shoe. Billie Holiday stretching into her last chorus, the drummer giving it a few good whomps as the band closed round her for the final bars. Two minutes, thirty-odd seconds. Resnick swallowed cold coffee, headed for the door.

"Stephen Shepperd, sir. Fifty-two. His wife, Joan, teaches part-time at Emily Morrison's school. Kevin interviewed her there this afternoon; that was when he saw Stephen. They live off Derby Road, on the right going up the hill."

"Near the flats?"

"Three streets away."

Resnick could picture them, thirties semis with watered-down art deco features, privet hedge to the front and small, neat gardens behind; concrete bollards set across the centre of long cross streets to stop the traffic racing through.

As they passed Canning Circus there were still lights burning in the police station, but not so many. Five pubs within spitting distance, customers jostling by now at the bar, getting in another round before the call for last orders. A few students, hands in pockets, beginning the trudge back out to the university campus. Lynn Kellogg slowed as she indicated left, turning into the Shepperds' road.

It was a third of the way along, facing west down the hill. A view over Queens Medical Centre, the university beyond that; much closer, a hop, skip and a jump and little more, the high-rise blocks that had been Gloria Summers's home. Naylor had parked fifty yards further on, the opposite side of the street, and now he walked towards them, eyes on the Shepperd house.

"Again," Resnick said. "How certain are you?"

"Well, it wasn't a photograph."

"Which doesn't mean you're changing your mind?"

A quick shake of the head. "No way. Just, you know, those drawings, that's all they are. A sketch. Likeness."

"And the one you saw, that's what it was, a likeness?"

"Yes, sir."

"Fair enough."

The lower third of the house was yellowing brick, the rest a creamy pebble-dash that would soon be in need of some repair. Except in the larger upstairs window, where it looked as if double glazing had been fitted, the windows were divided into small squares of glass. Lined curtains had been pulled neatly across. A light shone from beneath a brass shade above the porch.

"No sense going in mob-handed," Resnick said.

Lynn took a pace off to the side, leaving the two men to approach the door.

What had happened was this. "Quick," Joan had called, hearing her husband's slow approach along the hall, "it's already started." Well, didn't she think he realised that? No sense rushing if it meant tumbling rear over tip and losing their supper. Besides, what would it be tonight? The main item? Even money something about what used to be called the Eastern Bloc. Not so many years ago, Stephen clearly recalled, the world and his wife were beside themselves with how marvellous it was, everything changing, people throwing off their shackles, thirsting to vote. The democratic process. Stephen had been voting now for more than thirty years and he hadn't noticed it improving his life a great deal.

"Stephen!"

"Coming!"

He did wish she wouldn't shout at him as if he were one of her five-year-olds. Though, come to think of it, she was a sight more patient with them.

"Ste—"

"I'm here."

On the screen the newsreader's head—that woman, the dark one, not the very dark one, really black, he knew who she was, but this one, the other, light-skinned but dark all the same, equal opportunities, not before time he supposed, but that didn't help him to remember her name—anyway, there it was, superimposed over tanks trundling along the road to somewhere.

"I thought you were never coming," Joan said, as he set the tray down on the nest of tables she had pulled out ready.

"Where is it this time, then?" Stephen asked. "Croatia? Czechoslovakia?"

"Belfast."

Stephen squinted at the screen.

"Bit mean with the apricot jam, Stephen," his wife said.

"What took me so long, scraping the jar." He took his own plate and balanced it on the arm of his chair before sitting down.

"Ooh, I do wish you wouldn't do that."

"What?"

"It's going to come flying off there one time, all over the carpet."

"Well, it hasn't yet."

The newscaster was announcing an important new development in the investigation into the disappearance of six-year-old Emily Morrison.

"I want to see this," Stephen said.

"Then do sit down."

One hand resting on the side of his chair, Stephen started to turn. Before he was fully round, the artist's impression filled the screen. Stephen jolted upright, away from the chair, backs of his legs colliding with the tray. Joan's mug of Horlicks went flying, hot malted milk splashing over the front of her skirt before the remainder emptied out across the carpet.

"Stephen! What on earth . . . ?"

"I'm sorry, I'm sorry." He flailed his arms for balance, struck his shins sharply against the table nest, swore and backed away, reaching down to rub his leg, cheese biscuits tumbling to the floor as he banged into the chair.

"Anyone who thinks they know the identity of this man should contact their nearest police station . . ."

Joan was on her feet, shaking the front of her dress; Stephen on his knees, rescuing the biscuits, the plate, the empty mug. Every inch of his skin felt like ice. He held the mug between his fingers and dropped it again.

"That lovely new carpet," Joan was saying, dismayed, "it's ruined."

"It's only milk, it'll come out."

"Nonsense. That's the worst thing of all. You can never get rid of it." Joan shuddered. "That awful sour smell, it's there forever."

The newsreader had progressed to the next item: the cost of first- and second-class post was about to rise again. Another twenty minutes passed in which damp cloths were pressed against the carpet, the dustpan and brush brought out from under the sink to deal with the crumbs, another cloth, dry, to deal with the smears of butter; more biscuits were prepared, a second helping of Horlicks, half and half this time or the milk would run out before the milkman called. The set had been switched off and when Stephen had put Manuel and his Music of the Mountains on the record player, his hand had shaken so much he had scraped the needle twice, once across the grooves, the second time not on the record at all but over the antistatic mat. "Stephen, you're ruining my birthday present!"

So it was that when Resnick rang the front doorbell, they were sitting in the front room in steely silence, the stain on the carpet darkening between them.

"Whoever is that at this time of night?"

"How do you expect me to know?"

"Stephen!"

"What?"

"What are we going to do?"

"Nothing."

The bell rang again, longer this time, followed by a double knock against the door.

"We can't simply sit here and do nothing."

"I don't see why not. It's getting on for eleven o'clock for heaven's sake. There's no law says you have to go answering your door to any Tom, Dick or Harry at this time of night. What if we were already in bed?"

"But we're not. And whoever's out there can see that we're not."

The letter flap rattled insistently.

"Stephen . . ."

"All right, I'm going. You stay here." And he closed the door behind him.

Resnick and Naylor had their warrant cards at the ready, clearly visible in the overhead light. "Detective Inspector Resnick, local CID. This is Detective Constable Naylor. Mr. Shepperd?"

Stephen mumbled yes, nodded.

"Mr. Stephen Shepperd?"

"You do know what time of night this is?"

"I wonder if we might have a word?"

"My wife and I were ready for bed."

"It might be better inside."

Stephen didn't move. "What is it about?"

"You didn't by any chance see the news tonight?" Resnick asked.

"Yes. I mean, not all of it. But, yes, why? What's happened? Has something happened?"

"I do think it would be easier if we asked you questions inside, Mr. Shepperd."

"Whatever is it, Stephen?" said his wife from the living room doorway. "Whatever's the matter?"

"We simply want to ask your husband some questions," said Resnick.

"I know you," Joan Shepperd said, looking, not at Resnick, but at Naylor alongside him.

"This afternoon," Naylor said.

"Yes," coming towards the front door, "at the school. Stephen, you remember, he was at the school. Asking about Emily. This isn't about Emily, is it?"

"If we could step inside," Resnick said.

"Of course, of course. Whatever are you thinking of, Stephen, not inviting them in? Stand here in the hall with that door open much longer, we'll all catch our deaths."

Resnick and Naylor came into the house and Stephen closed the door behind them.

"It is to do with Emily?" Joan Shepperd asked Naylor.

"Yes."

"I thought it must be. Stephen, why don't you go and put on the kettle while we go through to the front room?"

"Thing is," Resnick said, "it's your husband we've come to see."

"Stephen? I don't understand."

"All right, Joan," Stephen said. "We'll go in there and talk. Why don't you make the tea or whatever it is we're having?"

"I shall do no such thing."

Stephen held his wife's gaze for a moment before stepping past her to open the living room door, holding it while the others went inside. He and his wife took their usual chairs, leaving Resnick and Naylor to sit, less than comfortably, on the two-seater sofa, side by side.

"Last Sunday afternoon," Resnick began, "the day that Emily Morrison went missing, someone was seen running close to her home."

"Stephen . . ."

"Be quiet," Stephen said.

"Obviously, one of the things we're concerned to do is identify anyone who was in the vicinity at the time Emily disappeared . . ."

"Ste—"

"I said, be quiet."

"Not because their being there is, in itself, in any way a cause for suspicion, but so that we can remove them from our inquiries. And because they might well have noticed something that could be of importance."

Joan sat watching her husband, mouth slightly open, saying nothing.

"You do understand?" Resnick asked.

Stephen nodded quickly. "Yes, I understand."

"You aren't that person?"

"The one you were just talking about, the one running?"

"Correct."

"No."

"You're sure?"

"Of course, I'm sure."

"You do run, though?"

"No."

Joan's fingers pressed deeper into the upholstery of the cushion on which she was sitting.

"You're saying that you never go running, Mr. Shepperd? Jogging?"

Stephen was having difficulty freeing his tongue from the roof of his mouth. "I didn't say never."

"You do jog, then? To keep fit."

"Mostly I swim."

"Mostly?"

"Yes, I prefer it. And it's better exercise. For me, that is. Running, I never seem to go fast enough, you know, to do any good. Swimming, I suppose it suits me better."

"Do you mind if I ask where you were on Sunday afternoon?"

Stephen's eyes sought Joan's before he answered. "Swimming."

"You went swimming?"

"Yes."

"Sunday afternoon?"

"Yes, I said."

"I heard you, Mr. Shepperd. I just wanted to be sure."

Stephen clasped his hands together, crossed his legs, cradled his knee, loosened his grip, uncrossed his legs, laid both hands flat along his thighs.

"Ask my wife," Stephen said.

Resnick glanced across at Joan Shepperd, but asked nothing.

"You didn't see," asked Naylor, leaning forward, "when you were watching the news, a drawing of a man in a track suit?"

"No. I'm afraid I didn't. We didn't, did we, Joan?"

"It must have been when there was all that kerfuffle."

"Kerfuffle?"

"My drink got knocked over. Look, you can see, on the carpet, there. The stain."

"A shame," Resnick said.

"Yes," Joan Shepperd said. "We've not so long had it down."

"I know it's only a sketch," Resnick said, looking straight at Stephen, "a quick impression. But I would have to say, it looked an awful lot like you."

33

Lynn Kellogg had been thinking about what Kevin had said, Debbie walking out and taking the baby. The look on his face in the pub when he had told her, what it had cost him to blurt out the words: how he must be feeling. The front door of the house opened and she saw him, outlined for a moment against the light. Then Resnick was there with him, half-turned back towards the house, saying something she could not catch; the two of them heading back towards the cars.

Lynn went several paces to meet them, asking the question with her eyes.

"Denied it," Kevin Naylor said. "Out of hand."

Lynn shifted her gaze to Resnick's face.

"Says he was swimming," Resnick said.

"All afternoon?"

Resnick shrugged and smiled.

"What got me," said Naylor, "reckons they were in there watching *News at Ten*, never saw the face."

"Got distracted," Resnick said.

"Spilt the bedtime drink."

"At the crucial moment."

"Convenient."

Between the two men, Lynn could see the house, porch light still shining, a movement of the front room curtains, someone peering out, curious to know if they were still there. "What are we going to do, sir?" she asked.

"Have a go at him again in the morning, maybe he'll remember things differently. Till then, let him stew."

As they turned, Lynn glanced at Naylor, wanting to say, Look, come round and have some coffee, it's not late, we could talk. But there was Resnick, standing by her car, expecting a lift back home. There was still the taint of whisky on his breath and she knew why he hadn't wanted to drive himself.

"Good night, Kevin," she said.

"Night. Night, sir."

Firm closing of doors, firing of engines, acceleration and a changing of gears. The Shepperds' curtains twitched open, fell closed.

Stephen Shepperd backed away from the window, managed to step back into the room without once, even though she was staring at him intently, looking into his wife's face.

"Where do you think you're going?" He was almost at the door, fingers reaching out.

"Up to bed," not turning. "It's late."

"Sit down."

Stephen unmoving: allowing his hand to swing back to his side, his shoulders to slump.

"Sit down and talk."

He wanted to ignore her, carry on through the door and not even up to the bed they shared, but out, out into the street, he didn't know where and didn't care, as long as he didn't have to turn and face her.

Once, still a boy, twelve, thirteen, nothing more, he had waited in his room for his mother to confront him. Lying there in the narrowness of his bed, sheet and blankets high above his head, muting the click of the door as it opened and closed and the slight edge of her breathing as she stood there, prepared to be patient, knowing that he could not stay like that forever.

"Stephen."

Head down, he turned back into the room and crossed towards his chair.

The two of them sitting there.

"What do you have to tell me, Stephen?"

You can tell me anything, I'm your mother.

"Stephen?"

Anything: and slowly she had drawn the truth from him and as the words fell from his mouth he had seen the muscles of her face tense, her eyes tighten and her colour change until she was suffused with shame.

"I'm waiting, Stephen."

"No."

"You can't not tell me."

"But there's nothing to tell."

"Isn't there?"

"No."

She was shaking her head, slowly, the twist of her mouth might almost have suggested that she was smiling. "You know you can't lie to me, Stephen."

"I'm not lying."

And she made that little gesture of the hands, like someone brushing away crumbs: what was he doing, imagining he might fool her? Didn't she know him better than he knew himself?

"I was swimming. Sunday afternoon. You know I was. Whatever it is they're suggesting, I wasn't there."

"And the drawing?"

"We didn't see any drawing."

"Other people did. Isn't that enough?"

"Why is it?" Voice shaking with anger, frustration, getting less than steadily to his feet. "Why is it, whatever happens, I'm the last one you'll believe?"

"That's simply not true, Stephen. It isn't fair."

"Isn't it?"

"If you were out running that afternoon, why not say so? What's the crime?"

"Joan, listen, look at me, listen. I was not running, not on Sunday. I was at the leisure centre, swimming. I don't see why you can't be-lieve me."

"Stephen, I took your things out of the bag when you got back home. In case anything needed washing. Your costume wasn't even damp."

On the drive home across the centre of the city, Resnick said little, but Lynn had felt the tension accumulating inside him. If, as seemed likely, Stephen Shepperd spent some of his spare time in his wife's classroom, putting his now redundant skills to work, he would have come into contact with Emily; as important, she would have known him. It would have been a simple matter for him to have found her address in the register; an address sufficiently close that even a middle-aged man, not especially fit, could include it in the itinerary of his afternoon run.

But Resnick voiced none of these things: instead he asked Lynn about her parents, her father's health, the poultry farm. Nodding at her responses, anticipating, no doubt, the plump capon that would make the journey back from her pre-Christmas visit and find its way from the waste bin of Resnick's office, first into his refrigerator and eventually his oven. Lynn slowed to a halt outside Resnick's home.

"Early start, sir?"

"Absolutely." A quick smile and he was gone, a blur of white as his hand came up to stroke the first of his cats to run along the wall.

Lynn brought the car around and headed back along the Woodborough Road, the night suddenly clear and pitted with stars. Naylor's car was parked at the kerb between the Lace Market theatre and the probation service car park, waiting.

"I shouldn't have come."

"Nonsense. Of course you should."

Behind the housing association flats where Lynn lived, someone, probably the Old Angel, had applied for an extension and the throb of bass was overridden at intervals by the shrill screech of overamplified guitar.

"Someone's idea of a good time." Lynn smiled.

Nervous, Kevin Naylor said nothing.

There was a single can of Heineken in the fridge and Lynn offered to share it, but Naylor shook his head. She put on the kettle instead and found some music that might be more appropriate, Joan Armatrading, though she doubted it was Kevin's cup of tea.

"How long ago did it happen?" Lynn asked, and, as he toyed with a tipped Rothmans and his lighter, passed him a saucer and said, "Here, use that."

"I know it sounds stupid, but it's hard to say. I mean, it's not as if I came off shift one day and she'd got everything packed up and gone. It was more gradual, months. First off, she'd take the baby there, leave it longer and longer each time. Fair enough, I mean, I didn't like it, not a whole lot, still, fair enough, she'd been, like, depressed, since the baby and she wasn't getting much sleep, so if it was over there, well, at least Debbie caught a few hours' rest, we both did."

The kettle whistled and Lynn went to the kitchen. "Don't stop. I can hear what you're saying."

But he waited, anyway, till she was back in the room.

"Sugar?"

"Thanks, two."

"You were saying, the baby was sleeping over at Debbie's mother's."

"Right. Next thing, she was staying there herself. Evenings, I'd get back . . ."

After a pint or two with Divine, Lynn thought.

". . . and she'd not be there. In a while she'd phone, say she'd gone over to collect the baby, but she was fast off, asking for trouble to wake her, why didn't she just stay the night, come back in the morning?" He glanced across at Lynn's attentive face. "I'm not sure when it was she stopped coming back. I don't know. We were snowed under. To be honest I was glad to get home and not have to bother, not with Debbie, not with the baby, not with anything. Just sit there for a bit, you know, let your mind clear, off to bed knowing no one was going to be shaking you awake this side of morning."

Lynn was looking at the patterns in the rug. "Sounds to me as if maybe you got what you wanted."

"It wasn't what I wanted."

"You didn't try to stop it."

"I told you, I didn't know . . ."

"Your own wife and kid?"

"All right," on his feet, "I didn't come here for this."

Lynn, standing, facing him. "What did you come here for?"

The richness of the singer's voice, the same phrase over and over, slow build of intensity. All either of them had to do was take that first forward step, reach out and touch the other's skin.

"Well?" Lynn said.

"I don't know. I thought . . ."

"Yes?"

"No, I don't know." With a shake of the head, he moved back across the small room and sat down.

"You wanted to pour it all out, how badly she's treated you, and me to sit here and listen, agree with you."

"Probably."

"Well, what I've heard, I do agree with you. Up to a point. Whatever Debbie's playing at, it doesn't sound as if facing up to things is one of them. But it also sounds as if you let her go."

"She didn't need much letting."

"No, maybe. But what she did need, what she just might've wanted from you, was somebody saying no. I suppose it hasn't occurred to you that what she was waiting for all along was for you to tell her what you felt."

"And what's that?"

"I'm afraid I don't know, Kevin, and if you don't either, well, maybe that's part of the problem. But my guess is, all the time she was waiting for you to say, Look, don't do this. I want you here. I want us to be here, together."

Naylor lit a fresh cigarette from the butt of the other.

"When you didn't . . ."

"How d'you know I didn't?"

"Oh, Kevin." Lynn shaking her head. "When you didn't say anything, she thought that meant you didn't want her. Her or the baby. So it was easier to stay with someone who did. And with someone who would help."

"I did help."

"With the baby?"

"Yes."

"What? Helped with the feeding? Played with her? Changed her?"

"Yes. If I was there."

Despite herself, Lynn knew that she was smiling.

"I don't see what's so funny."

"Nothing. Nothing's funny."

"Then what the hell're you laughing for?"

"I'm not laughing." But she was; laughing until she leaned forward and steadied herself by holding his hand.

"Oh, Lynn," he said, voice thickening as he gave her hand a squeeze.

"Kevin," she said, "nice as it might be, it wouldn't solve anything."

"What? I didn't . . ."

Lynn laughed again and got to her feet, releasing herself. "Have you talked to her? Recently, I mean."

"I've tried."

"How often?"

"Once."

"Do you want me to talk to her?"

"No."

"Why not?"

"It's our business, we've got to sort it out for ourselves."

"I don't want to be nasty, Kevin, but it doesn't sound as if you're making a great job of it."

"Thanks very much!"

"Kevin, you're impossible!" Bending low, she kissed him deftly near the top of his head. "I'll give her a call, see if she'll meet me for coffee, a drink."

"She'll only think I've put you up to it."

"So? If nothing else, it'll mean you're trying to do something. It'll mean that you care."

Kevin sat and finished his drink and his cigarette; Joan Armatrading clicked off into silence. "I'd better make a move," he said.

"Sure," Lynn said, relieved that the one he was finally making was the one towards the door.

In his sleep, Stephen Shepperd turned towards the person lying beside him and slipped an arm around her, cuddling close against her warmth. "I'm sorry, Mummy," he breathed into her back. "I'm sorry." And although Joan Shepperd lightly stirred, it is unlikely that she heard.

34

Resnick had been up since before six, padding around the house between bathroom and bedroom and back again, persuading Pepper out from the airing cupboard, where the cat had made a nest for himself in the deep blue of the towels. Downstairs, he unbolted the door and let Dizzy in out of the still-black morning. Cats fed and coffee ground, he went in search of a clean shirt. If Stephen Shepperd had almost collided with Vivien Nathanson, why had he lied? If he had been there in the crescent, would there have been time and opportunity enough for him to have abducted Emily Morrison? Where could he have taken her and why? Resnick sliced rye bread with caraway, three small rounds, and set them in the toaster, side by side. Sighed as he saw both Dizzy and Miles eating from Bud's bowl, the smallest of his four cats destined to be smaller still. Push them away with his foot, they'd be back seconds later. Instead he scooped Bud up in one hand, nuzzled him under his chin and sprinkled a handful of dry food on the work surface, standing the cat down next to it to eat. Coffee not quite ready, he began to slice the Jarlsberg for his toast. What he wanted to know, what they hadn't yet asked, exactly when that Sunday afternoon Stephen Shepperd had arrived back home, the time his wife had next seen him. He spread margarine on the toast, scraped some back off with the knife and returned it to the packet; he overlapped the cheese across, cut a chunk of garlic sausage from the fridge and put that on top; what he would have liked, a tomato, but they had all gone, what he was tempted by, a smear of mayonnaise. A hand pressed against his stomach was enough to help him to resist. What had Stephen Shepperd said about swimming being good exercise? Maybe he should take it up? A few leisurely lengths each morning before work. He must send someone along with the Identikit picture, see if they recognised Stephen, if they could remember him being there on Sunday afternoon. He carried his toast and coffee through to the other room, wondering if Skelton would be up yet, whether he should call.

"Not exactly a lot to go on, Charlie. Our word against his he was there at all. And if he was, what does it prove?"

"If he was," Resnick said, "why's he lying?"

"Someone else, perhaps, illicit assignation. Last thing he wants to do, admit the truth in front of his wife."

"The whole of Lenton couldn't have been at it, sir. Sunday afternoon."

"According to my wife, who sees the world increasingly through the eyes of Andrea Newman's novels, it's what most people are doing any afternoon."

Skelton knew the dangers of making the wrong move too soon. Set against that, the almost certain knowledge that the more time passed before finding the girl, the lesser the chance of finding her alive, the more likely he was to come under criticism.

"We've not come up with a lot else, have we, Charlie?"

Slowly, Resnick shook his head. "Sod all, sir," he said.

Lorraine Morrison opened the door to Lynn while her finger was still pressed to the bell. Whatever Lorraine had tried doing to her hair that morning hadn't worked; a green-and-yellow rugby shirt hung loose outside her jeans, sports shoes on her feet.

"Have you found her?"

Lynn shook her head.

"But you've got some news?"

"Not really, not much."

"We saw the drawing last night on the news; it was in the paper as well. There must be something."

"A lot of phone calls, yes. We're sorting through them now."

"Well, then."

"Lorraine, what you have to realise, people who respond to items like that, they do so for, oh, a whole lot of reasons. Some think it's a way to get noticed, some want to get their own back on their neighbours, others call in and suggest something stupid just for a joke, a laugh. Never mind somebody has to check them all out."

The disappointment in Lorraine's face was so palpable you could reach out and touch it.

"There is one possibility, though. Look, I mean, nothing to get your hopes up about, not really. But we think we might have a line on somebody. Probably only a witness, though, at best."

Now it was clear Lorraine didn't know what to feel, and Lynn, who knew she'd overstepped the line saying anything this early, felt responsible for offering the girl something that she'd immediately taken away.

"How's Michael?" she said.

"He went to work. Decided last night and then, this morning, changed his mind. I had to push him out of the house in the end, but anything will be better for him than moping around."

Lynn glanced at her watch. "How about a quick coffee, then? I've just got time."

There was no doubting the small look of pleasure on Lorraine's face as Lynn eased the front door to and they started towards the kitchen.

"Michael's brother phoned not long before you came," Lorraine said. "I was glad Michael was out. I suppose he's full of the right intentions, but all Geoffrey seems to do somehow is put Michael into an even worse mood." She gestured for Lynn to sit down. "But perhaps that's the way families are? I don't know, I was the only one. How about you?"

"Afraid so," Lynn said. "Just me."

"You don't like it?"

"When you're growing up, I suppose it's not so bad. All that love and attention. It's when you're older, when your parents are getting older, that's when it can get a bit more worrying." That's when, she thought, the chickens start coming home to roost.

Joan Shepperd had woken that morning to the faint electrical sound of drilling, pushed out a hand and felt the pillow on her husband's side of the bed, still damp. Down in the cellar which he had equipped as a workshop, Stephen was bending, not over a drill, but a plane, turning lengths of timber. On one of the shelves his old portable radio was tuned to Radio Two, Sarah Vaughan and Billy Eckstein, that song that used to be so popular all those years ago. They must be dead now, the pair of them, Joan thought, either that or in their seventies. Eighties, even. She seemed to recall hearing that one of them had died, couldn't for the life of her remember which one.

"Stephen, do you want any breakfast?"

Very well, let him pretend he hadn't heard. Stay down there all day if that was the way he felt. She closed the cellar door as the whine of the tool Stephen was using drowned the final chorus of the song.

"Passing Strangers," is that what it had been?

Today, Joan thought, would be a good day for All-Bran and some dried fruit, apricots and prunes.

"What d'you call that?" Millington had asked, setting the *Mail* aside to lean over the book his wife was looking at so earnestly.

"What the artist calls it is *Double Nude Portrait.*"

What Millington could see, opened out over their breakfast table, was a middle-aged woman, not a stitch on her, leaning back in front of a gas fire, breasts sliding sideways in either direction, legs apart and one knee raised. Seated behind her and gazing down through a pair of round-framed spectacles, was this equally naked bloke with a vaguely hairy chest and what looked like the leftovers of an erection.

"Nice thing to have on the breakfast table," Millington said.

"I think they're on the floor, Graham."

"I can see that, toasting themselves in front of the gas."

"I think it's oil, Graham."

"Gas."

"The tutor said it was oil; a Vector oil heater. It was the artist's own."

"Yes? So what else did he have to say about this? Your tutor."

"*She* said it was an act of religious contemplation."

"Um. So what's this, down here at the bottom? Looks like a piece of raw meat."

"It's a leg of lamb. Or was it mutton?"

"Religious, too, is it?"

"I think it's suggesting a contrast between the two, the one just for eating and the other . . ." She stopped, a faint blush showing on her neck. "I'm really not sure, Graham."

"No, well, you've got it nearly right, I reckon." He leaned closer to the title. "Stanley Spencer. *Double Nude Portrait: The Artist and his Second Wife.* Didn't say anything, your tutor, as to how he disposed of the first one?"

The exterior of the Victoria Leisure Centre, on the corner above the wholesale market, smelled of rotting vegetables and poverty; inside the smell was of chlorine and Brut. Divine held his identification up to the glass panel at Reception and when he had the girl's attention, slipped a copy of the drawing through the opening.

"What about him?" the girl asked, trying not to notice Divine doing his best to get a good look down her front.

"Know him? Regular or anything?"

She picked it up and held it closer to her face. Can't be much more than eighteen, Divine thought, eyesight should be better than that.

"I think so," she said.

"He comes here?"

"Yes, I'm pretty sure."

"Well, you're pretty," Divine said.

She gave him a look that would have stopped a ferret at fifty feet.

"What, then?" Divine carried on, undeterred. If you never gave it a go, you never knew. "He use the baths or what?"

"Swimming, yes, I'm pretty . . . I'm almost certain." Leaning back in her chair, she called through to the inner office. "Les, this bloke's a regular, isn't he?"

Les came out with a bundle of towels in both arms, a well-built man in his fifties with greying hair. "Never seen him before," he said, looking through the glass at Divine.

"No," said the girl, "not him. Him."

"Oh." Les dumped the towels and took hold of the drawing. "Yes, him, two or three times a week. Main pool."

"Any idea when he was here last?" Divine asked.

Les and the girl exchanged glances, both shook their heads.

"Sunday?"

Les reached for his towels. "Could've been Sunday."

"You working then?"

"Me, not Sunday, no. One in four and that's one too many." He pointed at the book on the counter. "See who was on Sunday. Morning," he said to Divine, "or afternoon?"

"Afternoon."

"Freda," said the girl. "It was Freda."

They found Freda in the women's changing rooms, doing duty with a long-handled broom. "Get all kinds left in here, you know. Everything from Tesco's chicken tikka sandwiches, still cellophane-wrapped, untouched, to a pack of contraceptive pills with only six missing. There's someone'll be going white round the gills come the end of the month."

Divine showed her the picture.

"Stephen," she said. "Nice bloke. Always time for a bit of a chat. What about him?"

"Was he in Sunday?" Les asked. "Afternoon?"

"Not unless he's been practising limbo dancing. Wouldn't get past me any other way. 'Sides, like I say, liked to chat. No, he wasn't in this weekend. If he was, I'd've seen him."

"You're sure of that?" Divine asked.

Freda leaned forward against her broom, fixed Divine with her eyes. "What do you think?" she said.

Patel and Naylor spent the best part of the day sorting through the responses to the artist's impression, throwing out the too obviously false, the one who claimed it was his father-in-law, another who swore that it was the bastard of a manager who'd refused him a loan at the bank. Four pointed in the direction of Stephen Shepperd; one, a neighbour, mentioning the fact that he'd seen him running round Lenton Rec; a man who used to work with him identifying him by name.

Jogged by the fresh publicity, two people contacted the station about the unaccounted-for Ford Sierra. As a result Naylor delved into the phone book for the address of a Bernard Kilpatrick, owner of a sports shop out at Bulwell, currently living round the corner from the White Hart.

At the shop it appeared to be half-day closing and no one was picking up the home phone and answering, so Naylor was all for going round there, get him out to the station, but Millington's hand on his shoulder kept him where he was.

"You sit tight with that little lot. I'll see if I can run Mr. Kilpatrick to ground. Never know, might sink a quick half in the White Hart while I'm about it."

As it was, Millington never got his drink. Bernard Kilpatrick, engine oil on his arms and state-of-the-art tool kit spread over the pavement, was making some minor adjustments to the carburetor. He straightened up as Millington drew nearer and prepared to swop stories about the unpredictability of cars generally, engines in particular. Even something as normally reliable as a G registration Ford Sierra.

35

"What I want to know, car's that close Randall could hit it with a throw from cover point, how come none of our lot spotted it? Even if they weren't using their eyes, what was wrong with questions? Ford Sierra owners, isn't that what we've been looking for? Whatever happened to checking vehicle ownership through the damned national computer? God alone knows how many man-hours, how much overtime's gone into this already, and it takes some civilian to tip us off.

"Well, thanks very much to Joe Public, thanks indeed, but meanwhile, what in hell's name's been going on?"

Jack Skelton was not a happy man. He'd summoned his senior officers first thing and it wasn't to pass out commendations. Skelton had dispensed with his normal shirt-sleeve order, brisk and businesslike yet approachable, and was standing there glowering at them from behind his desk in a suit sharp as battle armour, tie knotted so tight as to endanger his blood supply.

"All right, let's make up for sloppy work with some hard graft, some application, a sight more diligence. Charlie, I want that lecturer in here this afternoon if you have to carry her in on your shoulders, let's get Shepperd in an identification parade sharpish. Meantime, background on him and his wife; as many questions asked about this couple as we can. Neighbours, friends, colleagues, let's pay particular attention to the people who responded to the Identikit. Bit of an odd setup, from what Charlie's said, sounds as if the wife might know more than she's letting on. Let's get her on her own, see if she'll open up. Rattle her if you have to, rattle anyone and everyone. There's one child on this patch dead, another missing. For Christ's sake, let's do what we're paid for and do something about it."

Millington intercepted Resnick on his way back to CID. "How'd it go?" he asked and, seeing Resnick's face, wished he hadn't. "That bad?" he said, sympathetically.

"Worse."

Resnick pushed into his office, Millington following. "You," he said, turning to prod the sergeant with his finger, "for now, Kilpatrick's yours. By the end of the day you're going to know everything about him from where he takes his holidays to if he flosses his teeth and how. Right?"

"Sir." Millington was already on his way.

"And send Lynn in here."

"Not sure if she's back, sir."

"Then get her back."

According to Millington, Bernard Kilpatrick had been smooth as silk and about as slippery. Yes, as a matter of fact, he had parked his car on the crescent on Sunday. To be quite honest, he'd spent most of lunchtime in the Rose and Crown, anyone had breathalysed him, he'd have turned the thing the colours of the rainbow. Even so, he'd got in the car and started for home, turned into the crescent and before he knew what he was at, one of his wheels had been up on the kerb. He hadn't needed a second warning. Straight out of the driving seat and walked. Went back for the car later. Condition he was in, all he could do was to pull off his shoes and collapse on the settee. No, he didn't know when he woke up, nor when he went back to get the car, but he was pretty sure it was dark. Well, this time of the year, that's mostly what it was.

The Rose and Crown was a biggish pub, Sundays it might well be pretty crowded, but if Kilpatrick had been there long enough to get good and drunk, someone should have noticed him.

"Graham," Resnick called into the main office.

"Sir?"

"We have checked Kilpatrick's lunchtime binge, I suppose?"

"Divine's down there now, sir."

God! thought Resnick. Like sending a kleptomaniac into Sainsbury's in a power strike.

Eight o'clock, nine, ten o'clock, eleven. Whenever Stephen switched off the power, he could hear Joan moving around overhead, her footsteps filtered through the strings and muted brass of daytime easy listening. Once, she had called down the steps to inquire if he wanted coffee and he had failed to answer. Coffee meant more questions and they would come soon enough without his meeting them head on.

In the event, it was not so far short of twelve.

"Stephen," his wife shouted down. "You'll have to come up. The police are here to talk to you again."

The inspector was on his own this time, the heavy-looking one, the one with the unusual name.

"Sorry to interrupt, Mr. Shepperd, it's just one thing. Last night, you seemed certain that you'd been swimming on Sunday, Sunday afternoon. Now you've perhaps had a chance to think about that a little, I wondered whether you'd changed your mind?"

Stephen blinked. "No."

"You weren't jogging?" Resnick asked.

"No, I told you . . ."

"Not running, but swimming?"

"That's correct."

"At Victoria Baths?"

"Yes."

"It couldn't have been anywhere else? You wouldn't have . . ."

Stephen shook his head. "It's where I always go. Why don't you ask them? They know me."

"Thank you, Mr. Shepperd." Resnick smiled. "We already have."

Stephen stood tense, waiting for what was to come next, but that, apparently, was that. He was starting to breathe more freely when Resnick turned at the door.

"We'd like you to take part in an identification parade this afternoon. Formality, really. Settle the matter once and for all."

"But I was at the pool, ask them, you said you asked . . ."

"And so we did, Mr. Shepperd. This is simply for confirmation." Resnick looked at him squarely. "There can't be any reason for you to refuse?"

"No," Stephen agreed, his voice oddly distant, not a voice that he recognised. "No, of course not."

"Good. Three o'clock, then. Oh, and you can have somebody present with you, if you wish."

"Somebody . . . ?"

"You know, a friend. A solicitor even." Resnick turned the handle of the door. "Till this afternoon, then, Mr. Shepperd. Three o'clock. Perhaps you'd like us to send a car?"

"No, thank you. No. That won't be necessary."

Resnick nodded and closed the door; without turning, Stephen knew that Joan was standing behind him, watching.

Millington didn't know where they got the nerve, close to a hundred quid for a pair of plimsolls, gym shoes. That's all they were. All right, there was a lot of fancy work down the sides, purple and black and that, ludicrous tongues that poked out the front the size of shin pads, but when you got down to it, gym shoes is what they were. Plimsolls.

"Sell a lot of these, do you?"

Kilpatrick took the trainer from the sergeant's hand and gave it a look of glowing admiration. "Can't get enough."

"At that price?"

"Word goes round we've got a few in stock, they're on the bus out here from all over. Rarity value, you see. None of the big boys stock them."

Millington looked bemused. "That matters?"

"Look at it this way, you're seventeen, eighteen, what do you do, most of the time, not a lot of money to spend, you go walking round town with your mates. Bunch of lads, always running across other lads. What're you doing? Checking one another out. The trousers, the hair, the T-shirt, more than anything else, the trainers. You go strutting along Bridlesmith Gate or round the Broad Marsh in a pair of those, maybe there's only a dozen more pairs in the city, tops, people are going to be looking at you, thinking, Hello, he's a bit special. See what I mean?"

"Yes," Millington said, "but are they comfortable?"

Two youths, black, one with a jagged razor line along one side of his close-cut hair, the other with dreadlocks caught up in the kind of hair net Millington's gran had used to wear, were checking out the shell suits near the back of the shop. A man in his late twenties, with the minimal dress sense and mixture of earnestness and confusion which led Millington to mark him down as a social worker, was spending forever deciding which colour badminton shuttle was right for his game.

Millington had been forced to work with men like that, pious as piss about sexism and racism and ageism and the rights of the individual, couldn't wait to get you out on some godforsaken council estate at six in the morning, hammering on doors and hauling kids off into care, never mind the rights of the sodding families.

He'd argued with the boss about it a time or two, Resnick, ever since he had that thing going with that social worker, bending over backwards to see their side of things. Nice woman, Rachel Chaplin, shame she'd not stuck around longer. Came close to being a statistic in one of Resnick's murder cases, got a transfer down to the West Country, Exeter, Bristol, somewhere like that, anything for a quieter life.

Bernard Kilpatrick hit the cash register and a moment later the doorbell jangled. "Bloke who bought the shuttles," Millington asked. "Don't happen to know what he does?"

"Vicar," Kilpatrick said. "Nice enough, but can't he waffle. Sort for whom crossing the street's a moral dilemma."

"Where's his get-up, then?" Millington asked.

"Saints' days and Sundays."

Millington shook his head sorrowfully. Surely it wasn't so long ago that clergymen all wore black suits and dog collars and sports shoes were something you bought in Woolies, dead white and change back from a pound?

"Only thing we're still not too clear about," Millington said, almost as an afterthought. "The time you went back and picked up the car."

Kilpatrick shrugged. "No more am I."

"But roughly?"

"Depends how long I slept. Hour, maybe more."

"And you got home when? Three?"

"Around then."

"So you could have collected the car as early as four?"

Another shrug, his full attention not on the sergeant, watching out for what the couple at the back might be trying to boost. "Could be. Is it important?"

"Probably not," said Millington. "We'll let you know."

Lynn Kellogg hung back, watching as Joan Shepperd got out of the car, refusing her husband's offer to help carry her various bags and books into school. She watched Stephen watching his wife making her way between the shrieking, racing children to the classroom. Only when he had driven away did Lynn enter the school herself.

Joan Shepperd was taking something from a cupboard as Lynn stepped into the room, warrant card in hand.

Felt-tip pens fell between her fingers as she turned. "My husband's due at the police station this afternoon."

"I know, Mrs. Shepperd, it's just . . ."

"The children are about to come into school."

"What your husband said about Sunday afternoon, going swimming . . ."

"This isn't fair."

"We wondered if you thought he remembered wrongly? Perhaps there was a reason for him to be confused?"

She bent down and began to retrieve the pens; there were voices outside the door, an impatient scuffling of feet. "If Stephen says he was swimming then that's where he was."

Lynn stooped towards her, placing a card into her hand. "If there's anything you think of, anything you want to talk about, to me, possibly, rather than anybody else, you can contact me on that number." Straightening, Lynn began to back towards the door. "Sorry to have disturbed you, Mrs. Shepperd. Perhaps I'll speak to you again."

Small children pressed around Lynn's legs as she left the room.

36

The department office was in a long, low building, dingy and scuffed walls and a sloping corrugated roof; as a centre for learning it had the presence and authority of a converted cow shed. But perhaps if you were teaching American and Canadian Studies you liked it that way. A sense of the vast outdoors, the pioneering spirit. The secretary treated Resnick to a smile that would have seemed at home in the expanses of Saskatchewan or Manitoba and directed him outside again, along to a lecture room at the end of the block. Inside the room, Vivien Nathanson wasn't lecturing, at least not in any way that Resnick recognised it; she was sitting in one corner with seven or so students, chairs pulled clear of the tables and formed into a circle. Waiting for the Indians, Resnick thought, smiling, slipping into a seat near the door.

"If you need a central text," Vivien was saying, "you could do worse than the McAdam we were looking at earlier."

When we met, I thought knowledge had limits, that in love
we were finite beasts who shared known boundaries

but watching you touch objects for which I have no desire
I see a measure of longing in your eyes

that forces me to say, I don't know you yet. That forces me
to say, there are places in you I may not wish to know

"Anybody remember how that goes on?"

After some shuffling of papers and sudden interest in footwear, a girl with corn-blonde hair ventured: "Is it the bit about infinity?"

Vivien smiled encouragingly.

"Beasts of infinity?"

"That's right."

In love we are beasts of infinity, crude in our longing
for things that may carry us apart.

"What's interesting, one of the things that's interesting, is the way desire and sexuality are discussed in terms of distance, place, boundaries. That's the focus I think you should take for your essays. All right?"

A quick smile and a closing of the book to show that it was over.

"Aren't you going to give us an actual title?" asked one of the young men, the savagery of his haircut at odds with the soft correctness of his accent.

"Oh, very well." Standing, Vivien's eyes flicked towards Resnick at the far end of the room, the first acknowledgment that he was there. "How about 'Desire and Place: The Erotics of Distance in Canadian Poetry'? Is that posey enough for you?"

Two or three students laughed; the youth who'd asked the question blushed and shuffled his feet.

"Do we have to restrict ourselves to the poets we've talked about?" The girl with cornsilk hair was walking with Vivien towards the door.

"No, not at all. But Rhona McAdam, Susan Musgrave, you might start there. After that," she smiled, "the possibilities are infinite."

With scarcely a glance at Resnick, the students filed from the room.

"I was waiting for a dramatic intervention," Vivien said, the smile still not faded from her face. "A quick three minutes on personal safety and care of belongings, at least."

Resnick nodded in the direction of the door. "God knows what they thought I was doing here. Someone from the board of works, come to size the place up for a paint job. Not that they seemed that interested anyway."

"Ah, they're just being cool. It doesn't do to demonstrate a great deal of interest in anything. Least of all work or strange men. But if your ego's bruised, they probably thought you were my lover. I'm sure they think I have one somewhere." She chuckled, low in her throat. "At least, I certainly hope so."

So, Resnick thought, come on, what's the answer, do you or not? And, as if she knew what he was thinking, the light of mischief moved across her eyes.

"That poem you were reading?" Resnick asked. "It was a poem?"

"Yes."

"Does it have a title?"

" 'Infinite Beasts.' Here, take this. Borrow it."

Resnick looked from her face to the book in his hand. "It's all right."

"No, do. I've finished using it for now. You can return it later."

The cover of the book was pale pink, overprinted in black and grey; he wondered if her lenses were tinted blue or if that was the natural colour of her eyes. "The man you saw out running . . ."

"You've found him."

"We think so. We'd like you to come and identify him, if you can."

"You mean one of those parades, where you can see them but they can't see you?"

"Not quite so high-tech," Resnick said. "No one-way mirror, just a room big enough for everyone to stand in and stare at one another."

"That sounds more intimidating," said Vivien.

"It is. But you'll manage." Without really needing to, he looked at his watch. "If we make a move now, everything should be more or less set up."

"Then let's go."

Passing the secretary's office, she said, "If we go in your car, does that mean you get to drive me back?"

"Not necessarily. But it does mean somebody will."

However she viewed that prospect, Vivien Nathanson kept it to herself.

Stephen Shepperd arrived at the station wearing a patched tweed jacket and brown cords. Patel did his best to put him at his ease while they were waiting for Resnick to return, but Shepperd was not going to be calmed down with politeness and inquiries about the outside temperature.

When Resnick entered the room where they were waiting, Shepperd opened his mouth to say something, reconsidered, and bit the inside of his lower lip instead.

"You know you have the right to have somebody else present?" Resnick said.

Shepperd shook his head.

"You understand it's within your rights to refuse to take part in this parade, but that if you make that choice, we may arrange to have you confronted by a witness?"

Shepperd nodded.

"Also, that should you exercise your right not to participate, that fact may be offered in evidence in any subsequent trial?"

"What trial?"

"We don't know yet, Mr. Shepperd. Any trial that might ensue."

Shepperd pressed one hand to the side of his face and teased with his teeth the place where he had bitten his lip. Resnick nodded at Patel, who handed Shepperd a copy of the form outlining the procedure in detail.

"When you've read that through, Mr. Shepperd, sign it at the bottom and indicate where it says that you're waiving your right to have anyone else present."

Shepperd read the form with difficulty, the hand holding it less than steady; his signature little more than a scrawl.

Outside the door to the room where the parade was going to take place, Resnick made him pause. "There are eight men in there, all chosen because of a physical similarity to yourself. Now you can choose to stand anywhere between them, anywhere in the line. You'll see there are numbers on cards placed on the floor at intervals, one for each of you. When the witness comes in, they'll be asked to identify the person they saw previously if possible and to do so by the number in question."

Shepperd's eyes were moving everywhere, never settling on Resnick's face.

"Is that clear?"

"Yes."

"Since you're not having anyone present, a photograph will be taken of the parade before the witness comes in. A copy of that will be made available to yourself or your solicitor if it becomes necessary."

Resnick stepped back, leaving Patel to take Shepperd inside. He found Vivien Nathanson in close discussion with Lynn Kellogg and whatever it was they were talking about cut off as soon as Resnick approached.

"I have to tell you," Resnick said to Vivien, heading back towards the room, "the person you saw may or may not be in this parade. If you can't make a positive identification that's fine, you just have to say so.

If you do recognise anyone, the way to indicate that is by referring to their number."

"They have numbers?"

"Uh-huh."

"Round their necks?"

"In front of them. Where they stand."

A moment later they were inside the room. Stephen Shepperd had chosen to stand third in line. Five of the others had been persuaded in off the streets to perform their civic duty, the remainder were uniformed men who'd changed back into their street clothes.

"Take your time," Resnick said. "Walk along the line at least twice and then, if you can, if you're quite certain, I want you to indicate whether the person you saw running across the crescent on Sunday afternoon last is in this room."

Vivien Nathanson had thought it was going to be easy; she hadn't imagined herself as being under any pressure. After all, she was just the witness; she was the one who had come forward, conscientious, anxious to help. Why then, as she looked along the line of men, did her mouth feel suddenly dry, the muscles of her stomach wall begin to tighten and contract?

37

Divine was chuffed as a pig in muck. Get me something on Kilpatrick, the sergeant had said, and a couple of jars with Tom Haddon from the vice squad and there it was. There they were, Millington and himself, off out to Bulwell, Millington whistling, looking dapper in the passenger seat, prepared to be pleased. Only trimmed his bloody moustache, Divine grinned, bugger's fancying his picture in the paper already.

Bernard Kilpatrick was serving someone when they went in, a youth in denim jacket and jeans trying on a pair of size-eight Nikes.

"With you in a sec." Kilpatrick frowned. About the last thing he'd expected, the CID back in the shop so sharpish, and with reinforcements.

"No, sorry. Don't feel right." The lad handed Kilpatrick back the trainer and wandered out onto the street.

"Something to do," Kilpatrick explained, returning the shoe to its box. "Third time he's been in here this week. Perfect fit, he'd never afford it."

Over to the side, Divine had lifted down one of the cricket bats and was practising a lofted drive over the head of cover.

"Lovely bat," Kilpatrick said, encouragingly. "Duncan Fearnley. If you're looking for something with a bit of extra weight, that's the one. Look, try it with just the one hand, test the balance."

"What time," Millington said, "were you thinking of closing?"

Kilpatrick blinked. "Five-thirty, six, why?"

"Thought today you might make an exception."

Kilpatrick had taken the bat from Divine and now he was patting it gently against the outside of his leg. "Maybe you better tell me what's going on," he said.

"Didn't want someone barging in, interrupting."

"Interrupting what?"

"Oh, just a few questions."

"Such as?"

"Look," Millington said, moving towards the door. "Why don't we turn this around?"

"Here, you can't . . ."

But the sergeant had already swung OPEN round to CLOSED. Divine was quickly alongside Kilpatrick, taking the cricket bat from his hand.

"Look, I . . ." Kilpatrick, turning back towards the counter, eying the phone.

Divine stooped low to the socket, disconnecting the plug.

"Better," said Millington. "No chance we'll be disturbed."

"Right." Divine smiled. "Sudden order from the local scouts for Ping-Pong balls."

"This is bloody harassment," said Kilpatrick.

"Is it heck," Millington said.

"Whatever's going on, I want to call my solicitor."

"No," Divine passing close in front of him, "I don't think so. Not really."

"Not yet," Millington added.

"D'you want to sit down?" Divine asked.

"Or would you rather stand?"

"What I'd rather do, I'd rather know what the fuck's going on?"

"Right." Millington nodded.

"Right." Divine nodded.

"February twenty-third," Millington said. "That'd do for a start."

Kilpatrick backed up against the counter, sweat beginning to form inside the track suit that he wore at work, showing it off for the customers, loose drawstring trousers and a zip-through top, silver and blue.

"You remember the twenty-third."

"February?"

"The twenty-third."

"Is that this year?"

"Don't," Millington advised, "piss us around."

"I'm not, I wasn't, I . . ."

A couple of Asian youths rattled the door and Divine signalled for them to take a hike.

"How about the thirteenth?"

"February?"

"June."

"How the fuck do I know? How the . . ."

"Steady," cautioned Millington.

"Temper, temper." Divine grinned.

"Come on now, try harder."

"June thirteenth."

"Unlucky thirteen."

"Unlucky for some."

"Then, so was the ninth."

"September as I recall."

"That's it, September."

"First full month of the season."

"Same month Gloria Summers went missing."

"Who?" Kilpatrick said.

"Gloria Summers."

"Six years old."

"Missing from where she was playing."

"Found her a couple of months later."

"Likely you read about it."

"Over Sneinton way."

"Railway sidings."

"Dead."

"All right." Kilpatrick spread his hands, pushed his way between them, almost at the shop door before he turned to face them. "I don't know what all this is about. I don't have a clue. But you come barging in here with this whole Little and Large, Cannon and Ball routine. One minute you're asking me about a whole string of dates that don't mean a thing, next up it's some kid got herself murdered. Well, I want to know what it's all about and I want to talk to my solicitor now. Before I say another thing."

Divine looked over at Millington, who inclined his head fractionally, at which Divine took hold of the telephone lead and renewed the connection. Lifting the receiver from the cradle, he held it out in Kilpatrick's direction.

Kilpatrick made no move towards it.

"September the ninth," Millington said, "you were stopped in your car in the area of Radford Road. Two officers from the vice squad informed you that they had been watching you for the best part of an hour, during the course of which time you had slowed down by and approached several women whom they had reason to believe were soliciting for prostitution. They had also observed you driving up and down past a house which they suspected was being used as a common brothel. You were told that the details of your name, address and vehicle registration would be noted down and kept on file and you were warned as to your future behaviour. Remember now?"

"Yes."

"And do you remember receiving similar warnings on the thirteenth of June and the twenty-third of February?"

"Yes."

"According to certain of your neighbours, you have been in the habit of receiving home visits from a succession of young women, believed to be providing a massage service."

Kilpatrick scowled. "Some people'd do well to mind their own business."

"Others might be advised to steer clear of women on the game."

"It's been a bad time for me, a bad year. My wife and I separated . . ."

"After which you moved in with a seventeen-year-old bimbo, who dumped you after a month." Divine was warming to his task, really beginning to enjoy himself, feel the edge.

"Eighteen. She was eighteen."

Divine laughed in his face. "Seventeen years, seven months, and capable of looking younger. A lot younger. If there was a demand for it."

Kilpatrick turned his head but there was no stopping Divine now. Tom Haddon had set him up with the girl that lunchtime, earning a few quid giving relief massage at a place off the Carlton Road.

"When you met her she was working the hotels. Tip the security staff a quick freebie or a tenner and prowl the corridors with a smile and a bottle of massage lotion in her bag. Wonder what it was turned you on that first time, that innocent schoolgirl smile?"

Kilpatrick swung fast and for a moment, maybe two, he was going to deck Divine, punch him hard in the middle of that smug, smiling face.

"Play school, Kilpatrick." Divine leered.

"Stop this!" Kilpatrick yelled. "You can fucking stop this! You can put an end to this right fucking now!"

"Navy school skirts," Divine taunted, "hair up in bunches. Classroom games."

"Bastard!"

"You be the naughty little schoolgirl, I'll be the teacher."

Kilpatrick grabbed for the phone, fumbling it against his chest while he flipped back the pages of the address book open on the counter.

Divine turned towards Millington and winked.

"Suzanne Olds," Kilpatrick said into the telephone.

"Ninth of September," said Millington, "you were stopped by the police out looking to buy sex. Second week in September. Same week Gloria Summers was abducted, sexually assaulted, murdered."

"No, I don't want her secretary!" Kilpatrick shouted. "I want her in person and if that means hauling her out of court, that's what you'd better do."

Vivien Nathanson hesitated before Stephen Shepperd for the second time. The man who had bumped into her almost a week ago had been looking back over his shoulder, she had only seen his face for—what?— a minute. Less. Enough for the police artist to have teased out the basic features; seeing the drawing she had been certain, yes, that was the way he had looked, yes. But now in the sweat of that closed room: looking at those eight men, one to one to another; those men looking back at her. The others, watching and waiting.

She thought about the missing girl.

The photographs she had seen reproduced.

The enormity of what seemed to have been done.

She moved along to the end of the line before she turned away; slowly, she crossed towards Resnick shaking her head.

"The man you saw last Sunday, do you see him here now?"

The slightest of hesitations and then: "I'm not sure."

Resnick was staring at her, willing her to say something different.

"I'm not sure," she said again.

Gravely he nodded. "Very well. Thank you for coming in. DC Patel will take you wherever you want to go."

She hesitated, looking for something other than anger or disappointment in his eyes.

Patel gestured towards the door.

When it had closed behind them, Resnick approached Shepperd, whose arms were now folded across his chest to stop himself from shaking. "If you've any comments about the way this parade was conducted, the time to make them is now."

38

"What is it, then, Charlie? What've you taken to feeding them? Raw steak, all of a sudden?"

Resnick picked at a blob of mayonnaise that had somehow found its way onto the lapel of his jacket. Second time on the super's carpet in twelve hours wasn't his favourite location. "Maybe went in a bit hard and fast, sir, got their *t*'s crossed and their *i*'s dotted too soon."

"What they did, Charlie, chased down a lead with some good police work, then buggered it up with bully-boy tactics that'd give some judge down the road the chance to throw the whole shebang out of court."

"Only Kilpatrick's word for that, sir."

"You don't believe him?"

Resnick didn't answer.

"Intimidation, verbal certainly, not so far off the physical; refusing a request to contact his solicitor—and you know who that is, I suppose?"

Resnick knew: he and Suzanne Olds were frequent sparring partners who occasionally drank espresso together at the coffee stall in the market. They treated one another with a grudging respect and never flinched from the chance to score points.

"Ms. Olds is out there now, counting her fee, rubbing her hands as if she can't quite believe what we've handed her on a plate."

"It's still only Kilpatrick's word against ours."

"And whose are we taking?"

Resnick looked past Skelton's head towards the window, the sky settling into that blue blackness that is never truly black, the darkness of cities. Another day and Emily Morrison not found. Was it so difficult to understand his officers acting as they did, their frustration?

"Not hard to see what happened, Charlie. Days of routine and dead ends and then this. The adrenaline takes over. Judgment? Scraped away like shit off the bottom of a shoe."

Resnick nodded agreement. "Divine, I'm not surprised. But Graham . . ."

"Coppers like Millington, Charlie, next rung up the ladder, it's out there like the end of the rainbow. All they can see, all they think they need, that one result, that one big case that's going to leave them covered in glory. Now, one way or another, you're going to be giving his bollocks a dusting and the resentment's going to be so thick you can taste it."

Neither of them spoke for several moments; traffic came over the brow of the hill and past fast enough to make the walls of the building vibrate. Not so far down that same hill, Resnick could see Lorraine Morrison in her kitchen, glancing at the clock, gauging the time, her husband's mood. Maybe he'd had an extra beer on the train, two scotches as against the usual one. What would they talk about before dinner and after, filling the silence that would so recently have been broken by their daughter's shouts and laughter?

"What if they're right, sir? About Kilpatrick?"

Skelton shook his head. "You've seen labourers on a building site, Charlie. Downing tools every time a schoolgirl walks along the street. My Kate, she was whistled at and worse from when she was twelve, more often in her uniform than out of it. God knows what it is about ankle socks and pleated skirts and I'm glad I don't, but if we pulled in every man who had that for a fantasy, we'd have half the male population behind bars. More. And if this Kilpatrick's been spending good money getting women to act it out for him, I'd reckon he was less likely to be our man rather than more."

Resnick nodded, wondering whether Skelton had been borrowing a couple of books on sexual behaviour, or merely reading his wife's copies of *Company* and *Cosmopolitan*.

"His car was parked near the Morrisons' house, sir. Around the time the girl disappeared."

"For which he has a reason. What we don't have, unless I'm much mistaken, is anything linking him to the girl."

Resnick pinched the bridge of his nose; his eyes were starting to smart and he couldn't remember the last night he'd had that had passed undisturbed. "Kick him loose, then?"

"Let Millington's interview run its course. He just might unearth something, I suppose, and if he does I'll gladly eat my words. After that, let's have him out of here as quickly and politely as we can. Hope that forty-eight hours or so'll calm him down sufficiently that he forgets any ideas he might have about suing for harassment or false arrest."

"And Millington? Divine?"

Skelton allowed himself something close to a smile. "Chain of command, Charlie. You know how it goes."

Right, Resnick thought, I know exactly how it works. You panic and bawl me out for nothing getting done, I give my team a going-over in turn and the result is they go rushing round like a bunch of headless chickens, desperate for a result. The result is this. At least, now the interviews were taped, they wouldn't be so keen on manufacturing evidence, changing answers, responding to pressure down the chain of command.

He got to his feet and turned towards the door.

"Pity about the identification parade," Skelton said.

"I still think he was there, sir. That afternoon, Stephen Shepperd."

"What if he was, Charlie? What did he do? Tuck the kid under his arm and run off with her?"

"Maybe."

"Charlie."

"Somebody did. If not that exactly, something close. He did have the car, remember. Drove off to go swimming. Changed his mind and went for a run, must've parked it somewhere. If he did grab her, he need not have carried her too far."

"Sunday afternoon, Charlie. People at home. She'd have screamed, struggled. Somebody would have heard."

"Not if she knew him. Which almost certainly she did. In and out of the school, the classroom, helping his wife out. Shepperd might've spoken to her any number of times. What was to stop him speaking to her again, that Sunday? Both her parents indoors, their door shut, curtains drawn. So easy for her to have been fed up, bored; easy for someone she knew to have beckoned her over, come and look at this, he could have walked Emily Morrison away from there holding her hand."

Skelton had nodded several times while Resnick was talking, but now he leaned back in his chair, hands in his trouser pockets, shaking his head. "The only witness we've come up with, the only one that might have placed Shepperd near the scene, failed to identify him. We can't even place him there."

"Why did he lie about going swimming?"

"If he did."

"I'm sure of it."

"Even if we know he wasn't at the baths, even if we know he lied about that, we don't know for certain what else he did. The rest is supposition and rumour and whatever may be twisting away inside your gut."

"Isn't that all it often is?"

Skelton nodded. "Agreed. But before we can do anything, we need something more substantial. Because if you are right, the last thing we want to do is give him the same kind of get-out we just handed to Kilpatrick."

Resnick nodded and got to his feet. "Kid gloves, sir."

"Better be."

Outside in the corridor, Suzanne Olds was taking a break from the interview room, smoking a cigarette. A tall woman wearing a light grey tailored suit, an expensive leather bag hanging from one shoulder, she watched Resnick's approach with interest, one eyebrow quizzically crooked. Head down, Resnick walked past, only just hearing the solicitor's quiet "I see crash courses in terrorising the innocent are back in the manual." He didn't turn, didn't falter; in the CID room he left instructions that Graham Millington should under no circumstances leave the station without seeing him first. The kettle was warm and he made himself coffee, taking it into his office with the intention of reviewing his conversations with Stephen Shepperd. Unwillingly, he found himself thinking of Vivien Nathanson instead; of the poem she had read. Reluctantly, he opened the drawer and took out the book, turning to the page. Infinite, unfathomable desires.

39

Lorraine had spoken to her mother three times that day; Michael had called twice from work, the second occasion on a portable phone that had kept breaking up, reducing his conversation to a sequence of barely related sounds. The same person claiming to represent one of the national tabloids had offered her fifteen thousand for her story of a young mum's grief, conditional on exclusivity, a thousand now, four more when the body was found, the remainder on publication. As usual, Val Patterson called round for a coffee and a chat, stayed long enough to eat half a packet of Lorraine's chocolate digestives—"The last one, I swear, not doing a thing for my figure"—and smoke her own cigarettes—"Last one, I swear it, ruining my lungs." The assistant manager at the bank had rung to see how she was—"No, you stay out, stay at home until you feel you want to come back in. Your decision, your decision absolutely." Lorraine had tried to speak to Lynn Kellogg at the police station, either her or Inspector Resnick, but both had been busy. She had taken down the curtains in the bedroom in order to reline them, something she had been meaning to do for ages, and now they lay in swirls around the sewing machine, unpicked and, since then, untouched.

When the doorbell sounded, her first thought was that it was Michael, home early, although, as she hurried down the stairs, why hadn't he got his key? She blinked at the woman she found standing there, not recognising her, shorn of context, as one of Emily's teachers.

"Mrs. Morrison, Joan Shepperd. I hope you don't mind my calling?"

"Oh. No. Of course not. I . . ."

"I was going to sooner. I wanted to, only . . ."

The two stood there looking at one another self-consciously, for all the world like mother and daughter. "Please," Lorraine said, stepping back, "won't you come in?"

"Thank you, I didn't mean . . ."

"No, please, come in."

While Lorraine boiled the kettle for tea, Joan Shepperd passed complimentary remarks about the house, the neatness of the kitchen, the pattern on the china, wondering all the while just why it was she had come, what, exactly, she was hoping to find.

"Emily was a . . ." she began, stumbling to correct herself. "She is a bright child, interested in everything. Since the term began, you can really see the progress."

Lorraine smiled a reply.

"Nothing's been heard?"

"I'm afraid not."

"And you've no idea . . . ?"

"Not really. None at all."

Joan tasted the tea, asked Lorraine about Michael, about Emily's mother. "She's in hospital," Lorraine said. "She's not been well for some time. I don't think she knows what's happened."

When Joan Shepperd looked up, tears were sliding down Lorraine's face. "I'm sorry," Joan said. "I really shouldn't have come. It was thoughtless of me, it's only upsetting you."

"No," Lorraine shaking her head, "I'm afraid I do this all the time. Sometimes, I don't even notice." She pulled a crumpled tissue from her pocket and began opening it out. "I went to pay the window cleaner yesterday and the same thing happened; he stood there, looking at me gone out. I just hadn't realised."

She dabbed her cheeks and patted her eyes, blew her nose and asked Joan Shepperd if she wanted another cup of tea.

"No, thank you. That was lovely." She surprised herself by reaching for Lorraine's hand. "I wanted you to know how sorry I am, about Emily. I do think about her a lot."

Tears returned to Lorraine's eyes and she moved away to stand by the sink, turning on the tap so that the water dribbled out. *Emily was;*

Michael had said the same himself only last night, there in that room. *Emily was.* Was it only the police, then, who thought there was some chance she might yet be found alive? Or were they, too, merely going through the motions, unable to admit what in their hearts and minds they knew, that wherever she now was, Emily was surely dead?

"It can't go on."

"I don't know what you mean."

"Like this. Ignoring me."

Stephen was standing at his workbench, in the cellar, back towards the stairs. "I'm not ignoring you, I'm working."

Joan looked at the fleshiness of his neck, the breadth of his shoulders, hunching forward, despising him. Promises he had made and broken.

"What did the police say?"

"Nothing."

"Then what happened this afternoon?"

"Nothing. They made me stand in a parade, a line of men to see if this woman recognised me."

"Which woman?"

"I don't know. How should I know? Anyway, it was all a mistake."

"What do you mean?"

Turning now to face her, swivelling from the waist. "What I said, she didn't recognise me. She couldn't. I wasn't there."

"Where?"

Stephen had swung back again and was reaching towards the bench. "I was swimming," he said, and bent over his bench, working the wood steadily until he heard his wife's feet moving away, the door closing. There was something so special about the touch of newly turned wood, its smoothness, the slight warmth left from the lathe, like blood beneath young skin.

The Partridge was busy enough for all the seats to be taken, both bars with groups standing, the occasional lone drinker nursing his pint of mixed between both hands. It had been Vivien's suggestion, a pub she knew and sometimes used, one which had long been a favourite of Resnick's, one of the diminishing few where all attempt at conversation wasn't lost to karaoke and disco. They found a space near the rear wall between a group of adult education students practising their Spanish—

how did you ask for a pint of mild and a packet of cheese and onion crisps in Madrid?—and the usual collection from the Poly, wearing Oxfam overcoats and wingeing on about the cost of CDs and how difficult it was to get decently pissed on a grant.

"I used to teach a class round the corner," Vivien said.

"Canadian Studies?"

"Not exactly. Women and Utopia. Or was it Utopias? I can't remember."

She was wearing a green cord skirt and a rust-coloured sweater with a crew neck; a light cotton coat hung open from her shoulders. She had surprised Resnick, who had almost gone ahead and ordered a dry white wine, by asking for vodka and tonic.

"You don't work there anymore, then?"

She shook her head. "I was just filling in. Working at the university part-time and waiting for somebody to move on or die."

Resnick smiled. "I've got a sergeant who's a bit like that."

Vivien drank some more of her vodka. "I'm sorry about this afternoon. That's why I wanted to see you. Apologise."

"No need."

"You were angry."

"I was disappointed."

"Do you think he's the one? I mean, do you think he's responsible? Whatever's happened to the girl."

"Who?"

"Number three."

A little of Resnick's beer spilled over his hand, began to drip towards the floor. "You did recognise him."

"No. I didn't. Not really. Otherwise I would have said."

"Then what did you mean, number three?"

"Well . . ." More vodka. "He was the one who looked like the man I saw the most, no doubting that."

"Then I don't see why . . ."

"Yes, you do. I had to be positive. I had to be prepared to go into court . . ."

"Not necessarily."

"But quite probably. And say, under oath, that was the man. What use, if all I could say was, 'Well, I think it was,' or, 'It might have been'?"

Resnick sighed and supped some beer. To his left one of the party had taken out her snapshots of Barcelona and was passing them round.

"You're telling me now."

"That's different."

"Is it?"

"Will you arrest him because of what I'm telling you now?"

"Probably not."

"And if I'd picked him out this afternoon?"

Resnick looked across the room. "More than likely."

Vivien drained her glass. "Besides," she said, "it's not exactly a fair system."

"Whyever not?"

"The perspiration coming off that man this afternoon, he was scared half out of his wits. None of the others was anything but bored."

Resnick finished his beer. "Another?" he said, expecting her to say no. But she handed him her glass and let him shoulder his way through to the bar to buy a second round. Maybe that was one of the things about women and Utopias? Men waiting on them hand and foot, always sodding off to pay for the drinks.

Her flat was high up in one of those vast Victorian houses near the city centre, dormer windows pushing out from the shallow slope of roof. The main room she had painted white, tall walls without decoration save for pictures no more than postcard size, black-and-white photographs or etchings, each mounted inside a considerably larger frame.

"My colleagues laugh at me," Vivien said. "Accuse me of trying to re-create Canada right here at home."

Resnick had been surprised when she had suggested he call in for coffee; from her expression, she was almost equally surprised when he accepted. As it turned out, she hadn't brought her car. "I thought I might get you to drive me home," she said, "sooner or later."

She put on some music, a woman singing something classical, but low enough that it didn't matter. There were fewer books than Resnick had anticipated and those were scattered in half-neat piles around the floor. A round table beneath the window was covered in piles of papers, photocopied articles, magazines. Aside from a low two-seater settee, the only chairs were wood and canvas, painted black. The television, if there was one, Resnick guessed to be in the bedroom; he wondered if that room was as austere.

Coffee came in tall, narrow cups, black on the outside, white within.

"Milk or sugar?"

Resnick shook his head.

Vivien sat opposite him on the settee, legs pulled up beneath her skirt. "Nobody you should be rushing back to?" she asked.

To say only the cats smacked of self-pity. "No," Resnick said.

"Isn't there some kind of appalling statistic about the number of police marriages which end in divorce?"

"Is there?"

She could tell from the sharpness of his voice that she'd started down the wrong track, but retreat wasn't a tactic she was used to employing. "You were married?"

"A long time ago."

"Long enough to have children?"

His face said it all. No need for words and Resnick was staring back across the room at her, not saying a thing. He finished his coffee and stood up. Was he angrier with her for asking or himself for getting so instantly, so irreversibly upset?

"Look," Vivien said, "it's meeting people in classes, tutorials, some weeks I swear it's the only talking I do. It gets you out of practice for normal conversation."

"That's all right," Resnick said. "It's probably good for me to be on the other side of an interrogation for a change."

"Is that really what it was?"

"Why don't we just forget about it?" he said, leaving Vivien standing there, a coffee cup and saucer in either hand.

40

"I went to see the Morrisons yesterday afternoon."

Stephen's spoon hovered short of his mouth, Joan behind him, close to his right shoulder, still warm from her bath, wearing her dressing gown.

"After school. The father wasn't there, but the mother, I talked to the mother, told her how upset I was, we all were, at the school. Not her mother, really, stepmother, but even so." She passed in front of Stephen, reaching for the cereal packet on the shelf. "The dreadful time that young woman's been going through. She didn't seem to be able to stop crying. Terrible."

Stephen, head bowed, carried on chewing his prunes.

"I'm surprised you haven't been, Stephen . . ."

"Me? Why should I . . . ?"

"It's not as though you didn't know Emily."

"I suppose I knew who she was."

"I always thought she was one of your favourites."

Stephen staring at her now, not eating, breakfast forgotten.

"One of the ones you always made a point of talking to. Well, she was certainly a pretty girl, everyone said. I mean, you weren't alone in noticing that."

Stephen twisted round on his chair. What did she think she was playing at, sitting there with her bowl of Fruit and Fibre, chattering on, matter-of-fact?

"You should go, Stephen. Why not this morning? I've got one or two little bits of shopping to do, you could go then. Walk over, if you didn't want to take the car. It's not far, the other side of Gregory Street; but I keep forgetting, you know that."

Without his meaning it to, one of Stephen's hands jerked out, overturning his bowl, prune stones and juice across the Formica-covered table, spoon skittering to the linoleum-covered floor.

"A nice house, where the Morrisons live, garden front and back. Quite a view of the rear garden from the road, lawn mostly; I suppose with both of the parents working they don't have a great deal of time to do much else. And besides, it must make a lovely space for Emily to play." She dabbed at the corners of her mouth with a paper napkin. "Don't you think so, Stephen?"

Stephen was running water at the sink, fidgeting cutlery through his hands, spoons, forks, knives. A dribble of sweat ran from his eyebrow into the corner of his eye.

"So much nicer for Emily than anywhere that other poor little soul had to play. Aside from the rec, of course. I always wonder, don't you, Stephen, what they can get up to, cooped up in one of those tall flats with only a balcony to run along? Balcony and, I suppose, the stairs."

A spiral of blood ribboned up from where the tine of the fork had pierced Stephen's thumb, staining the water pink.

"What was her name, Stephen? You remember, that pretty blonde child? The one you were so taken with."

But Stephen was no longer there to answer. Door slam after door slam and finally the bolt inside the cellar workroom being drawn across. Joan Shepperd drained the soiled water from the sink and ran new, never liking to get on with the rest of the day before the breakfast things were washed and stacked away. Gloria, that was right, Gloria Summers. She had known all along.

Since the new greengrocer's had opened where the butcher's used to be, Joan Shepperd seldom bothered to shop further afield in the week. With three Asian shops, each staying open late into the evening, it was always possible to pop back out for anything she might have forgotten. This morning it was tomatoes, a pound of apples, easier now it was all right to buy South African, orange juice, a book of stamps from the post office, second-class. She couldn't believe that she was feeling this calm. Lying awake in the night, listening to Stephen, his even breathing beside her, undisturbed, sleeping the sleep of the just. Lorraine Morrison's face, her tears. She had to wait for the telephone, two kiosks but only one of them functioning, nothing new. "Hello," she said, connected, "I'd like to speak to a Detective Constable Kellogg. Yes, that's right, Lynn."

"You sure it was her? Shepperd's wife?"

"She didn't say. Like I said, wouldn't leave a name. But, yes, I'm pretty sure. Though I only spoke to her the once."

"Well." Resnick brushed crumbs from his front as he stood, a toasted ham and cheese filling the gap between breakfast and lunch. "For now that's not the most important thing. The most important thing is the information, right?"

Lynn nodded. "I called the education office and checked. You'd have thought I was asking them to divulge state secrets, but finally we got there: Joan Shepperd was at Gloria Summers's school for most of the summer term before she disappeared. On supply. Gloria's regular teacher went abseiling in Derbyshire and broke her leg in three places."

"Joan Shepperd stepped into the breach."

"She'd worked there before, two years previously. Seems they were pleased to have her back. Experienced, reliable."

"An otherwise unemployed husband, who's got a way with a hammer and nails." Resnick looked at Lynn sharply. "I wonder if he drove her to work there, too? Collected her?"

"I could check."

"Do it now."

Resnick followed Lynn into the main office. "Kevin," he called. "Downstairs with a car, five minutes."

At first, they couldn't get anyone to come to the door, though the intermittent whine of an electrical motor told them someone was in the house. When Stephen Shepperd finally appeared, he was wearing his old white coveralls, a bandage taped around the end of his left thumb.

"Thought that was the thing separated out you professionals from amateurs like me," Resnick said, nodding towards Shepperd's hand, "never hit themselves with a hammer."

Shepperd looked from Resnick to Naylor and back again, saying nothing.

"Maybe you should nip back down," Resnick said, "make sure everything's switched off. If she's not here, you might want to leave your wife a note."

"Are you arresting me?" Shepperd asked.

"Should we be?"

A nerve began ticking at the far corner of Stephen Shepperd's eye.

"What we'd like you to do," Resnick said, "is come with us to the station, answer some more questions."

"Why can't I do that here?"

"You're not frightened of us, Mr. Shepperd? Nothing about the way you were treated yesterday?"

"No, but . . ."

"No special call to be worried about anything we might ask?"

"No, of course not, but . . ."

"Then we'll just wait here while you do whatever it is you need to do."

Shepperd hesitated beyond the moment when he might have refused; he turned back into the house, hand reaching out to close the door behind him, but Naylor got there first.

"No need to shut that, Mr. Shepperd," Naylor said. "I'm sure you won't be that long."

Lynn Kellogg intercepted Resnick on the stairs, drew him off to one side while Naylor escorted Shepperd towards the interview room. "Drove her there every day, there and back, regular as clockwork. The staff used to remark on it, tease her a little the head said, how she had her husband so well trained. 'Lend him to me for the weekend, Joan, so's he can do a few odd jobs for me.' That kind of thing."

"And did he do a few odd jobs for the school?"

"Wonderful, the head teacher reckons. Repaired equipment, all sorts. Got so she started to feel quite guilty about it, wanted to give him something out of the school fund. Wouldn't accept a penny. Said helping them out, that was reward enough."

"Right." Resnick nodded. "But maybe not quite enough."

He made to move on, but Lynn detained him with a touch on the arm. "Seems there was this one occasion, sir. Mrs. Shepperd got held up, talking to a parent in her classroom after school. Head happened to pass through the cloakroom and there were three or four children still hanging around. Shepperd was there, talking to them. No suggestion of anything, you know, at all funny. Wrong. But she does think Gloria Summers was one of them."

"She *thinks*?"

"She can't remember for certain."

"Did she say anything about this at the time?"

"No, sir. Didn't seem important, I suppose. Relevant."

"Fax that drawing out to Mablethorpe. Wherever the nearest station is with a fax machine. Get someone to take it round to Mrs. Summers, see if she can remember him hanging around the school, talking to Gloria."

Lynn nodded and was on her way. By the time Resnick got to the interview room, Stephen Shepperd was sitting at the table, staring at the burn marks left by a score of cigarettes. Naylor was slipping a pair of fresh tapes into the machine.

"Do we have to use that?" Shepperd asked, looking towards the recorder. "I hate those things."

"Keeps an accurate record of what's said," Resnick explained. "More reliable than struggling to get it all written down. Quicker, too. In your interests, I'd say."

Shepperd wiped the palms of his hands along the legs of his trousers and, for a moment, closed his eyes. When he opened them again, Resnick was standing immediately before him, directly across the table. "We're going to ask you some questions relating to the disappearance of Emily Morrison, Mr. Shepperd, also to the murder of Gloria Summers."

Shepperd's hands ceased to move, gripped his thighs.

"As I told you before, you are not under arrest at this time. Which means you have the right to leave at any time you choose. It also means if you wish to have a solicitor present or want to obtain legal advice, you're free to do so. Do you understand all of that?"

Drawing in air through his mouth, Stephen Shepperd nodded.

"In that case," Resnick continued, "I am cautioning you that you do not have to say anything in relation to these matters unless you wish to do so, but what you do say may, at some later stage, be given in evidence. All right, Mr. Shepperd? Stephen?"

Using his fingers to still the nerve that had begun to beat again alongside his head, Stephen Shepperd murmured, "All right."

Joan put the tomatoes and the orange juice in the fridge, the apples into a bowl. She took one of the stamps from the book and stuck it to the corner of the envelope that was addressed and waiting, a letter to her friend in Redruth, just about the only friend from college with whom she still kept in touch. Stephen's note was on the table, held down by a jar of basil he had taken from the shelf. She read it with neither surprise nor passion. She knew that she had let things slide for far too long, taken assurances at face value, looked the other way, she could acknowledge that. Well, now matters must take their course. The tranquilisers her doctor had prescribed that autumn she had never taken, not until last night, and she thought she might take another now, swill it down with some water before her mid-morning cup of tea. One: maybe even two.

41

"Michael!" Lorraine had called. "Michael! Michael!" From the foot of the stairs, the landing, finally a foot inside the bedroom door. Michael Morrison broke from his heavy, sweated sleep thinking that the urgency and the clamour were due to news about Emily, but one look at Lorraine's face was sufficient to give a lie to that. He groaned and slumped back down, hauling the covers over his head.

"Michael, you'll be late for work."

From beneath the duvet came sounds she deciphered as "That's because I'm not going to bloody work!"

The cup of tea she'd brought him up half an hour earlier sat beside the bed, untouched and close to cold. The room smelled of drink and cigarettes: Michael sitting up till past twelve watching videos he'd fetched from the corner store, one after another, end to end. Finally, he'd insisted on hooking up the VCR to the portable set they kept in the bedroom, sitting propped against the pillows with the umpteenth bottle of wine by his side, an ashtray in between his legs, watching something loud and dreadful with Eddie Murphy.

Lorraine had lain with her back to him, telling herself over and over to remember what had happened, that we all dealt with trauma in our different ways; telling herself why it was she had married him. Trying to remember.

She had slept fitfully, disturbed by the sound of punches being faked, by Michael's occasional laughter and later his trips to the bathroom; by dreams in which Emily was on a train pulling away from the station and she, Lorraine, was somehow trapped outside, screaming, banging her fists against her stepdaughter's bewildered face at the other side of the glass. In the morning there were ash and cigarette butts on the carpet, wine stains on the bed. Michael's hair lay flattened like tar across his head. Emily's picture smiled down at them from the top of the chest of drawers: soon it would be a week.

When Michael finally appeared it was ten minutes short of eleven. Lorraine was sitting in the living room at the back of the house, scissoring recipes she intended to make from magazines. On the low table was the scrapbook she had bought to put them in, the paste.

"My mouth feels like a toilet," Michael said.

"Serves you right," said Lorraine, deciding to pass over Cod Mornay.

"Bitch," Michael said, heading for the kitchen.

Diplomatically, Lorraine decided she hadn't heard him.

When the doorbell sounded, she was spreading her recipes out along the table, considering the order; Michael was drinking instant coffee with sugar, waiting for the sliced bread to pop up from the toaster. Both arrived at the front door at roughly the same time.

"Hello," said the woman in green duffle coat and glasses. "You don't know me, but I'm Jacqueline Verdon. Jackie. I'm a friend of Diana's."

"My Diana?" said Michael, surprised.

"Well," Jackie Verdon said, "not anymore."

"She's not . . . ?"

"Oh, no. She's all right. I didn't mean . . . I just meant it was a funny way to describe her. Yours."

"Won't you come in?" said Lorraine, stepping back.

"Yes. Yes, I would like to. Thanks very much. Thanks."

"Live round here, do you?" Michael asked. Something inside his head seemed to reverberate each time he spoke.

Jackie shook her head. "West Yorkshire. Hebden Bridge. I've a book shop there. You know, secondhand."

"Oh, I thought when you said you were a friend of Diana's . . ."

"We met up on a walking holiday. Not a holiday, really. A weekend. In the Lakes. B and B, guided tours, that kind of thing."

"I never knew Diana was much interested in walking."

"No, well, I daresay there's quite a lot you don't know about Diana. Oh, I'm sorry, that sounds dreadful. I didn't mean to be so . . . I didn't intend to be rude."

" 'S fine," Michael said huffily.

"It's just that over the last six months or so, Diana's gone through a lot of changes. Started to take some control of her life."

"Which is why she's back in hospital, I suppose?"

"Maybe she pushed a little too fast too soon; maybe I tried pushing her too fast, I don't know. But what's happening now, I think it's temporary. Not even a step back; one to the side. I think Diana's going to be fine."

"You do?"

"I've seen her recently. Today. Have you?"

"I've had other things on my mind."

"I know. And I'm sorry. But Emily is Diana's child, too."

Lorraine came through with coffee and two kinds of biscuits, chocolate digestive and lemon creams. There were some polite inquiries about milk and sugar, some discussion of the onset of Christmas, how it seemed to start earlier each year, a little nonconversation about the weather.

"Does Diana *know*?" Michael asked.

"About Emily? No. And it's important that she doesn't. Not yet. Not now. That's the principal reason I'm here. The hospital has been very good about keeping her sheltered from the newspapers, anything like that. Of course, they can't do that forever and when Diana herself is feeling stronger, well, it simply wouldn't be possible." Jackie Verdon looked at them and smiled. "By that time, of course, Emily might well be safe and sound." She breathed out deeply. "If she's not, I think I should be the one to break it to her."

Michael glanced at Lorraine, began to say something but couldn't choose the words.

"I think it's fair to say I'm the closest to her now. Aside from Emily herself. I want you to agree that it's all right for me to tell her, that you won't go in and do it yourself. Afterwards, of course, if that's what Diana wants, it's only natural that it's something you should share."

"Look," Michael snorted, "you've got a hell of a nerve. Waltzing in here, laying down the law about what I can and can't say to someone you've known less than six months."

"How long were you married to Diana?"

"Never mind."

"And you think you knew her? In that time, you think you spent a lot of time and energy getting to know Diana?"

"Of course I bloody did!"

"When it was all over I doubt if you knew the size of her shoes or the colour of her eyes, never mind anything that really mattered."

The way Michael got to his feet, Jackie Verdon was convinced he was going to hit her; she rocked back in her chair, arms thrown up to protect her face. By the time she had lowered them, Michael was on his way from the room.

Jackie and Lorraine looked at one another across the overlapping circle of digestives and lemon creams.

"I'm really sorry," Jackie said. "I don't know what got into me. I should never, ever have said that."

"Michael's been under a lot of strain."

"Of course. It's just, with Diana, I get so protective. You know?" Lorraine nodded. "I think so."

Jackie reached for her hands. "There's no news about Emily?"

Lorraine withdrew her hands, shook her head.

"I wish there was something I could say."

"There isn't."

Jackie gave her a printed card. "I'm staying there for the next few days, till Monday or Tuesday of next week. If anything does happen, please let me know. If I think, after talking to the doctor, that Diana's up to it, I'll tell her about Emily before I go back to Yorkshire. Tell her something anyway." She looked away. "Prepare her, I suppose, for the worst."

Lorraine walked her to the door. The TV had been switched on upstairs, a rerun of an old Western series, the rigours of family life on the frontier.

"Tell your husband, tell Michael, I apologise for what I said. He's more than enough to cope with to have to put up with my jealousy and bad temper."

"Jealousy?"

"All that time when, even though they'd parted, Diana was still tied to Michael, emotionally. Time I would have wanted her with me."

She brushed her cheek against Lorraine's and opened the front door. "I hope there's news of Emily soon, good news."

Lorraine stood there, watching Jacqueline Verdon until she was out of sight, closing the door only then and wandering off into the living room to collect the coffee things, thinking about the relationship, Diana's and Jackie's, how protective, how fiercely caring the older woman had seemed. She knew she should go upstairs to Michael now, even if it was simply to sit with him and watch the movement of horses, dogs and men, hold, if that was what he wanted, Michael's hand. You'll live to regret it, her mother had said, you mark my words. But she could never, Lorraine thought, not even bothering to stem the tears, never ever have meant this.

42

Naylor negotiated the tray without spilling overmuch: two teas and a coffee, sugar, packets of UHT milk, plastic spoons. Resnick was by the window, looking out. Shepperd had barely moved in his chair, shoulders slumped forward, arms extended between his legs, fingers touching but not entwined. Not long into the first session, Resnick had felt Shepperd becoming overanxious, words stumbling into one another, the accelerated tremor near the eye, the sweat. Either he was about to shut down altogether, refuse to answer, or start asking for a solicitor, legal representation. There and then, Resnick wanted neither.

"How's the tea, Stephen?" Sitting opposite him, the pair of them, Naylor's chair pulled slightly further back and round.

"Stephen? Tea?"

"Fine."

"Good." Resnick grimaced at his own coffee, decided adding milk was the better part of valour. He angled his eyes towards Naylor and the tape machine. "All right, then, Stephen, what do you say we push on?"

No reply.

Naylor set the mechanism in motion, twin tapes beginning to wind on simultaneously. "This interview," Resnick said, "continued at eleven forty-seven. The same officers present." He shuffled back in his chair, wanting to appear relaxed, needing to be comfortable. "Let's forget about Emily Morrison for a while; let's talk about Gloria instead."

Shepperd's body jerked. "I've already told you . . ."

"Not about Gloria, Stephen."

"I've told you, I don't know her."

"Gloria."

"Yes."

"But you know who we mean?"

Shepperd's head was lowered towards the table, his voice indistinct. "You mean the girl who was . . . who was killed."

"That's right. Gloria Summers."

"I don't know her."

"But she was in your wife's class."

"Not for long."

"Sorry?"

"She wasn't there for long, Joan. She was hardly there any time at all."

"Half a term."

"No."

"According to the head teacher, your wife taught there for almost half a term. What's that? Six weeks? Eight?"

Shepperd was shaking his head strongly. "She was never there that length of time, never."

"But while she was there, however long, you went with her, to the school."

"I drove her, yes, usually. She can't drive."

"You carried her things inside."

"No."

"Never?"

"Not hardly."

"All those things infant teachers take with them: egg boxes and cartons and pictures and heaven knows what else. I can't see you just sitting in the car and watching your wife struggle with all of that on her own."

"All right, I helped, sometimes, when there was a need, I helped."

"And you helped around the school as well." Resnick brisker now, beginning, lightly, to bear down. "The head teacher could scarcely stop singing your praises. All of that free time you put in, the expertise. So much there was even talk of a presentation . . ."

"There wasn't any presentation."

"Only because you declined."

"There wasn't any presentation."

"They considered what you'd done worthy of one. They were deeply grateful. Equipment mended, new pegs in the cloakrooms . . ."

"Look, what I did, it was nothing. Took me no time at all. That's why I wasn't having them give me anything for it."

Resnick realised that he was sitting too far forward, arms on the table; slowly, he levered himself back and smiled. "You're a modest man, Stephen. You don't like people to make a fuss."

Shepperd looked at the ceiling, slowly closed his eyes.

"When, later on, after your wife had left the school, when Gloria disappeared, all that in the papers, everyone talking about it, your wife talking about it as she must have been, you did know who they meant?"

Shepperd's hands were back between his legs, wrists locked tight.

"When she talked to you about it, you knew who she meant?"

"Of course I did."

"You did know her, then?"

"Not know her, no, but when she said Gloria, course then I knew who it was."

"You remembered her?"

"Her picture was everywhere. You could hardly look in a shop window in town without it was there."

"And you didn't recall her from the school, your wife's class?"

"No, not specially."

"I wonder, Stephen, can you remember what she looked like now?"

"What for? I mean, I don't see the point, I . . ."

"What did she look like, Stephen? Gloria?"

The nerve at the side of his head had started to tick again. "She was, I don't know, how would you describe her? Pretty, I suppose. Fair hair, sort of long. I don't know what else there is to say."

"Pretty, though, you would say that?"

"Yes."

"Prettier than Emily Morrison?"

"What?"

"I said was she prettier than Emily Morrison? You know, of the two of them, which one would you say was the more attractive? Which did you prefer?"

"Now you're being stupid. You think you're being clever, but you're being stupid. Playing games."

"What kind of games, Stephen? What kind of games are these?"

"You know damn well."

"Then tell me."

"Trying to trick me, that's what you're doing. Trick me into admitting something that isn't true."

"Admitting, Stephen? What do you think I want you to admit? That you find one girl prettier than another? Hardly a crime."

"All right," Shepperd said, pushing his chair back from the table, standing. "All right, that's enough."

Resnick and Naylor looked back up at him, neither responding.

"You asked me about Emily and I agreed, yes, I knew who she was, once or twice I'd talked to her in Joan's class. You've tried all manner of ways to get me to say I was near her house on the day she went missing and it hasn't worked because I just wasn't there. And now you want me to say I knew this Gloria, like I knew Emily, and it isn't true. It isn't. And that's all there is to it. I'm not going to talk about it anymore. And you said, you can't make me. Not without you arresting me, isn't that what you said?"

Resnick signalled to Naylor to switch off the tape.

"I'm asking you now," Shepperd said, "is that what you're going to do?"

"Not now," Resnick said. "Not yet."

"Christ, that was stupid! So bloody . . . he even said it himself, Shepperd, think you're being clever, but you're being stupid, and, God, he was right. I pushed, I prodded him too hard and in the wrong direction and what I got was the opposite of what I wanted. Now he's not going to give us a thing without us arresting him and we can't arrest him unless he gives us more than we've already got. Jesus, what a mess!"

Skelton walked round from his desk towards the coffee machine. "The wife, Charlie. That's where it is. The answer. If she's the one who phoned."

"We don't know that for certain."

Skelton shrugged. "Kellogg seemed pretty sure. You've got to talk to her at least. Meantime, get this down you."

Resnick accepted the mug of coffee, holding it between both hands.

"If it is him, Charlie, Shepperd; if it's him and you're right, you know what that means for the Morrison girl?"

Nodding slowly, Resnick closed his eyes. The coffee Skelton had given him was stale and bitter and he drank it down, every mouthful.

Diana had made a point of asking Jacqueline to fetch the photo albums and the scrapbooks from home and eventually there were no other excuses to be made. Although she'd learned the truth, a version of it, from neighbours eager to outdo one another with tales about a drunken husband, ambulances, police and knives, Jacqueline elected for a lie: some youths had broken in and left the place in a bit of mess, next to nothing taken. Together, she and Diana sat in a corner of the day room, setting the books back as close as possible to how they'd been.

"Do you think," Diana asked, holding a picture of Emily in one hand, "once I'm a little better, Michael will let her come to see me?"

"I hope so," Jackie said, inclining her face away. "I think he should."

Diana smiled. Of course, that was the way it had to be. After all, wasn't it because of Emily that she was here? Because she wanted it to be all right between them; a precaution she had had to take to ensure nothing went wrong.

"Who's this?" Jackie asked. "I thought it was Michael at first, but now I can see it's not."

Diana took the photograph and looked: a man sitting on a painted horse, a roundabout at the fair. Emily with her legs around the horse's neck in front of him. In the whirl of movement, one thing is clear, the joy on the girl's face as she angles back her head to laugh at the man behind her, holding her safe, her laughter and his smile.

"Geoffrey," she said.

"Who?"

"Michael's brother, Geoffrey. He used to come over every year, from where he lives, the Isle of Man, just to take Emily to Goose Fair." Diana smiled again. She was smiling a lot today, Jacqueline noticed, the way she did when they were in Yorkshire; she took it as a good sign. "He couldn't have been nicer to Emily if she'd been his own. I think Michael used to get quite jealous sometimes, but then isn't that the way it always is, with brothers?"

"Men." Jackie laughed. "Any men will do. Brothers enough, most of them, beneath the skin."

Although they lived close by, Joan Shepperd hardly ever went into the rec. Oh, cutting through between Church Street and the Derby Road, especially if it was a nice day. But seldom to sit, as she was now, a bench down by the bowling green, near where the magnolia tree would blossom so beautifully in the spring. Such a shame it never lasted long. Some years one good wind was all it would take.

She could hear the voices of children from the swings, two sets now, the one beside the green, the other further up towards the gate. Always children there, it hardly seemed to matter the weather. A lot of them knowing her, of course, calling out if she passed by. "Mrs. Shepperd! Mrs. Shepperd! Miss! Miss!" Older children playing rounders, football. Men in track suits lapping round the path, circuit upon circuit, timing themselves. Others, like Stephen, not out to break any records, content simply to jog slowly, watch whatever was going on.

When she saw Resnick walking towards her, rounding the edge of the bowling green, raincoat flapping shapelessly about him, her first instinct was to look away, pretend that if she didn't notice him, then he would never recognise her. But she knew it was too late for that; knew, unlike the children she taught, that when you took your hands away from your face and opened your eyes, the bogeyman would not have disappeared.

Resnick sat alongside her, pulling his coat free. For some little time, neither spoke. Behind them, a sprinter train carried a fortunate few towards Mansfield, a town Resnick only visited when County were in the same division and playing away. On the last occasion, the snow had clamoured in off the hills aboard a wind that had made a mockery of the game and threatened to cleave Resnick in two. Only by buying pasties, one after the other, and eating them from between gloved hands, had he preserved his fingers from frostbite.

"Somebody contacted us this morning," Resnick said, "with some information. It had to do with your work and, by inference, your husband."

Joan Shepperd continued to watch a mother pushing her child, no more than three, back and forth on one of the swings. The same repetitive rhythm.

"It was helpful, of course it was. We were truly grateful. Only I'm not sure it's going to be enough."

The mother was careful, Joan noticed, never to let the swing sail too high so that the child might become frightened, never to push it too hard.

"I would never give evidence against my husband, Inspector, even if I were convinced he had done wrong. Even if he had done terrible things. I could never bring myself to do that. Not in court and not to you. I'm sorry."

Resnick sat there several moments longer, testing all the questions he might further ask inside his head. When he was sure none of them was right, he got to his feet and walked away.

43

This was the bit of the city Raymond hated most, from Millets and Marks all the way down to where Sara worked, past C&A. And as the week wore on it got worse. What with the veggie lot outside the church, pushing petitions in your face about political prisoners or factory farming, all the lefties expecting you to pay good money for a paper that didn't have sport or tell you what was on tele, and then the cranks carrying placards and reading from the Bible, it was a regular nightmare. "Whole bloody lot of them," his dad said, "want locking up." Raymond didn't usually go a bomb on what his father had to say, but in this case he'd got it about right.

He didn't spot Sara at first, disappointed, thinking maybe she'd taken the day off, but then there she was, coming into the shop from the storeroom at the back. Raymond waited till she was refilling the sections before going inside.

Sara, who'd already seen him, seen him through the glass, carried on with what she was doing, even when he was standing at her shoulder.

"What's going on?" Raymond asked.

"What d'you mean?"

"Why aren't you talking to us?"

"You can see," using the metal scoop to round out the strawberry delights, "I'm doing this." Turning to face him: "Raymond, I'm busy."

"I was only saying hello."

"Hello."

"Seemed stupid hanging around at home, you know, I was ready. I thought I'd come and see you, hang around outside."

Sara glanced over at the manageress, who was watching them with a face like alabaster; she moved along three bins and began to restock the old-fashioned bull's-eyes. "There's no need you waiting around anyway," she said.

"I thought we were going out?"

"Yes, well, we're not."

"What d'you mean?"

"Raymond, keep your voice down, do."

"You said tonight was all right."

"So it was. Only now it's not."

"Why not?"

"I've got to help my mum."

Raymond grabbed hold of her arm. "You mean you don't want to see me. That's it, isn't it? Except you haven't got the guts to come right out and say it."

The manageress was coming towards them, a beeline across the floor; Raymond's fingers were poking hard into Sara's arm and she was sure they'd left a bruise already.

"Sara?" the manageress called.

"Tomorrow," Sara said. "After work tomorrow. I promise. Now go. Go."

"Sara," the manageress said, "you know we have a rule about this sort of thing."

"Yes, Miss Trencher," Sara said, colouring visibly.

Miss Trencher, Raymond thought, was an ugly cow in need of a good shagging. From behind, face down in a tub of tripes. Hands in pockets, Raymond slouched towards the exit, taking his time.

"Is he a friend of yours, Sara?"

"Not really," said Sara, still blushing.

"Because I don't want him in this shop again. Apart from anything else, he smells."

Some days Resnick was happy enough to stand in line at the delicatessen counter while one or another of the assistants chattered in Polish to an elderly man in an ill-fitting suit, a plump woman with a string shopping bag, choosing seven different kinds of sausage and telling the latest about her cousin in Lodz. This particular afternoon, he fretted and fussed and finally interrupted, earning himself no goodwill observing that the sell-by date on marinated herrings might be reached before he got the chance to buy them.

By the time he lowered his carrier bag—half a pound of herring, three-quarters of liver sausage, a quarter of black olives, cheesecake, sour cream—to the floor by the coffee stall and climbed onto his stool, he was in no mood to find Suzanne Olds smiling her supercilious smile from the opposite side of the counter.

"Cappuccino?" asked Marcia, a hefty, good-humoured girl who rode a motorcycle and played bass guitar in a rock band.

"Espresso."

"Small or full?"

"Full."

"I'll get this," Suzanne Olds said, coming round to take the stool alongside him.

"No, it's okay," Resnick said.

Suzanne Olds slid her shoulder bag onto the shelf beneath the counter. "Something to go with it?" she asked, indicating the stacks of doughnuts and scones under their plastic cover.

Resnick shook his head.

"Hmm." She smiled, eying the way his stomach seemed to fold over his waistline. "Probably just as well."

Resnick sat straighter and sucked himself in. Marcia set his espresso in front of him and Suzanne Olds gave her a five-pound note, keeping her hand out for the change. "If my client goes ahead with taking you to court, you might need every penny you possess."

"Kilpatrick?"

"Uh-hum."

"I'm sure you're giving him better advice than that. And besides, from what I hear I doubt if he'd want his sexual preferences all over the news."

Suzanne Olds slowly raised an eyebrow. "I didn't have you marked down as a prude."

Resnick tasted his espresso. "One more mistake," he said.

Suzanne Olds laughed but sensed that probably it was true. In a half-drunken moment once, too much champagne too fast after a famous victory, she had not as much propositioned him as made it clear were he to proposition her, she would be neither shocked nor offended. Resnick had made it clear that their relationship, limited and professional as it was, was already close to the boundaries of what he could take.

"Emily Morrison," Suzanne Olds said. "Still not been found?"

Another shake of the head.

"No closer to getting a lead?"

Gloria's grandmother had thought she'd recognised the drawing of Stephen Shepperd as someone she remembered from the school, but had no sense of ever seeing him with Gloria. The head teacher had been pushed again over the cloakroom incident, with the result that now she was becoming uncertain whether Gloria had been there at all. Lynn Kellogg had met Joan Shepperd at the end of the school day and earned pursed lips and frosty stares. "No," Resnick said. "Not a lot."

He was finishing his espresso as he reached down for his bag. "Thanks for the coffee," he said, hurrying away.

"I'm here to see Debbie," Lynn Kellogg said, Debbie's mother implacable in crimplene on the doorstep.

"Are you a friend?"

"Not exactly. I do know her though."

"You're a friend of Kevin's." It wasn't quite like being accused of carrying a contagious disease, but similar.

"Kevin and I work together, yes."

"I don't think Debbie will want to see you."

Lynn adopted a stance which said she wasn't about to be got rid of easily. "I think she should," she said.

If there had been anywhere to walk to, that's what they would have done, but they sat in Lynn's car instead. Debbie, Lynn thought, was partly pleased to be out of the house, away from her mother, partly disturbed, as if uncertain how she should act, what she should say.

As it grew colder and darker around them, they talked about the baby, about Debbie's attempts to get another part-time job, clothes, anything other than what each knew they were there to talk about.

"How's Kevin?" Lynn said suddenly, right across the middle of something Debbie was saying about teething rings.

"I don't know," she faltered.

"You've seen him though?"

"Once. Only once, recently. It wasn't any good. It was hopeless."

"How d'you mean?"

"We rowed. We just rowed."

"What did you expect?" said Lynn sharply.

"Well . . ."

"Well, what?"

"What's the point, if when we do see one another, after all that time, all we do is fight?"

"Surely, that's because it has been all that time."

"What d'you mean?"

"Look," turning square-on in her seat, an arm close to Debbie's head, "why you split up, reasons, who left who, none of that's my business. But given that's happened, I don't see what you can expect to do but argue. Least, at first."

"Then what's the point?"

"The point is to try and sort things out. Argue them through. Things went wrong. You're not about to fall into one another's arms, lovey-dovey. It's got to be worked at and that's not going to be easy, but it's got to be done." She waited for Debbie to look at her again. "Unless you really do want it to be over. In which case I think you should be honest and say so, get on with getting a divorce."

"No."

"Why not?"

Debbie didn't answer; she looked out of the window instead, at the line of almost identical houses in which lights shone. At a twelve-year-old boy with a red-and-white wool hat, skateboarding along the pavement, rocking himself up and down over the kerb. It was cold enough inside the car for gooseflesh to have formed along the length of her arms; at least, she thought it was the cold.

"He's the baby's father," Lynn said.

"He doesn't act like it."

"Then maybe that's what you should talk about, then give him another chance."

Debbie looked away again, staring straight through the windscreen now, a pretty face with a small mouth and a tiny scar to the left of her chin.

"He came round to see me the other night," Lynn said quietly. "Round to my place, it was late." Debbie was looking at her now, right at her, not missing a look, a word. "Oh, nothing happened. We had coffee, talked. Talked about you. But it could have, and someday soon it will. Not with me, I don't mean that. But someone. And not because Kevin wants that, but he wants somebody. He wants you and he wants the baby and he can't find the way to say it." Lynn smiled. "Debbie, you married him, you know what he's like. He needs your help, he has to know that you want him back and right now all he can see is that you're shutting him out."

Lynn touched Debbie's forearm lightly. "I think you should phone him. One way or another, that's what you ought to do. And Debbie, don't leave it too long."

Almost out of the building, Resnick turned right around and went back up to his office. He found the university number in the book and Vivien's home number also, V. Nathanson, nice and neutral. The other night at her flat he had been a grouch and a bore and it wouldn't hurt him to call her up and tell her so. Apologise and suggest, perhaps, another meeting, another drink.

It took him ten minutes to realise that he was going to do no such thing. Screwing up the piece of paper on which he had written both numbers, Resnick tossed it into his wastebin as he switched out the light.

"Great!" Lynn Kellogg said, stepping into her flat and looking round. "Just great!" There were piles of washing on both of the chairs, waiting to be ironed. Bills behind the clock waiting to be paid and the clock itself had stopped around an hour and twenty minutes earlier, battery run down. On the table were the only two letters she'd received in the past week, both from her mother and both waiting to be answered. She knew without looking that there was a can of Diet Pepsi in the fridge, a wrinkled tube of tomato puree and little else. "Such an authority on other people's lives, it's a shame you can't do something about your own!"

44

Resnick had been lying there for several minutes, awake without fully realising it, slivers of conversation loose inside his head, loose and unattached. *Kerfuffle*. Dizzy, gracing Resnick's bed by virtue of the gathering frost outside, pushed a paw into the sheet over Resnick's arm and began to delve with his claws, purring loudly. Strange word: *kerfuffle*. *All that kerfuffle*. Carefully, he extricated Dizzy's claws and got a nip at his fingers for his pains. The Shepperds opposite him in their front room, explaining why they had missed the Identikit on TV. *My drink*. Who was it, Stephen or Joan? One of their drinks had been knocked over. That was it. Convenient, Resnick remembered thinking, that or the opposite. Their bedtime drink all over the carpet and there, pointed out to him as proof and, yes, he could remember that too, the stain. His own polite expression of regret, made without thinking, the whole business a distraction from the matter at hand. The stain.

"A shame," he had said. And Joan Shepperd had replied, "Yes, we've not long . . . we've not so long had it down."

Resnick was as awake now as he had ever been.

From underneath Gloria Summers's nails, the forensic team had prised tiny pieces of carpet fibre, red and green. Whatever had happened to Gloria, she had struggled against her attacker. Where? On the carpet of that thirties living room, safe behind patterned lace? And if he had attacked her there, the first of many blows? The blood. The stain. *We've not so long had it down.* Resnick wanted to know when. And once the old carpet had been taken up, what had been done with it, where had it gone?

Twenty minutes later, unshaven, pouches around his eyes, Resnick was standing on Skelton's front porch, waiting to be let in.

It's still not light. The two men sit in the small room off the hall that gets called Skelton's study, when it's called anything at all. There are, in fact, shelves of books: a carefully alphabetised collection of professional surveys and memoirs, Alderson and Holdaway, McNee and Whitaker; official reports from the Home Office and the Police Foundation; back issues of *Police* and *Police Review*, correctly bound. There are also, to Resnick's surprise, sections covering motor mechanics, home improvements and Japanese art and culture; less surprisingly, drug abuse and treatment, juvenile offenders, running and diet. The box files in neat order along one side of the floor are labelled Receipts and Insurance, Holidays and Statements. There is a green two-tier filing cabinet: A–N, O–Z. It is into the bottom half of this that Skelton reaches for the bottle, S for scotch or W for whisky, Resnick isn't sure. Either way, he nods as the superintendent holds it over his mug of instant coffee, ready to pour.

"Run it past me, Charlie."

Resnick does so. The suspect had ample opportunity to know both girls, by his own admission did know one of them; his position within the schools, both as someone who did jobs there and through his close association with one of the teachers, made him someone the children would be aware of in some vague official capacity and would be likely to trust. It was an occasional practice to run in the recreation ground where both children were known to have played and from which one of them disappeared. There was a supposition, strong but not definite, that he had been running in the vicinity of the second girl's house at approximately the time she had gone missing. The suspect had denied this, giving an alibi which didn't hold water. Furthermore, someone— possibly the suspect's own wife—had drawn the attention of the police to the fact that he had contact with the first child as well as the second. She had implied that there was evidence she might have against the suspect, although refusing to say what this was. Wasn't it as though she were saying, Look, the answers are here if only you'll look closely enough to find them out?

Skelton tastes his coffee, strengthens it with a touch more scotch. Muffled, from above, the sound of a toilet flushing, his daughter or his wife.

"Warrant, then, Charlie, car as well as the house?"

"Yes," Resnick says, "house and car both."

Just short of seven the cars entered the road, a cold morning, shrouded in darkness and frost. A milk float further along on the opposite side; a nurse peddling past, on her way to begin the morning shift at Queens. Resnick intercepted the paper girl with a smile and, with only a questioning look, she passed the Shepperds' *Telegraph* into his outstretched hand. A nod and Graham Millington knocked sharply on the door, pushed his thumb against the bell and held it there. Inside the house, lights went on, footsteps and anxious voices were heard.

"Mrs. Shepperd . . ."

Joan Shepperd stared out at a half-dozen topcoated men, a single woman, immobile, faint blurs of their breath across the air.

"Mrs. Shepperd," Resnick said, "we have a warrant to search . . ."

Holding her dressing gown close at the collar, she took a step back inside the house and turned aside to let them in.

"Joan, what on earth . . . ?" Three risers from the foot of the stairs, Stephen Shepperd, striped pyjama jacket loose over regular grey trousers, carpet slippers on his feet.

"I think," Resnick said, officers moving past him, "it might be a good idea if you and your wife sat down somewhere until we're through."

Shepperd hesitated, eyes wild, settling finally in his wife's implacable stare.

"Mr. Shepperd."

He came the rest of the way into the hall, moving towards the front room.

"Perhaps not in there," Resnick said. "I expect we'll be rather busy in there. Here . . ." pushing the newspaper towards him, ". . . why not take this through to the kitchen?"

Unspeaking, the couple did as they were told, sitting self-consciously at the small table, Mark Divine, arms folded in the doorway, smirk on his face.

Patel and Lynn were going through the upstairs, room at a time, drawers and cupboards first, the obvious places. In the front, Millington and Naylor were moving pieces of furniture towards the centre, all the easier to prise the carpet from the boards. "I wonder," Resnick said past Divine's shoulder, "if you'd be good enough to let us have the keys to your car?"

DC Hansen, borrowed for the occasion for his skills with things mechanical, caught the keys with a grin and turned his attentions to the E registration Metro at the kerb.

Thirty minutes later, neither of the Shepperds had moved, the paper rested, folded and unread, between them; Stephen's eyes were either closed or focused on his hands, thick ridges of hard skin at the corners of the palms, the ends of the fingers. All that Joan did was stare at him.

Divine sighed from time to time, shifted his weight from one foot to another, amused himself with scenarios of what would happen to a man like Shepperd if he ended up in prison.

"The carpet in the front room," Resnick said, "when was it laid?"

"Sometime last summer," Stephen said.

"September," said his wife.

"And the old one?"

"What about it?"

"What happened to it?"

"Do you mean, to make us replace it?"

"If you like."

Stephen coughed and fidgeted on his chair, three people watching him and he didn't want to look any of them in the face.

"I was working on the brakes," he said. "The Metro."

"In the living room?"

"I didn't want all the fuss of carrying things downstairs."

"He didn't want to get filthy oil over his precious tools," said Joan. "He got it all over the carpet instead."

"It was unfortunate," Stephen said.

"It was a horrible mess. Ruined the carpet, the rug, everything."

"We'd been talking about getting a new carpet for ages," said Stephen.

"What was that about a rug?" Resnick asked. "There was a rug as well as a carpet?"

Joan nodded. "Stephen's right, the old carpet was worn and thin; we bought the rug a year or so ago to help cover it up, make it look more respectable."

"What colour was the carpet?" Resnick asked.

"Oh, blue. But it had faded, you know. A sort of greyish blue."

"And the rug?"

"Tartan. I wouldn't know which one, it may not have been a real tartan at all, of course, but that kind of a pattern." Resnick was on the point of asking her which colours predominated, when she added: "Not dark at all, green and red."

"What did you do with them?" Resnick asked. "The carpet and the rug?"

"Took them to the tip," Stephen said.

"Which one?"

"The nearest, Dunkirk."

"Not easy, moving a carpet for a room that size."

"Tied on top of the car," Stephen explained.

"After you'd refitted the brakes, I hope." Resnick smiled, causing Divine to snigger into the back of his hand.

"And the rug?" Resnick asked. "Did you fasten that to the roof as well?"

Stephen shook his head. "I put that in the boot."

The clothes that Stephen Shepperd wore for running were in the linen basket in the bathroom, waiting to be washed, a dark blue track suit with red-and-white piping round the collar, St. Michael label inside. A white singlet, white socks with reinforced soles. A pair of Reebok running shoes, earth and ash in the grooves, rested alongside his other shoes at the bottom of the wardrobe. All were bagged and labelled carefully.

Diptak found the camera at the front of Shepperd's shirt drawer, a small single-lens reflex, Olympus AF-10, the kind that can easily be carried in the pocket, held in the palm of a hand.

In the cupboard on Joan Shepperd's side of the bed, Lynn found a bottle with printed label, a childproof top, diazepam, 10 mg. Inside, there seemed to be twenty or so remaining. On the opposite side, she found the photograph of Joan Shepperd's class, the last afternoon of the summer term, thirty-plus children gathered around her in the playground, Joan looking round and maternal, smiling at the camera; sitting at the front, cross-legged and squinting a little into the sun, unmistakably, Gloria Summers.

DC Hansen's white coveralls were smeared with black, he was already on his second pair of gloves. Pay special attention to the boot, the message had come out, and paying special attention to the boot was what he was doing.

For fuck's sake, Divine was thinking, how long are they going to sit there like something out of the wax museum? Not as much as a pillocking piece of toast, a cup of tea!

Millington had left Naylor to mark out the boards near the fireplace where there was some slight discolouring, as if maybe, just maybe, something had seeped through the carpet and its underlay. How recent, it was impossible for the naked eye to tell. Forensic, when they arrived, would be able to form a better idea.

Now the sergeant had joined Resnick in the cellar, moving around the workbench, the shiny woodworking tools with care.

"Put this lot on show," Millington marvelled. "Bugger must spend more time cleaning them than he does putting them to use."

Resnick recalled the fastidious manner in which the pathologist had set his spectacles back in place. *A severe fracture at the rear of the skull, acute extradural and subdural haematoma. Almost certainly a blow.* "Tag them," Resnick said. "Every one."

While the sergeant was doing that, Resnick began working through the bank of narrow drawers: brass-headed screws, six different sizes of nails, drill bits, squares of sandpaper from coarse to ultrafine. It was between these that Resnick found the photographs. Squeezing back his breath, he laid them out on the work top, like a deck of cards.

"Bloody Christ!" Millington gasped.

Resnick said nothing.

There were twenty-seven pictures, postcard size. Many of them were slightly blurred, unfocused; either the subject had moved or they had been taken with a less than steady hand. Most, but not all, had been shot in open space, some kind of a park with swings. Young girls in jeans or swimming costumes, bare-chested, wearing only shorts; girls waving back at the camera, laughing, dancing, turning somersaults. There was one photograph, too dark to decipher clearly, which seemed to have been taken in a corridor; another, in which the flash had come into play, inside a school classroom. The last four that Resnick had set out were in a swimming pool and in the final one of these a skinny girl with visible ribs stood at the edge, fingers pressing her nose closed, the instant before jumping in.

At first sight, Gloria Summers was in none of these, but Emily, Emily Morrison, there she was at the centre of a group here, towards the rear of another there; kicking her legs high on the swing with her mouth open wide in a shout of terror and delight; turning as if at the sound of a voice she recognised, pale movement of her face, dark widening eyes.

Resnick placed the photographs, one over another, into a careful pile and slid them into a plastic evidence bag, which he then put in the inside pocket of his jacket, together with his wallet.

"Finish up here," he said to Millington, already heading for the stairs.

Lynn Kellogg met him in the hall, the class photograph in her hand. Resnick glanced at it and nodded. "Stay behind and question Mrs. Shepperd," he said. "Keep Diptak with you."

Divine moved aside in the kitchen doorway to let him through. Resnick stepped around Joan Shepperd and rested his hand, not lightly, on her husband's shoulder.

"Stephen Shepperd, I am arresting you in connection with the murder of Gloria Summers and the suspected murder of Emily Morrison. You do not have to say anything unless you wish to do so, but what you do say may be given in evidence."

Shepperd's body, which had gone tense under Resnick's grip, slowly relaxed as his breathing grew harsher and the tears began to slide down his face. Less than an arm's length away from him, Joan Shepperd's face curdled with contempt.

45

"I thought you might have lent a hand today, Jack," Skelton's wife said, "today of all days."

Skelton nodded glumly. Tomorrow was actually the day of all days, his father-in-law's birthday, his eighty-first; today was simply the day you chased round like blue-arsed flies getting things prepared. The old man was due to arrive that afternoon, the five twenty-seven from Coventry; the year back, his eightieth, Leeds had been Saturday afternoon visitors, and both Skelton's wife and father-in-law had been forced to take refuge in the ladies' toilet while soccer supporters waged a pitched battle up and down the platforms.

From early on Sunday morning, the rest of the family would start arriving: cousins from Uttoxeter and Rhyl, from Widmerpool the un-married triplets, a Methodist clergyman from Goole.

"I thought the least you'd do is collect the sparkling wine we ordered from Threshers. I promised we'd pick up the cake from Birds before midday."

Skelton was moved to kiss her forehead. It would be hectic, but he was certain she'd manage; all the better, most likely, without him being involved.

"I'm sorry, love," he said. "I didn't make this happen today on purpose."

The look she gave him back suggested she might be having difficulty believing that. As Skelton was halfway to the garage, he stopped and turned, wondering if his wife was still there. Instead, there was Kate, staring at him from the doorway in that half-mocking, entirely disparaging way of hers, black jeans torn across both knees, a duffle bag slung over one shoulder. Skelton realised he didn't know if she was coming home or just leaving.

"Twenty-four hours, then, Charlie."

"Twenty-three," Resnick said, a quick glance at his watch, "give or take ten minutes."

"Thirty-six, thirty-five, if we need them."

"We'll have him charged before then, sir."

"Genuine hope or just optimism?"

"Face him with the photographs, I think he'll start talking."

"And if he doesn't?"

"Fibres that Hansen found down by the spare in the boot, we've got Forensic earning their overtime, trying for a match with the ones found with Gloria's body. They're also analysing the stains on the front room floor, hammers and the like from the cellar. One of that lot's got to come up trumps, surely?"

"Waste of time trying the tip, I suppose? Rug'll have made the trip to the incinerator long since."

"More than likely. But I've shipped Mark Divine off down there just in case."

Skelton fiddled with the cap of his fountain pen. "Does he have a solicitor?"

"On his way back from Stoke apparently. Arnold Bennett Festival."

"Who?"

Resnick wasn't sure; the only thing he knew about Arnold Bennett, he had a damned good omelette named after him.

"Turn the screw easy, now, Charlie. Remember what happened yesterday."

"Yes, sir." No two ways about that, Resnick thought, he had no intention of misjudging Shepperd twice.

What Joan Shepperd normally did Saturdays: collect up the towels and tea towels and decide which needed to be soaked in bleach, which could go into the washing machine straight off; hoover the house from top to bottom, dust in reverse order; put on her outdoor clothes and walk along the boulevard and round by the marina, over the bridge to Sainsbury's— walking back with the shopping, she would stop off at the Homebase cafeteria for a pot of tea and Danish pastry.

This Saturday, by nine-fifteen, she had done none of those things. True, there had been the chance of a cup of tea, Lynn Kellogg had asked permission to make it, but Joan had no more than sipped at hers.

"You should have something," Lynn said.

Joan looked at her slowly. "I'll have one of my tablets in a minute," she said.

Lynn went up to the bedroom and brought down the bottle; stood it on the table beside a glass of water.

"There was a photograph of you with one of your classes in the cupboard beside your husband's bed," Lynn said, sitting on the chair Stephen had occupied before. "You've no idea what it was doing there?"

Joan Shepperd tipped one of the pills into her hand. "No idea at all." She placed the pill an inch back on her tongue and drank a mouthful of water, swallowing hard. "I expect it got put there by mistake," she said.

Millington was holding the photograph with both hands. "Who do you recognise in this?" he asked.

Stephen Shepperd blinked. "Joan, of course, my wife."

"Who else?"

"I don't know if there's anyone."

"Look again."

Shepperd appeared to do as he was told; time passed without an answer.

"Are you looking, Mr. Shepperd?" Millington said.

"I must ask you not to badger my client," Shepperd's solicitor interrupted, earning himself a sudden, once-and-for-all-time look from Resnick that would have stripped several coats of paint.

"Look closer," Millington suggested, moving the photo towards him. "Say, along the bottom row."

"Remember," Resnick said, "who you were talking about yesterday. It's on the tape."

Shepperd made a show of screwing up his eyes. "Is that her?"

"Who?"

"The girl. Gloria."

"You tell me."

"I suppose it could be. It doesn't look a great deal like her."

All right, Resnick thought, play it this way, drag it out, we'll see which of us is the more patient in the end. "What were you doing with this photograph beside your bed, Mr. Shepperd?"

"It wasn't beside my bed."

"It was in the cupboard beside your bed."

"That's not the same."

"It's close."

"It's still not the same . . ."

"As what?"

"What you said, it makes it sound as if, well, I had it there to look at it."

"What else would anyone do with a photograph?"

Shepperd started to answer, finished up looking at his solicitor instead. Resnick and Millington looked at him also, as if daring him to intervene. He was a slender man in his late fifties, dark-rimmed spectacles and grey hair. His blue suit was rumpled from the journey back by car and he had forgotten to remove his Arnold Bennett Festival delegate's badge from his lapel. Most of his professional life was spent conveyancing and processing small claims for compensation.

"I tell you what, Stephen," said Resnick, getting to his feet and allowing himself a stretch or two, "it's not so far from when we might take a break. I wonder though, before we do, those other photographs, perhaps you could tell us something about those?"

Shepperd set both hands to his temples and Resnick guessed that behind them, that telltale nerve was beginning to beat. Slowly, he took the plastic wallet from his pocket; slowly, he slid the batch of photos down into his other hand.

"This, for instance," dropping the first onto the table under Shepperd's nose. "Or this. Or this. Or this."

Stephen Shepperd's eyes were closed, screwed tight. Even so, Resnick assumed, he knew the contents of each photograph in detail, like well-remembered dreams.

After three-quarters of an hour trying to get Mrs. Shepperd to cooperate, Lynn was certain she was wasting her time. She called in to speak to Resnick, but he was in the interview room, so she asked for the superintendent instead.

"Absolutely," Skelton agreed. "Come back in."

"How about the Morrisons, sir? Do you think I should call in, let them know we've a suspect under arrest?"

"No." Skelton was definite. "Far too early in the day for that."

But by that time of the day, Lorraine and Michael Morrison already knew.

All good crime reporters have friends in the right places and one of the local man's particular friends had been on duty at the desk when Stephen Shepperd was brought in. One phone call, quick and discreet, and the reporter was on his way to the Morrisons' house, a nod in his line of work every bit as good as a wink.

The only way Michael Morrison had got to sleep the night before had been with the aid of a bottle of Bulgarian red and a video of *The Last Picture Show*. Fortunately for Lorraine, the VCR had been moved back downstairs. Michael had fallen asleep on the settee, woken to find himself sprawled half on the floor, Timothy Bottoms flattened on a dusty street. He had stumbled up to bed and hogged most of the duvet, which was where he still was when the reporter called to get the Morrisons' reactions to the news.

Lorraine had been astonished, briefly elated and now was mooching about the kitchen, picking up jars and cartons and putting them back down. Whatever she was feeling, she didn't understand it. No, she did. The man who'd been arrested had been charged with both crimes. Lorraine didn't want to remember the details she'd read about Gloria Summers's body when it had been found, but there was no way she could prevent herself.

The reporter had gone off to file his story, no doubt intent upon getting an exclusive placed in the nationals before Wapping woke up to what was going on. Lorraine had given him a couple of quotes, not as much as he would have liked, but promised that Michael and herself would talk to him again later on. Before that, she would have to wake Michael and tell him the news.

She found the number of the police station and asked for Lynn Kellogg.

"Hello," the voice said, "DC Kellogg speaking."

"I thought you were going to let us know," Lorraine said. "Keep us informed."

Lynn was quiet; she should have gone round there, never mind what Skelton had said; she should have gone round there first.

"You've arrested somebody, haven't you?"

"Yes, but . . ."

"It's the man that killed that other girl, isn't it?"

"We don't know that."

"But that's what you think?"

"It's a possibility, yes."

"Then what does that mean for Emily? What does that mean?"

Lynn's answer was lost in the fumbled slamming of the receiver. Lorraine's head smacked forward against the wall and from nowhere great sobs were shaking her as if she were in the grip of a fever. When Michael touched her she jumped, not having heard him on the stairs. "It's okay," he said as she gasped for air against his chest. "Come on, it's all right."

"They've found her, haven't they?" he said as Lorraine finally pushed herself away.

She shook her head, easing wet hair from her mouth and eyes. "They've got the man they think killed the other little girl."

"Oh, God!" breathed Michael. "And they think he killed Emily, too."

Divine had drawn a blank at the household tip; Forensic was still working on the floorboards, the fibres found in the car. Preliminary examination of the tools from Shepperd's workshop promised nothing, but they were trying again. The solicitor had boned up on his crib to PACE and forced a refreshment break at the end of the first two hours. Sometimes, Stephen Shepperd had said, I take the camera with me when I run. I take pictures, what's wrong with that?

"All of little girls?" Resnick had asked.

"They waved at me," Shepperd said. "They knew who I was. 'Stephen, take our picture,' they shouted out. They were all in Joan's class. There's nothing wrong in that."

Joan Shepperd had called ahead to the health centre, the tablets that Dr. Hazid had prescribed for her, oh, some time ago now. She would like to pick up a repeat prescription if she could. Some kind of tranquiliser. Dia . . . dia . . . diazepam, yes, that was it. The receptionist checked her name and address: Joan assured her she would be in to collect the prescription before they closed.

46

It was almost four in the afternoon when Lynn Kellogg knocked on the interview room door; one look at her face was enough to tell Resnick that something had happened.

"Forensic just rang through, sir," she said in the corridor. "Nothing from the flooring, but they have got a partial make on the fibres. They're the same as the ones found with Gloria Summers's body."

"That's positive?"

"You know what they're like, sir, cagey. Probably fight shy of taking it to court till they've done more tests. But it sounds pretty certain."

"The super know?"

Lynn shook her head.

"Tell him. Tell him I'm going to lean on Shepperd for a confession."

"Good luck, sir."

For the first time in a long while, Resnick smiled.

Lorraine and Michael Morrison sat on either side of the table, holding hands. Aside from an ambulance siren heading for the hospital, the only sound was that of children on the pavement, playing.

Shepperd looked significantly older each time the interview was resumed, the tapes timed and set in motion. His abrasive outburst at Resnick on the previous day had been the last time he had seemed to be in any kind of control. Now and then there were still occasional flashes when his voice was raised, as if a particular insinuation had offended him; the rest of the time he answered sullenly, head bowed, declining to look his questioners in the eye.

"How did you get her to come with you?" Resnick asked. "Did you tell her her teacher was there? Is that what you said?"

Shepperd moved his head slightly; his hands were back between his legs, wrists between his knees.

"Mrs. Shepperd asked me to come and get you, invite you back for tea, is that the way it was?"

In Resnick's imagination he could see the girl hesitating, uncertain, looking round for her grandmother. Shepperd saying, "Don't worry about your nan, I'll come back for her in a minute." Or, "Your gran is it you're looking for? That's where she is. Round our house now."

Stephen Shepperd glanced up, head angled towards Millington, the sergeant staring back at him with scorn, the way his wife had looked at him earlier. Was that only this morning? It didn't seem possible it could still be the same day.

"What was the bribe, Stephen? Cream cakes? Ice cream? Don't tell me it was anything as banal as sweets."

"Look . . ."

"Yes?"

"None of this, what you're saying, none of it ever happened."

"Stephen," Resnick said, "I don't believe there's anyone in this room who thinks that's the truth."

Shepperd's hands passed across his face. He turned towards his solicitor and his solicitor turned his head away. A man caught out of his depth, back in the Potteries he would be sitting in a seminar called "Bennett and a Sense of Place," looking forward with anticipation to that evening's screening of *The Card*, that wonderful moment at the end when Alec Guinness sees through Glynis Johns's airs and graces and rushes off to the sincere and simple charms of Petula Clark.

"Of course," Resnick said, "it's possible you could have taken her somewhere else first, especially if you used the car, but sooner or later you would have had to have got her into the house. Into the front room. Onto the carpet. Onto the rug."

"No. You can't, you can't . . ."

"Prove anything? Stephen, the report from the police lab is on the fax machine right now."

Shepperd's head came up slowly, slowly until, for the first time in a long while, he was looking directly into Resnick's face.

"It wasn't only photographs we took this morning, you know. There were other things: from the cellar, for instance; from the car."

"The car?"

"The boot of the car."

At night, at night it would have had to have been, carrying Gloria's body, wrapped inside that tartan rug and laying her in the already open boot.

"You'd done a pretty thorough job of cleaning it out, vacuum, I don't doubt. Even so a few fibres had worked their way into the well of the spare tyre."

Oh, he had Shepperd's attention now, hanging on his every word.

"Fibres from the rug, Stephen, the tartan rug, red and green."

"That's right. That's right. I thought I'd said. That was how I took it to the dump. In the boot."

"Eventually, Stephen, I'm quite sure that you did."

"Eventually? I don't understand."

"When we found Gloria's body, Stephen, in the cold of that railway siding, nestled up in bin liners and plastic, alone there with the rats, we found some other things. Fibres, for instance, red and green, the kind that come from a rug."

If the nerve beating inside Shepperd's head accelerated any more, it might burst through the skin.

"Just a few, Stephen, only a very few, but still enough to make comparisons. Lucky for us that she struggled, Gloria, when you were doing whatever it was you did to her, lucky that she fought and tried to get away . . ."

"Don't!"

"Otherwise we might never've found those scrapings . . ."

"Please don't!"

"Trapped beneath her nails, pressed fast against the skin."

"No! No, no, oh, God, oh, God, no, no, please, no. No." Shepperd pushed himself back from the table, twisted sideways on his chair, threw himself at his solicitor, clinging to his arms as his words degenerated into a broken succession of cries and moans.

Frightened, embarrassed, the solicitor seemed to be pushing Shepperd away with one hand, holding on to him with the other. Over Shepperd's shoulder, his expression appealed to Resnick for assistance.

"Graham," Resnick said.

Millington went round the table and tapped Shepperd on the shoulder, careful to treat him gently now, any hint of physical coercion to be avoided at all costs.

Only when Shepperd was upright in his chair, his clothing set to rights, his breathing back to almost normal, did Resnick, sitting opposite him, softly say, "Wouldn't you like to tell us about it, Stephen? Don't you think you'd feel better if you could do that?"

And Stephen Shepperd horrified Resnick by grabbing at his hand and clutching it tight, his voice as quiet as Resnick's own. "Yes," he said. "Yes."

47

"Fuckin' 'ell, Ray! You gone to sleep in there or what?"

"Got the tweezers out again. Trying to find his prick."

"Come on, Raymond, give us all a break. It is sodding Saturday night."

Back in his room, Raymond eased himself into his black jeans, tucked down the tail of his shirt before zipping up his fly. Front of the shirt unbuttoned, he took the deodorant from the end of the bed and sprayed again under his arms. Money in his back pocket, keys. Before leaving he tugged at the front of his shirt so that it was hung loosely over his waist. Like someone who can't stop themselves touching their tongue to a painful tooth, he pressed the ends of his fingers close against his nose. Nothing would get rid of the faint ripeness of fresh blood, raw meat.

Sara came out of the shop wearing low heels, black skirt inches over the knee; underneath her coat Raymond caught the gleam of a white blouse. Tonight they'd be like twins.

He waited in the doorway across the broad swathe of pedestrianised street; Sara chattering to two of the other girls, one with a cigarette already in her hand, the other lighting up as she spoke. Just when

Raymond was starting to get restless, scuffing his feet, the other pair turned and walked off towards the city, arm in arm. Sara waited a couple of moments, acknowledging Raymond only when he stepped out of the doorway and began, hands in pockets, to walk towards her.

"What's up?" he asked.

"Nothing. Why?"

Raymond sniffed and shrugged. They stood close, facing in opposite directions, movement on either side of them, groups of youths walking up from the station, in by train from the suburbs, the surrounding towns. Saturday night.

"What you want to do then?" Raymond said.

"I don't know, do I?"

A few more moments of silent indecision. No more than fifteen, a lad, jostled by his mates, bumped into Raymond and Raymond whirled round, angry. "Watch where you're fucking going!" The boy backing away, laughing it off. "Sorry, mate. Sorry." Fear in his eyes. His friends gathering him up and sweeping him away.

"Raymond, what'd you do that for? It was only an accident."

"Not going to let him push me around for nothing," Raymond said. "Bastard! He wants to fucking watch out."

"What is he like, this boy?" Sara's mum had said. "You haven't told us much about him."

"You hungry?" Raymond said.

Sara was looking over towards HMV, the posters for the new George Michael album in the window; maybe she'd get that before the end of the week if her money held out. "No," she said, "not really."

"Come on, then," Raymond said, starting to move away. "Might as well get a drink."

The ground floor of the restaurant was small and already quite crowded, the waiters either asking newcomers if they minded sitting upstairs or if they would like to try again in an hour, an hour and a half. Patel and Alison were in the corner, behind the door, next to two couples who had greeted the owner familiarly and proceeded to talk loudly through their meal, spraying advice on the relative hotness of the curries and details about their planned winter holiday round all and sundry.

"I've embarrassed you, haven't I?" Alison grinned, spooning lime pickle onto a piece of popadum.

Patel shook his head. "You? No, I don't see how."

The grin broadened. "Wearing this."

"This" was a low-cut chenille top beneath which it was impossible to disguise the fact that she'd elected not to wear a bra. The top was the colour of cream, worn over raspberry culottes in cotton velour. Patel was wearing dark grey trousers, brown leather shoes, shirt and tie under a burgundy jacket. He was trying not to stare each time Alison leaned forward towards the pickle jar.

"Not at all," he said.

Alison laughed, not unkindly. "The girls at work said you'd take one look and run a mile. Either that or put me under arrest for offending public decency."

Patel's turn to smile: by the standards of a normal city Saturday she was quite conservatively dressed.

"You have arrested someone, haven't you? It was on the news."

"For the murder of the little girl, yes, that's right."

"I thought there were two," Alison said. "Two girls."

The waiter squeezed his way between the tables with their portions of chicken tikka, shami kebab.

"So far, I think he's only been charged with the first murder. I don't know about the second."

"But he did do it?"

Patel nodded thanks to the waiter and realised that their noisy neighbours at the next table had fallen quiet to listen.

"I don't know," Patel said. "I haven't really been that involved. Look at all the chicken tikka you've got, you'll never be able to finish your main course."

Stephen Shepperd lay on a plain, thin mattress in the police cell, a continuous period of eight hours' rest, free from questioning, travel or any interruption. Whenever the duty officer looked through the door, Shepperd was a moving tangle beneath his blanket, the shallowness of broken sleep.

"Remorse, then, Charlie, that what'd you'd say he was feeling?"

Resnick sighed. Since his first waking thoughts about the Shepperds' new carpet, he had been functioning for close on sixteen hours. "Oh, yes, remorse by the bucketload. Even then not above trying to twist the blame."

"How do you mean?"

"You know, so beautiful, so lovely I couldn't stop myself from touching her. The way she smiled, not like a little girl at all. Always smiling, clinging to my hand. As if somehow she'd been egging him on." A shudder ran through him and he struck his fist against the side of Skelton's desk. "Trying to make her complicit. Six years of age. What kind of a twisted mind can convince itself of that?"

Skelton's father-in-law had arrived long since, replete with urinary sheath, leg bag and new three-piece suit in Donegal tweed; three times his wife had phoned to inquire when he would be home. "Nothing about the Morrison girl?" Skelton said.

Resnick shook his head. "Still reckons to know nothing about her. Beyond who she is, stuff he'd agreed to before."

"Think he's waiting till we've proof there as well?"

"Possible. Either that or he's telling the truth."

Skelton was on his feet, taking his jacket from the hanger back of the door. "Charlie, look at what we already know. Look at the facts. Chances he didn't do for the other kiddie, thousand to one against."

"I'm sorry," Lynn Kellogg had said, "there's still no information about Emily, nothing new at all. We'll let you know the moment there is."

Michael and Lorraine, not really focusing on Lynn's face, exhausted, cried out, gazing past her into the night.

"Raymond, however many's that you've had?"

"What difference it make? Just 'cause you want to sit all night over one lager and black."

It was her second but Sara didn't argue; she didn't know what had gotten into Raymond, but it obviously wasn't going to pay to argue with him about anything. He'd already had one shouting match with a bloke who'd splashed beer over his shoe.

"What d'you reckon then? This place, all right, isn't it?"

" 'S all right."

They were pressed against the balcony, looking down over the crowds milling round the bar below, squeezing between pillars or sprawled along bench seats down the sides. At the bar itself they were five deep, calling for attention, waving ten-, twenty-pound notes. Up where Raymond and Sara were, there was as much dancing as space would allow, a DJ playing Top Forty and regular soul mixed with swingbeat. Raymond promised himself that if the bastard DJ played "I Wanna Sex You Up" once more, he'd go over and stiff him one. Bastards with their big mouths and big dicks.

"Raymond!"

He had been absentmindedly stroking Sara's behind and she wriggled away, giving him one of those reproachful, wait till later and even then you'll be lucky, specials.

Raymond thought they'd make a move pretty soon, after he'd finished this pint, see about the long walk home. Some other night, he'd try and get her back to his place, room to stretch out, take your time. Not tonight though, he could tell she was in a mood about something. Not like some blokes, Raymond thought, no sensitivity at all, didn't matter what the girl was feeling, still wanted to pork it.

Patel looked along the room to where Alison was sitting, toying with her wineglass, waiting for him to return; he still couldn't take it in, that she wanted to be here with him. The warmth of her smile as he sat down beside her. The thrum of conversation, the thud of the speakers made anything less than a shout a waste of breath.

She finished her drink and pointed with her glass towards the door. "Let's go," she mouthed, reaching for her bag.

They walked along the narrow platform of tables where they had been sitting, underneath the paintings and the potted plants and out through the swing doors into the street. It was like stepping out into the middle of rush hour. A group of ten or twelve came down the centre of the road at a slow trot, blocking traffic, arms linked, singing at the tops of their voices. In the alley leading to the Caribbean restaurant, a couple necked furiously while a few yards further along a youth in a Forest shirt leaned back against the wall and pissed.

At the corner of George Street, Alison took Patel's hand.

"I was watching this programme," she said, "about arranged marriages. I'm surprised you're still walking round free."

"You can say no, you know?"

"I didn't think it was that easy, family pressure and all."

"It's easier if you're a man."

"Isn't it always."

Three young women in fancy dress came hurtling into the street in front of them: one was wearing a police tunic and hat, a pair of white ski pants and four-inch heels; the other two were dressed as schoolgirls, gym slips, black stockings and white suspender belts. One was holding a jumbo sausage wrapped in paper, the others were carrying chips and gravy in open cartons.

"Stick 'em up!" called the policewoman to Patel, waving her sausage into his face. "You're under arrest."

Patel sidestepped and the woman lurched away into the arms of her friends, the three of them bent double by hysterical laughter, chips spilling across the pavement.

"You can't say you don't see life," Alison said, linking her arm through Patel's and steering him away.

"Agreed," Patel said as they started down the hill, "but do you have to see so much?"

Alison laughed and moved closer against him as they walked.

Raymond had fancied one last drink in the Thurland. Sara had argued with him for fully five minutes on the pavement outside before finally giving in. It had taken them twice that long to get served, another age for Raymond to force his way into the Gents and when he got there someone had blocked one of the toilets and he had to stand ankle-deep at the stalls, water and worse.

Sara was being chatted up by some lad when he got back, black sweatshirt and hair tied behind in a little ponytail, gold ring in one ear.

"What'd he want?"

"What d'you think?"

Raymond looked over at the youth, laughing now with two of his mates. "Must've made a mistake, reckoned you for the wrong sex."

"What's that supposed to mean?"

"Bloody shirtlifter, isn't he?"

"He's not."

"Fucking fancy him then, do you?" Pushing her in their direction. "Go fucking on then, see if I sodding care!"

"Raymond, leave off! I've told you before about mauling me around."

"Yeh? Yeh? Right, if that's the way you feel, get home on your fucking own. Or get that poncey bastard over there to take you."

"Raymond!"

But he was barging his way towards the door, hands hard down into his pockets, head lowered. Sara took a few halfhearted steps after him and stopped. She could see the lad with the ponytail grinning at her, then one of his mates making that wanking movement with his hand. Sara sucked in her cheeks and hurried after Raymond.

Raymond had come out of the pub so fast, not looking, that he was almost off the wide corner of pavement before thinking about where he was going. For a few moments he considered going back for Sara, waiting for her at least. No, why the hell should he? He was alongside the telephone box across the street and starting down to the square when he saw them coming up the other way, the four who had attacked him outside Debenham's. Nearly two months back, but no way was he going to forget. Loose white shirts, sleeves rolled back, dark trousers, pleated at the waist, shiny shoes. One of them turning into the doorway of the jeans shop, shouting for the others to hang on, lowering his head to light a cigarette. In the flare of the lighter Raymond could clearly see his face: the one that had stared back at him in the Bell, had screamed with anger as he stabbed Raymond with his knife.

"Hey!" Raymond called, hurrying towards them. "Hey, you!" Closing fast.

The youth was slow to react, slow after all those weeks to recall Raymond's face.

"You!" Raymond pointing. "I'm having you!"

One of the youth's friends laughed in disbelief, another called out a warning; the one who tried to intercept got a fist in the face for his pains.

"Raymond! Ray-o!" If he heard Sara's voice, he gave no sign.

She was making her way across the road, not quite breaking into a run, when the youth realised Raymond was serious, possibly recalled who he was.

"Get the fuck away and don't be so fucking daft!"

Raymond threw a punch at his face and kicked high at his body, aiming for the groin, the toe of his shoe catching him above the knee. Hands grabbed for Raymond and he elbowed them away.

"What the fuck d'you think . . . ?" the youth began, but Raymond lowered his head and jerked it forward, forehead smack into the centre of the youth's startled face.

"Raymond! Don't!"

One of them grabbed Sara's arm and swung her aside, stumbling back towards the entrance of the Cookie Club, losing her balance and tumbling to her knees. One of the others kicked Raymond in the back of the leg but he scarcely seemed to notice.

"Right," he said, seizing hold of the youth's blood-spattered shirt. "You got this coming. Raymond Cooke, remember?" As recognition dawned, the blade of Raymond's Stanley knife gouged a chunk from the youth's face, beside his broken nose.

From where they had been looking at the futons in the window of the Japanese shop higher up, Patel and Alison heard the shouts, the scream.

"Don't," Alison said, hanging onto Patel's arm. "Please don't get involved."

Patel touched her hand, lightly prised her fingers away. "I have to," he said.

There seemed to be one person on his back in the doorway, another bending over him, two or three more attacking from behind. Patel began to run. A shoulder rocked Raymond hard against the shop window, making it vibrate. Fists flew round his face and he threw up both arms to protect himself, lashing out with his feet as he tried to break away. On the ground, hands to his head, the youth was alternately crying and moaning.

"All right," Patel said, taking hold of the nearest youth by the arm and pulling him away. "Put a stop to this."

"Fuck off, Paki!" the youth shouted, and punched Patel's shoulder. "Yeh, fuck off!" And they swarmed round him.

"I'm a police officer," Patel just had time to call out, before Raymond jumped towards him, the force of the attack knocking him back, knocking him down, the blade of the knife that was still in Raymond's hand severing the carotid artery alongside Patel's chin.

Within moments all the youths were gone. Only Patel lay there, Alison gazing helplessly down, blood across her culottes and her shoes, beginning to run between the paving stones. On the edge of the crowd that was slowly forming, Sara picked herself up from grazed knees and started to run haphazardly away, vomiting into her hands.

48

Resnick was still numb. Even though he had seen the body, it was difficult to believe. CONSTABLE KILLED IN KNIFE ATTACK. POLICEMAN SLAIN IN CITY BRAWL. The headlines were there behind him, Sunday tabloids bunched on the back seat of the car. *Detective Constable Diptak Patel was stabbed and fatally wounded when he sought to intervene in a vicious fight between armed youths late last night. Constable Patel, who was off duty at the time* . . . Since the early editions, the front pages had been changed, reports that Stephen Shepperd had been charged with murder relegated to page 2. On the feature pages articles charting the rise of violence and the decline of the inner cities vied with psychologists profiling the kind of man most likely to engage in paedophilia.

"Why? Why? Why?" Patel's mother had cried in the hospital, over and over again. "Why would anyone do this to my son?"

"Stop this!" his father had interrupted, stilling her with the fierceness of his anger. "Stop this now! We know, all of us, the reason why."

No, Resnick thought, none of it is that simple: not what happened to Patel, what happened to Gloria Summers; neither what made Shepperd the person he became, nor the youth who lashed out in ignorance and fear, a knife blade in his hand. He saw that he had missed his turning, drove to the end of the street and doubled back, the pebble-dash bungalow one block along to the right.

He was sitting with Edith Summers on the promenade, staring out over the North Sea, grey as the folds of an old man's neck. What they sold on the front was daylight robbery, Edith had said, and anyway, at that time of the year most of the places would be closed. So they sat there, drinking tea from a thermos, wrapped up against the cold.

"It was good of you to come and tell me," Edith said. "Good of you to come and talk. It's not everyone as would."

Suddenly, Resnick had to turn his head aside, afraid of tears.

"When he'd done what he'd done," Edith said falteringly, "to Gloria, did he tell you why he had to . . . to take her life as well?"

. . . all of a sudden there was this screaming and at first I didn't realise, I mean I hadn't meant to, the last thing in all the world, I hadn't meant to hurt her, but she was staring at me and screaming and, oh, God, I hadn't meant to hurt her, I promise, I promise, I tried to get her to be quiet, I was frightened someone would hear but she went on and on and . . .

"I think he got carried away," Resnick said, "this time. I think with girls before he'd only looked, perhaps touched, but nothing, you know, nothing too serious. This time, when he realised what had happened, I think he was shocked, ashamed; scared of what Gloria would say and do, who she might tell."

"You sound almost as if you feel sorry for him," Edith said.

"Do I?" said Resnick. "I don't think that was what I meant." Though there are times, he thought, with someone like Shepperd, when perhaps I might. Oh, less than for Gloria, or for you, but a little, a residue of sympathy. But not today: today all the sorrow that I have is used up.

"They won't hang him, will they?" Edith said. "They don't do that anymore. They'll put him in some place instead, Broadmoor, look after him with doctors, keep him locked away. People will write to him, it's what happens. Say it's not really his fault, let on they understand."

Resnick reached out and took her hand. An elderly woman, grey-haired, walking her dog, looked at them compassionately as she passed. How nice to see, she thought, a couple like that still acting so affectionately towards one another after all those years.

"Okay, if I take him a tea?"

The custody sergeant looked up from his desk and nodded Millington through.

Shepperd was sitting on the edge of the bed, arms between his legs in that now familiar position. He was muttering to himself, something Millington couldn't make out, falling silent as the cell door closed.

"My wife . . ." Shepperd began.

"We spoke to her yesterday, said she didn't want to see you. Since then nothing's changed."

"Can't you ask . . ."

"She knows where you are."

"Please ask her again."

"We'll see."

You self-pitying bastard, Millington thought, I'd like to wipe your face with the wall. "Interested in this?" he said, indicating the mug. "Tea?"

Shepperd reached out a hand.

"There's two people waiting on you," Millington said. "Desperate. Emily Morrison's mum and dad. Waiting for you to tell them what you did with their daughter, where she is."

"I told you," Shepperd moaned, "so many times. I haven't any idea."

Millington hurled the contents of the mug high above Shepperd's head and let himself out of the cell fast, fearful of the damage he might cause.

The blade passed like fire across the throat and as if opening a tap the blood poured down, splashing back up boot-high, chasing in circles down the drain. Raymond turned and pressed the sheet to his face and the sheet stank sweet with his sweat. The body of the calf continued to shake. A cut the length of the underside and the guts fell out. He had locked the door and run the chest against it, flush. For what seemed hours now he had been dimly aware of movement, voices below. The second cut opened the animal from the rear legs to the sternum. Sweat and urine: sweat and shit. Tubs of coiled pink guts, pink and grey. Raymond crying, frightened his mother would find out and tell him off, didn't know how it had happened, hadn't done it on purpose, honest, he hadn't meant to mess the bed. He felt between his legs. The last he'd seen of Sara, she'd been on her knees and crying. Stupid bitch! Serve her right, should have listened, done what he'd said. He could feel himself beginning to harden in his hand. Intestines sliding along a stainless steel chute, slithering down. On the news last night, they'd caught the bloke that had that girl, the one he'd liked to watch. Two-ball. Kiss chase.

Laughing at him from across the street. "Ray-o! Ray-o! Ray-o! Ray!" Legs kicking up beneath her little skirt. When he'd got her off on her own, what had he done? Raymond pulled the sheet up over his face and closed his eyes. Sweet stink. He spat into his hand and brought it back down to his cock.

Resnick got back to the station late afternoon. Millington looked up at him from where he was sitting and slowly shook his head. "Shepperd's solicitor's been on the phone again," Lynn Kellogg said. "Been trying to get in touch with Shepperd's wife. Won't pick up the phone or come to the door."

"Get the keys," Resnick said.

She'd hoovered the house and dusted, later than usual, but still it had been done. Her bedtime drink she'd made for herself, rinsing out the saucepan and the cup and leaving them on the side to drain. She had poured a glass of water and taken it upstairs to bed. The two medicine bottles were empty on the cabinet.

Lynn looked at Resnick and went back down to the phone.

She hadn't left a note.

Instead, on the pillow next to her, where her husband's head more usually would have lain, there was a yellow wallet, Stephen Shepperd's final batch of photographs, the last few taken almost exactly a week ago: blurred but recognisable, Emily with her doll's pram, waving from her front lawn.

49

The detective sergeant who met Resnick at the airport was stocky and bald, bundled into a dark green anorak, black-and-white trainers below heavy cotton trousers.

"Good flight?" he asked, leaving Resnick to open the passenger door.

"Short," Resnick said.

They drove the rest of the way in silence.

The house was beyond the edge of the village, high on the headland. "Let me out here," Resnick said.

"I'll take you right up . . ."

"Here. And wait."

Hands in pockets, he walked past low stone walls and the dark massed green of rhododendron bushes. Here and there the sea was visible through the mist; somewhere out there was Ireland. The house had been built from iron-grey stone, turrets pointing towards the flat grey of the sky: someone's idea of a castle.

Geoffrey Morrison, a heavy arran sweater over green cords, was leaning on his putter near the foot of the large, sloping garden, talking into a radio phone. His wife, Claire, was higher up, near the conservatory, kneeling in a padded leisure suit to tie off some new growth on the loganberry bushes. Between them, cheeks puffed out and red from the wind, Emily was working herself back and forth on a bright green metal swing.

Happy family, Resnick thought.

Geoffrey Morrison broke off his call. He had only seen Resnick once before but recognised him immediately. In the back of his mind he had been waiting for Resnick to walk around the corner, pass through that gate, Resnick or someone like him.

"How did you know?" Morrison asked.

"What you do," Resnick said, "you and your wife. You get Emily ready. No fuss. I don't know what you've said to her already, but all she needs to know for now, the holiday's over, her mum and dad are coming to take her back. They'll be over on the next flight. Right?"

There were half a hundred things Morrison wanted to say and he said none of them.

Resnick held out a hand. "The phone," he said.

Morrison gave it to him and turned towards where his wife was slowly walking towards him, holding Emily's hand.

There had been five photographs of Emily altogether, taken by Stephen Shepperd as he jogged past the Morrison house, the Sunday afternoon that he came close to colliding with Vivien Nathanson. In one of these all that could be seen of Emily was a gloved hand, continuing to wave. At the far side of that picture, visible just inside the frame, the number plate of a car, a Ford Orion otherwise unaccounted for. A computer check had shown it as a hire car, based at Birmingham Airport, less than an hour and a half away. The rest of the details had been simple to obtain.

Geoffrey Morrison sat in one of the leather armchairs, waiting for his brother and sister-in-law to arrive. Emily was upstairs with Claire, excited, packing her things. Every now and then, a peal of laughter would invade the quiet of the L-shaped room, one wall of which was double-glazed and looked out across the garden to the sea.

"He's a loser," Geoffrey said, "Michael, always has been. Marriage in tatters, Diana likely to spend the rest of her life in and out of bloody loony bins, any chance he ever had of a career, earning real money, down the bloody toilet. Can't hold a thing together, act like a bloody man, why else does he go and marry some kid half his age? Nobody else'd give him an ounce of respect, that's why. Poor bloody Lorraine, doesn't know any better, but, mark my words, she'll learn if she hasn't already."

He ignored Resnick's disapproving look and refilled his brandy glass.

"You want to see what's possible, look at this. Place like this, any idea what it cost? Just to keep it up's a sight more than Michael's pathetic little mortgage. Two fortunes I've made in my lifetime, two. And what's he got to show? That wonderful brother of mine. It's not as if I haven't asked him, begged him. Come in with me. The two of us together, family. He wouldn't listen, wouldn't bloody listen. The blue-eyed boy. What's he ended up with? Nothing."

"Not quite," Claire Morrison said from the doorway, one hand holding a new suitcase, the other Emily's hand. "Not exactly."

Geoffrey swallowed his brandy and glared.

"You couldn't have children," Resnick said.

Claire squeezed Emily's hand. "Ironic, isn't it? Everything else money could buy. Oh, we had the advice, the treatment, hormone injections. And there's Michael and Diana, halfway round the twist and one step from a pauper's grave . . ."

"For God's sake, stop running off at the mouth," Geoffrey said.

"Bingo!" said Claire. "Pregnant first time."

"Shut up!" Geoffrey threatened, standing in front of the chair.

" 'Course, we could have adopted, heavens, we could have bought a child. But, no, that wasn't good enough, not for Geoffrey, that wasn't family, and even though poor Michael wasn't apparently good for much else, it seemed the boy could be counted on in the sperm stakes . . ."

He rushed at her and Resnick grabbed his arm and held him back, but Claire stood her ground.

"I told you . . ." he began, but his heart was no longer in it.

"Geoffrey," Claire said, "you've told me what to do for the last time. Come on, sweetheart, let's go down to the road, see if we can see Mummy and Daddy's car." And she ushered Emily from the room.

Resnick released Geoffrey and watched as he subsided into his chair like yesterday's balloon.

"I don't know," Resnick said, "if you ever really thought you could get away with this, or for how long. If all the money's blinded you to the point where you think you can do whatever you want; take over a child like you would anything else, and bugger the rules. Anything to teach Michael a lesson, exact some kind of revenge."

Morrison wasn't looking at him, but Resnick knew he was listening all the same.

"I don't know," he said, "if you have the remotest idea what you've been responsible for, the amount of unnecessary pain."

Resnick moved closer, willing Morrison, if only for a moment, to look him in the face.

"Geoffrey Morrison," Resnick said, "I am arresting you in connection with the abduction of Emily Morrison. I must warn you that you do not have to say anything at this time, but if you choose to do so, anything that you say will be written down and may be given in evidence against you."

Standing outside the house, clouds shuttling across the greying sky, Resnick watched Emily beyond the bottom of the path, holding Claire Morrison's hand. When Claire bent towards her and pointed into the distance, Emily began to jump up and down and then ran a few paces towards the approaching car, her cries of excitement rising on the winter air.